"This is a heavy book, that invokes deep thoughts and feelings and raise questions of morality. This book brings up deeper themes of grace and mercy, and justice. It is so easy to judge actions without knowing the pain behind the choices. But you see the choices. You know the people. And you start to realize that justice without grace and mercy misses the mark."

—Brianna Lynn Campbell author of *Moments Late*

"Perrie takes readers through thick and thin within a war ridden world, alongside dynamic characters in this clean fantasy that has it all along with a message that walks along with reality: hope in the light of darkness. An enthralling sequel to Partin: The Chosen, Partin: The Taken showed that even hero's must face the consequences . . . fortunate or tragic."

—J Bruckner, *Goodreads* review

Partin: the Taken

IN THE KING'S ARMY CHRONICLES: BOOK 2

Partin: the Taken

RILEY J. PERRIE

Hardcover: 979-8-9871189-8-6
Paperback: 979-8-9871189-9-3

First paperback edition August 2025.

Edited by Sera Amaroso
Map by Braeden Perrie
Photographs by Gaelle Perrie
Interior Formatting by Riley Perrie
Header Art by Quaid Perrie
Interior Character Art by Raphiel Diederich
Paperback Art by Kyannah Durocher

Printed in the United States of America

Keys to Kingdoms Publications

authorrileyperrie.com

I would like to dedicate this book
to My Lord and Savior Jesus Christ
for without Whom this book wouldn't
be possible.

To those who have ever felt afraid.

Author's Note And Content Warning

Hello,

Thank you for picking up this book. I am leaving this note as a warning to all who might be reading. This book has some very dark and hard subjects to read. I recommend that if you aren't above the age of 16, please do not read this book.

Some trigger warnings that may be helpful for you to know before reading if you are older than 16 are: Heavy themes of war, death, and loss. Romantic tension that never goes past kissing and brief mentions of sexual desire. Abuse and domestic violence are mentioned through one character's arc. Intense, but not graphic, battles and fight scenes with some blood and injuries mentioned. Mention of a miscarriage. Brief mention of some characters dealing with depression and thoughts of suicide. Please proceed to read with caution.

Thank you.

—Riley

Pronunciation Guide

Characters:

Aleetha of Färrin: (Al-ee-th-a) Queen of Färrin. Rahuin's mother

A'zre Re'San: (As-rear Ray-Shan) King of Sun'Ar

Connan Brachs: Admiral of Casta. Married to Esther

Dais Verne: (Day-us Vern) King of Casta. Married to Rahuin

David Verne: Prince of Casta. Dais's brother. Esther's twin brother. Cursed human who struggles with a gift of fear

Ellenora Verne: Married to the late King Timothy of Casta. Mother to Dais, David, and Esther

Esther Verne: Princess of Casta. Dais's sister. David's twin sister. Married to Connan. Cursed human who has the gift of foresight that allows her to randomly see memories of anyone she touches.

Frobin D'Leoni: (Fro-bin D-leo-nee) Peggy's brother. Cursed human who has the gift of shapeshifting

Glena: Shapeshifter. Zenz's daughter

Henry of Färrin: King of Färrin. Rahuin's Father

Jarret D'Arvent: (Jare-ret Dar-vent) Garon Prince. Rahuin's adopted brother. Thesa and Jet's son

Peggy D'Leoni: Frobin's sister. Cursed human who has the gift of fire

Rahuin D'Arvent: (Ray-hoon Dar-vent) Princess of Färrin. Believed to be the chosen one prophesied to bring the King of Light back. Married to Dais

Renell Oslehan: (Ren-ell Os-le-han) Princess of Lanckest. Cursed human with the gift of death that transforms her into a unicorn that kills anything it touches.

Thesa Organsi: (Th-es-a Or-gan-sigh) Princess of Treía. Loyal guardian to Rahuin. Mated to Jet

Timothy Verne: Late king of Casta. Killed by Rahuin. Father to Dais, David, and Esther

Wen: Previous second-hand-man to the Darkness. Powerful sorcerer believed to be the original chosen one until Rahuin appeared

Zenz: Leader of the shapeshifters and Fenrir

King Dais Verne

Princess Rahuin Verne

Wen

Jet Ganai

Princess Thesa Organsi

Princess Renell Oslehan

Jarret Organsi-Ganai

Princess Esther Brachs

Admiral Connan Brachs

Carrie Haligun or Xin

Aiden Brachus

Peggy D'Leoni

Prince David Verne

Glena

Frobin D' Leoni

King A'zre Rè San

Zenz

Countries and Places:

Casta (Kas-ta): *Morough* (More-Row)
Sun'Ar (Sōn-Are): *Ren'R* (Ren-are)
Lanckest (Lān-kest): *Lanckest* (Lān-kest)
Onar (O-nar): *Oberin* (Ob-er-rin)
Otherworlds: Alternate worlds suspended in time and space
Cay-Llek (Kay-Yek): *Cizarrél* (Siza-rel)
Färrin (Fair-rin): *Silfräs* (Sil-frās)
Treía (Tray-ah)
Vyl'ein (V-yell-in)
Y'rheim (Ya-reem)
Ganhiem (Gan-hime)
Nüvrom (New-V-Rom)
Nnilmsh (Nil-mm-sh)
Qnnomk (K-nom-k)
Wädnn (Va-den)
Gra'lore (Gray-lore)
Ei-kar (I-car)
Seran (Sir-ran)
T'sash (Sash)

Words:

Aihha (I-ha) = Elven word meaning daughter
Belemè (Belem) = Sun'Arian word equivalent to holy moly or oh crud
Caldig (Cal-dig) = Cay-Llek word meaning female dog
Cola Sorenta de Nu (Cola Soren-ta day new) = Sun'Arian slogan meaning The Sun Still Shines
Dir flak (Der flak) = Lan word meaning smart ass
Eid (Eed) = Sun'Arian cuss word meaning damn
Eoth (Ee-oth) = Färrin word meaning hell
Elleha (Eh-lay-ha) = Färrin term of endearment meaning mother
Gizzek (Gee-zek) = Sz-karian word meaning bastard
Hevakseni (Have-ek-sen-i) = Farrin word meaning congratulations
Hidà (Heeda) = Sun'Arain word meaning dear
Jerè (Hair-ray)= Lan word meaning overseer

Kide (Key-day) = Käsian word meaning crap
Maerk (Mar-rk) = Castian cuss word meaning bastard
Ne'rns (Naarns) = Sun'Arian word meaning morons
Phyn (Fin) = Dwarven word meaning close friend
Rlébe (Releeb) = Treían cuss word used in terms meaning the worst of the worst
Shiev (Sheeve) = Castian cuss word meaning asshole
Sh'lles (Sheells) = Sun'Arian word meaning idiots
Sev (Sev) = Castian cuss word—equivalent of shoot, darn, dang it, and damn
Velk (Velk) = heavier version of sev
Velkan (Velk-an) = Castian cuss word equivalent to bullcrap
Xeh rer (Ze-reer) = Färrin cuss word meaning smartass
Xin . . . Yel . . . Zer (Zin . . . Yell . . . Zer) = Käsian meaning three, two, one

Things:

Greint (Greent) = Treían rainbow stones unrelated to helns
Heighle (High-el) = female Sun'Arian traditional wedding garment
Heighe (Hee-g) = male Sun'Arian traditional wedding garment
Helns = Treián stones that have been tethered in pairs and given to mated couples for communication
M'laj (Malaj) = Sun'Arian savory tea,
Reiis (Rees) = a form of Lan traditional scarring used to show commitment between married couples

Races and Creatures:

Brownies: Little hairy men that grow anywhere from 10 inches to 25 inches tall. They help with small tasks like intricate weaving or painting. In some areas, they are even used as spies.
Dwarfs: Warrior mountain people who live in clans
Elves: Humanoid people with pointed ears that can wield magic and are highly connected to nature.
Fairies: Fae people who live hundreds of years and can conjure magic. They can grow themselves to be human-sized or coin-sized.

Fates: Ancient magic users that are positioned to keep the balance between time and events.

Fenrir: (Fen-Rear) Giant wolves and, unlike common lore, cannot shapeshift.

Garons: (Gare-ron) Dragon shapeshifters that descended from dragons. They are smaller than real dragons, but still large, and can change at will from human to dragon (Garon… as they will be referred to). They cannot shift halfway (i.e., use only scales or wings or heightened sight), so they are either only human or Garon.

Ghorrok: (Gore-Rock) Beings that grow anywhere from 8 feet tall to 15 feet tall and can live from 100 to 400 years. They are built similar to a cockroach with a carapace and cordon fibers that make up their limbs. Both their carapace and cordons are different colors. They eat mineral rocks and find precious gemstones to be a delicacy. They usually travel alone and do not have a gender.

Goblin: Smaller form of hobgoblins.

Giants: Self-explanatory, but they speak a language called *Knargk* (Nark).

Hellions: Devised the same as Horrors, only they are giants and don't ride horses.

Hobgoblins: (Hob-goblins) Smaller and more deformed version of orcs.

Horrors: Horsemen that are made of nothing by nightmares and shadows. They wear a silver or brass ring around their neck to connect them to the physical world. Otherwise, they would be invisible and unable to touch or harm physical things. They feed off the nightmares and fears of other races.

Humans: (Obviously) Cannot wield magic but can be cursed with "gifts".

Nymphs: Monstrous Fae creatures that can harness the power of the elements.

Orcs: (Or-cs) Brute humanoids usually 10 to 12 feet tall with prominent jaws and fangs.

Sirens: Mer-people who can curse sailors to a watery grave after a night of bliss.

Trolls: Smaller form of goblins.

Walks: People in the alternate Otherworlds who have magical abilities separated by class. Each have a claim to the royal bloodline in some way or another. i.e. A Death walker controls death. A Lifewalker controls life, and so on.

Witches: Sinister humans who have "sold" themselves to gain their magic ability.

Wraiths: Devised the same as Horrors and Hellions, but they can fly or remain on the ground.

Map of Partin:

Previously in Partin: the Chosen

Partin: the Chosen (In The King's Army Chronicles Book 1) spoilers ahead.

After a night of betrayal from her lover, Wen, that forces her to leave her only home in Castlehaven behind, Rahuin is taken to safety by The League of Light: Zenz, a shapeshifter; Grimall, a dwarf; Klash, a ghorrok; Glena, a shapeshifter and Zenz's daughter; Frobin, a shapeshifter; Thesa, a Garon princess; and Jarret, Rahuin's adopted brother; who have been watching over her and protecting her since she was born. They tell her of ancient prophecies about light against dark and why they believe she's the chosen one. She accepts her calling and trains to become the savior who will help bring back the King of Light and defeat the Darkness.

Jarret, while teaching his sister, morphs for the first time in his life and finds out that he's a Garon prince, which shocks Thesa as she realizes he's her long lost son but can't find the heart to tell him the truth right away.

Deemed the 'Mysterious Knights' by their allies, Rahuin and the League battle the forces of the Darkness until one fateful battle sends a wounded Rahuin to the city of Morough in Casta. The League come with, hiding under aliases to protect their mission. Here her fate entwines with Prince Dais, the crown prince of Casta who does his best to protect his country. He saves her life due to the special bond of Vessel that they share.

While in Casta, Thesa reunites with her lost love Jet. Frobin finds his sister Peggy, who escaped with the long-lost Prince David from a camp that enslaved cursed humans.

Princess Esther has lived her entire life under the will of her father, King Timothy. Her special gift which can see the future or past of anyone she touches is a valuable gift that has led her into dangerous and scandalous situations. Two years ago, she and her twin brother, David, were taken by the Darkness and locked away. During that time, she gave birth to her son, Aiden, who was then taken away from her.

Admiral Connan Brachus crosses paths with recently escaped

Peggy and David and helps them get to Morough so they can be re-united with their family. Connan, who has been in love with Esther for the last three years, hopes that this act of kindness will get him back into her good graces and that she'll finally tell him what happened two years ago and explain why she disappeared. Due to a misunderstanding caused by Esther's father, the young lovers were forced apart, and Esther was left to bear their child alone. While he's there, he meets up with the League of Light and reunites with his old acquaintance, Grimall.

Princess Renell of Lanckest, betrothed to Prince Dais, travels to Morough harboring secrets of her own. She's cursed with a gift she received from her mother that transforms her into a harbinger of death. She fears the curse will be her and Lanckest's undoing, until she meets and falls in love with Jarret, whose presence helps her control the curse.

The Darkness haunts Rahuin while she recovers in Morough and soon exposes her secret and the League to the world, but this doesn't deter their mission. They continue to fight as they should, until Rahuin is captured by the Darkness and then rescued by Dais, whose love for her saves her life. Once they're safe, Dais calls off his engagement to Renell but is reprimanded by his father. He learns that Casta and Lanckest have been standing on a very slim line of war with the other nations—Cay-Llek, Sun'Ar, and Onar, and they need a peaceful union through marriage to keep the other countries appeased.

Rahuin, struggling from the after effects of being taken by the Darkness, runs away from Dais when he confesses his love for her because the Darkness has promised to harm those she loves. To protect Dais, she goes back to Wen and the Darkness and asks them to teach her.

During Rahuin's absence, King Henry and Queen Aleetha of Färrin visit Casta for Prince Dais's impending nuptials. Once Dais sees them though, he believes them to be Rahuin's parents and after some questions, he finds out the truth. They gave Rahuin away during the Färrin civil war to protect her. Toward the end of the war, they had their second child, a boy, but he was taken from them and they learned about the existence of the Otherworlds—a place where children and people disappear and never return. They decided to leave Rahuin in the safe place until she came of age but never got to retrieve her because she was attacked by the Darkness's forces in Castlehaven.

After a vision that shows Dais's death, Rahuin heads back to Morough to protect him. However, she is unsuccessful and must go to the Pool of the Lost to acquire an antidote. Once she arrives, the Fates there tell her that she can only save Dais if she gives up her ability to be loved. She agrees and heals Dais, but he and everyone who care for her, forget she even exists.

King A'zre of Sun'Ar, who is in league with the Darkness, begins his campaign against Casta and Lanckest so he can rule all of Partin; and after the battle for Dais's life, declares war on Casta. Dais once again calls off his engagement with Renell, and Esther and Connan get married instead as a way for King Timothy to start making amends for all the things he forced Esther to do. Rahuin visits the party, and Dais remembers her once they start to speak. He breaks her curse by saying he loves her, and they are soon married in a secret ceremony. Renell and Jarret have a falling out and she goes back to Lanckest.

After heading back to Lanckest, Renell makes a deal with King A'zre of Sun'Ar, who promises he can help her control her curse and will allow her to keep Lanckest once he takes over all of Partin. All she has to do is be ready to kill on his command. She accepts.

A few months later, the war isn't going well for Casta and their ally, Lanckest. Rahuin, convinced that she's the only one who can put an end to the war, makes a deal with King Timothy, promising that she will kill him as a performance for the Darkness to accept her back so he can show her how to defeat his armies. King Timothy agrees as he's already dying of a disease and believes this will be the best way to serve his country.

Thesa, involved with Rahuin's plan, goes to Treía to meet her father, King Grelik, and asks for the Garon's help in the war. King Grelik agrees and makes amends with Jet, who he exiled and punished several years ago after finding out about his love affair with Thesa.

Dais returns to Morough from the battle wounded and in shock. Through a series of letters, he learns about his father and Rahuin's plan. He is soon crowned king and begins training his people for a last stand. He sends Thesa and Grimall to find dwarven allies until Grimall must go alone, and then sends Thesa and Zenz to find the Fenrir wolves, the ancestors of the shapeshifters. Zenz succeeds and convinces the giants of old to help as well.

While this happens, Dais sends Connan on his own mission to acquire help from the sirens. They agree but start to drain Connan's life from him so he ages faster than he should. Esther is grieved by this but wants to spend all the time she has left with him.

Rahuin, now in the clutches of the Darkness, begins training with Wen again, and after an almost fatal use of her magic, finds out she's pregnant. To keep the Darkness from knowing that the child is Dais's, she convinces Wen that she still loves him and uses him to keep her child safe. While she's there, A'zre sends Renell after Rahuin with a command to kill her, but Renell can't do it when she finds out about the pregnancy. Rahuin catches her, and they create their own plan to have Renell help Dais protect Casta and find all of the Darkness's hidden armies.

Once everything has been set in motion, Renell relays Rahuin's plan to Dais. While she's in Morough, she makes amends with Jarret and he comes with her. Dais hears of Rahuin's plan and agrees. He will hold the Darkness's armies in the mountains once Rahuin gives a signal. Rahuin, while on the battlefield, collapses, and Wen takes her to safety, only to learn about her pregnancy.

Dais takes this as the signal and pushes his men to hold the Darkness's armies. Rahuin gets Wen to rest and then leaves him to Renell, who has been tasked to kill him. Renell, however, can't kill Wen when she realizes that he still holds too much light in his heart. She convinces Jarret to help her save him, and they escape.

Rahuin, using her newfound power that she learned from Wen and the Darkness, destroys the Darkness's army. Thesa and Dais find her and take her home where she tells Dais of her betrayal to their marriage and to Casta. He has a hard time hearing it but decides to work toward forgiveness because she came back home to him.

Back with Jarret and Renell, Wen wakes up to find himself shackled, and they tell him what happened and convince him to start fighting for the light. After some struggle, he agrees. Book one ends with an epilogue that visits Zenz being killed by a Hellion.

Chapter 1

Ravenous Wolves

Dais

The council room erupts with angry shouts as I enter, limping as my foot drags with my cane along marble floors.

"Why is she here?"

"She murdered our king!"

"—should be tried!"

"Thrown in prison!"

I close my eyes. The noise is deafening and my lingering headache from last night becomes worse. It feels like someone keeps slamming a mace against my head. I hobble to the middle of the room, where a centered stage sits below rows of seated officials looking down at me through angry glares, masked deceptions, and thin lips spewing blasphemes. I step up to the podium, meeting their harsh faces contorted in self-righteous hatred. I raise my hands, and their shouts fall silent, but even the silence is deafening. Can't they see I don't have the strength? I don't need to deal with this on top of everything else. This war is far from over, and we have more important things to deal with than the validity of my wife's crimes.

My shoulders slump like someone tied a boulder around my neck and forced me to walk with it. I take a moment to lean against the platform, the solid wood under my fingers is a cool comfort grounding me to reality—reality that I felt slipping too much these days. My racing heart is the only evidence that I've survived these last few weeks. Taking a deep breath, I reach a trembling hand into the inner pocket of my silver and dark blue embroidered jacket. The slip of paper is smooth against my calloused fingers, and my touch lingers on it for a moment too long, remembering that not so long ago, my father held this very paper. It brings a little solace in the face of this adversity, because it can never bring him back.

I clear my throat. "I would like to read a letter my father left behind as instructions for this day he believed would come." I clear my throat before continuing and the action makes my head protest with a spike of pain down my spine. "I've written this letter for all the nobles and councilmen who might believe what Rahuin did was wrong. I assure you. She did all she could to protect Casta. As a few of you know, I was already on my deathbed. My illness was something I tried to conceal, but it was catching up to me. When Rahuin told me her plan, she needed to do something that would compel the Darkness to trust her and take her into his lair. It was my idea that she kill me for all to see. At first, she protested, promising she would never do anything to hurt Casta like that. After I explained there was no other way, she finally agreed."

I swallow, choking on the next words. My fingers tremble so much I can barely read. "I want you to grant a full pardon for her sins. If anyone is to blame, it is me for the treachery I have caused this nation. I know many of you will still be skeptical, and for that, I applaud you. You have the best interest of Casta at heart, but please understand that this young woman does too. I hope you all find it in your hearts to forgive her." I flip the letter around, showing it toward the council so they can see my father's seal embedded in the blue wax. "As you can see, it was officially sealed by my father to prevent the likelihood of forgery." I set the letter down, meeting their gazes.

Some stare back with menacing eyes full of hatred and others wear shocked expressions that can't easily be concealed. The wooden stands whirl around me and the cerulean blue banners sporting Casta's crest of crashing ocean waves blur in a sickening array. I grip the podium with one hand to ground me.

"Some of us received letters similar to that one," Lord Hev—a man known by his nasally voice and big nose that sniffed in other people's business—states.

"How do we know that letter is real?" a voice calls from the back.

"Exactly," another echoes.

"It could be a forgery. You could be in league with her. After all, she is your wife." Lord Concer snorts, blurry eyes dripping down into sallow skin that he keeps dabbing with a handkerchief.

More accusatory words fly around the room, but I don't have the strength to discern them.

Lord Morrlok stands, drawing attention to his broad figure. Once upon a time, he'd been one of my father's closest advisers. His comforting form seems to take precedence over the seated nobles. "I was in the room when he wrote that." He looks over the council. "Lord Gervios and Lord Rëtt were present as well. That letter is not forged."

Lord Gervios and Lord Rëtt nod as he speaks.

"We all read it." Lord Rëtt stands. "That letter our *king* holds, is most definitely not forgery. Our late King Timothy made sure of that."

Lord Gervios speaks, "We know this letter isn't foraged, in fact, we know all of the letters aren't, but . . . how can we find it easy to believe the circumstances written? How can we forgive this person who once promised she meant no harm to our king? How can we ever trust her again?"

Many around the room nod at his words,

"How can we trust her around you? Even if she is your wife, you can't expect us to trust her."

Sir Ury leaps to his feet. "Blood has to be paid for blood!"

"Aye," someone yells.

"I agree."

Shouts rise in a clamor at Sir Ury's statement, growing in malice as their words form daggers that plunge into my head, tearing through my temples as the world I was once familiar with threatens to tear me to shreds. I grit my teeth, trying to soothe the anger bubbling under the surface of my skin, but I am done being patient.

I slam my cane into the wood of the podium, calling the men's increasingly short attention spans back to me. Honestly, they're like overgrown children calling for their mothers.

"Blood has already been paid!" I scream—my anger on display for their amusement. "So much blood has already been shed! Yes, Rahuin killed my father, but because of it, she saved us all. You heard witnesses from the battlefield testify that the enemy army was completely destroyed. Men are still out there digging mass graves to put the bodies in! Their families will never get the chance to give their loved ones a proper burial! War is not a thing to be taken lightly! Yes, my father sacrificed himself so she could learn how to stop the enemy, and that is exactly what she did! The blood has already been paid! Not hers, I know, but theirs! Their blood has been spilled to protect us. Shouldn't that be enough?" I spit. How many times do I have to say it? How loud do I have to scream for them to hear me?

A foul taste settles in my mouth as I look at the smug faces of those surrounding me. I want to vomit. Most of these men have never seen battle. Most of them don't understand the horrors that can take place out there. But most of them have lost someone before; and those who haven't are the ones who still speak,

"She should be tried!" Lord Ury screams, silver beard billowing with his uproarious movements as he tries to gain more support for his contention.

"Publicly." Lord Concer's sanctimonious gaze pierces mine with the venom of poisonous darts.

"We can't even trust our king! He wants to keep a murderer in our palace!" someone to my right hollers, I think it's Lord Xifer. Father mentioned that I should watch out for him as he often raises animosity among the nobles and even staked his claim for Casta's crown after my father was appointed king years ago.

I study their faces. They repulse me. All I see are greedy vipers with bared fangs ready to inject their venom. "Your palace? Nothing in this castle is yours. It's not even mine."

Their faces blanch as they realize the enormity of their mistake. They've overstepped, and will continue to do so, unless they are stopped. My father told me that a few in his council weren't trustworthy and were only after the crown or their own greedy advancements. He mentioned I should be wary and learn who they are. Because once they make a mistake, I will have grounds to force them out of court. I know who they are now, and I am coming for them, one way or another.

"If I must try my wife. I must try you as well, but I don't think you will stand as strong as she will. You are spineless! In your attempts that I—my father's approved heir—might make a mistake so you can replace me! I will not let your corruption stand." I look around the room, studying the hall for faces that squirm.

Some stand strong, but others don't. The ones who fidget know what's coming for them, and I hope they realize that. I hope they realize what their thirst for blood means. I hope they realize their blood will be spilled now. I don't have time to deal with their corruption. I have more important things to do.

"I will not hear another word uttered about a public punishment for my wife. Her dues have been paid and she will live with the consequences. Those of you who have seen battle know she will never forget those faces. Even if she never got to see them in detail, they will haunt her every breath. This meeting is adjourned." I turn to Jet, who has been by my side since the meeting began, as the men start filing out of the room. "Keep a close eye on the ones who spoke against me or Rahuin. I know with the country in turmoil, they won't take long to make their move. I am at my weakest, and they know it."

He grips my shoulder, dark eyes narrow. "Of course Your Majesty, I will get every available man I can to watch them. I'm doubling the guard around you and Rahuin as well."

I nod. I want to tell him that extra protection won't be necessary, but he's right. In my and Rahuin's weakened state, we are in no position to keep ourselves safe. Rahuin hardly has the strength to leave her room most days. I don't blame her, not when these vultures circle. I wish I had the luxury. I run my fingers over my curls, blaming my wife isn't going to get me anywhere.

"Have you heard anything from Zenz?" I ask, quieting the doubts that rise in my soul waiting to destroy everything I hold dear.

"Not yet, Your Majesty."

I sigh. With Rahuin defeating the army in the mountains, the amphibious attack on the coast proved to be the most difficult one as our ships were easily overrun. Connan had to retreat. After the men regrouped and were joined with our other forces, the enemy didn't stand a chance once they made it to the shoreline. It's been two weeks since I sent Zenz to the Tunnel of Gra'Lore. He should have at least dispatched a shapeshifter with a report, but we've heard nothing. I'd hoped they'd meet minimal resistance, but I fear I may have been wrong.

"I am going to rest," I mumble, squeezing the bridge of my nose. My headache is worse now after my outburst.

"Of course. I will wake you if anything changes."

Rahuin

I sit out on the balcony, looking at the frozen world below me and letting the icy air wash over my skin. The last two days have become mercilessly cold, and I wonder how the men still fighting for Casta are faring. Lanckest gave us every textile they could spare when their people crossed our border as refugees, but I fear it isn't enough. Nothing is ever enough. Not when there is a war taking place. Even though I destroyed most of the Darkness's army, I know men are still out there securing the border and preparing to take back Lanckest in the spring. We haven't even heard anything from Zenz, and I don't want to think about what that could mean.

From my perch, I watch the cerulean breakers crash against the golden shoreline; seafoam stretches across in blinding white. The tumultuous waves match the conflict surrounding my heart. Out in the bay, ships sway in the tempestuous waters. Men bustle over them like crazed ants as they work to repair the vessels that were damaged in the attack two weeks ago. Charred, broken masts stick out like desolate reminders of the war we've been forced into. The setting sun's glistening rays cling to the edge of the horizon as if waiting for an encore.

Maybe I should stay out here. Maybe the cold will cleanse my darkness.

"We've found no survivors . . ." The words ring through my head once more. I still see them, thousands of them. Thousands of lives I didn't even think twice about murdering. They were on the enemy's side, but that doesn't make it any better.

Why?

Because I thought I could come home? Because I thought I was doing the right thing? Tears well in my eyes as I imagine the families who have lost a husband, a father, a brother, a son. Those men will never get another chance to breathe, dream, love, hope . . . Never again. Bile wells up in my throat. I swallow to keep it down. I don't deserve to live. The transformation should have killed me out there. It should have—

Sira . . .

The name floods my thoughts and I place my hand against my stomach. Is she the only reason I am still alive? Do two lives matter compared to thousands? I don't know anymore. I used to think every life was precious. That's why I did it. That's why I saved Casta and came home, but does it really matter when you have to be reminded of your actions? Does it really matter when you have to live with the fact that you murdered thousands? Every life is precious, and I took away thousands. The chilly wind freezes the tears streaming down my cheeks, opening my eyes to the setting dusk. Darkness consumes the sky, chasing the sun away, but I just want it to stay. I'm so tired of the dark.

The door opens behind me, and I hastily wipe my tears.

"Rahuin!" Thesa's voice breaks through the crashing waves down below me. "Get inside or you'll catch your death!"

"Perhaps I should die," I whisper.

Thesa stands in front of me, her jade eyes piercing mine. Black, silver, and purple streams of hair whip around her face in the angsty wind. Her pale hand swipes away the errant strands. "Now I know you didn't do what you did just so you could kill yourself and your child out here. That is not who you are."

I clench my fists, looking away from her hardened gaze. "Then who am I, Thesa? How can you be so sure when I don't even know who I am anymore? I don't even know what I fight for. I used to, but now I don't!" The tears are back. "I killed thousands, so I could save thousands? I fought so I could come home to a husband and a kingdom I betrayed? To a kingdom who sees me as scum of the earth?"

Thesa looks away from me. "They don—"

"Don't lie to me!" The broken words scrub my throat raw, but maybe it's just the cold. "I'm tired of people lying to me! I'm not a baby to be coddled! I'm a twisted warrior who deserved to die out there! Not them! Their blood will be on my hands until the day I die, and nothing will ever be able to atone for those sins." I take a shuddering breath as my shaking finger points toward the Plain of Ei-Kar where my life forever changed.

I drop my hand. "Maybe you're right. I didn't do all of this just so I could kill myself out here. I came back so I could live with the consequences of my sins forever. I came back because death . . . death would be a mercy. A mercy I don't deserve." The frigid air chills my bones, and I know Thesa feels it as she gathers her arms closer to her sides before raising her fingers toward me, stopping just before her pale hand connects with my shoulder.

I watch her throat bob as tears glisten in her jade eyes.

"Don't say that. It was us. It was our fault. We let you carry the burden all alone, and we didn't even try to stop you," Thesa pleads.

I growl, nails digging into my palms. "That's another lie! I would have done it all on my own, and you know that. Nothing and no one would have been able to stop me. Even if you told me the consequences. Even if you told me all I would be feeling right now, I still would have done it. Isn't that crazy? Here I am thinking I deserve to die for my sins, and yet, I would do it all over again. I would kill thousands all over again. I would kill them for her." I nod at my belly. Approaching footfalls and the tap of a cane echo on the quartz floors behind me. Dais. I tilt my chin back toward him. "I would kill them for him."

Thesa looks up at him, her gaze pleading. She must think I'm crazy. Everyone thinks I'm crazy. Who am I kidding? I think I'm crazy.

A sickening feeling twists my gut and I place a hand on my stomach as if that would settle the burning nausea. Nothing feels real anymore. The burden of my sins has become an aching hole I'll never be able to climb out of. Perhaps reality is a tragic idea I can't fathom. What if I never understand it? What if I'm stuck here forever? Maybe the Darkness is fulfilling his promise to cause me the same amount of suffering I assured to those I loved. Maybe there's no way to stop my descent into insanity.

"Rahuin." Dais's hand rests on my shoulder. "Let's go inside. It's too cold out here."

I look up at him and nod.

Thesa shoots him a grateful smile, which I pretend not to notice. She's worried about me. I know she believes she has every right to be, but I wish she wouldn't. No one should waste their energy fretting over me. I don't deserve it.

Dais helps me out of the chair and ushers me back inside. Light blue drapes welcome us inside, leading to sky colored walls covered in amber filigree of flitting birds, open meadows, and large trees. He leads me past the four-poster bed to the fireplace. Crackling flames lick at the dry wood, sending sparks up the chimney.

I watch them dance behind the grate as Dais helps me into one of the blue cushioned chairs. Everything in this room is blue. Usually, the color calms me, but today all I find is extreme annoyance. I chew on the inside of my cheek, trying to ignore the twisting in my gut.

Thesa secures the balcony doors before announcing that she'll be back with some hot tea. She's out the door before I can even decline. I don't want anything right now, least of all hot tea.

Dais sits down across from me. His warm fingers caress my cold ones. I don't deserve his comfort. I don't deserve a fire to warm myself. This room is becoming a prison I can't break free from. "You should have listened to Thesa."

"I probably should have listened to a lot of people, and did I?"

He falls silent, his lips drawing a thin line.

I look away. What is wrong with me? Dais doesn't deserve my anger. He hasn't done anything wrong, but I have, and I don't know how to make it right. I can never . . . I shake the thought away as I look back at him. The dark circles under his brilliant blue eyes seem to have gotten broader since he left for the council meeting earlier. I study his gaunt face, reading the thoughts he has written on his features. He isn't very good at hiding anything. I'm partially grateful for it, but at the same time, I hate that I see everything he thinks. It means I see when I hurt him too, and I've been hurting him too much lately.

"They want my blood, don't they?" I ask.

He nods.

"Of course they do. Greedy men always want everything to bend to their will."

He squeezes my hand, and I hate the sympathy in his expression. "I won't let them."

"Maybe you should. I deserve it for what I did to you. For what I did to . . ." I trail off. I'm losing my grip again. The fire in front of us pops loudly, and I jump.

The warmth of his hands leaves mine as he stands. "Stop saying that! I don't have the strength to fight you and them!" He glares, his lips upturned in a snarl. "Stop feeling sorry for yourself! You wanted this! You left without consulting anyone. You did this on your own, and now you must deal with the consequences." He runs a hand over his golden curls, blue eyes drowning me as he points toward the door. "But now that you are back like you promised, I will do everything in my power to keep you and her from being harmed by those ravenous wolves!"

Tears trail down my cheeks once more.

"You said you did it for her and me. You said you would do it all over again. She doesn't deserve to die because you feel sorry," he spits and then grasps his head in his hands. Perhaps we are both losing our grip on reality.

"I'm sorry." I reach for him and pull him down until he lies against my chest. I stroke his curls.

He swallows. "I'm sorry too. I—"

"I know," I whisper as I kiss his forehead. "It's all too much for the both of us to bear."

"At least not alone."

He's right.

Together.

It was part of our vows when we eloped.

He lifts his head. "Let's have our wedding ceremony." His cyan eyes are full of hope in this dark world.

"But—"

"For the people. For the enemy. A way to say, 'you haven't broken us, and you never will.' A way to remind me . . . remind us of what we're fighting for."

I caress his chin. "But they'll hate you even more. The people they don't—" No one outside of the palace knows that Dais and I are married. We eloped in a secret ceremony before we went to war. Thinking back on it now, I realize how foolish it was. How eager we were and how it has led us to this—hurting each other with every word and action. Maybe we should think about this more. Why would he want me after all that's happened . . . after I betrayed him? Should he want me? It'll be better for both of us if he lets me go now. "If we have it soon, they'll think I manipulated you into marrying me after what I did to your father. They won't forgive so easily."

He kisses my hand, the tender touch radiating along my skin. My heart swells and my fears disappear in an instant. How did I ever get the chance to love him? He's another thing I don't deserve.

"I know, but we do it together. Always."

A'zre

I crumple the report in my fist.

Dead! All dead! Fifty-thousand Sun'Arian troops—dead. All because of her.

I scream and fling my arms across my desk, sending parchments flying around the room. Red and gold tiles blur around me and the mosaics of lions on my walls are lost in my fury. The Darkness promised he would do his part and he hasn't. This is exactly why I never trust anyone. They never complete the task they promise—not my generals, not my troops, no one! Untrustworthy! Vile! Incompetent!

Now all of my troops are dead! The Darkness promised I would have all of Partin, but what do I have now? Fifty-thousand dead men. Generals destroying themselves over power grabs in Cay-Llek. Onarian parliament demanding their compensation. A war-torn Lanckest. And Casta . . . the country rubbing its victory in my face by announcing a royal wedding of all things.

The air shifts, sending a chill across my skin, and I know it's not from the desert night just outside my windows.

His voice fills the room. "If you wouldn't have failed your task, this wouldn't have happened."

I turn to glare at his dark human form. His black eyes set into harsh gray skin gaze at me in contempt. "If I hadn't failed my task . . . If I—" I scoff. "If you would have done what you promised, none of this would have happened."

"You went against me." His presence fills the space with a palpable heaviness.

"For good reason! I had to have insurance, but even that back-fired on me." Renell was supposed to kill Rahuin and Wen, but did she accomplish that simple task? No. Even though I warned her of the consequences, she still chose to let them live. "You promised that once Rahuin was with you, you would have complete control of her! I trusted you!"

His soulless eyes flash, and he sweeps across the room, his gray hand grabbing my throat. His fingers are cold against my skin, and despite the fact that he holds my life in his palm, he doesn't choke me. It's just a reminder of all he controls. "I trusted you. You didn't give me enough time to completely take command of Rahuin. I almost had her, but because she met with Renell, she was able to force me out of her head!" He releases me like I'm filth he has to step over. He won't kill me . . . not yet anyway.

"The men were prepared! You promised she would be ready when my armies were in place, and she wasn't because you didn't have full control of her. I sent Renell to protect my investments, and even she failed! But don't worry, she will receive her due punishment." I move to the middle of the room, swinging my arms around as if that'll dispel my anger. I still feel his fingers gripping my skin even though he's not holding me anymore. I swallow to make it go away, resisting the urge to rub it.

The Darkness's black eyes shift over me, but he doesn't take the opportunity to remind me of his authority. "Mark my words, Your Majesty, you will receive your due punishment as well for crossing me."

"Do you think I care? Casta is still out of my reach. Go ahead, kill me. I've already been disgraced enough."

A sick smile spreads over the Darkness's face, but after all I've lost—men, land, pride—it does little to scare me. "Killing you would be a mercy. Oh no, I have something much more sinister in mind for you, but maybe the punishment can be lessened if you do exactly as I say. Casta is not completely out of your reach. If you want it, don't cross me again, and pay very close attention to what I'm about to say."

Chapter 2
An Ode to Retreat

Zenz

Wake up! Zenz! Wake up!

The smell of smoke and seared flesh reaches my nostrils, forcing my eyes open. I taste blood in my mouth. I have to move. I have to . . . I hear a growl behind me as something grabs the back of my neck. I howl as the movement sends pain up and down my spine. What has happened? How did I—the thought dies as I'm forced to look on the horrifying face of a hellion. He laughs at me as my eyes connect with his soulless black ones that are consumed by hate and fire.

"You're finished." His growl grates my ears.

"I'm still alive," I spit, blood spilling over my lips. I have to shift, but into what? My vision blurs. I'm not strong enough to shift, not right now.

"Are you?" He laughs.

Zenz . . . *I hear a voice speak over him.*

"What?" I try turning my head to look around.

Zenz! *The voice is louder now.*

"You are dead! There is nothing you can do. We will prevail!" The

world shakes as the hellion moves. He moves enough so I can see my body lying dead at his feet . . .

"Zenz!" The voice finally reaches my ears, and everything comes rushing back.

The sky is gray, almost black, as fire falls down in large projectiles. Swirling onyx smoke rolls off my silver armor in waves as the Hellion that holds me tries to take my soul. The monster growls, glowing red embers churn as the composition of his form underneath the obsidian smog. Sulphur stings my nose, and the brass ringlet around his neck that binds him in physical form shimmers slightly in the glow of fire.

Wake up! I hear Kali, my Fenrir second-in-command, in my head now. *It's a dream! It's all in your head! Don't let the fear get a hold of you!*

My heart pounds as the Hellion's eyes, immersed by fire, burn into my soul. His brass ringlet is close—so close. If I can destroy it, I can finish this.

A flash of gray and white flies beside me in my peripheral vision—Kali. She slams against the side of the Hellion, distracting him as I shift into a sparrow and slip through his dark fingers. I feel my armor reform around me as I circle the beast.

A yelp sounds from Kali as the Hellion flings her to the ground. He reaches for me again.

I dodge his shadowy fingers and fly toward his ringlet. With the last bit of my strength I shift into my dragon form. My huge jaws grab the brass and rip it apart.

The Hellion shrieks as his massive form vanishes into dust.

I look at the ground.

Kali.

Her limp form lies frozen on the scorched earth. I race to her side, shifting back to human as I do so. My boots crunch under the dry ground as I reach her.

"No," I whimper as my shaking, wrinkled fingers gently sweep her fur.

Her terrified dark eyes search me. *Zenz!* She screams my name into my head. *I can't move. I can't—*

I run my hand over her coat. *It's okay. You're going to be okay.*

The ground shakes as a boulder crashes a few feet away.

Tears fill her fear encapsulated eyes. *I don't want to die. I don't want—* Black shadows and darkness start to swirl around her gray and white fur.

I dig my fingers into her thick hair. "Kali!" I shout her name, but she doesn't seem to hear me.

Instead she repeats the same thing over and over again . . . *I don't want to die. I don't want to die.* The darkness grows thicker until I can't even see her anymore, just a black cloud where she used to be.

I release her, backing away from her body. "Kali! Wake up! Look around yo—" My screams die in my throat as the earth under my feet shakes again, but this time, it comes from in front of me. My entire body's paralyzed as I watch the black mass that used to be Kali transform into the smoke and fire of a Hellion.

No. My heart sinks in my chest. This can't be. This—have we been fighting our own kind this entire time? No, that doesn't make any sense, but how, why?

I notice a brass ringlet on the Hellion's wrist, holding Kali's new form present to the earth. A sickening feeling overwhelms my gut. I can't. There is no way I can save Kali now, but I can't kill her.

It's not her! My head screams. *Not anymore . . .* I swallow the bile that rises in my throat as the Hellion locks eyes with me. If I don't move now, I will be its next victim. I urge my worn body to shift into a dragon one more time.

For Kali.

I fly toward the Hellion's brass bracelet, leather wings beating against the heat rising from the battlefield below me. I clip the metal with my teeth once more, smashing it. The Hellion shrieks, and I swear I hear a hint of Kali's voice mixed in before it disappears into ash.

Tears run down my face as I look over the battlefield. Men fight valiantly across the once-beautiful mountainous plains that have now been torn apart by blood and fire, but there are too many enemies. There is no way we are going to win this. The Hellions, Horrors, Wraiths, and others are winning, and if we don't retreat now, there will be no one left to save. I glance at the spot Kali transformed. Until we know what we are dealing with here, we can't afford to keep fighting.

I turn my head to the skies and bellow the call to retreat.

Frobin

The ground shakes under my feet as another ball of fire lands a little ways away from where I'm fighting a Wraith. It attacks with the sharp spikes on the ends of its leathery wings. The rest of its body is cloaked in black smoke and its head looks like a snake. It screeches, onyx spikes parrying a blow from my ax. The sound of screaming men creates a cacophony that I've tried to drown out for the last few hours. Smoke chokes my nostrils as the ground around me burns.

I lift my ax again as I try to attack and my weary muscles scream in protest. Sweat and smoke aggravate my eyes, making it hard to see my opponents. This fight has to end soon, but the enemies seem to be renewed with a never-ending stream of reinforcements. Aside from the Wraiths, Horrors, and Hellions I've fought in the past, different shadowy monsters have joined their ranks. I don't know what the new figures are called or if they even have a name, but they're defeated the same way.

The Wraith's metal neck brace glints, almost as if it's made of gold, and the reflection momentarily blinds me. I blink to get the spots out of my vision. I swing my ax at the figure hoping that I will strike the gold band. My sight clears, and standing in the Wraith's spot is my dead best friend . . . Crin. I blink again, thinking that what I'm seeing must be wrong, but it's not.

Crin stands in front of me.

He's dead. The words echo in my head as I lower my ax.

What if he's not? What if he never died? What if we all thought he was dead because of the avalanche?

A blow from Crin's mace sends me flying onto my back, denting my chest plate. The ground meets me in an unforgiving embrace, and my head rings with an echo. Pain erupts across my body, and I feel the pressure of my warped armor digging into my chest. I gasp as I try to find enough breath to move again, but I can't breathe. Panic makes my blood race faster.

I can't breathe. I can't breathe. I can't—

Crin stands above me, his mace ready to strike. Spots of white light blind my vision. This is it. This is the end. I gasp for air, anything to get me motivated to move again, but the fight has left. Out of the corner of my eye, I see a figure block Crin's blow with their spear.

Glena.

Her silver armor glints in the dim light, striking in contrast to the dark gray skies above us.

The fight ignites in my veins. I can't let her do this alone. I can't—

Morph . . . The word enters my head. I have to get out of here. I have to try. I shift into a bird and my armor changes with me, allowing me just a split-second of glorious air. But pain still stabs my chest, leaving me frozen on the trampled ground. I see Glena fighting Crin, the echo of their weapons reverberates in my ringing head. I want them to stop. I want everything to stop. I don't want this to be real. I morph back to my human form and the shifting has caused my armor to expand slightly, but not enough so I can get up.

Glena, I call out to her mind. *Stop it—it's Crin.* I try to move. I have to stop them. I can't lose them. I can't lose them again.

Frobin, snap out of it! I hear Glena's voice, as I roll to my knees. *Open your eyes! It's not Crin!*

The sound of metal on metal crunches against my ears as I watch them fight. What did she mean by open my eyes? My eyes are open! They see Crin, and they see Glena and Crin fighting. How are my eyes not open?

The tip of Glena's spear pierces Crin's side and he bellows in fury.

Glena st—

The call to retreat fills the air, cutting through my thoughts. Glena's spear whips toward Crin's neck, and before I know it, he dissolves into ashes. My heart stops. What has she done?

Glena races toward me and pulls me up. "We have to go!" she screams, dragging me forward, but my feet don't move. I can't take my eyes off the spot where Crin had been.

"Wha—"

"Frobin!" Glena shakes me, flipping her visor open so I can't see anything but her aquamarine eyes. "It wasn't him. It wasn't—" Tears stream out of those blue eyes, and I realize . . . she thought it might be him too. "W—we have to go."

I nod this time, understanding her now, understanding her pain.

She morphs into a bird, and I follow her as we hurry to catch up with the others.

Glena

"Yeah, it got you good," I say, after I've finished examining the wound on Frobin's chest. His purple, almost black, bruises have spots of yellow and red encircling them. He still can't breathe very well, and I am worried that his lungs are bleeding, but there is no way to tell. Part of me thinks I should make a small incision against his ribs to alleviate the pressure he's feeling, because I'm almost certain that's why he's having difficulty breathing. I push an errant strand of white hair behind my ear.

"Thanks for the diagnosis," Frobin wheezes from his spot on the ground, shakily running a hand through his orange hair.

A fire crackles a little ways away, sending sparks into the night sky. Other shifters and Fenrir mill about in the late dusk, making an evening meal and wearily setting up tents for the night. The murmur of commands and small talk reaches my ears, but I don't focus enough to hear any conversation.

"You might be bleeding internally. I can't flag down one of the healers yet. They're still helping the most critically hurt from the battle, and you're not one of their top priorities." I start wrapping bandages around his chest.

"Well, thank you for putting me in my place."

I try not to smile at his off-hand comment but fail. "I can always cut an incision if you wan—"

"No, I think I will wait for the healers, thanks." He winces as I secure the bandages.

I shoot him a look. "You sure about that?"

"Certain." He nods with a sarcastic grin.

I roll my eyes. Is there no end to his *velkan*? "I'm finished."

He drops his shirt.

I sit down beside him and stare into the little fire we built. The warmth covers my skin but can't erase the jittery thoughts. After my father, Zenz, called us to retreat, I tried to talk to him about the battle to confirm what I'd witnessed. I hoped he'd have a reason, but he ignored me and everyone else demanding an answer for what they saw. His behavior was understandable considering what happened out there, but what *had* happened was the question. No one really knows.

Crin.

His deep brown eyes and oval face appear in my mind again. I can't stop the tears that clench my throat. I swallow to keep them away. It wasn't him. It wasn't real. But he looked so real . . .

My heart shatters in my chest as realization sinks in. Crin is still gone. He never survived. Almost two years later, and I still hope—believe he really didn't die in that landslide. I still believe he somehow survived after saving me. If only I hadn— The smoke thickens, making me think about the battlefield. It's closing in on me. It will suffocate me.

"Thank you."

I jump at the sound of Frobin's voice as it draws me back to the present, crackling fire. I'm not there anymore. The nightmare is over, for now. I look at him.

"Thank you for helping me with the wound, and for . . . getting me out of there. I—" He takes a shaky, shallow breath. "Was that—was that really not Crin out there?" His shimmering eyes meet mine.

"No," I whisper, trying to keep my own tears away. "It definitely wasn't Crin. Crin never—" I was about to say that Crin would never hurt him like that, and it's true. Crin never would have hurt Frobin physically, but he had hurt him emotionally. *We* hurt him emotionally. "Whatever that thing was . . . whatever it did to become Crin, it somehow knew we would react that way. It knew we wouldn't know how or—or want to fight back, e—especially not against someone we both loved so dearly."

Frobin nods. "Is it selfish to think to—to believe that it could have been him? That he really hadn't died?"

"No, of course not but . . . if that thing would have been what Crin became, even if it was him, he wouldn't have been the same Crin I knew and loved. He would never try to kill the people he loved." I look into Frobin's eyes so he can see my tears. "You have no idea how much I truly wanted to believe it was him, but there was nothing, no emotion behind those eyes. And I knew, it could never be him." I smile sadly. "Crin always had such life behind his eyes."

Tears stream down Frobin's face, and he looks up at the sky, as if that would hide what I already saw.

"You don't have to hide," I say. "I miss him too."

He looks back at me, and I know he understands.

I take a shaky breath. "I lost everything but my father because of that avalanche. I lost my mate. I lost you. I lost my friends, because they thought I was . . . and they had every right to think that, because it was true."

"Glena—"

"I'm not saying this so you pity me. I'm saying this, so you understand how much I loved Crin. Yes, I know I hurt you, and if I could change time, I would go back and tell you that I didn't want our relationship to continue because I loved someone else. But I was a coward, and I dragged Crin into my cowardice. And if I—I had come clean, he wouldn't be dead. We would have had a proper ceremony. We would have never been up there. I killed him. He died trying to save me. We were up there because of me." I break down into sobs, but Frobin doesn't try to comfort me. I'm glad he doesn't. I don't deserve it, but now I think he's angry at the things I just confessed. If he's angry . . . he'll never forgive me, and I'll never get one of my closest friends back.

"And then I made it harder," he whispers.

I sniffle as I try to look at him through blurry eyes. Those aren't the words I expected him to say. My silence speaks for me.

"I take that as a yes." He reaches his hand out.

Hesitantly, I take it.

"I don't know if I forgive you yet, but I understand."

I nod, because I understand too. I can't even forgive myself, so what makes me think he will forgive me?

The grip of his hand loosens in mine as his eyes roll into his head and he falls backward against the earth.

"Frobin!" My heart sinks, settling in my stomach like a crushing anchor. I lean over to his mouth and place my ear against his nose and lips, but no air rushes forward. He's not breathing. I think of the damage to his chest. His lungs have to be full of fluid. I pull his shirt up and rip my knife from its sheath at my side. I place my fingers against his gauzed ribs and start to count. If I insert the knife into the wrong rib, it will kill him, but if I don't do anything, he'll suffocate. I've counted enough. I try to keep my hand from shaking as I puncture the space in between the ribs.

The knife comes out clean, and clear fluid spills all over the bandages and my fingers. I gag at the smell, watching his chest to see if he starts to breathe, but nothing happens.

No.

Not again.

I drop my knife and entwine my palms together as I slam them down against his chest.

"No!" The cry escapes my lips, as I do it again and again. "You. Can't. Do. This. To. Me!"

He gasps and his gaping mouth fills with air.

"Frobin!" I sigh in relief. His eyes look into mine, as he starts to breathe freely. I help him sit up, resisting the urge to hug him. He's alive. Tears stream down my face as I awkwardly place my hands into my lap.

"I told you we should have punctured my ribs," he croaks, and I try not to chuckle.

I wipe my tears. "You idiot."

He laughs.

David

You have failed . . .

Failed . . .

The voice rings through my head. I didn't do anything to stop her . . . Instead, she has destroyed everything. Instead—instead what? What was I thinking about again?

Failure.

The voice is back, taunting my dreams. What dreams? I open my eyes, but all I see is darkness. It's cold here, but in the cold I feel warmth. I turn my head to the right, and through the darkness, I see a pair of aquamarine eyes staring at me. They're the only thing I find in the pitch black.

Peggy.

"David," I hear her voice, but it seems distant and far away.

You have failed. You allowed her to succeed. She will take everything you love. Piece by piece. Little by little . . . The voice starts again, but I'm not sure who it's talking about.

"David!" Peggy calls.

Is the voice talking about Peggy? Or is the voice talking about someone else? Peggy is one of those people I love. It can't be her. Can it? Flames leap in my peripheral vision, but they don't burn me. I close my eyes to block out the sight. The cold starts to dissipate. The warmth changes into a fervent heat, and this time when I open my eyes, I see Peggy with her lips against mine. A wall of fire surrounds us. I push her away, and the flames disappear with a blast against stone walls before disappearing into darkness.

"Peggy?" I ask into the dark after a moment.

"I'm here." I feel her hand touch mine.

"Where? What happened?"

"I took you down to one of the servant's tunnels so your gift didn't freeze anyone's fears. It was the safest, quickest place I could think of, but I don't know if it helped."

I gulp. I lost control of my gift again? Obviously, there is no other explanation for the voice I heard earlier. What was it trying to tell me? I shake my head. It doesn't matter now. "Is everyone else okay?"

"I don't know. I haven't been able to find out yet."

I turn my hand, gripping Peggy's. "Thank you." Even with her stiff right leg, she managed to get me down here. It couldn't have been easy, but I'm grateful she did. Peg was born crippled but she's never let her disability drag her down—it's one of the reasons I love her so much.

I reach my other hand up to caress her face, but then think better of it, dropping it back to the ground. Knowing me, I will miscalculate where her face is and poke her in the eye. It will be a gentle poke, of course, but the romance of the moment will be lost. "I'm sorry to lay all this on you. I should be taking care of you, not the other way around."

"Nonsense. I'm free to leave whenever I want to, but I choose to stay." She sits down on my lap, her hand against my chest.

I can feel the cold stone of the servant's tunnel against my back. "I know, and I'm so grateful for it. I'm sure everyone in the castle is grateful for it." It's a lame attempt at a joke, but I still receive a chuckle for it. I can see Peggy's silhouette now. I reach up and caress her cheek—without poking her eye out.

"Peggy, so many things are uncertain right now, and who knows what will happen within the next few weeks. But, I—"

"Yes," she blurts and then starts giggling. I know she can't see my expression, but if she could, it would be stuck somewhere between amused and concerned.

"Yes, what?" Genuinely, I'm curious as to what she agreed to.

"Never mind," she mumbles between giggles. "Perhaps, I should have let you finish."

"Perhaps? No, you can't get out of this one that easily. Pray tell, what are you saying yes to?"

She groans. "Fine, but you have to promise you won't patronize me if I'm wrong."

"Cross my heart."

"Yes, I will marry you."

I raise my eyebrows. She's right. I wanted to ask her to marry me, but she didn't even give me a chance to say the words. Now, I can give her impatience a taste of its own medicine. I don't say anything for what feels like an hour, but in reality is an excruciating twenty seconds.

"David?"

I stay silent.

"David?" She snaps her fingers, and I burst out laughing. "Why are you laughing?" Her finger pokes my cheek. "It's not funny."

"What's not funny?"

"Stop it," she huffs, getting off my lap.

"Woah, woah, wait a minute." I grab her waist and pull her back down on top of me. "I was laughing because you read my mind. You didn't give me a chance to ask, but I love you and I want you to marry me."

I hear the smile in her voice as she answers. "Good."

And then her lips are against mine again.

Esther

"You have to find me."

"This isn't what I wanted."

"I never wanted this to happen."

"I did it to protect you . . ."

"Why did you let them take me?"

The voices bombard my head, filling it with doubts and fear. Fear I had tried for years to rid myself of, but fear never truly goes away . . . not really.

I wake with a gasp, my heart hammering in my chest. Darkness surrounds the room like a suffocating blanket, reminding me of the dark I suffered through three years ago when I was taken and left alone for several months . . . when they waited to take my newborn son, Aiden. All this time and I still have no idea who took me or what they did to him.

I have to get up. I have to get out. There must be a way out.

I feel a hand on my shoulder. "Esther?"

A short, terrified yelp escapes my lips, blood rushing in my ears before I realize that it's just my husband, Connan. Relief floods me. I'm not in that place anymore. I'm safe, but the voices—I heard my son's among them. I've never heard his voice, but in my heart I know it was him.

"Did I wake you?" I whisper, tracing his face in the midnight haze.

"No. I . . . had a nightmare as well." He gathers me into his arms. The cool metal of his left arm brushes my skin with shivers as I melt into the warmth of his chest.

"Tell me."

He sighs. "It's nothing new really. I was walking alone on the shore, sand under my toes, but as I walked, the beach became frozen. I knew I was taunting them—the sirens." His breath hitches as he grips me a little closer. "It's the only reason I was there. Then they appeared, jumping out of the water and reaching for me. They took ahold of me, and just before my body hit the water, someone pulled me back. Then I woke up. What about yours?"

I take a deep breath. "Nothing new either. I was in that room again, but this time, the voices were yours and my parents and David and Dais and . . . Aiden. He accused me of letting them take him away. I wanted to tell him that it wasn't my fault, but then I woke up, and"—tears clog my throat—"and it felt like he was being ripped from me. I'm so tired of things being ripped from me."

"Esther—"

"I know what you're going to say . . . It's not your fault. I know that, but it feels like a punishment—like I'm bound to lose everyone I love."

"That's not true." His fingers dig into my skin as if it will keep him from being taken from me.

"Don't tell me it's not. You're here now, but soon you will be claimed by the sea. You won't be able to hold out. Already, I'm watching you grow older. I'm watching you die. I'm watching you disappear like the years you gave them—years you should have had with me. Just like my years with Aiden were stolen too. If David can't learn to control his gift, I will lose him too. I've already seen Dais's downfall, and the worst part, I can't do anything to stop it." I wrap my arms around his thick shoulders, crying into the crook of his neck. I feel his cheek rest against my head.

"If I could go back—"

"Don't. I know you would do the same thing again because it was your way of protecting me—of protecting your men. There is no way to go back. What's done is done, and you can't regret your choice because of a few tears shed by your wife. Just promise me I will be able to say goodbye before you go. I've never . . . I've never been given the chance to say goodbye. That's all I want."

It's really not all I want, because what I want, I can't have. I want Connan to be okay. I want him to live. I want my son. I want peace . . . but those are all things I can't have. It's as useless as holding onto the broken fragments of a lost dream. I feel his gentle intake of breath, the pulse of his heartbeat underneath my fingertips—the only solid evidence that he's still here.

"I promise. I love you."

I raise my head, cupping his chin. "I love you."

Chapter 3

With All the Finery in the World

A'zre

I don't have time for this. I pace the room. Back and forth, back and forth. My lawyers promised that the proposal would be done tonight, but they are just liars who like to try my patience. Chilly night air sweeps across my study, but I refuse to close the floor-to-ceiling windows that lead out to the terrace. The cold keeps me awake while I wait in never-ending agony.

A gentle knock on my study's door takes my mind off the thought of having them publicly executed for lying to their king. I glare at the door engraved with emerald and ruby rhinestones that have been inlaid with gold. I don't want to open it, but it could be one of my stupid lawyers with the promised treaties.

"Come in," I bark, picking up the cup of *M'laj* a servant left me a while ago. Of course it's already cold, but my guest doesn't need to know that.

Lami steps over the threshold, her bright gold eyes that compliment long silver hair look over me and linger on my cup. "Would you like me to replace your tea?"

I wrinkle my nose, placing the cup down. If anyone besides Lami had opened the door and not addressed me as "Your Majesty" I would have had them killed right on the spot.

She was my nurse and caregiver while I was a child. She's one of the few people I truly know . . . and one of the few people still alive who knows everything about me. I don't like it when others are familiar with my past because they can always use that information against me. But Lami is different, just like I am different to her as well.

I am the only son she ever had, not biologically, of course, unless my father was lying about my mother, which wouldn't surprise me. No, she isn't the woman who gave birth to me, but she is the woman who raised me. Unfortunately, she couldn't protect me from the horrors my father inflicted, but before he physically made me his abused little puppet, she took plenty of beatings to keep me safe. I guess it was all for naught though, because he still came for me.

"Never mind that. I'm not thirsty anyway," I say.

Lami raises a silver eyebrow but keeps her mouth in a tight line. The silence kills me, and she knows that.

"Fine. I'll drink it." I gulp down the remaining liquid. How wonderful, a king who has to drink cold tea. "Why have you come to see me?" My eyes flicker along the lion mosaics on the wall to the right.

Lami sighs, but I pretend not to notice. "R'sha has given birth to a son. Your fourteenth child. Your sixth boy. Congratulations."

I nod. "And R'sha?" She is my fifth wife out of six.

"Resting, but it was a difficult birth. You will need to give her at least three months' rest."

I nod stiffly. I hate being at the birth of my children. I hate it because . . . I feel the hand holding my throat at the memory. The hand that tore me from the woman I loved and forced me to destroy the beautiful bond I had with her. After that fateful day, I can't bring myself to be present at births. They remind me of all I have, and all I have to lose. Sons are good, but one day they will be forced to destroy each other for power—for the kingdom. Fortunately, I won't be able to see it. Just like I won't see them come into the world, I won't see them leave it, but I will be there through the middle.

I meet Lami's star-streaked eyes. "I will have to think of a good name for him before the ceremony. Thank you."

She nods. "Are you really heading to Casta soon?"

I stare out toward the balcony. Red curtains sway in the breeze. I shiver, still refusing to close the windows. Where are those incompetent *Sh'lles*? "Yes, I leave the day after tomorrow."

"I wish you a safe journey then. Please come home," she whispers, clearing my tea cup and rushing out of the room before I can answer.

I hate that she cares for me. Not because of pity, but because I don't deserve her devotion. Just like I don't deserve a healthy son. I grunt before starting for the door. Those *Ne'rns* will just have to wait for me. I am the king after all. I can do whatever I want, and right now, I want to meet my new son.

Ellenora

Those bumbling buffoons! I think as I scramble down the hall after being confronted by one of the lords on Dais's council. Bright chandeliers light my way even though the sun shines through the windows this morning. I'm so angry I can't even remember which lord it was. As if I would ever side with him compared to my own son!

"Your husband was killed by your son's murderous wife, correct?" His stupid words ring through my head once more, making my blood boil. What an idiot! Oh, how I wish I could remember who it was just so Dais can put him on the traitor list! Oh! That's good. Why didn't I tell the moron that sooner? My son needs patriots to help run this country not fools.

I stop in front of the gold gilded double doors that lead to Dais and Rahuin's room. Two guards flank the sides, and I startle for a minute, before remembering that Jet doubled their guard. I sigh in an attempt to calm my temper. I haven't gotten angry like that in such a long time. In some ways, it feels good, freeing even, but in others, it feels ridiculous and not at all graceful, let alone poised!

Temper.

I take a few deep breaths before opening the door. I step inside. Sunlight floods through the windows on the adjacent side of the room, illuminating sky blue walls gilded in amber filigree. Rahuin sits at a little table positioned in the warm light from the windows, caressing a cup of tea. The smoky tendrils curl around her chin and frowning mouth. Her blurry green eyes laden with dark circles widen at my unannounced visit.

"Ellenora." She starts to stand.

I rush forward. "Sit, sit, my dear. I'm only here to join you for tea." I take a seat across the table.

She rings the bell for a servant to bring me a cup. "To what do I owe this visit?" Her voice hitches up at the end like she's nervous. Her red hair has been pinned into a haphazard bun with frizzy curls escaping all over the place and framing her pale face.

I reach for her hands. They're warm compared to my own. "I know you've been home for a few days now, and I wanted to wait until you felt well enough to speak with me. I'm here because I want you to understand that I don't blame you for what happened."

Tears well in her eyes, and it's like I'm watching porcelain crack as her brow furrows. "Out of everyone, I thought you would be the last to forgive me."

"Timothy . . ." I swallow. "He was sick for a long time. So much so, that I prayed it would take him away and end his suffering, but suffering was the reason he became ill."

"I know about his sickness, but it still doesn't change what I did."

My thumbs rub circles over her hands. "Timothy used you to end his pain and save his country. If he hadn't been willing, you wouldn't have been able to get into the Darkness's lair."

Her hand squeezes mine. "A lot of good it did . . . I'm not proud of what I had to do just to save Casta. I hate myself for it."

"Tell me what happened." A sick knot twists my stomach. What horrible things did she endure for her to say such things?

"Not—I—while I was with the Darkness, I found out I was pregnant, but to keep her safe, I had to sleep with—with someone else." Her voice cracks as the tears rain down her cheeks. "I betrayed Dais. Then, I used what the Darkness taught me and murdered thousands of men. I—I cut so many lives short. M—me." She starts sobbing, shattering with the weight of all she carries.

"No one should have to go through that. No one should have to carry the weight of thousands of lives on their hands, but war and death are merciless masters. I know you will never forget those atrocities, but maybe one day you'll be able to forgive yourself." I gently reach up, rubbing away a tear on her cheek.

"Do you believe I can be forgiven for what I've done?" Her eyes search mine, looking for a ray of hope in the world of hurt she's in.

"I've forgiven you because I realize that there was no other way Casta would have had a chance. If you hadn't done it, we would all be slaves under the Darkness's ruthless hand. Who knows how many more lives would have been lost? Then you would hate yourself for not doing anything. I know if there had been any way to resolve this without excessive bloodshed, you would have done it, but that wasn't the case. Your bravery and their sacrifice saved us all."

"But what happens if it doesn't?" she whispers. "I did this to fulfill the prophecy, but what happens if the Darkness still enslaves us all? What happens if he comes for everyone I love because I defied him? To join him, I—I had to promise that I would bring you all endless suffering, and he—he promised he would do the same to me if—if he found out I was lying. What if I made everything worse?" Her voice cracks as her eyes grow wild with paranoia.

My heart clenches in my chest. "Don't believe any of those lies. You didn't make anything wors—"

"I gambled with your lives! The Darkness knows whom I love. He knows what will break me the most, and i—it won't be long before he comes for all of—of you." She breaks down into sobs again.

I stand and rush to the other side of the table, taking her into my arms. We fall to the floor as she cries against my shoulder. I hush her, my fingers stroking her cheek. I feel like I'm trying to keep her broken pieces together before she shatters. "You didn't gamble with our lives. You're not the only one who has fought the Darkness and you won't be the only one carrying on the fight. You're not alone. Not anymore."

She trembles in my arms. "I just—I don't want to lose what—everything I have fought for. I'm just—I'm so scared I'll lose everyone I love, and that I won't be able to stop it because it was all my fault."

I rub small circles into her back as she weeps, taking a moment of silence. "You won't lose us. Like I said, you're not the only one fighting. You've done the hardest part. Now, it is time for us to fight for you. It is time for us to take care of you." I place my cheek against her head of ruby red curls.

After a second, she lifts her head, her tear-stained eyes taking me in. "You're right." She sits up, wiping her face. She seems stronger now, her resolve put back together. "I'm sorry I broke down like that. I—my emotions are all over the place."

I smile. "Carrying a child in your womb will do that to you."

She takes my hands into her own. "Thank you, Ellenora. Your kindness and forgiveness mean the world to me." Tears smart in her eyes again, but she blinks them away. "Perhaps we should finish our tea." She stands and helps me up beside her.

"It's probably cold now." I laugh as we take our seats. I was right, the tea is cold.

"I have to tell you," Rahuin starts after ringing for more tea. "Dais and I have decided to host an actual wedding ceremony." She smiles.

I gape at her. "You have?"

A servant enters and places steaming hot cups filled with delectable tea in front of us.

Rahuin waits until she's gone to speak, "Last night."

"But—"

"I know. Perhaps it isn't the best time, but we want to show the people that Casta isn't defeated. We want to give them something to celebrate, but I'm skeptical about how many will actually celebrate."

She's right. How many will accept her and Dais's engagement? Yes, many of the nobles and workers in the palace already know they're married, but the people don't. They already hate Rahuin's part in Timothy's death. How many will see their marriage as manipulation by a murderer? How many will accept them?

"Then why are you doing it? Why do you want to have the celebration right now? Perhaps, you should wait until the baby is born and give the people a little bit of time to calm themselves over the events of Timothy's death." I take a sip of tea, the mild, earthy tones calming my nerves.

"I doubt anyone will ever understand why I had to kill him, but I'm hoping the celebration will become a way for me to prove to the people that I mean them no harm . . . that I did what I had to to keep them safe."

I look away. "They won't see it that way."

"Maybe not, but no one ever got anywhere by not trying. We plan to read the letters King Timothy left. Maybe they'll help bring understanding, or maybe they'll cause more hatred. Whichever it is, I still plan to marry Dais publicly. He is my husband, and I want to tell the world."

I sigh at her words. I understand what she means, I just don't accept it. I don't think a celebration is what the people need right now. They are thirsty for blood, and at this rate, they don't care whose blood it is. They want someone to pay, and I fear my son and Rahuin will bear the brunt of their pain.

Carrie

ÄLBRECT CASTLE—OTHERWORLD KINGDOM—KÄS

Moving a tapestry aside, I step into the King's quarters. King Rave stands in front of a quadrilateral mirror with seven different attendants helping him into a black, indigo, purple, and gray suit. The different colors shimmer in certain areas around the black so it looks like he has the wings of a raven. The last thing they attach to him is a giant cape made of actual raven feathers that drapes down his back and trails out behind him in a train that ruffles when he walks toward me. A smirk lights his face, his dark eyes sweeping over me in the bright room. Gold chandeliers from King Rave's great inventor host glorious electricity to illuminate the space.

I bow my head.

"What do you think, Xin?" He does a little spin, his hands splaying in front of him.

I look him up and down. "Marvelous, Your Majesty."

"I thought so." He glances behind him, dismissing his attendants with a nod of his head.

My heart starts to pound as they make for the door. I hate being alone with the King. He's not exactly a man of . . . honor.

His sharp eyes examine me once they're gone, and the good-natured smirk lifting his face immediately disappears, replaced with a gaze that could freeze the sun. I force myself to meet those frigid eyes, letting him know that no matter what, I won't cower in his presence.

He smiles, but it's cold and dead. How fitting. As a Deathwalker, he's able to control death. He can hold the balance of someone's life literally in his hands. Just like he holds mine. If I were ever to defy him, I would die. I suffer from a rare disease. One that attacks my heart. If King Rave didn't use his power to keep it at bay, my heart would shatter, and I would give in to death.

"I'm glad you made it, Carrie."

My blood boils at the use of my name on his tongue. I hate it. I hate the way he says it, like it's poison he has to spit out.

"Anything to honor Your Majesty. How can I be of assistance?"

He moves around the room, pouring liquor out of a gold decanter into a black crystal glass. He nods to it, asking if I would like some, and I shake my head.

"In the room behind that door is a dress. Put it on. I have a special mission for you tonight." He takes a sip of his drink, his head tilting toward a little white and gold painted door lying to my right.

My mouth goes dry. "Your Majesty?"

"Don't question me and do as you're told." The ice in his voice forces me to move.

I step into the room to find several servants bustling around an enormous green dress. My jaw drops as they immediately pull me inside and start undressing me.

I bite my tongue to keep myself from speaking. I hate it when people touch me, especially when my clothes are being taken off and replaced. Somehow they wiggle me into the gown and cinch the bodice tight, accentuating cleavage I didn't even know I had. Why would the king want me to wear this contraption? What special mission involves a dress? My stomach curls at the thought that he wants me to accompany him to his Bicentennial Celebration. I hope not. I don't think I can tolerate his frozen demeanor for a whole night. My transactions with King Rave are often short and precise—my mission, my target, my reward. They never involve keeping him company.

After applying a bit of makeup to my face and combing my short brown hair, the servants breeze out of the room, and I'm forced to head back into the King's main quarters.

His dead-eye gaze looks me over as slow as he possibly can. "Hmm, look at that. A special soldier can clean up well. You even look rather beautiful."

Bile rolls in my throat, but I swallow it down as the dread from earlier fills my stomach again. "Thank you, Your Majesty."

Something besides coldness lights his gaze, and the shift sends gooseflesh across my skin as every sense in me screams, *"Danger! Run!"*

He downs the last bit of his drink before stepping toward me. "Your mission for tonight . . ."

Please don't say accompany you. Please don't tell me to accompany you.

". . . I want you to keep an eye on a very special someone." His voice fades back into my thoughts. "His name is Aiden Brachus. He's a new recruit of mine, and he holds an exceptional ability. I need him, and I need someone I can trust to stand close by his side."

I barely keep my relieved sigh from escaping. At least he doesn't want me to accompany him, but now I have to babysit a Walk? I thought he hated Walks—well, he hates them unless they prove to be useful to him.

"How will I find him?"

"He'll be at tonight's celebration wearing a black and gold suit. I'll have Juda give you a full description. Gain his trust and keep him close to your side. He's a Lifewalker, but I have yet to discover the true nature of his ability. I want you to figure it out for me."

"You think I can do it all in one night?"

"No." Rave shakes his head, amusement crossing his face. "Of course not. You will continue any regular missions through Commander Li, but I want you to gain his trust by being Carrie. Just Carrie."

Just Carrie . . . Who even is that? I don't know her, and I'm certain she doesn't know me, even though we're the same.

"I will do as you ask, Your Majesty." I lower my head.

"Of course you will."

Aiden

ÄLBRECT CASTLE—OTHERWORLD KINGDOM—KÄS

Lights flicker without the use of fire, shining down on the ballroom with effortless beauty. Electricity. I'm told. I frown. Of course, King Rave would be the only person to have it in Käs. I'm sure the invention would be a great asset to everyone, but the king isn't concerned with anyone but himself. My stomach tightens as I walk past ushers in gold and blue embroidered jackets with masks obscuring their eyes. Their greeting is lost on me as I step toward the edge of the balcony that overlooks the ballroom below. My eyes take in the ivory and gold walls.

Filigree in the shapes of ravens, vines, and flowers snake up the pillars that are half-set into the walls. Obsidian floors sustain guests clad in Käsian finery—silks, gossamer, velvet. They mingle around the ballroom, talking about whatever strikes their fancy. In the center, some dance to the lilting music being played by musicians at the front of the room directly across from me.

I turn to the left and follow the grand staircase down to the main floor. Guests look up as I descend, appraising me behind their elegant masks. Even though I don't know they're thoughts, I know they must be wondering about me. *Who is this man? We've never seen him here before. Why is he here at the most prestigious celebration of the year? He doesn't look like anything special.* I smirk as my silver-tipped boots hit the obsidian floor. Maybe they won't see me as special, but that's the reason why I'm here. Because a certain someone found out how special I am.

I usually don't brag about myself, but this party is solely for people who intend to brag about themselves. Of course, we can never outshine the person of honor—King Rave—but we all try our best to come second, and maybe that's why I decided to grace this party with my presence. *You graced it only because a certain Deathwalker would kill you if you didn't . . .* That's probably true, I like my head. It'd be a shame to part with it now, all because I didn't go to a masquerade ball?

He requested my presence so specifically he even sent a black and gold embroidered jacket and mask to my clinic with explicit instructions that I wear them—as if that wasn't obvious. What else do you do with a jacket and mask? Burn them? Give them to someone else? He'd probably see it as treason and use his particular power to send me into the depths of Astyria, or wherever you go after you die.

"You look lost," a woman, clad in a silk green dress, says. The tight corset top cinches her cleavage silhouetting her thin waist before furling down in emerald-green waves, burying her in a sea of fabric. Though she is quite beautiful in the contraption, I can't help but think she looks like the dress is wearing her, not the other way around. Short brown hair curls gently around a sharp chin. Bright red lips smile at me, shimmering in a welcoming facade.

Her gaze tells a different story, and I realize why my earlier observation makes sense. Her dark brown eyes look like a caged animal trying to claw their way out. I wonder who hides inside the cage? Who is this woman? Is she allowed to say, to be who she really is? Or is she caged because she can't be anything more than what she's forced to be? But who's she being forced to be? Obviously, she hates it.

"Funny, I was going to say the same for you." I take a step closer to her, but not too close. I'm afraid I'll trip over her dress. Perhaps it's something she was commanded to wear, just like me.

She smiles wider, but her eyes narrow in suspicion. "You didn't even see me before I gained your attention."

"I'm certain you would have gained my attention at some point during the night." I lean forward a little.

"Are you trying to flirt with me?"

"Maybe. Is it working?" I smirk.

Her lips quirk as she raises a perfect brow. "Definitely not."

I roll back on my heels, standing up straight again. "Well, that shoots my next question out of the water . . ." I trail off, refusing to give up so easily, and if I say my question right now, she won't want to know what it is.

This time, she leans in. "And the next question would be?"

Got her.

"Would you like to dance?"

"I don't dance with strangers."

"Then what are you doing at a masquerade ball?"

"The food." She smiles.

I make a show of looking around. "There's food? Shoot. I should have arrived earlier."

She rolls her eyes. "It hasn't even been served yet . . ."

"Well then, you have a while to wait. Let's dance." I hold my hand toward her.

"I don't even know your name."

"That's an easy fix—Aiden Brachus." I fold my hand over my mouth, leaning in close to her so I can whisper. "And I don't think I'm supposed to tell anyone, but I'm a Lifewalker. Gasp. So we all know why I'm here." I lean back. "It's your turn."

"Carrie Haligun." She leans in close, folding her hand over her mouth as well. "And I'm not a Walk at all. So why do you think I'm here?"

"The food obviously."

She finally laughs, the sound pulling at my heartstrings. *Get a grip, Aiden. You've heard women laugh before.*

"You're a quick one, Aiden Brachus." She takes my hand, and I lead her to the dance floor. I have to extend my arm all the way out to keep from tripping over the layers of her dress.

"So what do you do if you don't belong to the king's menagerie of Walks?" I ask, pulling her closer for our dance, one hand on her waist and the other gripping her slender fingers.

A smirk lights up her features, and for a moment, her eyes don't look so lost anymore. "I'm a dancer. You know, one of those fancy ones."

I grimace. Dear Lifewalker, I finally find an interesting woman whose laugh intrigues me and she's one of the king's—

She starts to giggle. "You should see your face. I never knew someone could look so disgusted."

I spin her to the music, trying to hide my exasperation. "Very funny."

"Entertaining men is a very worthy profession, I've heard."

"I'm sure." I lean closer to her face. "If you're entertaining me, I'd rather not know."

She giggles. "If I am?" Her dark brown eyes study mine. My heart stops. A fire now lights that gaze, and I begin to wonder if our banter has put it there.

"I think I'd be very disappointed." I swallow. Couples dance around us in colorful swishes of fabric like waving flower petals, reminding me we aren't the only two mesmerized in the steps.

"Why?" Her voice drops, almost as if she's the one disappointed with my answer.

"Because if you're just playing a part to entertain me, then this very interesting, beautiful woman I met at a party once doesn't exist."

"Beautiful?" She smiles. "If she did exist? What would you do then?" She sways closer to me, her lips near my ear.

I turn my gaze to meet her eyes. "I would invite her to tea with me and my uncle. I would get her family's permission to court her. I would fall in love, and I'd hope she'd love me back."

"What a romantic you are." She bats brown lashes, a smile lifting the corners of her lips as she looks up at me, and I see my blue eyes reflected in hers.

"And you aren't?" I ask as she steps back.

"Not like I used to be." She looks away, and the little fire that appeared vanishes again. "Would you believe me if I say . . ." She pauses, taking in a deep breath as her eyes bounce around the room. I notice her taking in every guard around us. Is she being watched? Who is she that she's too scared to tell me the truth—that she's so scared of who she is?

She smiles. "I wish I could tell you who I am. I wish I could be the girl who goes to tea for a boy. I wish I had a family you could ask for permission, but in answer to your question, I'm not an entertainer."

The song ends, and she steps away from me, her eyes narrowing around the room before they finally settle on me. A gentleness lights her gaze before she dips her head and says, "Thank you for the dance. I should really be going." She turns to leave.

"Wait." I reach for her. "Please just leave me a way to contact you." This is stupid. I shouldn't pursue her. Obviously she has secrets of her own. Secrets she's not willing to share, but I can't help myself. I have to try, even though I know she'll say no.

She starts to shake her head. "You don— all right. Ask for me at Thirty-First West Tier Street. Mrs. Hilde will help you. It was nice meeting you, Mr. Brachus." She disappears, leaving me dumbfounded in the middle of a grand ballroom.

I smile. *Thirty-First West Tier Street* . . . Suddenly, I can't wait for it to be tomorrow.

Chapter 4
Regret is the Worst Mistress

Rahuin

My fingers shake as they hold Dais's. The white balcony doors engraved with gold leaves and flowers stand before us. Two ushers hold the handles ready to announce us to the people of Casta. The glass windows outside the door show a view of the white-washed balcony spiraled in cerulean ribbon. I'm grateful I can't see the crowd below it.

I never thought I would be this terrified to face the people I call my own. People I killed others to save. People who hate me for killing someone they all loved and adored. The irony of it. I killed to keep them safe, only to come home—not a hero, but a murderer in their eyes. They don't see the sacrifice it took. They don't care because they've lost as well. They need someone to blame, and that's who I've become.

Dais squeezes my hand, steadying it in the depression of his palm. "It's going to be all right. Once they hear the letters my father left, everything will be fine."

I nod, swallowing the bad taste in my mouth. Sometimes I think he's too optimistic. How can people who don't even know me forgive my sins when I can't forgive myself?

"You don't have to speak if you don't want to. I'll do all the talking. They just need to see you," he whispers, but I hear the hesitation in his voice—the anxiety that pulls at his gentle words. He hates public speaking. He told me once that it terrifies him more than facing a ruthless enemy on the battlefield.

I squeeze his hand back, hoping he can find some comfort in my presence, just as I find comfort in him.

"I can speak too. We do it together." I gaze up into his blue eyes, which are turned to the sky just outside the windows. I don't have long to get lost in them because the call for "His Majesty the King" rings outside, sparking fanfare and cries of jubilation from the people. My heart jumps as those filigree doors open wide. Frost-bitten air greets my skin, and I pull my wool wrap tighter in my gloved fist.

My legs shake as we step out onto the balcony. The screams become deafening as Dais comes into view, but the cheering dies out as they start to recognize who I am. My heart thrums in my chest as if begging to be let out so it doesn't have to sit here, caged and broken and on display for all the world to see. Even from up here, I see a mix of confusion and anger set into the eyes of the people closest to the balcony. *You shouldn't be here. They hate you . . .*

"Great people of Casta!" Dais starts as criers call out his message to the masses. "By now most of you have heard the rumor that this warrior, Lady Rahuin D'Arvent, killed my father on the battlefield in cold blood. We stand before you today with a new message, one I hope in time you will accept. She—"

"Let me tell it," I gasp.

Dais glances at me before stepping away so I can face them in the center. I swallow. "I made a deal with King Timothy because I wanted to infiltrate the Darkness. The only way to gain his trust was to kill the entire royal family or turn them all over to him. I could never do that. So King Timothy and I came up with a plan. That I . . ." I can't breathe. I can't do this. I thought I could. I thought— Dais's hand slips into mine once more, and I finally take a breath.

"That I would kill him publicly on the battlefield. It worked. I was able to infiltrate the Darkness and destroy his armies. I know many of you saw the light that brightened the sky several nights ago and heard reports of the men who were k—killed in the blast. I used magic to destroy the enemy's army. That's how I was able to justify my actions in killing King Timothy. It was the only way I was able to return home." My voice drops down to a whimper I know they'll never hear. "I'm sorry it was the only way to save you."

Murmurs ripple through the crowd, and a light breeze tousles my red locks. Even though I'm freezing, I feel sweat sliding down my back.

"How can this be true? How can we know you actually made this deal with the King?" I hear the shout above the rest in the crowd, followed by others affirming the man's question.

Dais takes over for me. "My father wrote several letters explaining what happened to me, my mother, and several noblemen. Out of their good will, we have decided to release these letters. They will be announced in public squares and published on the bulletins of every city and village. They will affirm Rahuin's innocence. I hope you will accept them and find it in your hearts to forgive her for the actions she had to display in order to save all of Casta."

The people are incredibly silent at his words, as if he enraptured them in a spell of silence. My heart swells as I listen to him. I don't know why he's so afraid to speak to his people. They love him so much.

"Her sacrifice has deterred the enemy enough so we can regroup and continue to train more men. I know you wish this war to be over, but we have much to prepare for in the coming months. I ask for your steadfast courage and hope to continue forward until we are free of the lingering threat posed by this enemy that wants our peaceful country!" he finishes with a shout, and the people meet his enthusiasm, raising their hands and cheering for their king. He lifts his hands, calling them to silence.

"There is one more thing I have to address before we leave you today. Many have heard the rumor that Lady Rahuin and I are more than just comrades in battle, and I want to tell you that the rumors are true." He takes my hand once more. "Rahuin and I have fallen in love over the last year, and I have asked for her hand in marriage."

Cries rise up among the crowd—disbelief, shock, jubilation, anger. It's a deafening roar that strikes my heart. *They'll never accept you . . .*

Dais raises his hands again. "Our wedding will be held in two months' time. And before any rumors surface saying I advocated for my father's death, I want to tell you that I had no idea of their plan at the time. I was very hurt when they both left, but I love Rahuin and I loved my father. I trusted that they knew what they were doing. Rahuin was able to accomplish her mission, and I was able to forgive her for what she did. I urge you all to find it in your hearts to forgive her as well, for she will be my wife, and in turn, the queen of this nation."

The people don't even wait for him to finish speaking before they throw their opinions out into the wind. I grip Dais's hand tighter as my breaths come to quick. I hear them calling for my blood. I hear them saying I don't deserve to be queen. I will never be queen in their eyes. They will make Dais and the entire royal family pay for this mistrust of faith. How can I protect Dais now? Sira? The rest of his family and the League? They will turn against us. They will come for my head.

In trying to secure the country, we've caused a civil war. The thoughts consume me, and I feel cold tears making their way down my face.

"Rahuin, Rahuin . . ." Someone shakes me. I blink away the tears, turning my head to meet Dais's eyes. Everything comes back into focus, and I can hear the shouts behind his blue eyes. "Long live the king! Long live the queen!"

A smile lights his face. "We did it. I told you it would be all right."

I nod, forcing a smile because I'm not sure what's real and what isn't anymore. I'm not sure if my fears speak truth, or if the cheers are really the sound of acceptance. Are they just tolerating us for a new day?

Jarret

The spyglass in my fingers quivers as I look out over the snow-covered valley. There are hundreds of them. Hundreds of soldiers training over the trampled earth of Lanckest's once beautiful grasslands and fields. I pull the glass away from my face and look at Renell, who stands beside me in her cursed form of a black unicorn. A long flowing mane spills over her silky coat and her tail swishes, kicking up snow flurries.

Renell is a creature of death—a gift that kills anything she touches or that touches her when she's in her full cursed form. Sometimes she uses a small portion of her gift to see life flowing in other's veins. She tried to describe it to me once, and it sounded beautiful. She explained that everyone has a different color she watches flow through their veins like water.

Darkness swirls at the edges of her mane, making her look more menacing than she actually is as she stares down into the valley. I know she sees the same thing I did through the spyglass, and she doesn't look happy about it.

"Renell, come on, we won't learn anything much up here. We have to get down there and figure out who is in charge of these operations."

I already know who is in charge. Her voice appears in my head.

"Still, three of us can't do anything against five thousand men."

Six thousand.

"Excuse me?"

There are six thousand men down there, not five thousand.

I frown, and she laughs as she changes back into her human form. Her dark green eyes tease mine as she takes a step closer to me. She pats my chest with gloved fingers before pulling her jacket tighter around her shoulders. Her black hair blows in the wind, faming her brown skin and the pale tattoos of the moon that encircle her face. "I don't plan on fighting these men . . . at least not yet. I honestly can't believe they have this many men training here already. Rahuin ju—"

"They never stopped training," I answer as I study the valley that crawls with men who look like nothing more than dark cockroaches.

It's Renell's turn to frown. "Okay, *dir flak*." She turns to walk away.

I chuckle and start after her. I honestly have no idea where she thinks she's going to go. We're standing on a mountain peak, and she needs me to help her get back down safely, unless she plans on rolling down the mountain. Which I guess isn't an entirely implausible idea.

I race after her and snatch her into my arms, morphing into my dragon form before we tumble off the side of the mountain. Dark blue scales appear from my skin as my body lengthens and wings sprout from my back.

She gasps as we launch into the air. "Jarret!"

I laugh as she twists in my arms. *Don't squirm, or I'll drop you.*

"Don't. You. Dare." She hisses, and I hold her tighter to my chest.

I won't, I assure, as I bank towards our camp. I honestly don't want to receive the brunt of Renell's wrath. No thank you, I prefer to keep my head attached to my body. Snow covered evergreens reach for us as I glide over the tops. I see a small fire glowing in the snowy clearing of our camp as we draw near, but Wen is nowhere to be found. Great . . . Bed rolls are already laid out around the fire with our bags lying at the foot of them.

The white haired demon probably disappeared and is long gone by now. Why did Renell trust him to stay alone while we went scouting? At least he didn't steal our bags.

I set Renell down before I land, but there is still no sign of the missing demon.

Renell immediately starts rummaging through our supplies for something to eat.

"Excuse me, but isn't someone missing here?" I ask once I've morphed back to my human form. I run a gloved hand through my long hair.

"Something missing where?" Wen's voice sneaks up from behind me as he passes with an armful of kindling. White tattoos on his neck and face standout against his tawny skin as a smirk plays across his features.

I glare daggers into the back of his white head as I step forward.

The little *flak* is going to get it.

Renell steps in front of me, placing a hand to my chest. "Let it go."

I look down at her and huff. I can never say no to her. "I'm sorry. He just gets on my nerves." I gently cup her face with my hands, my thumbs rubbing circles against her cheeks and moon tattoos.

"I know, but you have to learn to control your temper. He has decided to change, and I have given him every opportunity to falsify his claims. So far, he hasn't failed those tests yet. You have to give him a little grace. At least, he hasn't killed us in our sleep." She smiles brightly, and I feel like the sun has appeared on our camp, even though it just set in a blur of hazy orange and pink.

"Comforting."

Her smile widens, dark green eyes glistening as her fingers run along my stubbled jaw. It sends shivers down my skin. "That I am." She lifts her lips for a kiss, and I can't refuse.

"Hey, lovebirds!" Wen yells, separating us before our lips meet. "The eggs are burning." He points to the fire that indeed holds a pan of smoking eggs. Now I'm really going to kill him.

Renell, sensing my anger once more, kisses my cheek before leaving me to go fix the mess that should have been dinner.

Renell

"I will kill everyone you are close to, right before your very eyes . . ." The red gaze looms and grows larger until it seems like it'll swallow me whole. He's watching me. He sees me. He knows. He's coming . . .

I gasp as I wake, the lingering memory of his eyes haunt my thoughts and the darkness surrounding me does little to shake the image away. The warmth of Jarret's arm across my torso fills me with a little comfort.

But what if it's not Jarret? The thought creeps into my mind before I can stop it, and now I can't see his face because the fire has burnt down to embers.

I have to see his face. I have to know it's him.

I push his hand off me and tap into my gift. His veins ignite in a beautiful glowing blue, like his Garon form. Relief washes over me. It's fine. It's him. Wen glows white a little ways away on the other side of the coals, sitting on watch with his back turned to me.

I move over to him, letting my curse fall away. Snow crunches under my booted feet, the cold seeping into my toes. Dark silhouettes of trees tower in the distance, their thick branches offering a little buffer from the frosty winter wind.

"Can't sleep?" he whispers as I sit down on the log he's taken residence.

"Nightmare."

He looks at me, gray eyes glimmering in the shadow of the firelight behind us. "Do you want to talk about it?"

I rub my gloved hands together to chase away the cold. "It was about Lanckest. About what I did, how I lost them, and King A'zre's promise to take them all away from me if I failed . . . terms I agreed to and can't take back now. I was hoping with all the confusion caused by Rahuin, that I could take Lanckest back, but . . . after seeing all those men down there, I don't think I can, at least not yet."

He nods. "Regret, it's the worst mistress. It begs for attention and steals all your hope for a peaceful tomorrow."

"And a peaceful night," I agree. "You speak like someone who holds deep regrets."

He shrugs. "Well, it might seem silly in comparison to your situation. Because my deepest regret doesn't involve losing an entire country, it involves losing one person." His voice falls away for a second as he sighs. "I don't regret meeting her. I don't regret falling in love with her, but I regret lying to her. I regret losing her. If things were different, maybe she would be my wife, and not someone else's . . ." He looks toward the solemn stars, an audience eavesdropping on our woes.

"Unfortunately, we are left to bear the weight of those regrets until we die, because there is no way we can change the past. All we can do is forgive ourselves and keep moving forward, and hopefully earn the forgiveness of those we've wronged as well. Hopefully, in time, we can make things righ—"

"Shh," Wen cuts me off, and I fall silent. That's when I hear it—a crunch over the crisp snow. I know it's not Jarret because I didn't hear him stir. Someone else is here. I slip into my curse once more so I can see who is out there in the darkness. It's pitch black for a second before, one by one, men in their glowing veins appear out of the dark foliage. It looks like an entire rainbow decided to explode over the forest, as every glowing body sports a different color.

Wen tenses beside me. "How many?"

"More than fifty, at least. They're not headed toward us though. They're headed east toward Lanckest," I whisper as I slip out of my curse.

"We should wake Jarret and leave. We don't know who they are or why they're here. If they find us, they might not be very kind."

I nod at Wen's words and turn to wake Jarret, but he's gone. My heart jumps into my throat.

No!

I race over the snow and fall against his bedroll. It's still warm. He was just he— The cool metal of a thin blade presses against my neck, freezing my next thoughts.

"Look what we have here," a voice whispers in Sz-kar, hot breath blowing against my skin.

Cay-Llek.

These men are from Cay-Llek, but what are they doing in Lanckest? Shuffles, and the sound of blows landing, breakout against the crunchy snow. In the commotion, I sense the edge of my curse bursting to be let out, but I can't. Not yet.

"Renell!" Jarret's voice cuts across the skirmish, followed by another blow. He groans, and I know he's been hit.

"Jarret!" I call into the darkness, as if that will save him. Where is Wen? Has he made a run for it? Even if he has, I still have to protect Jarret. I still have to find a way to get us out of this alive. The monster inside me begs to be free. I don't want to indulge it, but if it can help me save Jarret, then so be it. I know Jarret will save me in return. I know he will help lock my curse away again . . . I stop fighting and let the monster free. It crawls over my skin in a gale of darkness, taking over my entire being as I transform. The shouts of frightened men crescendo as the darkness consumes me.

Esther

Cool sea-spray saturates my skin and sends strands of blonde hair spinning around my face. I breathe in the salty air. In all honesty, it doesn't smell or feel any different from standing on the shore . . . but Connan loves the sea. He always has. Oh, the irony that it's the reason he now has to die. The bitter thoughts grip my mind like a vice. Marriage, what a terrible thing—brutal when you have to stand by and watch your husband die. *The Grandier* creeks underneath me, the wood groaning as we hit another wave.

Rahuin and Dais are having their public marriage in two months. David informed me that he and Peggy have decided to get married too. I want to tell them not to do it. That it's not worth it, but will they ever listen? Probably not. I'm done trying to protect my siblings. If they want to invest in something especially dangerous and heartbreaking, then it's on them. I'm finished. I don't have much time left to spend with my husband, and I have to repress my pain long enough to hold him for the little while that remains. I don't have time to worry about anything else—just him.

I glance at Connan, who stands beside me at the helm of his ship. To escape the fact that my brother is marrying his wife again in front of the entire nation, Connan decided to take me to the fairies' home island of Is'Er for a little while. He was raised by fairies after his mother was beaten to death by his father. Besides me, they are all he has. I glance at his metal left arm as it shimmers in the low-hanging sunlight. He lost his arm that day too, but the fairies saved him and raised him until he could come back and take his birthright as Castian Admiral from his father. I sigh. With any luck, we won't make it back to Casta in time for my older brother's wedding.

Maybe I'm just being petty, but I think it's stupid. I think Dais is just asking for someone to kill him. It's like he has a death wish—

maybe he does, and who am I to stop him? I already tried that once, and he still married her. The damage has already been done, but it doesn't mean I have to sit back and pretend to be happy for them in front of all of Casta. Especially since I haven't forgiven Rahuin for what she did to my father. In all honesty, I hoped she wouldn't come back for Dais. I hoped she would die trying. Maybe that makes me a horrible person, but I've lost too much to care.

Connan's ice blue eyes meet mine when he finally turns his gaze from the sea. They seem so much dimmer than they used to. It's the life draining from his body. Dirty blond and gray hair whips around his face. Wrinkles outline the skin around his eyes and mouth, making him look much older than he actually is. He stands with a stoop in his shoulders now, as if the weight of his choices is too much to carry. He looks almost as old as my father would have been if he were still here. I shiver against the cool breeze as the sun hangs low over the horizon.

He stands behind me, pulling me into the warmth of his chest. "Did I ever tell you that the sunset reminds me of your smile."

I grin at his words, before craning my neck to look at him. "Really?"

"Yes, every time I believed I forgot you, I would see the sunset and be stuck thinking about you all over again. So much so, I tried to avoid the sunset as much as possible, but it seemed to hang in the sky longer when I didn't want to see it. Or maybe *The Grandier* was just heading toward it. I can never be sure."

"That started out as really romantic and then took a major decline."

He laughs, rumbling my back with the motion. "You know I try."

"What? To not be romantic?"

"Exactly." He kisses my cheek, before trailing along my exposed neck. "Let's get inside. It's starting to get cold."

I nod but don't move as my eyes focus on the brown spots and blue veins starting to appear along his arm. I sigh as the present comes crashing down around me. For a brief moment, our banter helped me forget the truth of our situation.

"Let's not be sad. The island will be good for me. The fairies will help ground me a bit, help me . . ." *live longer.* I hear the words even if he doesn't say them.

I turn in his arms, running my hands up his chest and twining my fingers into his gray-streaked blond hair. "As you've already said, I won't be sad. I can't afford to be."

"Good. Let's forget for a minute, even if it's just a fantasy."

"Already doing that."

He smirks before bending down to meet my lips.

"Yikes," a voice says behind us. "You two should have a warning sign when you're being all affectionate on deck."

Connan sighs, taking a step back from me. "It's not like you haven't seen this before, Maud."

Maud stands beside him, raised eyebrows etched into her delicate face. Black hair falls down her back, whipping around her translucent pink wings. Maud is his fairy mother who healed him after his father took his arm. She practically raised him. "Just because I've seen it doesn't mean I want to see more." She rolls her salmon-colored eyes that appear more vibrant with the sunset. "The images will never go away now. Thank you."

"Any time." Connan bows slightly, a youthful expression trapped in his aged gaze.

Maud glances at me. "How do you put up with this *dir flak*?"

"It's not like I have much choice, now do I?" I banter, brushing blond strands from Connan's forehead.

"Ouch, you make me sound like a chore."

"You are. Maud can attest." I wrap my arms around his waist, burying my head in his chest.

Maud sighs. "I can attest, but I'm not going to sit here and watch you two. I just wanted to let you know dinner is ready. Is'Er will be in sight by early morning. A few scouts just let me know, and they recommend we cloak the ship."

"Why?" The concern in Connan's voice causes me to lift my head.

Maud glances around at the growing shadows, her pink eyes reflecting the last remnants of the sun's rays. "Sun'Arian ships have been scouted around the archipelago. Many patrols pass beside Is'Er, and although the ocean is anyone's waters, I'm afraid if they find *The Grandier . . .*"

"They won't be very merciful," Connan finishes.

Maud nods. "We successfully defeated their fleet, but we don't need to come across a captain whose pride has been hurt by recent events."

"That would be wise. Sev, this little trip was supposed to be fun," Connan grumbles.

"I'm not sure war is a good time for fun," I mutter.

Connan shoots me a look before addressing Maud, "If you and the others can handle it, let's cloak the ship. I'm assuming the island's magic will help us when we get there?"

"Yes, it should be enough." Maud nods. "I'll let the others know. Enjoy your"—she wrinkles her nose—"affection."

Connan squeezes me close. "Of course."

She rolls her eyes once more before disappearing into the inching shadows.

Chapter 5

Will You Give in or Overcome?

Jarret

The shouts of battle have long since stopped, but I don't know how long I've been lying on the snow-covered earth. I open my eyes to find the stars still twinkling above me. My stomach sinks as I realize that I'm not sure how I got here. The men from Cay-Llek came and then . . .

Silence stifles the air, and I wait, listening for anything besides my own pounding heart. The sound of hooves falling against the frozen ground reaches my ears. I stumble to my feet, even though they feel like lead and take a second to obey. I reach for my sword that should be strapped to my back, but the scabbard is empty. *Velk!* If the Cay-Llek men are back, I have nothing to defend myself with, especially since I have no clue where Renell or Wen went.

A horse as black as the night appears from the tree line to my right. Just one.

Renell.

It has to be. The tension in my shoulders relaxes as the unicorn—not horse—rushes toward me. It's angry—bloodthirsty. But I know

Renell is under that skin, just waiting to be released from her cursed prison. Sometimes when she allows her curse to fight, it overtakes her until she can't gain control again. I'm the only one who has ever been able to help her without the monster killing me. I reach my hand toward the animal as it draws near. It rears its head before starting to circle around me.

"Renell," I call to the animal as I turn with it. "I'm here. I won't let it hold you." I move toward the unicorn with my hand outstretched. A shrill whinny pierces the cold air and I freeze. The unicorn sniffs my hand, and I wrap my arms around its neck, not caring if its curse kills me. I just want Renell back. The taunt muscles fade away into Renell's familiar shape. My beautiful Renell. Her tired body collapses into mine, and I hold her tight against me.

"I—"

"I know," I whisper, rubbing circles into her back. "I know. They're gone. Come on, let's sit down." I lead her to what used to be our camp. Food, pots, and coals now litter the frozen mud and snow—the stars the only witnesses to tonight's atrocities. I wonder if my sword is somewhere in this mess. I set Renell down on a bedroll, holding her close to my chest for a moment. She's here. She's safe. She made it through. I tamper down the intrusive thoughts that nag at the back of my mind, taunting me with what ifs. What if I can't help her next time? What if one day I lose her to the curse? What if I'm too late? The what ifs are useless—a problem for another day. I kiss the top of her head, before leaving to grab wood for a fire.

There is no sign of Wen. Typical. I'm sure he ran as soon as Renell transformed. I stumble over something, and when I look down, I find a shriveled hand leading to the corpse of a Cay-Llek man. His skin has been pulled tight against his bones, leaving his body emaciated. His mouth hangs open in a gaping, horrified state.

I shudder and glance away. I can't allow Renell to see him. Her curse did this. I reach down, grab a fistful of his garment, and pull him away from the camp.

"I missed one." I hear a voice grumble as I drop the body behind a snowbank just passed the towering evergreens. Wen appears from behind the bank.

"You were cleaning them up?" I ask, surprised that he's still around . . . and cleaning up dead bodies.

"I was trying to get our camp back together."

"How many?"

"Eighteen." He walks past me.

I gather some wood before following him. I reach the camp, dropping my armful of kindling and morphing to light it on fire. Once a fire is blazing, I sit down beside Renell, who hasn't moved since I left. Wen continues to work on salvaging the rest of the camp. I pull her into my arms, her head resting on my shoulder.

"How am I going to fight for them, Jarret?" she asks. "I can't release my curse against every army in the world. If that happens, I'll never be able to stop. You'll never be able to pull me out of the deep end again. How are we supposed to fight six thousand men? How am I supposed to fight for Lanckest? I—I should have never given them away." Despair laces her voice as she buries her face in my neck.

I pull her closer as if the motion would secure her. We both know she's right. "How could you have known it was going to come to this? It's not your fault that all this happened. You didn't start this war and you aren't going to end it." I run my fingers through her black hair.

"I know." She sighs, the weight of her worries falling from her shoulders as she wraps her arms around my waist. "I have an idea, but I don't think you are going to like it."

"What do you mean?" I swallow, trying to keep my mind from racing with possible scenarios. She's not going to make another deal is she? The last one didn't end so well, and it caused her to lose Lanckest. Hopefully, that's enough to keep her from wanting to do something immensely stupid, right? A breeze blows by, sending ice particles swirling around us.

"I want to challenge the High Chief of Cay-Llek."

She can't be serious. I look into her eyes. "You what? But . . . if you fail—"

"I know, but if I win, I will become the leader of all of Cay-Llek's tribes. I'll have full control of their army. Their rules state that anyone regardless of nationality can become the High Chief. If I rule them, their alliance with Sun'Ar won't stand. I'll have Lanckest back in my control before I know it."

"Until somebody else challenges you," I snarl as I release her and stand. Clenching my teeth, I try to ignore my tightening chest as I pace in front of her. Is she crazy? She knows she can't win against the Cay-Llek High Chief. He's the High Chief because he triumphed over all the other chiefs who wanted control. Even if she wins, how will she continue to combat the endless bloodshed that will ensue if she becomes their leader? Someone stronger will always come fight for the position. That's how it works. She'll never have peace.

"I've thought a lot about it. I gave Lanckest away, but maybe I can save it by becoming Cay-Llek's leader," she mutters, almost as if trying to convince herself and me.

"No, I don't think you've thought about this enough. Even if you win, you'll constantly be challenged. How can you expect to hold onto the position long enough to command their armies to save Lanckest? They'll never respect you, and before you know it, you'll be dead. Then how can you fight for Lanckest?" I glare at her.

How could she make this choice without talking to me? I know she'll always choose Lanckest before me, but she could have told me what she was thinking before now. A haunting wind whistles through the trees like a defiant howl, but I can't tell if it's agreeing with me or Renell.

She glares as she stands, her mouth set in a defiant line, dark green eyes leaping in the reflection of the fire. "I knew you would react this way. You think I'm not strong enough to do this on my own. You think I'm a reckless princess who is going to foolishly sacrifice her life in vain." She steps closer, jabbing me in the chest.

"That's not what I said!" I step back, throwing my hands up. My chest aches as it pulls on my already exhausted muscles. I don't want to fight her over this. I just want her to be safe. "I'm saying I don't want you to do something that will get you killed. Cay-Llek chiefs have been training their entire lives! How do you think you can beat them?"

She steps back, throwing her hands out. "See! You don't believe in me. You don't think I can do thi—"

I move closer, towering over her. "You're right I don't! Because I have no desire to sit back and watch you kill yourself." I sigh, running my hands through my hair and swallowing the lump in my throat. Why can't she see it the way I do? Why can't she see that I don't want to watch her die in this endeavor? How come all she hears is that I don't believe in her?

"I have my curse. That's how I will win!" Her wide gaze searches mine, daring me to continue the fight.

I reach for her, my hands gripping her shoulders. "You just said you couldn't rely on your curse! Either way, it'll get you killed"—my voice cracks—"either way, I'll lose you."

Renell looks away, and her voice is as cold as winter's night surrounding us as she spits, "It's not about you is it?" She tries to wrench out of my grasp.

The words feel like a kick to my gut, and I hate the memories that flood my mind, reminding me of what she said on the night she apologized. *If I wasn't a princess, I would have never been raised to sacrifice my happiness for everyone else's . . .*

"Let me go, Jarret!" She grabs my hands, trying to pry my fingers off her. "Jarret!"

I release her. Her wide eyes search my face, but I don't feel the need to explain myself. She can't trust me enough to tell me her thoughts, so why should I do the same for her?

"You're right. It's not about me," I say as I brush past her, clipping my shoulder with hers.

"Jarret!" she yells after me, but I don't care. She's right. It's about Lanckest. It'll always be about Lanckest. I'll never mean as much to her. I'll never be able to stop her.

I morph once I'm away from camp. Gone is the fear. Gone is the concern. Instead a darker, more sinister force screams in my veins, begging to be let out. I need to destroy something. I need something to hurt as much as I hurt, and I don't care what it is. *No! You do care.* Another voice screams, but I'm done listening to the voice of reason. I'm done holding myself back. I'm done being useless. The Darkness that Renell once saw in me is becoming a monster I can't control. I think she helps keep it at bay, but I can't even look at her right now. I glare back at the camp before I take to the ice-filled skies.

Renell

I sit down in a huff as I watch Jarret fly away. Part of me wishes I could morph too so I can go after him, but I know arguing won't make him understand my reasoning. He needs time to think. I just hope he comes back. I shake my head. Of course he'll come back. Or will he? I made it clear—again—that I am a queen and will always care for my people first. Of course, those aren't the words he wants to hear, but it's true. Jarret will always be second compared to my duty . . . and I hate myself for it. I dig my boot into the snow, kicking up a little bit of dirt with it.

I love Jarret, but I told him before he came with me that I would do all I could to get my people back, especially since my foolish decision to trust A'zre. I have to right my wrongs. I have to do what I should have done in the first place—fight, and if Jarret stands in the way of that . . . well, I have to remove him from the situation. He wanted to come with me. If he isn't strong enough to handle my rejection, then that's on him.

But . . .

But the way he reacted to my plan scares me. The darkness I saw in him when we rescued Wen has started to grow. I saw it in his eyes while we fought, and the way he gripped me . . . He's never done that before. It's like he was lost in the dark that I've seen fighting for his soul. Maybe he was.

A cold wind howls around me, whipping in a frenzy like demons laughing at my fears. I pull my cloak tighter around me. It feels like a vice trying to consume me, pointing fingers and saying that it's all my fault. I did this to him. My rejection will continue to fuel his darkness. I hoped my love would help, but what if I'm making it worse? What if he does something terrible in an effort to make the darkness dissipate? How will I keep him from snuffing the light out and embracing the dark?

I wish he would talk to me about it, but now he's angry with me.

I know he won't even come back until he calms down. What if he doesn't come back? The thought stabs me in the gut. What if I've lost him for good? What if I sent him off the deep end and the darkness has already taken hold? What will happen then?

I drop my head into my hands, nails digging into my scalp. My chest feels like it's about to cave in. I can't do this. I can't keep him safe. Why did I tell him he could come with me? Why did I— my breaths come too quickly. I can't breathe. *Relax, Renell. Give him some time. He'll come back. Give him a chance. He's just worried about you.*

I lift my head, inhaling cold air as I stare at the stars. Jarret's up there somewhere. He'll take a breath and come back. He has to. But what if he doesn't? Will I go after him or continue my mission? I shouldn't have to think about this. I shouldn't have to choose. I wish I didn't have to. I told him when he joined me that my people would come first. He said he understood, so why does it feel like I've lost something so important?

Wen sits down beside me, his eyes turned to the sky. "Do you want me to go after him?"

I look at him. "No. He needs time. He'll come back when he's ready." I swallow the fears that rattle in my chest saying he won't— saying I'm alone and I've lost him.

He nods, white eyebrows raising. "You're really going to fight the Cay-Llek High Chief?"

"Yes. Even if Jarret tries to stop me, I'll do it. We can't take on the army ourselves, and I know Dais doesn't have the resources to fight more battles right now. I have to do what I can to save my own people—to give them back their homes, their livelihoods." I remember how happy my people used to be. We were a simple farming nation, but we had festivals and dances for everything from the moon to the sun to the rain to the harvest. I miss the way it used to be—simple, with no fear of war or death.

"Has it crossed your mind that maybe that's not what your people want?"

"No one's happy without a home, Wen," I whisper and stand, crossing my arms over my chest. I'm extremely cold now that Jarret isn't here to wrap his warm arms around me. "I would have thought you out of all people would know that."

He scoffs. "Right." He stands and faces me, silver eyes flashing in the firelight. "My home isn't a place, Renell. It's a person, and I think you're pushing your home away."

I open my mouth to retort, but Wen stomps past me without another word. I want to tell him I have no home, but that's not true. I had a home, and I gave it away because of my selfishness—a choice I could've prevented if I'd been putting my country first. A choice I wouldn't have made if Jarret had been by my side. Wen is right. I am pushing away my home.

Thesa

I worry a hole through my lip and wince. I didn't realize I was chewing on it. I haven't heard from my son, Jarret, in a few weeks. Before he left, I told him to keep me updated on his whereabouts, but I haven't received anything. What if he's been captured by the enemy, or worse? I don't think he's dead, but I fear something terrible has happened to him.

The cream and gold filigree walls surrounding me have transformed into little minions of doubt, poking holes in my chest and filling my heart with crippling pain. I don't notice the beautiful patterns of flowers or flying birds. The tea cup in my fingers quivers, sending searing droplets onto my skin, but I hardly feel it.

Maybe I should go out and find him. Maybe I shou— Rahuin's face swims in my mind, shattered green eyes, disheveled red hair. I sigh. I can't leave her. Not in her weakened state. *Sev,* she almost let herself freeze to death on a balcony yesterday because she thought she didn't deserve to live. I know she feels guilty for what happened, but she has more to protect now. She isn't making things easier on Dais either.

Another minion stabs my chest. Poor Dais. He's been through so much, barely taking care of himself when Rahuin was gone, and now he looks even worse off. Rahuin's betrayal, the doubt from the nobles, and this new development with the Darkness Jet told me about—the entire world is against him. I'm afraid he's going to snap soon. If I were Dais, I know I would have lost my mind long ago. He's strong, but I know that strength won't last.

Everything seems so pointless. I just want them to rely on me, but it feels like they're pushing me away, especially Rahuin. I don't know how to help her out of her grief, and I'm afraid that one day, I'll be too late.

A flash of color and movement just past the glass veranda doors catches my eye, and I stand to assess the distraction. Someone's out there, his hand on the handle as blue scales recede into his skin. Jarret. He's here. My heart soars with relief as I yank the doors open, nearly sending him tumbling to the ground.

I catch him in my arms, holding him close. "Jarret. Where have you been? Why haven't you written? How is everything? H—"

"I can only answer one question at a time you know." He pulls away, an amused smile on his face. It irks me how much he looks like Jet. He should have a little bit of me somewhere, right? But no. He has his father's black hair, albeit with streaks of blue, and sharp jaw-line. He does have a bit of my eyes though, even if they are brown like his father's.

"You wouldn't have to answer them all now if you had just sent a message or something. Do you know how worried I was?"

He takes my hands, squeezing them. "I'm sorry, Mother. I've just—we've been having a hard time." His brown eyes wander the space, taking in the cream walls and shining filigree in the shape of flowers. A chilly breeze slides into the room through the door we still haven't closed.

I move to shut it, keeping my eyes on him as if he might disappear if I look away. "What's wrong?"

"It's nothing really, but I—" His dark eyes search mine, and there is something about them that is unsettling, like they're trying to fight an unseen war. "How is Rahuin? Did she make it back okay?"

I nod, my throat constricting. "She did, but you didn't come here to ask about Rahuin. Tell me what's going on."

Tears suddenly appear in those divided eyes. "I've done something terrible. I did—I think—I should start at the beginning." He runs a hand through long black and blue locks. "Last night, Renell told me that she wants to challenge the Cay-Llek High Chief so she can control their armies. I tried to stop her, but we got into a fight and then . . . this feeling of darkness overwhelmed me. I couldn't fight it. I—it felt so welcoming, like an old friend, like it was trying to comfort me. I fled the camp, and I must have blacked out. When I woke up, I had . . ." he chokes. "I woke up surrounded by ashes. It was a village. A village I'm afraid I burned down." He clenches his jaw, swallowing to keep his tears at bay. "But I don't remember, and I'm terrified that I did a terrible thing."

"You didn't do anything wrong. I know you are good, Jarret. You would never do something to intentionally hurt someone."

"What if I did it because I thought I was protecting someone? It was a village in Cay-Llek. I don't even remember how I got there, but—but what if I burnt it down because I hoped it would keep her safe? Or change her mind, or make the possibility disappear?"

"Jarret, if anything happened, it was because of the Darkness, not you." I reach for his arm, squeezing him gently.

"I still let it take control of me. I still let it use me . . . to harm innocents." He pulls away and paces the room, his voice rugged from holding back his tears. This is the war I saw in his eyes. The duel between the darkness and the light. Both want a space in his heart, and he's terrified the Darkness will win.

I take his shoulders into my hands. "The Darkness won't win. We'll find a way to help you fight it."

"The only way I can fight it is if I leave Renell. I'd have to let her go alone, and I can't do that because I promised her and . . . we—I love her, but every time she says or does something that's going to get her killed, I lose it. I feel the Darkness crushing my thoughts because I know I can't stop her. Then the helplessness sets in and I need to do something to make the feeling go away, to make the pain disappear. So—"

"You give in," I answer.

He nods, stepping from my grip. "Yes, I don't want to give in. I want to be strong for her, but I can't make her see it the way I do. It's driving me insane. I refuse to leave her, but if I don't, what will happen if I lose it again? How many more innocents will I kill?"

"You can't let your hurt consume you. You say you want to be strong for her, but the second the fear grasps you, you give in. That's not being strong to protect the ones you love, that's taking the easy way out. Like when Rahuin left you here, and you turned to drinking. Now that Renell has pulled you out and given you a purpose, you still feel trapped because you can't change her mind. She doesn't need that Jarret, she just needs you to be there."

He throws his hands up, his voice quivering as he paces in front of me. "Will everyone stop telling me what I should and shouldn't be! Shouldn't I have a say in the matter too? Why should I be forced to sit back and watch the woman I love sacrifice herself again and again?"

"You knew this would happen! You tried to stay away from each other because you knew she would hurt you over her duty as a princess—queen—of her nation! But the hurt was still there, and it's always going to be there. Now you have to decide if the hurt is worth suffering with or without her. Are you going to be someone who gives into it or someone who overcomes it?"

Early morning sunlight filters through the windows to my right, washing his face and illuminating the dark circles under his eyes as he stares at me. His shoulders slump as he looks away. "I just want—I just want to keep everyone safe. I love Renell, and you're right, the hurt will always be there. Maybe I just feel lost because I think she doesn't want me to go through the pain with her anymore. I think she's pushing me away."

I take his hands into my own. "I can't speak for Renell, but she's probably trying to protect you too while also fighting for her country. She doesn't want to lose you, but she can't afford to let you stop her either. It's her choice. She has to choose between you and Lanckest. I know it's hard to watch her destroy herself, but it's her country after all. You either have to help her find another way to save Lanckest; or you go with her and support her every step of the way, even if it hurts. Maybe, just maybe, you'll find a better solution together."

He pulls me into a hug. "You're right. She already told me she would always choose Lanckest. I just thought I could handle it better than this. It hurts more without her, and I don't want to be a coward that runs away because it's hard to watch."

"When you love someone as much as you love Renell. It's hard to step back and let them do what they have to, but at least she trusted you enough to tell you the truth." I pull away, brushing black and blue hair out of his eyes.

"I know. Thank you. I just didn't know where to go."

"Well, I'm glad you chose to come here so I could have a chance to give you some motherly advice." I pat his cheek.

He smiles, lighting up his entire face. "I'm sorry I worried you. I'll keep you updated as much as I can."

"I would love that. Oh, and Jarret, there's been a new development with the Darkness. I just want to make you and Renell aware…"

His face remains stoic while I tell him all that Dais and Zenz had found out about the Darkness's armies.

He nods once I'm finished. "We'll be vigilant, and all the more reason for me to continue fighting my fear. If we find anything more about this along the way, we'll send word."

"That would be good." I nod, not knowing what else to say as I fold my hands together. "Well, give me one more hug." I try not to let him see the tears that have sprung to my eyes. How come it's so hard to say goodbye? To let him go when I know he could be hurt? But it's his choice, and I have to trust that he'll be all right.

"I love you," I whisper.

"I love you too, Mother."

Rahuin

"What should we have as flowers for our wedding? Roses or carnations or lilies, perhaps? Or maybe we should go with something smaller . . ." Dais mumbles under his breath staring down at a book that holds a history of Castian weddings, symbolization, and significance.

I smile at his antics. "Shouldn't someone else be deciding that?

You have so many other things to worry about." I take a small bite of my breakfast—eggs, scones, and canned fruit. I should be worrying about it, but flowers and a beautiful wedding are the farthest thing from my mind. I sigh as my eyes wander to the white framed glass veranda doors, where blinding sunshine seeps in over a thin layer of snow.

"It's our wedding." He laughs. "Shouldn't we have a say?" He reaches across the breakfast table, holding my hand in his. His blue eyes shine, and I just want to get lost in them forever. I missed his eyes so much when we had to be apart.

I swallow my food with the lump that has been slowly forming in my throat all morning. We were only apart because of me. The doubt from when I was talking with Ellenora comes back. I want to have our public nuptials, but I'm starting to agree with what she said. "Dais, you've just told me that our armies could potentially be destroyed by fear, yet you still want to have this ceremony." Zenz recently arrived with the army from Gra'Lore and explained to Dais what he thinks happened, but there is no evidence minus the eye witness accounts. We have no way of finding out how the Darkness consumes and uses bodies through fear. After giving his report, Zenz led his army of shapeshifters with Grimall and the dwarf clans to the mountains so they could bring the giants back home.

"I thought we agreed, Rahuin." His face falls with disappointment, and I look away, focusing on the sky blue walls that surround us. The decorations are supposed to give the illusion of a sunny warm day, but to me it seems to make the dark winter days more hopeless—just like my conversations with my husband.

"I agree. I just—I wonder—"

"Rahuin, they love you. We've been over this. We have to show them that we're strong. We have to show them that we can continue living our lives like normal. That all we've fought for in the past few months was not in vain. Everyone is guided by fear, and with the Darkness's new development, a country dominated by fear is a very dangerous place to be in."

"But what if they fear more because I marry you—fear what I will do to you?"

He stands up. "Those anxieties can easily be fixed once they hear my father's letters and see you mean no harm," he stops and looks away, running a hand through his unruly head of curls. "*Sev*, Rahuin, I'm so tired of what ifs. What if we win this? What if we do that? What if we can't make it through this? I can't take them anymore. So, we're going to get married and show our people a united front. Or… our marriage never happened, and I can fulfill the wishes of my nobles and make you leave." His voice trembles.

He doesn't really mean that. He can't. Tears appear in my eyes, blurring the vision of my husband standing against a background of blue. "Dais—"

"I want to marry you for the whole country to see. I want to crown you my queen because we've been through too much to give up now. I don't want them to win, so don't make them." He bends over and kisses my forehead.

I lean into his touch, craving the comfort I find there. He's right. We have no more time for what ifs. "I'm going to marry you, Dais. Yes, I don't think it's a good idea, but I'm starting to see that no matter what we do, there's always something that could go wrong. There's always something hard to overcome with no easy way out of it. I want to go through the hard times with you rather than without you. I've already gone through them without you, and it was torture," I whisper into his neck as I hug him to me. He smells like a combination of the sea and the honey he put into his tea this morning.

He sighs into my embrace. "I love you."

"I love you too."

The door opens behind us, and we pull away as a page stumbles over the threshold.

"Your Majesties." He bows his head. "Sir Jarret is here to see the queen."

I stand up, my eyes focused on the boy. "Please send him in." The boy scampers away, and I look at Dais. "I'll be late. I—"

"I know." He smiles. "I'll see you later." He's out the door, and before I know it, my brother stands in his place. His long black and blue hair hoods his eyes and blends in with the black cloak he wears over his shoulders. A silver sword hangs from his belt. He looks exhausted.

Jarret really isn't my biological brother, but we grew up together in Castlehaven when my parents left me with his adopted ones to protect me. We only recently found out that Thesa and Sir Jet are his real parents, and that King Henry and Queen Aleetha of Färrin are mine. So much has happened since Castlehaven was attacked. I can't believe it's only been a little over a year. It feels like ten years have passed since I was that naive girl who fell in love with her mentor and had to run for her life . . .

Wen. I shake my head to rid his gray eyes from my mind. I left him for dead. I killed him. I have no right to think about him. He's gone now, another life on my soul. Another I killed because of my selfishness. Because I couldn't be strong enough to choose.

"Jarret." I pull him into a hug. "When did you get here? Have you seen . . ." I trail off. It's still strange to call them his parents.

"I saw Thesa just now. How are you? How is"—he swallows—"the baby?"

I smile. "Did Renell tell you?"

"Yes, she had to because we . . ."

My heart clenches as Wen floods my mind once again. "Right. I'm all right—we're all right."

"Rahuin, we . . ."

"It's okay. You did what I asked."

"No, we didn't," he whispers, his brown eyes looking down at the quartz floor. The blue walls I had been admiring earlier suddenly seem to close in.

"What do you mean?" I try to ignore my pounding heart, but it beats like a war drum.

He finally meets my eyes. "We saved him. I—I didn't want to. I was ready to kill him for what he did, but Renell was convinced that he had too much light. She told me to save him instead."

Everything comes crashing down around me. I'm wrong. It isn't the walls that are closing in, it's my entire world. I can feel it now, sitting on my chest ready to crush me under its weight.

"But—" I start, but I don't even know what to say to him right now. I told Renell to complete her mission and get rid of Wen like she was supposed to. I set it all up. Especially, because there was no way I would have been able to kill him myself. Never. I thought it was all past. I thought he was gone so I could purge him from my heart. So I could be free of the chains I was wrapped in when it came to him, but now they're back, suffocating me, taunting me, reminding me that I will never truly be free. "Why? Why would you tell me this? I thought I could—I thought I could move on."

"I know it hurts, but I had to tell you the truth." His dark eyes are filled with a conviction I can't understand. "I couldn't just lie to you in case he ever came here."

"He's not with you? You left him with the Darkness? Why—"

"Of course he's with us. We're keeping an eye on him, but if he ever slipped away to come see you, I had to let you know the truth."

"He's not locked up?" Why would they let him roam free?

"It's not very forgiving of us to keep him locked up like a wild beast now is it? He has a long way to go to earn my trust, but for right now, he hasn't run back to the Darkness. He hasn't run here. He hasn't done anything except help us. I'm sorry that you can't let him go, but I think you have more important things to worry about," he snaps.

His words feel like a back-handed slap, and I can't stop the tears that flood my eyes. "It's not as easy as you think." I feel like I might explode with unsaid words. I want to scream that it's not true, but that would be a lie. He's right. I gave Wen over to Renell because I couldn't handle it. I just want my heart to pick a side. I'm tired of being so divided. It's not like I asked to love Wen and Dais. It's not like I wanted to be this torn apart, but when someone has already gripped a piece of your heart, it's too late to ask for it back. I think Wen stole a piece of it long ago, and the rest, I gave to Dais. I love Dais more than anything, but that lost fragment will always call for Wen. It will always want him.

Wiping my tears away, I look back at Jarret. "Thank you for telling me. I'm sorry I got upset. I just—I thought it would be easier to let him go if I believed he was dead."

"And did it?"

"Not really. It made it easier to leave, but afterwards, I—" *felt like a murderer.* I leave the words out. I only let death take its course to save others or defend myself, but Wen was another story. At first, I was so focused on destroying the Darkness's army that I didn't even think about leaving him for dead, but when I woke up after Thesa and Dais saved me, the memories haunted me. I saw his face when I tried to sleep. He appeared in my dreams, gray eyes glowing with tears because I killed him. Even though I didn't do the actual act, I still felt his blood drenching my hands.

"I didn't want him to die. Believing he was dead, did nothing to help me. It only made the fear—the agony worse because I believed it was my fault. Death or the thought of death, doesn't make anything easier, and I was a fool to believe that. Thank you for saving him. I know you never liked him."

Jarret nods. "I didn't like him because he was a liar. I didn't want to, but Renell was right, we couldn't snuff out a life that still had hope." His eyes grow sad. "I should get back to her. I only came to update you and Thesa."

I reach for his arm, brushing the dark fabric lightly. "Are you and Renell okay?"

"We could be better. I said some things I didn't mean." He runs a hand through his hair. "After talking to Thesa, I know how to fix it. So . . ."

I hug him tightly. "You better get going then. Be careful. I love you."

"Lots of 'I love you' going around." He smiles as he pulls away.

"I think we're starting to realize that we won't always have a chance to say them."

"I love you too, Rahuin."

With that, he's gone.

Chapter 6

Can You Trust Me Now?

Wen

"You're going to be a father." She smiles, those green eyes shining like the foliage surrounding us.

I can't believe my ears. She's pregnant. We're going to have a child. My heart soars, and I pull her into my arms, laughing in between her kisses. "I'm so happy. You've made me the happiest man in the world," I whisper against her red locks.

She starts to laugh, but it slowly turns into a cackle as the foliage around us shrinks into darkness. Her smile twists into a sick grin as her green eyes become as black as the night suffocating us. She lifts her hand, which holds my heart, beating and bloody against her palm. I scream, but no sound comes out. Pain erupts through my chest while I watch her crush my heart . . .

I scream, fighting my way out of the dream. Cold air steals my already labored breaths, causing pain to pulverize my lungs. I know it was just a dream, but it feels like my heart *has* been pulled out of my chest. Blood, muscle, and bone exposed for all the world to see. I feel

77

frozen tear-tracks on my cheeks.

Renell stands over me, dark green eyes that hold an ever-present darkness studying me. "Are you all right?"

Images flutter in my mind, replacing Renell's face with Rahuin's sinister smile. I see the blood. I hear the laugh. "No! I didn't do anything wrong! I didn't—" I stumble away from her, certain that my demons have come to consume me and drag me into the depths of the earth. Ironic that my fingers claw at the frozen ground to keep them from taking me.

"Wen! Wen, calm down. It's only me. You're not asleep anymore." Renell shakes my shoulders, pulling me from the freezing snow.

I shiver, my fingers digging into her warm skin. "They're coming. She's coming! I have to run before they find me. I have to get out of here!" I struggle against her hold.

She slaps my cheek. "Snap out of it! Nothing is coming for you! It was just a dream!"

I stare at her as the numb cold starts to seep into my body. Dawn breaks against the frozen world. I look around the snow-packed camp, staring at the trees clothed in frost as the sun shimmers against them, creating little rainbows of light. Renell is right. It was just a dream. I'm safe . . . for now. "It seemed so real." I stand up.

"Nightmares usually do. It's the dreams that seem less real—a haze that tells us this will never be reality, but nightmares—they take your soul and grip you so you can't move. So you can only relive the pain over and over," she says as we move closer to the crackling fire.

"Jarret's not back yet?"

Her brow draws at the mention of his name. "No, you were right. I believe something terrible has happened. I don't know how to make it right, or if there's even hope to make it right."

"Do any of us really know how to make it right? I think there is always hope because we're still alive to keep believing in it. Without hope, we'd just disappear. You're fueled by your hope to see Lanckest restored. I'm fueled by my hope that I can . . ." I trail off, because I'm not exactly sure what my hope is. I used to think it was seeing Rahuin again and making everything right with her, but that dream has started to vanish before my eyes like a phantom. I have a feeling she'll never want to see me again. I don't want to make her choose.

It's not like it'd really be a choice anyway. She'll choose him no matter what. I can only sit back and pretend that she truly cared for me like she cares for him. "I guess I'm fueled by the hope of figuring out where I belong in this world. To see the reason why so many want to fight for the light, even in the face of innumerable odds."

"Will you continue with us then?"

I shrug. "Do I have a choice?"

"We all have a choice, Wen, and in case you haven't noticed, we haven't been holding you hostage for a while. You're free to go where you please. You could have anything. I mean, do anything. Go anywhere. See what you want. You don't have to follow us."

Her words feel like a hammer to my chest. If I don't go with them, then I have nowhere to go. I have nothing, but the light keeps beckoning me forward, keeps telling me to stay with them. Even if I'm not sure what it means or where I go. "I have no other choice. I have no home. I—"

"Not even a home before the Darkness took you?"

I shake my head as memories of that day swirl through my mind. The day the old wizard, E'ok, died. The day the Darkness came to claim me as his own. "No, I never knew my father, and my mother was murdered by villagers in the little town we lived in on E'lmar." She stares at me with wide eyes. "They're superstitious. When I was born with white tattoos, they burned my mother at the stake and tried to sacrifice me to the sea, thinking that my father was some sea god or something. Anyway, an old wizard saved me and raised me until his death when I was twelve, that's when the Darkness came. All I had was the Darkness until I met Rahuin, and now I have nothing." I stare into the flames as they lick the morning air with warm tongues. "That's why I have to go with you."

"I can't say it'll be easy."

"Nothing is ever easy when you're fighting to restore what you've lost." I wring my hands together.

"That's true. I just hope I don't lose more trying to restore what I've already given up." Her eyes gain a faraway look.

"Like you and Jarret?"

She sighs. "Yes, I'm hoping Lanckest can be restored, but can Jarret and I?" She pokes the flames with a stick, shifting the coals. "I can't do this without him."

"Then tell him. Tell how much you love him. How much you need him, and maybe he needs you that much too. That's the hope you have in him. The hope that you will continue to want each other until you're both old and gray."

"If we even make it that far."

"You know we live in a world with so much hurt it doesn't really need your skepticism in the mix." The comment comes out a little off-hand, but at least I get her to smile. "It can be another hope you have—the hope that everything will be restored, and that you two can live out your days in peace."

"I hope so too. I want to marry him."

"Gee, as if it wasn't obvious." I smile as the sound of flapping wings fills the crisp air. Renell's face brightens as she sees him flying toward us in the distance. "Here's your chance to tell him. Don't let your home get pushed away," I whisper, standing up to get more firewood so I can leave them with some privacy and wishing that I hadn't destroyed what could have been my home.

Jarret

Renell waits for me in the clearing between tall conifers as I land. Smoke from the burning fire looms against the frosty morning. I morph, keeping my eyes on her as I transform. Tears glisten in her gaze, but I don't know if it's because of the cold breeze or because I've come home. I've done horrible things for the attention of this woman in front of me, but I don't want to be that person anymore. I just want to love her like she deserves to be loved. I don't want to lose her over her duty. I refuse to lose her that way again.

Now, it's my own actions that will destroy us. I know she fears the monster I could become, and I fear that I may have already become it.

"You came back," she whispers as I move close to her.

"Why wouldn't I?" I study her heart-shaped face—the smooth angle of her jaw, the curve of her lips, the tattoos of the moon cycles. Black hair whips around her face in the chill air.

She pulls her cloak tighter around her shoulders. "Because I pushed you away."

"No, I left because I didn't know what to do. I want to love you more than anything. I don't think your plan is a good idea, but I will follow you because I would rather be with you than without you."

Tears slide down her dark cheeks. "Me too, but I can't disregard my country. If I lose you again because of that—"

"You won't. I'm staying right here. You keep my darkness at bay, and I . . ." I trail off at the thought of the burning village, of the screaming residents that couldn't escape my wrath. "I fear that without you, I will do more I regret, and I would rather die than do that." I wrap my arms around her waist, pulling her close to me as I lean my forehead against hers. "I never want my frustration to overcome me again."

I tell her all that happened at the Cay-Llek village. Her fingers caress my chin afterwards. "I'm sorry my words made you lose control, and if it—"

"No, you can't tell me that I would be better off without you because I'm not. I'm lost when you're not there. I lose control. I lose everything. I'm not telling you this just so you will keep yourself at bay and not tell me what you're planning. I told you because I need to be honest. I told you because I love you, and I'm not giving up on us again."

She throws her arms around me. "I love you too. When I was afraid you wouldn't come back, I started thinking that I"—she swallows, pulling back to meet my eyes—"that I want to get married. Jarret D'Arvent, will you marry me?"

My heart leaps into my throat. What? Here I was thinking she would push me away or tell me it's too dangerous to be together and now—"I just told you that I burned down an entire village, and you want to marry me?" I ask, trying to be serious, but I can't stop the smile that spreads across my face.

She nods. "Well, I'm a death unicorn, so we're a match made in heaven."

I pull her closer to me. "That we are." I lean my head against hers again. "I will definitely marry you Renell Oslehan."

"Princess."

"Right, how could I forget that. I will marry you *Princess*"—I emphasize, garnering a giggle—"Renell Oslehan."

"I just wanted to hear you say my name again." I feel her fingers tangle into my hair.

"Of course you did." I lean down for a kiss that she doesn't hesitate to give.

Zenz

"If da shapeshifters and da giants 'elp us fights, we can take back Nnilmsh quickly. Once we's 'ave da stronghold, we's will 'ave da valley, 'nd we's will give its ta da giants 's—uh show of goodwill," Dwarven clan leader PPät of Nnilmsh says, chubby fingers pointing toward me and Drak—short for Drkkyn—the leader of the giants— whom I translate for since I'm the only one who knows Knargk.

Black, bushy eyebrows just over PPät's round face and cover dark blue eyes that shine in the firelight. A long black beard curls down into his boots. Orange flames from the fire we circle illuminates his hooded features and red tattoos morbidly. It's a dark light that reminds me of the Battle of Gra'Lore. The fire. The smoke. Kali . . .

I blink, forcing the images away and keeping my eyes trained on the faces around me instead of the sparks flying into the midnight blue.

"That is not what we were promised. We fight with the humans to be able to go home," Drak grumbles to me, his voice rumbling like an avalanche. The gray-skinned giant, easily as tall as two pine trees, scratches the side of his face, golden eyes narrowed over the small company present. I translate for the eight dwarven leaders. This situation is getting more hopeless by the second. Grimall has the clans somewhat united, but we can't get the giants to agree.

When I got the giants to fight for us, I promised to take them back to their ancestor's lands in Nnilmsh Valley, but now I'm on shaky ground since Drak might be thinking I lied to him. Nnilmsh joined the other clans when Grimall rallied them to fight, but their stronghold was taken over by another clan known as Vyl'ein. Now, we have to take it back to give the giants what I promised.

"We can't give ya a valley that we don't control," Grimall states, running a brown hand across his tattooed face. His umber eyes roam around the group. "The stronghold might not even need to be fought for. We have to remember that it could be abandoned like Y'rheim was. We should wait until the scouts get here to make any definite decisions. If the giants don't want to fight, they can wait until we've conquered the stronghold."

When Grimall started his search for dwarven allies for Casta, he'd started in his home clan of Y'rheim, but they had been raided—the stronghold left as a tomb for the dead.

"But it woulds be easier ta take it if dey giants 're wid us," Gnrishm, clan leader of Ganheim, states, gesturing toward Drak with a hairy fist.

"Yes, but we can't force them to fight. On behalf of my pack, I promised that I would give them Nnilmsh Valley. If that means we have to take it ourselves, then we will." I stand up. "Grimall is right, we should wait for all the information. It's lights-out soon. I'm going to retire." I translate for Drak.

He nods, his gold eyes narrowing in skepticism, causing the sallow gray skin around his face to bunch and droop like a discarded blanket. I don't really care what he thinks of me right now. As long as I keep him from acting on his suspicion, everything will be okay. I don't need him murdering my entire pack because of my incompetence. At least we allowed them to go back home, but I actually have to get them there.

I let my thoughts wander as I step away from the meeting. The slushy snow under my feet mixes into mud around the warm campfires. I run a hand against my face, stroking my silver beard as I step past dark tents that loom like small boulders around the camp. Normally, I don't let my facial hair get this long, but with the cold, it is a grateful comfort.

"Want a drink, *Phyn*?" Grimall asks, and I meet his eyes in the dim light of the moon. He holds up a bottle of *Xyr*—a nasty dwarven concoction only they know the ingredients of. I've never dared ask, and I'm not sure I want to know.

I smile. "Sure, just don't let me over drink like last time." Clouds of wispy air greet my lips as my words meet the cold night.

"I never let ya over drink." He laughs. "Yer just a lightweight." He claps me on the shoulder, steering us toward the edge of the camp, where we revive a dying fire abandoned by soldiers who already retired for the night. He takes a swig before handing it to me. I glare at the orange flames while I take a drink. I gag. It tastes like the smell of rotting guts.

He laughs.

"*Sev*, Grimall. What's in this?"

"I don't know. Gnrishm gave it to me." He takes it back.

"How convenient," I mutter, watching orange sparks fizzle and die in the darkness.

"What are you going to do once the giants get to the valley?" He belches.

"I'm taking the pack back to Morough. The war isn't over yet. Dais is going to need all the help he can get—the light is going to need all the help it can get." I grab the bottle again, chancing another swig that burns my throat like vomit going down instead of up.

He nods, his eyes looking far into the dark night. I wonder if he can see the silhouette of the trees and mountains off in the distance. "I know. That's why I'm trying to unite the clans. If they all realize that there are bigger things to fight for, maybe I can get them to fight for the light, but I have to get their strongholds back first. Once the other clans who didn't initially join us see that, they'll want our help too."

"You think they'll all want to continue fighting once you give each clan back their stronghold?" I'm skeptical to think that they would selflessly help each other.

"I don't know for sure, but I think a lot of the leaders are like me—they're tired of constantly fighting each other. I think they're ready for a change, but change can't happen unless they act. I'm hoping they won't revert to their old ways once we start getting strong-holds back. We finally did a good thing and achieved something that hasn't happened in years—unity. I'm hoping they realize that too and continue to fight for a better future. A better world where our women and children won't be murdered at the whim of someone else." He sighs, taking another draught.

I steal the bottle from him. "For your sake, I hope that too."

Thesa

I stare at the message on my glittering *heln*. The stone's shimmering surface boasts of handwritten swoops and curls in the beautiful Treían dialect. *Helns* are Treían stones that tether one way for communication. Mine swirls in cerulean and shimmering green that glows like it's alive. Usually, *helns* are tethered to another's mate, but since my union to Jet wasn't allowed, we never got one. Instead, my father gave me my mother's stone before he went back to Treía after the battle.

I pick it up, expecting it to be a message from my father, King Grelik, but to my surprise, it isn't. Immediately, I translate the words in my head as I read.

Dear Thesa,

I'm sending this message to let you know that your father is in poor health. The stubborn Heíb, wouldn't write you a message himself, despite my insistence. I fear a new monarch will be selected soon. I wish for you to come to Treía to be with him . . . that and the council needs to see you. If your blood-line gets chosen to carry on the monarchy, they will not take too kindly to your tainted line. If you come, you can start to show your competence. Some won't remember what happened all those years ago, but there are plenty who do, and they might do anything to keep you or Jarret from being chosen. However, if you show a strong presence and let your father publicly forgive you, perhaps they won't be so harsh. Or maybe these are just the rambling words of an old Garon. Send me a reply as soon as you can.

Your beloved friend,
Kyira

Kyira, one of the oldest Garons I know, has been one of Father's closest advisers for years. The only Garon who, although loyal to a fault, showed kindness and helped me escape Father's wishes for me all those years ago. I find myself ever grateful for her kindness and consideration. For if she hadn't sent this message, I would have been blindsided at the reality of my father's imminent passing. Father must have told her that he gave me Mother's *heln* to communicate with me after he went back to Treía.

My heart clenches. I thought he didn't look well when I last saw him. I should have known. Tears appear in my eyes. How can I lose him now? Now, after all these years? When we've finally made amends? Kyira is right. Even though he's forgiven me with his words and actions, he needs to pardon me officially in front of the council so they recognize me as an available heir. Not that I'm sure I want the monarchy, I just don't want those twisted brutes to come after me or Jarret because we might get chosen on the advent of Father's death.

I sigh, looking around my room. Shimmering candlelight glitters on chandeliers and lamps above my head, forcing the night sky away. I set the *heln* back onto its plush pedestal. It warps with spasms of green and blue.

How can I leave Rahuin? She's starting to get a little better. She's allowing herself to breathe and do what's best for her and the baby, but still, I worry about her. I worry she'll dive even farther off the deep end if I'm not here to help pull her out. She has Dais and Ellenora . . . they can take good care of her for a little while. The thought does little to ease my mind. Since I fled Treía all those years ago, Rahuin has been all I've ever known. I've never left her side, besides the time she was with the Darkness, but I've never left her willingly before—she's always left me.

How can I do that to her when she's in such a fragile state? I walk over to my vanity. In the top drawer inside a small box, I find little triangular purple flecks no bigger than my thumbnail—my facial scales. They're usually the last scales to recede when I transform, and therefore, one of the few types I can pick up after shedding, most of the others disappear with my transformation or fall off during flight.

Picking one, I walk over to the *heln* and wipe my hand across it, erasing her letters in an instant. I write with the scale, using the pointed end to inscribe my new message.

Dear Kyira,
I'm grateful to receive your message, howev—

I stop as my thoughts wander to Jarret. I sigh. I can't do this to him. I can't risk his safety just because he's part of a royal bloodline he hardly knows anything about.

Dear Kyira,
I'm grateful to have received your message. I'm sorry to hear about my father's health. I wish he would have told me sooner. As soon as I'm able, I will fly out to Treía. I will let you know the second I leave Casta. Thank you, my friend.
Your Princess,
Thesa

I sigh after finishing the message and then stuff the stone and scale into my vanity. With any luck, I will be able to leave for Treía soon. I'm worried that if I wait any longer, I'll never get the chance to say goodbye to Father. I just have to let Rahuin know. Hopefully, she will be all right without me for a few days.

Dais

"You think this will work?" I ask after Jarret told me what he was able to find out regarding the Corrupted. They finally have a name. A name I find all too fitting. We stand in my study and the giant map of Partin behind me seems to look down with foreshadowing of all I could lose. I'm tired of thinking about losing them. I'm already so tired of fighting.

"I don't know, Your Majesty, but it never hurts to find out. At least we have a name for them now," Jarret says, rolling back on his feet.

"And this source? The man who told you about them . . . can he be trusted?"

Jarret swallows, and I don't miss the glance he throws at Rahuin, who stands beside me.

Her posture becomes rigid, like she's readying herself to run.

I'm missing something here. Some secret they don't want me to know. The thought feels like a fist to my stomach. I hate it. Why can't we be honest with each other? Worse yet, how many more secrets does Rahuin have? How many more can she unveil that will tear me apart? Why hasn't she told me everything yet? Haven't we had enough secrets? Clearly, not.

"Yes," he says finally, dark eyes meeting mine with certainty.

I'm not sure he's telling the truth, but I don't think Jarret would lie either. Not when the fate of Lanckest could rest on the possibility of these words being true. If he loves Renell like he says he does, then he will do everything to keep her safe, but I can't shake the feeling that they've withheld something important. Something I should know.

My heart palpitates as I take a deep breath. "Fine. I will trust these words for now since it's the most information we've gotten about this new development." I call for a page to retrieve Thesa. I have to get word to Zenz and Grimall immediately, perhaps they can benefit from this new information. Thesa can fly there quickly. I turn to Jarret again. "I assume you won't be in Casta long."

"I head out immediately. But . . . how is her father?"

I lift my head. Renell's father, Fredrik, struggles with a horrible disease of the mind that has only gotten worse since he arrived from Lanckest with the refugees. "Not well. I have a few nurses watching over him. They say he slips deeper into madness every day. He doesn't even know who he is anymore, and I doubt he"—I swallow—"will know who Renell is either." I look away. Fredrik has always been a good man. I can't believe this terrible disease has come to destroy him, his memorie, and everything he stood for. At least, Renell will carry on his legacy, but his descent hurts more after my own father's passing.

Jarret nods. "She wanted him to know that she's getting Lanckest back, no matter what it takes, and . . ." His sad eyes fill with a joy so bright it practically lights up the room. "That we're getting married." He smiles.

"Jarret!" Rahuin exclaims, moving over to hug her brother. "That's wonderful."

"Yes, congratulations," I echo, feeling a little disconnected. All happy things become stripped away in the face of lies and secrets. I try not to think too much about it, but I hate that it feels like Rahuin doesn't trust me. I hate that I feel like I hardly know her even after all we've suffered through.

"What's wonderful?" Thesa enters the room with Jet, both of them beaming at their son.

"I'll tell you in just a moment, but I believe that Dais has something he needs to discuss with you first," Jarret says.

Thesa turns her attention to me. After a brief summary of the Corrupted, I tell her to head out and find Zenz and Grimall immediately. We have to know if the presence of love can really quell the transformation of fear.

"I'll deliver the message immediately, but I won't be coming back to Morough right away. I've received a message from one of my father's advisers. He's in poor health, and she fears that he won't last much longer. I would like to spend a few days with him before I come back. It won't be long," she says to me, but looks at Rahuin.

Rahuin nods, moving forward and hugging Thesa. "Of course. Go to your father. I'll be fine. If I have any trouble, I'll tell Dais or Ellenora. I'm not alone," she assures Thesa, though I'm not sure how true the words are. She can't even trust me with her secrets. Why does she think she'll share her struggles?

Thesa releases her. "All right. I'll be back soon." She smiles, looking toward Jet as she reaches a hand to him. He takes it, glancing briefly at me, and I nod. He has the right to celebrate with his family before Thesa leaves. They exit to hear Jarret's news.

I turn to Rahuin. She sees the question in my eyes. She knows I haven't heard the whole story, and by the look on her face, I can tell she isn't ready to say it. It hurts more than she'll ever understand. Every time I find another thing she can't trust me with, I see her leaving again. I see my father . . . I breathe in shakily, finding that I can't stand here in the same room with her right now.

I turn to the door. "I'm going out to the training fields. I need—"

"Dais, wait," she whispers, and I turn to meet those green eyes. Those eyes that always give me so much peace. The eyes that weren't there when she slit my father's throat.

She moves forward, placing a hand on my cheek. "I wasn't going to tell you, but I don't want to withhold the truth from you. I don't want to lie."

I gaze down at her, waiting for her to continue. She keeps her eyes trained on me, and it feels like a symbol of trust. Trust I was sure wasn't there a moment ago. How come I always give in so easily? Maybe it's because deep down, I know she truly doesn't want to hide from me . . . There are just incidents we never want to admit or remember until we're ready.

"The man Jarret was talking about, is a man I know very well. A man I left for dead. A man I thought was dead until yesterday. Jarret told me they saved him, and . . . I didn't know how to tell you. He's the man I—" she stops, looking away for a second.

My heart sinks in my chest. I saw the truth written plain as day in her gaze. A truth I don't want to acknowledge, but I asked for this. I asked for her to be honest, and honesty hurts. Honesty breaks down barriers and rewrites perception, bringing healing through its brutality.

She continues, meeting my eyes again, this time filled with tears, "the other man I love—my first love. I used him to—to keep Sira safe." She touches her stomach.

I breathe out slowly, trying to process the information, but it hurts. It hurts to know she loves someone else. It hurts that this person just brought his advice to me. It hurts that I accepted it without knowing exactly who he was. A person who loves my wife or used her like she used him? By the look on her face, I realize he loves her too, and she used that to keep our daughter safe. What a twisted reality I live in. I want to scream. I want to cry, but mostly, I just want to leave so I can clear my head and understand the whole thing.

She told me she had to sleep with someone else, but I didn't know it was someone she loved. Someone from her past whom she loved before I even met her. I feel doubly betrayed because she couldn't trust me with the truth before Jarret came to tell us what this man knew. At least, Jarret had the good judgment to not bring him here, because I don't know what I would have done. I know I wouldn't have let him live, or at least leave in one piece.

"What's his name?" I grunt, looking away from her and turning my eyes to the ceiling painted with epic battles against dragons and sea monsters. It's odd that I find myself wishing I could battle those monsters right now instead of facing the emotions coursing through me. I don't really care what his name is, but it's the only remaining thing I don't know about him.

"Wen," she whispers, and I can tell it's a name she never thought she'd utter again. Someone she already tried to bury. Someone she forsook so she could return home, so she could be with me. That has to stand for something.

I look back at her. "Thank you for telling me the truth." I form a fist at my side, digging nails into my palm. "I won't lie and say that I completely understand, so I need . . . a little time to think. I—I'm angry that you didn't tell he was someone you loved—still love. I know you came back for me. I know you left him and what he meant to you to keep what you have with me. I love you. I'm so happy you came back, but I need to—" I stare at the marble floor, wanting nothing more than to leave this conversation, leave the feelings I see warring over her heart.

"Go," she whispers. "Like I said, I told you not to hurt you, but so I can be honest with my husband. I could have easily withheld the fact that I love him, but I didn't because I love you. Because I'm trying to rebuild our trust. So go. Take all the time you need. I will be waiting for you, just like you waited for me." She clasps her hands in front of her, wringing them together as if that would take away the touch he left on her skin.

He *touched* her, *held* her. She's not solely mine anymore. We were each other's firsts. She made that clear on our wedding night, but not anymore . . . My heart feels like it's been torn open, or maybe it's a festering wound that hasn't had the chance to heal from all the abuse it's suffered in the last few months.

She starts toward the door, leaving me alone with thoughts and feelings that are too quiet to hear but too loud to ignore.

Chapter 7
Love Over Fear

Carrie

STREETS OF PËR, KÄS

The world seems so still. I don't know what it means yet, but maybe it will draw me closer . . . maybe I will finally find her. Maybe this is the place.

I gasp awake, moving my stiff muscles from the upright position I was resting in. Where am I again? Darkness surrounds me, but the cool night air and flickering gas street lamps in the distance tell me I'm outside. Oh right. I'm on a mission.

"Xin, are you in position?" A voice startles my thoughts, forcing grogginess from my mind.

No . . . I want to answer, but I know that will get me reprimanded, and we don't have time for that. My eyes adjust more on the buildings lined with coal soot and streets of grungy cobblestones start to appear.

"Yes," I whisper into the night because I know Zer can hear me. I stand, rushing along the boulevard, dodging piles of trash and sleeping dogs. Silent. Deadly. I can't afford to be heard or seen. Though, the second one might have already been compromised. I just hope they thought I was a homeless person.

I arrive at the warehouse—a grim-looking building that looks more like a barn than a warehouse. I glare at the grim slacks of wood. Golden light spills out through the cracks. Another figure lands on the roof, quiet and as stealthy as a cat. Someone else appears from the other side of the alley, positioning themselves at the door in the back.

My heart hammers in my chest as Zer's voice appears in my head again.

"Xin . . . yel . . . zer . . ."

I smash my boot into the door, swinging it open and catching the three men inside completely off-guard. My partner on the roof—Yel—smashes through a window, and the other—Wue—crashes through the back, appearing with his bow drawn, aiming at one of the men's hearts.

The startled traitors spring to their feet, taking in our threatening forms, but they don't seem scared, just surprised. A small kerosene lantern flickers at their feet where letters, documents, and other papers litter the ground.

"By order of the Raven Dynasty, you are under arrest for treason against King Rave," I say, but my voice sounds hollow, like I'm reciting lines from a novel. I don't even understand what they mean anymore.

"You don't know why you're here do you?" the man in the middle asks, his green eyes glow, studying me.

My eye twitches. "You are traitors. Traitors get tried and convicted." I leap forward, readying my knives, but before I can throw one, my limbs become frozen and I fall forward onto my face. The stone cold ground greets me in a frigid embrace.

What? They're Walks? Commander Li said they weren't anything special. Unless . . . they hid their powers. I try to move my hands, try to use my knife, but my limbs don't move. I glance around, finding my comrades lying on the floor as well.

"Convicted? You believe we're guilty even though you know nothing about us," the man on the right says, his deep voice rumbling the room like an earthquake. Brown eyes glare down at me.

"You're guilty of hiding your abilities, isn't that enough?" I spit.

"You're not a Walk. I can tell," the man on the left says, blue eyes shining in the lantern's light. He strokes his dark brown beard. "You have no idea what it's like to be gifted with powers and be told by a crazed king that we shouldn't have them. That we should die because of something we can't control."

Die?

"You don't die. We—"

"Is that what you think?" the middle one asks, green eyes unnaturally bright as he runs a hand through flaming red hair. "Have you ever been to the arena? Do you even know what goes on in that place?"

"I—"

"Don't let them speak, Xin! They're all liars," Zer says in my head. *"I'm a walk and I've never been treated like I was supposed to die. They hid their powers. They are liars."*

I glare up at the three men.

"Now you know," the middle one continues as the other two gather their papers.

"Catch us if you can," the left one says as they walk past us into the street. As soon as the middle one stops looking at us, our frozen limbs release.

"Move!" Zer shouts. *"Go! Before they're gone."*

I spring up, racing into the alleyway, but the second I do, the alley shifts, the buildings warping as they start coming after me. I blink, trying to correct my vision, but it's real. Everything's moving, even the ground feels like it's falling. I drop to my knees, willing everything to stop. To end. Sweat beads on my forehead as my chest seizes.

"Xin, get going. What are you doing?"

"I—I can't move. They're coming. They're coming for me!" I shout, closing my eyes as the fear closes in and leaves me in a world of darkness.

"Glena?" I call my sister's name as my eyes adjust to the stars shining above. We're lying on the grass covered ground. I inhale its sweet scent, the sounds of crickets overtaking the quiet.

"Shh," Glena mumbles, grabbing my hand and lifting it to the skies. "Don't say anything. Let's just listen."

"What for?"

"I said we're listening," she snaps with a sigh. "We're listening for the stars."

"Why? They have nothing to say."

"Not listening for them to say something, but we're listening like they do. Don't you think they hear and see everything way up there? See everything we deal with?" Her voice cracks.

"If they do, it must suck, because they can't do anything to help," I whisper, squeezing her hand that still holds mine.

"Yeah."

The scene fades. The stars disappear.

"Run, Carrie! Run! Don't stop running. Don't stop until you find us. Don't stop!"

I won't . . .

Aiden

STREETS OF PËR, KÄS

"What happened?" I ask as I arrive on the scene. Gas lamps illuminate the cobblestone streets in an eerie glow. I got the message about twenty minutes ago. Of course, I was fast asleep when the messenger got there.

Police lead me to a warehouse-like barn where someone lies on a make-shift pallet. Crates pile up around us, and I wonder why they chose this place.

"She collapsed during her mission. A Walk was manipulating her reality."

Manipulating reality? What an interesting ability. I'm sure she—I halt as I recognize the woman. It's her. The girl from the ball. Carrie. Her name feels like sweet syrup to my mind, but here she's sleeping fitfully, sweat beading over her pale face. Is this why she couldn't tell me who she was—a number soldier? I smirk at the thought. Very funny, the first woman I actually take any interest in and she's a Walk hunter. Figures.

"Thank you. I'll see what I can do for her," I tell the guard, and he shuffles out, leaving us alone.

I kneel beside her, observing her eyelids move like she's stuck watching something over and over again. Memories of her brown eyes fill my thoughts, but I shake them away. She finds and imprisons Walks, probably even kills them. *Forget her now, before it's too late.* I sigh. She was probably spying on me anyway. So she was just entertaining me. The thought hurts more than I care to admit. *Thirty-First West Tier Street . . .* Well, this new revelation takes away any giddiness I had for calling on her tomorrow.

Why do all my hopes have to be crushed before they ever become reality? At least I figured it out now instead of later.

I place a hand underneath her neck, gently cradling her head. Images fill my mind. Little girls running away. Carrie confronting King Rave. Her facing Walks—three of them. *Run, Carrie . . . Is that what you think . . . Just Carrie . . . Don't worry . . . I own you now.* Ethereal light glows around us as the warehouse comes back into focus. Warmth flows over my skin as my arms go limp. I release her and fall backwards.

My heart clenches in pain this time, and a sinking feeling rises in my chest. She's sick. I can feel the disease as it permeates through my body. My ability will absorb what little I took from her, but that's beside the point. Does she know she's sick? I doubt that's the case, because no disease hits me to the point of paralyzation, unless it's very serious.

I hear her stir, and shift my head to hopefully catch a glimpse of her waking up. *Kide.* I didn't really want her to see me, but it's not exactly my fault. Who knew she'd have a debilitating disease that would incapacitate me? Feeling slowly starts to come back to my limbs in little tingles. I lift my head to find her brown eyes staring at me.

They take in their surroundings very slowly, but those caged eyes grow wide as she registers where she is.

"Aiden?" Her voice is hoarse, nothing like the gentle lilt I'd heard only a few hours prior.

"Fancy meeting you here." I smirk, flexing my muscles as I try to sit up.

Guilt crosses her features for a moment. "I—"

"You don't have to explain. I understand. You couldn't tell me, and that's okay. I'm disappointed it was all a ploy though." I shrug, refusing to meet her eyes. I don't want her to see how much it hurts my pride. I'd like to keep anyone from knowing that.

"It wasn't just—"

"Please, let's not lie to each other. I've had enough of lies. I've been shrouded in them my entire life. Lie about who I am. Lie so they never find me."

She starts to sit up, massaging her head as she does so. "Forgive me, Aiden. I—"

"Had to. I know." I try to stand up, but my legs don't want to obey me. Stupid paralysis. I just want to get out of this warehouse as soon as possible. I don't want to find myself liking this woman more than I already do. I have to move on and forget about her *immediately.*

"Will you let me get one sentence in?"

"There you got one sentence in. While we're on the subject of lies, do you know that you are very sick?"

Even in the golden light from the kerosene lamps, her face pales, her brown eyes casting down to her heart. So she does know . . . "Yes, that's why I'm forced to lie."

"King Rave. He helps you."

"How do you know that?" She glances back at me, brushing strands of dark hair from her eyes.

"I'm a Lifewalker, and he's a Deathwalker. It's not too hard to figure out."

"Right." Her voice grows harsh. "I promise, I didn't want to lie to you. Yes, Rave told me to look for you, but when I saw you, when I figured out that you were my target, I didn't want to manipulate you anymore. That's why I slipped up. That's why I almost told you who I was."

"But it didn't matter, because you still couldn't tell me the truth," I whisper, finally being able to stand. I can get out of here. A meeting like this deserved to be under the vast expanse of the stars where failed dreams went to die, not here in the confines of cobwebbed ceilings and metal walls. Where the cool breeze could whisk away unfulfilled hopes, not where'd they'd be trapped in dusty, itchy gloom.

"Aiden, wait." She grabs my hand, and it feels like I've been bitten by fire, the warmth of her skin sending shivers up my arm.

I stare at her fingers on mine, and she gently releases me. Her brown eyes catch the light from the kerosene lamps, igniting something deep within my heart. I look away, ignoring the ache, the pull on my heartstrings, the yearning I can't name. I refuse to allow it to take hold. I refuse to feel anything for this woman. I refuse to let her change my mind. I'm leaving and never seeing her again. *That's what you like to think, isn't it?* I ignore my thoughts. *It is what I think, thank you very much.*

"I just told you why I had to lie." Her voice draws my gaze back to hers, and I can't help but think how beautiful her eyes are in the dim light. *Don't forget that you're leaving, Aiden. She doesn't care. No one ever will . . .* Might as well admire her beauty now.

"Yes, but how can I be certain if you'll ever tell the truth? You see, I don't know, and frankly, I'm not sure I want to know. When you spoke to me at the ball, you drew me in like a fly getting caught in a web. I didn't know it was a trap until it was too late. King Rave wants to know more about me—that much I understand. Unfortunately, he used a beautiful specimen to distract me." I scoff. "Even as I say this, I still want to get to know you more. I still want to unravel everything that makes up the intriguing woman I met at the masquerade ball, but I know I can't. Because I know nothing you say will ever be genuine. It will all be a lie. A false sense of security until you rat me out to King Rave. He'll just have to find another way to figure out who I am."

"And if he does?"

"What do you mean?"

"If King Rave already knew everything about you, would you still want to get to know me? If there were no risks involved, would you do that? Would you call on me? Would you court me?"

She does have a point . . . Shut up, thoughts. I sigh, trying to squander the smidge of hope that settles in my chest. I refuse to be the reason for my own downfall. Scratch that, I refuse to let her be the reason for my downfall. Because it's not just me I'm responsible for, it's hundreds of Walks' lives. Once King Rave knows the extent of my power, that will be the end of all Walks as we know it. If I fall for her . . . he'll use my love against me. I'm not stupid, and King Rave is too smart for his own good. All his plans are cinching on the idea that I start to care for this beguiling woman. So, I won't—for her sake, and for mine.

"Yes, I would. But I'm afraid that if anyone found out the secrets regarding my ability, it would be the end of all life as we know. So I hope no one ever does, especially you." I look away from the hint of sadness that takes over her face. "I should leave." I start for the door, and this time she doesn't reach for me.

"Thank you for saving me. I'm sorry this is all we could ever be."

I glance back at her, taking one more precious second to study the features of her face—to meet those caged eyes, but when she looks at me, it's like the chains fall away. She looks . . . free. My heart jumps in my chest, and I force the well of emotions down my throat. What a cruel world we lived in. I wish we'd met under different circumstances. I wish she was free from her enslavement, and I wish I could be the one to set her free. *Maybe you could.* I shake the thought away. There is no way King Rave would ever let her go. He has to release her for me to use my ability . . . and there is no guarantee I'll be able to sustain her. Just taking away her little faint had caused paralysis for a few minutes. I can't imagine what would happen to me if I tried to shoulder an extreme disease of the heart.

"It's not your fault. Though, I know it's easier to believe that. Goodbye, Carrie Haligun."

"Goodbye, Aiden Brachus."

The way she says my full name sends tremors along my skin, and I shiver, forcing them away because it's already too late for us.

Zenz

Abandoned. That's what the scouts told us before we decided to head into the Stronghold of Nnilmsh. I'll have to remind them what abandoned looks like. Abandoned strongholds do not have horrifying shadow monsters pouring out of the entrance—monsters I have no idea what to call. Because they aren't Horrors or Hellions, but they're made up of the same darkness. Created from the fear of those who must have inhabited the stronghold before we came to claim it—the same creatures we fought at Gra'Lore.

"Not again," I whisper, feeling my heartbeat rise in my chest. I don't know how we'll make it through this. It didn't go very well last time. Images of Kali flash in my head—of the dark swirling around her, of the monster she became.

Grimall stands beside me. "How do we defeat them?"

"I don't think we can," I say, more to myself than Grimall.

"Well, we don't have a choice, do we? I'm not leaving ya and yer pack to try to take this valley back all by yerselves just to appease the giants. Plus, we need to practice how to defeat them if the Darkness is going to be using these monsters to take apart all of Partin."

"Send the message to your troops. They cannot be afraid. If they get mortally wounded, they have to kill themselves, or else they will change into those monsters and kill their comrades." I hate the way my voice shakes as my armored fingers clutch the hilt of my sword for support.

"When ya put it like that . . ." Grimall glances at me. He knows something is wrong. He knows I'm reliving the last battle with these horrible creatures, but there is no way to pull me out.

"It was terrible, Grimall. I—"

He grips my shoulder. "We can't afford to be afraid, remember? Pull yerself together. We have work to do. The giants will have yer head if we don't get Nnilmsh, and I'm not gonna let yer death be on my shoulders."

"I expect no less, my friend." I nod, but the sick feeling in my stomach won't go away. I can't afford to let it win though. We can't be scared.

I raise the call of order to the other leaders present and tell them the plan. Hopefully, we will be forgiven for the choices we have to make to survive this. For the sake of my pack, I hope we don't fail.

We will be victorious, and we will leave no room for fear.

Glena

My spear slices the air, countering blows from the shadowy monsters that arrived from the stronghold. We learned that this particular brand of the Corrupted are called Dreads. They look like skeletons woke up out of the ground and started walking around with the help of black smoke to keep them going. They even sound like bones grinding against each other, though, their movements are far from any brainless, awkward monster. Every strike is intentional, cool, calculating, and merciless, cutting through my fellow warriors as if we are nothing but softened butter.

We have to use our love to fight. That's the call to order that Thesa brought with her. It seems so simple that love can overcome fear. Simple yet complicated, because sometimes love leads us to fear. Fear of screwing up. Fear of hurting each other. Fear of losing each other. I glance at Frobin, whom I have been fighting beside since we got here. He's the only reason I don't give into my fear. I love him and I want him to recognize my love again. He's the only reason I'm still grounded to this earth and haven't given into the fear that sits on the edge of my skin like a blanket covering me in warmth.

Though fear is anything but warm. It's haunting and broken. Damaging, and even more detrimental now that these Corrupted exist. But if he were to disappear, if his fear got the best of him, I'd go with him. The thought of losing him leaves a bitter taste in my mouth.

Two Corrupted come for me, and I shuffle back two steps, clipping the bracelet on one of the wrists before turning to battle the next. My muscles pull in exhaustion, but I can't give them a way to harm me.

I refuse to leave my father and Carrie alone in the world or worlds . . . or whatever we want to call it, but I have to hope that they will be okay. That Carrie will find her way to Father, and he will tell her what happened to me. That I went down with love in my heart. That I chose to follow someone who would never forgive me, but whom I loved nonetheless. Frobin would never expect it, giving me a chance to triumph over this war we declared against each other.

The smell of brimstone chokes every breath. My footsteps are heavy with mud from the little bit of snow that fell earlier as I back away from the Wraith in front of me for a moment's reprieve.

My last encounter with Frobin hasn't stopped playing in my mind. His laugh. His fear when we found out that the Corrupted had used a projected image of Crin against us. Our shared pain. Pain, he still blames me for. Pain, I blame on myself, but no more. Crin is gone and there is nothing I can do to change the past. All I can do is keep moving forward.

I thrust my spear forward, clipping the brass ringlet of the shadow monster in front of me. My stomach twists as I take in the gruesome creature. The sharp shriek of metal against metal and the shouts of fighting men echo across the expanse. Mud squishes under my feet, and the snow-capped mountains in the distance send relieving drafts of cold air on top of us.

I find myself back-to-back with Frobin. "How's it looking?" I holler over the din of clashing metal and dying screams. Screams that remind me to remain alert. The battle isn't over until the screams have disappeared—until we are left with irreversible silence.

"I'm sure it's not looking much different from where you stand."

He's right, as usual. Nothing has changed since we brandished the first blow. The enemies continue to multiply, and we continue to grow weaker and more afraid. Pain rips from my shoulder and my arm falls limp at my side as I scream, forcing me to drop my spear.

The Dread above me raises his battleax with cold black eyes, showing no sign of the dwarf that used to be behind the mask. I watch blood drip down my armor, falling to the ground in a pool of ruby droplets. I ignore the churning in my stomach as I fall to my knees, desperately trying to reach my spear. I'm not going to die. I'm not going to— Crin stands in front of me, that smirk that made me fall in love with him painting his lips.

"Say it, Glena. Come on, say it," he whispers, dark eyes shining before his lips meet mine . . .

"No!" I hear Frobin scream as his sword clashes with the Dread's ax. I blink. Crin is gone. It was just a hallucination. I can't give in. Not when I promised I would go with Frobin. The metallic smell of blood fills my senses and the fear dances in my stomach, begging me to join it in a broken union. My vision blurs, dark smoke rising around me. The darkness feels good. It feels safer than a battlefield littered with my fellow comrades.

"Glena!"

For a second, I think Crin is back, ready to bear me away with him; but that can't be possible, because I don't want to follow Crin. My vision sharpens and I see Frobin instead. His lips are moving, the words 'I love you' spilling between his mouth as his blue eyes shine bright like the sun. Brighter and more beautiful than I've ever seen them before. I want to kiss his eyes or fall into them and be lost forever. Forget this life of fighting and laying down my life—forget it all. Let me have him now because I squandered my chance before. I won't let it happen again.

I lean in, our lips meeting as I cut off his next words. The pain is forgotten. The fear. The darkness . . . because my heart explodes with a feeling of overwhelming love. I don't care about the war raging around us. I don't care about any of it. I just want him.

He meets my kiss, devouring me with hungry desperation. We've hidden behind regrets and betrayal for too long, and now it's consuming us. He pulls back, leaning his forehead against mine. "Don't give in. Don't let the Darkness take you."

His voice is clear now. The sounds of battle sharpen again, and the ache in my shoulder emerges, reminding me of my injury, but that doesn't matter. Together we have defeated the Darkness. I no longer feel the fear. I no longer see the black smoke consuming my body.

"I won't. I'm not. I won't leave you. Where you go, I will follow. I love you too much to let you go without me, and I refuse to go without you." I gasp as he helps me up. I lean against him, my shoulder throbbing at the movements. My head feels really light, and I'm sure that it's not just from our kiss.

He shifts into a horse. *You're going to be okay. I'm going to get you out of here.* I hear his voice in my mind as I get on his back. I nod against his mane, blood spilling onto a roan coat.

"Tell them," I whisper. "Tell them it worked."

Frobin

I stare at Glena as the healers look her over—white hair matted against her pale face from sweat. The gray tent above my head flaps with downdrafts from the mountains, sending a chill inside, and I notice it even more now that my energy has worn down from the fight.

The wound in her shoulder is deep, showing ivory bone. I don't even know if she'll be able to use her arm anymore. Her face is scrunched in pain as the healers continue to work and bandage it. Somehow she hasn't passed out yet. I think she's afraid to. Afraid that if she rests, the Darkness will come and take her away. I won't let that happen. I won't let the Darkness's sick and twisted game end with him as king. Never.

At least, we were able to prove the information Thesa brought as true. Love kept her from becoming Corrupted. My mind keeps replaying the scene where the dark smoke started to swirl around her— swirling just like that day we saw Crin. When I noticed it happening to her, even though I could tell she was fighting it, I couldn't hide behind my unforgiveness anymore. I had to tell her the truth. I had to tell her how much I still loved her . . . and when she kissed me—I smile at the thought. The world could have been ending around us and I wouldn't have missed that kiss.

I'm still hurt by what she did. Maybe I always will be, but I'm done punishing her for what happened between us. I guess that brings me one step closer to forgiveness. I can love her and still find it hard to forgive her, but I'm getting there. I'm realizing that it wasn't entirely her fault either. Crin could have told me how he was feeling. He could have confessed that he wanted her more than I did. If he had, I would have let them be. I would have stepped back if it meant keeping my best friend. Sure, I would have been angry for a time, but who wouldn't?

The healers move on, leaving a warm towel against her forehead.

I fall beside the small cot she lies on.

Her droopy aquamarine eyes focus on me. "Hi." She lifts her good hand, but hesitates, suspending her fingers in the air between us as if she's not sure she's allowed.

I take her hand, holding it to my cheek. It's cold. Too cold. I swallow the lump in my throat. She'll be fine. She has to be. "Hi." I kiss her palm, watching those gemstone eyes light up with joy-filled tears.

"It wasn't a dream?" Her tired green-blue eyes flutter. The gray canvas of the tent ripples once more, and I watch her shiver. I wish I knew where I could get something warmer to cover her. The healers only had a thin brown blanket smeared with dark stains that smelled like smoke—a scent I never want to smell again after today. "I was convinced I was dreaming, even though I haven't fallen asleep."

That's why she's afraid to close her eyes. She's afraid she'll lose me.

"It wasn't a dream. I'm here. I'm not going anywhere." My thumb caresses her ashen cheek, and she sighs, leaning into my touch. My heart flutters. I missed being this close to her, not that I really ever got this close to her before . . . I shake the thought away. I don't want the past to dim the newfound hope we have.

"I just had to make sure." A faint smile lights her lips.

"I'm glad I could clear things up for you." I squeeze her hand. "I sent a message to your father. He should be here soon." I lean back, but keep my hand tightly entwined with hers. Just like her, I'm afraid that if I let go, this dream will be over—this little solace we've found will vanish.

"Did you tell him Thesa was right?"

"Yes. I didn't—"

"Where is she?" I hear Zenz outside the tent, and before I know it, he stands on the other side of Glena, dark eyes taking in her bloody bandage. "Oh, my precious girl. How could I? How cou—"

"I'm all right." She glances at me, squeezing my hand. "It worked, Father. Thesa was right. The men need something to fight for—something they love."

Tears fill Zenz's eyes. "That's what I did wrong then. That's why…" He trails off, and we watch the weight he carries crush his frame. I've never seen him as small before, but right now he seems so fragile. Weak. Disheartened.

"Father, it wasn't your fault. You didn't kill them. We didn't know then, but now we do. Now, we can continue to fight. Now, we have hope beyond 'just survive'. We have hope that we will persevere."

Her words seem to give him strength because he transforms in front of my eyes—his shoulders straighten as his strong frame tenses with the anticipation of a renewed fight.

I sit up at seeing my leader rise up once more.

He stands, kissing his daughter's cheek. "You're right. We'll finish this, and then we're going back to Casta. The fight is nowhere near over, and we can't afford to wait any longer."

Glena nods, blue eyes shining even in her weariness.

Zenz glances at me, midnight eyes pouring over my soul. He nods toward the opening of the tent. "Are you ready?"

I smile at Glena before nodding at Zenz. I'm more ready than I've ever been because I'm no longer fighting out of anger or hurt—I'm fighting out of love.

Chapter 8

Facing the Vultures

Thesa

"Ah, the prodigal princess returns. She hears daddy dearest is dying and decides to come crawling home," Erix says, his snide voice echoing against the cave walls.

He's one of the most pompous princes I've ever laid eyes on. Black hair streaked with leaf green folds down to his shoulders. Golden eyes glare down at me. A thin nose leads to a black and green beard that hoods narrow lips formed into a sneer. A long time ago, I mated Jet instead of him. Clearly, he's still upset about the whole ordeal. I knew if I came here, I would see him again. Out of all the council members, he's the one I have to look out for the most. There's no telling what he'll do to be chosen as the next king.

Glowing stones in an array of rainbows shine down on top of us, illuminating the basalt cavern just outside my father's wing.

"Erix, how lovely to see you again. You must have been gone the day I came home to apologize to my father, but I guess I would expect nothing less from the laziest council member. What was it this time, chasing your tail in the clouds? Smelling flowers in the meadow—"

He steps close to me, one hand reaching for me, but stops, clenching his fist instead. Bright green and black strands of hair fall into his eyes as he leans forward. His hot breath tickles my neck, and it takes all my will-power to withstand his challenge

"Listen here, *voign*. You are nothing, and you will always be nothing. You're an outcast. No one will accept you as the queen, not even the stones. Maybe you'd have had a chance if you had followed your duty, but you couldn't even do that."

"You talk as if my father already died, Erix. If that's the case, you're talking treason. That's enough to make you an outcast too." I glance down at his clenched fist that still hovers just below my chin. "Good thing you didn't lay a hand on me. Otherwise, you would have given my father more incentive to banish you. My father has welcomed me home, and after today, all will know the truth—even you. The stones will choose when the time comes, and for the sake of our people, I hope it's not you," I reply, glaring into his bright gold eyes. Gold is highly revered in Treían culture, and someone as terrible as Erix doesn't deserve eyes like those.

"I guess we'll see, *princess*." He takes a step away from me, shuffling down the adjacent cave entrance. He reminds me of a rat, slinking back to his sad existence in his own filth and darkness. I just hope he stays there forever, but I know his ambition will drive him out of his hole eventually.

I take a deep breath after he's gone. I hadn't realized how terrified I was in his presence, my heart hasn't slowed down, even though the threat is gone. Somehow, I'd held my ground. I lift my chin at the thought. Jet will be proud of me. I can't wait to tell him.

My heart slumps at the thought. I wish Jet were here. He would have never let me handle Erix alone, though, and the altercation might have ended up with them fist-fighting and cursing each other until one of them gave in. I have a feeling neither of them would have given in and just fought each other to death.

I like to think that my mate would win before Erix. At least, Jet has been in more combat . . . Erix probably has never even seen a battlefield, let alone been in the middle of a fight. The thought makes me smile. I continue down the cave to my right, walking along the polychromatic pathway until I come to Prism Arch.

My father's wing.

Glimmering stones of all colors line the basalt in an arrangement of a rainbow. I step over the threshold, heading into the room. A huge table with several chairs and a giant map sit in the middle, behind it an altar of large vibrant stones rise up toward the ceiling. That's where I find Kyira. Her milky white eyes meet mine as if she can truly see me.

"Thesa." She smiles. "I recognize those footsteps anywhere. I'm glad you came."

I bow my head. "Thank you, Kyira . . . and my father?"

Her eyes dim a little, but she tilts a head back in the direction of his room. "He's been waiting for you."

I nod before stepping toward the carved stone door. Chills linger on my skin, but it's not because of the cold caves. What state is he in? Can he lift his head? Or move? Will he even acknowledge my presence?

I open the door to find him pacing the room in full battle armor. I halt. "Father?"

He glances at me, a smirk spreading across his face, his long salt and pepper beard shifting with the movement. He rubs thick hands together. "My daughter, you made it."

I stare, dumbfounded as golden light shines above our heads. His room is specifically decorated to show reverence to his royalty. "Aren't you—"

He waves a hand before gently placing it on my shoulder. "I fainted a few days ago, and Kyira made a big deal of the whole thing. I'm fine, as you can clearly tell." He starts to cough, causing the armor he wears to clash like a cymbal.

My heart goes into a frenzy. Is he serious? I take his hand and gently help him to his bed that shimmers with diamonds and gold framework.

He shakes his head, his coughing still not subsiding as his long milky white hair shifts over his wrinkled face like a curtain. "I—I'm fine."

"I don't think Kyira was making a big deal of it." I stare at him. "Why are you wearing battle armor?"

"Because, this is normal for me. I'm fine, and even if I was sick, I'm not going to get better holed up in here." His dual-colored eyes of orange and blue wander around the room.

"Actually, Father, that is the exact definition of recovering. You have to be holed away until you feel better."

He scoffs. "Not me! The rumors are already spreading, and I'm sure the vultures have come to prey."

I shudder, thinking about Erix's hot breath on my skin. "You're right. I met Erix in the hall outside Prism Arch. No doubt eavesdropping, and he ran into me, of all people."

"Of course he did. I hope you gave him a piece of your mind?" He raises his eyebrows, nudging me with his shoulder.

"I did my best, Father."

"Good, I don't need him and his bloodline thinking our posterity is weak. I have a feeling that when I decide to go on, you or Jarret will be chosen." He takes my hand, squeezing it tightly.

"Father—"

"Now, you know I'm not one for superstition, but I've heard the stones speak. Maybe when you live around them long enough, they start to talk. Or maybe the rumors are true—I'm losing my mind and I'll be dead before spring. Who knows, anything can happen."

"Don't say that. Words hold meaning," I huff, gazing around at the gold and white stones that adorn the walls of his room.

"You're probably right, but I do believe you or Jarret will ascend next, and that's why I told Kyira to send you a message."

Oh, so he told Kyira to send for me? The plot thickens. I narrow my eyes. "Kyira made a big deal about it, huh?"

"Well, I might have told her to exaggerate it."

I smile.

"I'm glad you came. Now, I can officially reinstate you as my daughter, fulfilling and restoring your bloodline. So all will not mock if you or Jarret are chosen and hopefully be a little lenient toward you two if you aren't chosen. It'll be another way of showing my remorse…" He trails off, his multicolored eyes growing distant.

"Father." My thumb rubs circles over the wrinkled ridges of his hand. Tears fill my eyes. If someone had told me a few months ago that I would get to hold my father's hand like this, I would have called them crazy.

"Don't cry for me, Thesa." He wipes my cheek with his thumb.

"I'm—I was just thinking that we never had the chance to sit like this before, and I'm sad that there is all this talk of you going. I—I know it's inevitable, but I wish we could have more times like this." I hate the way my voice shakes, but it's cruel to think he could leave me soon.

"I wish we could too, but you have your duties, and I have mine. Maybe all that will change soon, but . . . don't ever think it was your fault. If your stubborn-headed father hadn't forced you away, maybe we would have had more time." He gives my hand another squeeze as he sighs. "Well, unfortunately we can't freeze time forever. Let's get out there and face the vultures."

Rahuin

Dais hunches over his desk, blond curls falling in a wild array over his forehead. I can't help but think how adorable he is. The giant map of Partin hangs on the wall behind him. I sit to his left at the little desk he had brought in for me so I could be close to him. I know I'm supposed to be answering the letters from some of the civilians that were sent to his office. I should try to get some work done, but I can't stop watching him. He's too much of a distraction, and who knows how much time I'll have to study him, to remind myself that he's mine? The thought sends shivers across my skin. I don't intend to leave him ever again, so why did I think that?

"You know, if you're going to be in here with me, you actually have to get some work done." Dais says without lifting his head.

I blush, looking back down at the letter I was reading, but I don't focus on the words. I'm tired of deciphering handwriting anyway. "You weren't supposed to catch me looking."

He smirks, glancing at me, blue eyes flashing and making my heart race. "You're not very secretive, and I haven't heard a summary of a letter in over twenty minutes." He props his head on his hand, leaning toward me.

I mimic him with a smile. "In all honesty, I wasn't trying to be. I needed a little break from the squiggly lines and incongruent handwriting, and you were the perfect distraction."

He stands up, heading around my desk.

I lean back as he places his hands against the arms of my chair, standing over me. His face hovers over mine, and my smile widens as I melt into the cushion. I'm sure my face is as red as my hair.

"How's your distraction now?"

"P—perfect." I flutter my lashes as he leans in for a kiss, trailing along my jaw.

"Now you're my distraction," he mummers against my skin.

"Good." I catch his lips with my own, forgetting the world around us for a moment as my fingers caress his chin and move into his hair. But the moment doesn't last long as a knock sounds from the closed door.

Dais sighs, pulling away, blue eyes shining as he clears his throat and moves back behind his desk. "Come in."

I straighten, fanning my face to disperse the blush he left.

A page rushes in with two parchments clenched in his fists. He bows before Dais. "Your Majesty, I bring you word from the battlefield." He shoves his right hand forward. "Sir Zenz's messenger just left this. And this"—he holds up his other hand—"was brought by a Sun'Arian envoy."

My stomach clenches as I sit up. Sun'Ar? But—

"Thank you. Is the envoy still here?" Dais takes the messages.

"Yes, Your Majesty. Headmistress gave him a room for the night. He said he was only to bring the message for you."

Dais nods. "Good. You may go."

"Your Majesty." The boy bows again and is out the door.

Dais glances at the ominous messages. Both could be harbingers of sinister news, and I'm not sure how much more Dais can take.

I stand, leaning my arm over his shoulders as his hands tremble. I rub circles against his back. "Zenz first. Let's know of their fate. The envoy is resting. If he has to take a message back, he'll do so in the morning."

He takes a deep breath, opening the letter on his left. After a moment, he lifts his head, tears appearing in his eyes. My heart starts to pound. No. They're gone. It didn't work. The Corrupted won. The Darkness is coming.

"They're victorious. It worked. Love worked." He wraps shaking arms around my waist, pulling me closer.

I release the breath I was holding. "You scared me there for a minute. I thought for sure they were gone." I gently shake him. "But now we know. Now we know the Corrupted are beatable."

He nods, turning to face the other message. My relief is short-lived. Zenz and Grimall winning against the Corrupted is some of the best news we've received in a while, but now it might all come crashing down. He opens the Sun'Arian parchment. The blood-red sun sealed against the seams blinks at us with a sinister foreshadowing as Dais breaks it apart.

This one Dais reads out loud. "Your Majesty, King Dais. In extensive formalities, I assume this letter finds you well. In two weeks' time, I will grace the Castian border. I come in peace. I have a solution for your predicament. I hope we can extend each other a moment of grace. I understand we might not see eye to eye, but we are both monarchs of great countries. I'd hate to see either of us fall. If you agree to meet me, you'll allow my entourage to pass unencumbered. If you do not, I will take it as a sign that you want to continue fighting this war, and I will meet you eventually on the battlefield."

Dais folds the letter, looking back up at me. His blue eyes uncover something I can't place.

My heart starts to pound. We could end it. If we really wanted to, this war could be over. "You'll let him through?"

He scoffs, clenching the letter in his fist. "I have half a mind to ambush him. Destroy him before I can hear his ideas, but I'm tired of fighting. I'm tired of the destruction. Since he's in league with the Darkness, he could have endless possibilities to harm us. If I kill him, the Darkness could destroy us for good." I sigh. "I'll let him pass. Maybe he does have a solution, or maybe it's just a trick. We'll never know until we try."

I nod, swallowing the dark thoughts that swirl with the possibility of destroying the king of Sun'Ar before he even sets foot on Castian soil. "Sometimes that's all we can do."

Zenz

Frosty wind nips my face, sending little flakes of snow swirling around my head. My heart skips in wonder that we made it here. The battle was gruesome, but in the end we won. Tears fill my eyes, but I blink them away. The information Thesa sent came right when we needed it. The grateful part of my heart hasn't stopped thanking the King of Light. I was so afraid that we wouldn't make it, but He knew. He sent us the answer before it was too late.

The white tops of the mountains peak out above the fog and swirling snow, looming like an ominous message to any who dare to come closer. Drak stands beside me, his gold eyes dimmed with the foggy light as he looks at me. Below us, on the snow-covered ground is Nnilmsh Valley—the birthplace of the giants. They were driven out years ago due to forest fires and a human king who enslaved them for his wars. After the giants won their freedom, they settled in the Serash Mountains where they became good friends with the Fenrir. It worked well for them and us, until everything changed again.

I'm glad we could restore them back to their homeland. I was skeptical when I saw the Corrupted pour out of Nnilmsh stronghold. I breathe in shakily and let it out, sending a white puff of clouds into the air. I watch it dissipate, becoming one with the fog surrounding us. Though we lost some men to the Corrupted, we were able to completely defeat the army. Who would have thought that love would work? It makes sense. Maybe if I had figured it out sooner . . . I would have been able to save Kali.

My heart clenches as I think of her terrified eyes. If I had apologized for my actions and told her I still loved her immensely, would she be here? Would I have saved so many by inadvertently figuring out that we just need to give each other something to live for? Kali changed because she was scared—scared to die. I shake my head, trying to disperse the guilt that gnaws on my insides. She wouldn't be here anymore because her wounds were too severe, but I could have kept her from changing. I could have had her body to perform a death ceremony and say goodbye, but it's all too late now. I'll never get the chance.

I wonder if I'll ever forgive myself for not trying to save her sooner. If I'll ever be able to move on. When the Corrupted poured out of the stronghold, I saw it again. I saw everything happening over again. I saw the way I couldn't protect my men. I saw the way I had failed all of them. Kali believed in me to lead the pack, but now that she's gone, I fear her trust was misplaced. I can't do this. I can't watch them die over this war.

The realization chokes my throat, but I can't leave the war solely to Dais and his other allies. If this wasn't a war between light and dark, if the prophecies I had believed in for so long weren't being fulfilled before my very eyes, I would take the pack where we could live in quiet solitude. To a place with no fear of war or being transformed into a monster, but I know that will never happen.

Some of my subordinates might think differently. They might think we don't have to fight. That we should leave the humans to fight their own war. Surely, they're starting to see that this war is more than just a human squabble. What happens if the humans are conquered and the Darkness turns his eyes on all the races? What then? They won't be able to fight back if the Darkness gets his way and corrupts all human beings. He will have a massive army that is completely unstoppable.

That's why I will continue to force my pack to fight now while we still have help. Yes, some will die, and every life lost will weigh heavily on me, but we have no other choice. We have to fight now while we still have hope of victory. If we wait any longer, our hope will be squashed like the ground under a giant's foot. I won't let that become all that we are.

"You are deep thinking, my friends," Drak grumbles, his voice sounding like it might cause an avalanche, which wouldn't be good since we're standing on a mountain peak. No matter how many times

I correct him, he can't say the word 'friend.' Ever since we took the stronghold and valley back, he started speaking to me in Castian, but his knowledge of the language isn't exactly extensive.

"You can speak in Knargk. It's not like anyone else is going to hear you," I say. Both of our packs are busy hauling supplies into the valley. We're staying for one night to watch perimeters and make sure no more Corrupted are around, before we head back to Morough.

He switches to Knargk and it takes my brain a second to translate the booming language. "I'm trying to get better at it"—he pauses—"but thank you for upholding our deal." He touches his forehead and lifts it to the sky. "All is forgiven now, your debt has been paid. You and your pack are always welcome in Nnilmsh Valley. If this war becomes worse, don't hesitate to come for our help."

"Thank you, my friend. We'll stay the night, then head out tomorrow."

He nods. "Much luck, my friends."

I smile at his switch back to Castian. "You too."

Chapter 9

A King's Dance

Dais

"Do you truly believe his claim of peace?" Rahuin asks, her fingers gripping mine tightly as we wait on our respective thrones.

"No," I state as I watch the door, refusing to say more. If I do, I'll say something I regret, and I can't afford for my words to be overheard by the wrong ears. I hear the creak of the guards' armor as they shift in their standing positions. The clunk of feet walking up the massive halls of the castle echo through the throne room doors.

Sunlight streams in from floor-to-ceiling windows on my left, reflecting over quartz floors that giveway to light blue walls encased in copper filligree, but I can't take my eyes off the oak doors at the far end of the room. We've just heard from a messenger that King A'zre Re'San has arrived in Morough. It's been two weeks since his envoy came with his ominous message.

My mother enters with David and Peggy from the side door to my right. I glance at Mother and mouth Esther's name.

She shakes her head, her eyes growing sad. Great. Esther's not even here. How can I meet another king when my entire family isn't present? He knows I have a sister. What if he thinks it's an act of defiance if she's not here to receive him? That's nonsense, I tell myself, but I'm not so sure. Recent reports about King A'zre have led me to believe that the man is a little unhinged. Greed drives him, and usually, people blinded by that kind of ambition lack reason. I don't want to deal with a madman who might go into hysterics at any potential misunderstanding.

Trumpet fanfare echoes through the throne room as a crier opens the doors and announces, "King A'zre Re'San of Sun'Ar!"

The king appears in an entourage of guards with a sun pressed into their armored chest plates. Flag bearers take the lead, holding poles sporting the Sun'Arian flag—a blood-red sun against a background of yellow. The king walks proud amidst his guards. Black curly hair has been pinned up on his head, and a thin, trimmed beard lines his jaw and mouth. Black tattoos swirl around his face and down his neck. Red eyes meet mine, and I squeeze Rahuin's hand. He walks with an air of confidence—as if he already holds the whole of Partin in his hands, but the reins haven't been handed to him yet.

"Your Majesty," he says in almost perfect Castian, bowing low in a mock gesture of reverence I know is all for show.

I stand, bowing to him as well. "Welcome to Casta, King A'zre. I hope everything is to your liking?" I ask in An'R. A language a bit more pronounced compared to Castian. It hangs on my tongue like thick honey.

"Your pronunciation is quite good," he states in An'R.

"As is yours," I say in Castian. I saw my father move to the steps of this dance for almost fifteen years—now it's my turn. My family remains silent from their positions by my side.

"Everything is well," he answers my previous question in Castian. "I find Casta much to my liking."

"I'm sure you do," I want to spit, but that wouldn't be very peaceful of me.

Another step to our well-matched dance.

"Good, good." I turn to Rahuin, who stands as I hold a hand out to her. "I'd like you to meet my fiancé—Princess Rahuin of Färrin."

King A'zre meets her eyes with a glint of malice that strikes fear into my bones. He knows who she is—more importantly, he knows what she did.

She holds her other hand out to him, and he places a quick peck on it. "A pleasure, Your Majesty." She bows her head.

A rehearsed spin into a dip.

He nods, and I gesture to my mother and David, introducing them as I go.

"Lovely to meet you." A'zre's voice seems to take command of the room, as if he owns it.

I tamp down my anger and shoot the king a kind smile. I hate this dance we must step to, but I know he holds the power to crush Casta. I don't even know why he had the gall to come here. I permitted it in hopes that we could maybe work out a ceasefire agreement, assuming that's what his message meant when he said he had a solution to the war. Though, like I told Rahuin, I'm not entirely sure that's the whole reason he's here.

"I'll have the servants direct you to your quarter—"

"If you don't mind, Your Majesty, I'd like to get on with our business," he cuts me off, and I can't help the flash of frustration that spreads across my chest at his insolence. If I did that in his country, he most likely would have cut my tongue out, but in my position, I can't afford to make such rash decisions. Any act of aggression could leave us stuck in this war.

"Of course, Your Majesty, follow me." I head for my study, dismissing my family in the process. They know this meeting is for me and me alone—for now, at least. Who knows what intentions the king hides behind his abnormally red eyes?

Jet follows me closely as I lead King A'zre to my study and have him take a seat across from me.

Once we're settled, a maid brings forth piping hot cups of tea and sets them before us.

He takes a sip and then looks hard at me.

The music ends.

The dance is over.

"Let's not beat around the bush any longer," he states in Castian.

I keep my language. "I'm glad you agree. Our dance was starting to become exhausting."

His reddish-brown eyes glint with a hint of a smile. Maybe in another time we could have been good friends. How greed changes everything.

"Of course, I assume you already know why I am here?"

"I have an idea, but please don't hesitate to inform me further." I take a sip of my tea.

"As you know, Sun'Ar and I have prepared for a war. A war we believed would last at least a few years. I will be honest with you, your last defense crippled our supplies and troops, buying you a little time. While you and Casta spend the next—let's presume—five years rebuilding, Sun'Ar and I will be reenforcing our troops. The five years Casta was at peace will have all been in vain, because I will come for you and I will destroy you. However, I am pleased to offer you an alternative to end this inevitable bloodshed." He pauses and takes a drink of his tea.

I notice he has quite a flair for the dramatic. He should have become a theater actor instead of a king. I almost laugh at the idea, but he'll probably think I'm laughing at bloodshed, which I will never find humorous.

"Enter a marriage alliance with Sun'Ar, and I will spare our countries the heartache war brings. We've both lost enough, let's not continue this if we can avoid it."

My heart pounds in my chest as I clench my fists. I want to release the scream building in my throat. I want to say I will never allow Casta to be taken over, but he's right. Five years would hardly be a long enough time to get Casta back on its feet, let alone rebuild its military. I flex my hand. Who does he think he can enter into a marriage alliance with? I have no one to offer.

As if he can read my mind, he continues, "I heard your wife is pregnant with a girl . . ." He leaves the words hanging in the air. I try to keep my face blank, but I feel my neck flushing. First, how does he know Rahuin is my wife? Second, how does he know she's pregnant and with a girl? Third, he wants my daughter? Over my dead body . . . but if I don't come up with something to appease him, I will be dead before she's even born.

"Rahuin is pregnant with a girl," I agree, through clenched teeth. I'm not sure how he knows about my daughter, but if I had to guess, I'm sure it has to do with the Darkness.

He smiles. He seems to be enjoying this little game he's playing with me. The reports were right, the king walks a thin line between sanity and madness. "I've also heard Princess Esther's husband lies on his deathbed."

No fault of your own . . . I hold the words back, hating that I can't tell him to leave this place and never return, hating that I'm forced into this position. At least, he's trying to create an alliance with us, but at what cost? My sister is about to lose her husband. There's no way I'll let him have her. She's gone through too much already.

"What are you implying?" I ask, even though I know exactly what he's trying to say.

"Create an alliance with Sun'Ar through a betrothal of your daughter to one of my sons, or once the princess has completed her mourning, allow her to create an alliance through marriage to me. Those are my two options . . . unless you have some other unwed sister I don't know about?" He raises his eyebrows.

"No more sisters." I shake my head and take a deep breath as I stand. He follows suit. "Thank you, Your Majesty. I have heard your petition, allow me a day to think it over before I tell you my decision."

We bow our heads to each other.

He nods. "Of course, Your Majesty."

I open the door for him and address Jet who stands on guard. "Please make sure King A'zre is shown to his quarters safely."

I hobble back into my office as I hear Jet address two guards and a servant to show the king where he'll be staying.

I fall back into my chair, sighing deeply as Jet reappears, his dark eyes set in a firm, harsh line. "Should I call Esther and Rahuin?" he asks, after he shuts the door.

I look up at him and nod. "Bring Esther and Connan both. I know she didn't appear earlier because Connan is not well." They returned from Is'Er a few days ago. Unfortunately, the island didn't have the healing effect Connan was looking for.

Jet nods, and my thoughts wander. My father comes to mind. How did he do this? He dealt with this sort of thing every day. My mother was right. I should have spent more time here with him, but I was too pigheaded. I left all this to him, thinking I had more time. He wanted me to walk alongside him, and now it's all too late. I swallow the lump in my throat. I miss his council. I miss his courage. Most of all, I miss him. He would have known what to do in this situation. He would have known who to sacrifice to save his people . . . and that's what I have to do.

The door to the study opens, ushering Rahuin inside. The crease in her brow seems to have become a permanent fixture on her face. It overshadows her worried green eyes buried under dark circles as she steals a deep sigh. She wraps her arms around me and kisses me as if it could be our last.

I kiss her back, getting lost in her lips on mine and wishing that I didn't have to face marriage alliances and tyrannical kings. Wishing that we could— Someone clears their throat, breaking us apart.

"Did we come at a bad time?"

I look up at Connan and Esther, who entered without any announcement. I clear my throat as Rahuin buries her face in my chest, and even though I can't see her face, I know it's as red as a tomato.

"No, you're right on time," I answer as Rahuin falls into the chair at her desk.

Connan looks even more haggard than the last time I saw him. His hunched body leans heavily against my sister, and his once dark blond hair is nearly stark white. Dull blue eyes enclosed in a map of prominent wrinkles meet mine. He looks old enough to be Esther's grandfather, not her husband.

My heart clenches painfully for my sister. It must be killing her to see him this way. I gesture to have them sit, while I move back behind my desk.

"I've just met with the King of Sun'Ar. He shed some light on current situations." I look each of them in their eyes. "While our defense of Casta did limit his resources, he reminded me that Sun'Ar has been preparing for this war. He mentioned that while I am busy rebuilding Casta and its imports, he can be using every resource to strengthen his military. In five years' time, he could forcefully take Casta once and for all. To quell his ambitions, he placed an offer before me I'm afraid I can't refuse. He wants to create a marriage alliance with Casta. I haven't accepted since I need your counsel on this matter."

"A marriage alliance? Who will be getting married?" Connan asks, his husky voice grating around the room like a bellowing dragon.

"Well—"

"I will," Esther answers, cutting me off. "He wants me, doesn't he?"

"Or—"

"Sira," Rahuin responds.

I meet her eyes, but they are lost in thought. I swallow. "Yes, he wants Sira to be betrothed to one of his sons, or after, Connan . . ."

"He wants to marry Esther," Connan finishes.

I nod, looking at my sister and studying her expression. "He promised he would wait until Connan passed so you have a little time, but I have to tell him who we choose before he returns to Sun'Ar."

"You believe there is no other way to stop him? You believe there is no other way to fight?" Esther asks, her purple eyes shimmering with worry.

"If Casta fights, either now or in five years, it would all be in vain. Lives would be given for no reason. It would be a stalemate of fighting lasting until they overtake Casta. If there was no other way, I would beg my countrymen to fight till the death, but he's offered us another way." I sigh. "I don't want to do this to you. So . . ." I look at Rahuin. She studies me. She sees it in my eyes. She sees my decision. She nods. "We will offer him Sira, and hopefully she will be enough to save us all."

My heart drops. I don't want to do this to my daughter. I hate this. She's not even here to defend herself and make her own choice. My job as a father should be to protect her and allow her to choose her own path, but I guess that's neither of our faults. She'll be a princess, born to serve her country. That's a fate I can't protect her from.

"Dais," Esther starts, "You of all people know what it's like to be betrothed to someone you hardly know. You can't subject her to a life that has already been planned out for her."

The frustration I'd been tamping down since King A'zre was here bubbles to the surface and I can't stop it when I shout, "Does it look like I have a choice? Do you think I want to do this to her? Do yo—"

Connan stands to his feet, slamming his metal arm against my desk. "That's enough! We're supposed to be finding a solution, not yelling at each other!" He turns to look at Esther. He takes her hands into his. "My love, you're right. We shouldn't subject Sira to a life she never asked for." His blue eyes search hers, tears welling in their gazes.

"Connan, I—"

"I know, but I'm already a dead man. If you can save Casta and tell Dais what's happening on the other side, I think it would be best."

"But—"

"You won't be betraying me. I'm telling you to marry him," Connan says. Tears fall down Esther's cheeks. He kisses her forehead and turns to look at me. "I know she's not ready." He blinks away tears. "I'm not ready." Esther starts sobbing behind him. "But it would be best. I won't be here for much longer. Allow her some time to think before you give the king an answer." He turns to help his wife out of the study.

Rahuin takes a seat on my lap. I hug her to me, burying my face in her neck. "Do you think she'll do it?"

I nod against her shoulder. "Yes, that's why she was crying so hard. She knows Connan will let her go to make it less painful. This gives him the perfect opportunity to bow out silently so she doesn't have to see him die. I'm sure he's tired of putting Esther through this." I pull away, looking deep into my wife's eyes. I can see she doesn't want Esther to marry the king. I don't want her to marry him either, but I know that it's not my decision to make . . . it's Esther's. I know Esther will agree to protect Sira, to protect us all. I rub my hand up and down Rahuin's arm, drawing comfort from her presence.

She kisses the top of my head. "Don't dwell on it. The choice is up to her now. There is nothing more we can do, and if she says no, it's our duty to raise Sira to—" she stops, taking a deep breath, as if it pains her to finish the sentence.

I understand, because it hurts me too. "I know."

Connan

Esther and I head back to our room. I lean heavily against her because I can't trust myself to walk well anymore. It makes me feel ridiculous. I hate all of this. I hate doing this to her. I hate that I'm dying. I look at her, but she doesn't acknowledge me. Instead, she stares straight ahead, her eyes unfocused as she tries to hold back tears.

"My love." I hate how my voice grates along the arched hallways. The sconces flicker over the plastered and gold inlaid walls. Some would call the sight beautiful, even glorious, but all I see are monsters lining the hollow cavity, or perhaps the beams are a huge beast's rib-cage and we have already been swallowed whole. Either are terrifying enough for me to want to run, but I can't even walk without help, how will I run?

Esther stops, a shaky breath filling her lungs as she turns her red gaze to me. She looks so tired. So worried. So sad. Grief has become a veil she's forced to hide behind.

I swallow the knot in my stomach. Even though it hurts to see her this way, I have to remind myself that it's my fault. I'm the reason she's losing me.

"Connan, I—" She sobs, turning into my chest as she cries, her nails digging into my coat. I fear that we'll topple over from the weight of our pain, but I hold her steady. My legs don't fail me. One thing they're still good for . . . standing.

She looks up at me, her purple eyes appearing more vibrant with the red encircling her swollen eyelids. I know what she's going to say before the words leave her lips. "I can't. I can't marry him. I won't do it. I won't leave you. We p—promised until death do us part. We made a sacred covenant. W—we can't just throw that away. It means too much! I—" Her words become indistinguishable as cries overtake her again.

But Sira . . .

An innocent child doesn't deserve to shoulder the alliance of a war she is unfortunate enough to be born into. We both know it, whether we want to admit it or not.

"Esther, I'm—"

"No! Please don't remind me that you're dying. I'm reminded every time I look at you. I just—please don't make me do this. Let me finish this with you. Don't let me go." Her breath settles against my neck.

"I can't make you do anything. It has to be your choice. Just like it was my choice to give my life for Casta's safety. It all seems so pointless anyway. My sacrifice only bought us a little time that leaves you with a terrible choice—a choice that takes you straight to the lion's den. I should have never . . . I'm sorry I did this to you. I thought it would keep you safe. I thought I could make you happy. I thought and I hoped so much, but in the end, right now, it doesn't matter. I love you, Esther, but I can't protect you anymore. I don't want you to marry him either, but I fear you'll have to. I just—I don't want you to be there when I die." The words feel like a punch to my gut, and Esther gasps.

"But—"

"No, look at all the tears you've already shed over me. I can't take it anymore. I know I'm leaving you with so much pain, but there is nothing I can do to change it. We will get an annulment, because I don't want you to watch me take my final breath. I want to go out in your memory as the man you always loved, not an old man you didn't even recognize. I get weaker every day. I—"

"You're using this as an excuse to leave me? Even though the king said he would wait?" Her lips tremble.

"Yes." I hate myself as I utter the words. I did this. I did this to her, but I can't watch her pain anymore. I can't watch her continue to lose me. It's selfish, I know, but there is no other way she'll let me go.

She lifts her hand as if she's going to slap me but stops, and it's like I watch her body fill with strength. Her fingers roll into a fist, she blinks the tears away, and her face gains a hard edge—like a mask I know she'll use to keep her emotions intact, even if it means she'll wear it forever.

"Fine. Go. I will do as you ask. I will marry him. I will protect Casta because it's all I'll have left now. I promised I would stay by your side until the very end, but if you want to go, then I won't deny your wishes. I hate that you deny me, but I will do it." Her voice quivers, but the tears don't fall again.

I nod, tears welling in my eyes as I look at her, but she holds a hand up.

"Don't. You don't have any right to cry. You're the one leaving me, remember? We'll ask Dais to set up the papers to annul our marriage, and I will—I will become the king's new bride. He only has six wives already." Malice poisons her voice. She wraps her arms around me again, and this time, she holds me up instead.

I try to memorize how she feels against me. I run my fingers through her hair, remembering how my callouses snag on the silky strands. "I love you, Esther. I always will."

"I know. You loved me so much you lost yourself to save me. I wish you hadn't loved me so much. I hate you for it. Your sacrifice doesn't make me feel loved, it makes me feel alone and bitter. But maybe we were doomed from the very beginning, back when I was a foolish girl who fell in love with the boy on her balcony. I love you, and I will miss you every day I draw breath." She inhales deeply. "Do one last thing for me, since you are leaving . . ."

I hug her tighter, breathing in her scent. Oddly enough she smells like the sea, like it's been ingrained in her bones to draw me back time and time again. "Anything."

"Die with peace. Don't die with regret. Die knowing that, although I hate you for leaving me, I'm so proud to have been your wife. I'm proud you chose me and loved me through all my flaws." Her hands run up and down my back.

"I will die with no regrets, because, if given the chance, I would do it all again. I would love you again. I would sacrifice myself again. I don't regret it."

She pulls away, and I notice how the shadows draw harsh lines of darkness over her features. I wipe the streams of tears on her cheeks.

"I promise these are my final tears over you."

The words burden my heart, weighing it down in my chest, but I'll no longer be the cause of her pain. "Let's go tell Dais."

Ellenora

"With this act, I now annul the marriage between Princess Esther Verne and Admiral Connan Brachs," the priest announces, placing the cerulean blue veils they'd gotten married in back over Esther and Connan's heads.

Connan slowly releases Esther's fingers, and I watch his shoulders slump even more from my spot on the balcony. The priest stands at a podium with a rectangular pool sitting in front of it.

Tears well in my eyes as I watch them stand back into the pool and submerge themselves separately. The blue-clad priest helps them out, designating them to exit the chapel in the same fashion they had entered during their marriage ceremony—through the adjacent doors on the side. Cerulean and pastel blue shine down on them from the stained-glass window at the front of the church. The blue seems too cheerful for this sorrowful day.

My heart breaks for my daughter. I can't believe that after waiting for so long, she was finally able to be with Connan, only to have him ripped from her again. I couldn't have been half as strong as she is— not with the strength she has embodied in the last few hours. If I was her, I would have buried myself in a closet and never returned to the light of day. I know why she's doing this. I know why she thinks she can help Casta this way . . . but she's already lost so much because of her birthright. I wipe the tears from my eyes as Esther and Connan disappear. My other children start getting up from their balcony seats. The ceremony is over. We can leave now, but I don't move. I feel like waiting, but waiting for what? I'm not sure.

I hate my foolish heart. I hate that it chose to love a king. I hate that I cursed my children with the burden of caring for a kingdom. A kingdom they will die and sacrifice for. A kingdom that will never do the same for them. I hate that I raised them to love it. I hate that it will be the death of all they hold dear. Just like it killed Timothy, just like it's killing Connan, just like it's destroying Dais and Rahuin. It will be a curse that falls on my grandchildren and their children for generations to come, until another tyrant wages war against them and tries to take their birthright away.

It won't come to that . . . the voice calms my shattering heart. It's a voice I've found myself relying on time and time again throughout my life, and I believe with everything in me that it's the King of Light who speaks to me, comforting me when I have no hope to move forward. I know many don't believe in Him. Don't believe that He will come back as He promised, but I think He's around, just waiting for when He can finally return in all His glory and take back the land He was forced out of so long ago.

I repeat the words over and over in my head. If He says it won't come to that, then it won't. I hope that means He'll come soon and relieve my family of their suffering—relieve this land of suffering.

Chapter 10
For Casta . . . All for Casta

Esther

My heart palpitates in my chest as I wait in the garden. Spring has started to show its face in little bits of greenery—small plants and flowers poke through the dead foliage of winter. Servants peruse the grounds, cleaning the dead away and encouraging new growth to expand.

Birds twitter in the trees, almost too excited. How can they be happy when I'm in misery? They seem to announce his arrival. I meet my future husband today. A man I have to marry for the sake of Casta—not for love, but for country. I should be happy that I got the chance to marry the man I loved. I should be happy that I get to serve my country this way, but nothing about this situation makes me happy. I can't see the good in all this, and I wish I could. The swaying trees above me send whispers of fresh clacking leaves across the air, a hint of wet wood and salty air suspends around me. It's suffocating. The sea reminds me of him.

Dais appears to my right with King A'zre, their guards trailing behind them with careful, sure steps. It's the first time I've seen the King

131

of Sun'Ar. He has skin the color of chestnuts and long dark hair that falls down his back in thick, curly waves. A thin beard coats his chiseled chin and black tattoos line his face and eyes in complex swirls. Eyes the color of autumn foliage blaze as they meet mine. I've never seen eyes as red as his—they're bewitching.

I stand as they approach, bowing my head.

Dais turns to the king. "King A'zre, I'd like you to meet my sister, Princess Esther Verne," Dais says before turning to me. "Esther, I'd like you to meet King A'zre Re'San of Sun'Ar.

I meet his gaze, looking deep into his mysterious eyes, or perhaps he's only tried to make them a mystery. They hold a certain darkness, a weight burdening them. They strike me as familiar, almost like Connan's. Even though King A'zre looks nothing like Connan, they share the same darkness—a past drenched in abuse. How interesting that my next husband holds the same dark past as Connan.

King A'zre lifts his hand, and I place mine into it for a kiss. I wait for the onslaught of his memories to consume me, but nothing happens. This man is becoming more and more interesting by the second. Connan is the only other person I've never been able to read.

"It's a pleasure to meet you, Your Highness." His voice is smooth, like a gentle breeze on a warm day.

It throws me off. I'd always imagined his voice to be as callous and harsh as the wars he's raged against Casta. The thought fills my heart with venom as I'm reminded of all I've lost in this war, and this man standing before me is the reason. I can't be fooled by his misunderstood eyes or lilting voice. I have a mission to become his wife and appease a war that has already destroyed my life, my father, my husband, and my home.

"Please, Your Majesty, let's not waste each other's time. We both know there is nothing pleasant about this." I remove my hand from his.

Dais shoots me a look, but I ignore him, watching A'zre as he lifts his brows, an amused expression on his face.

"You are quite right, Your Highness." He glances at Dais. "I like your sister, Your Majesty. I don't want to waste my time either."

Dais nods. "I'm glad, Your Majesty. I will leave you two to it."

Dais tosses me a look that seems to say, *"You'll be all right?"*

I nod, and he departs. Of course I'll be all right. I don't exactly have a choice either. In a few hours, I'll be married to this man.

King A'zre offers me his arm, and I take it. We start strolling, weighted silence filling the space between us.

"You have nothing you want to know about me?" he asks in my silence.

"I could say the same for you." I raise a brow, glancing sideways at him. "Funny, we don't want to waste each other's time, but we can't even get to know each other before we get married."

"Tonight. Are you nervous?"

What an odd question. "Not really, even though I'm marrying an absolute stranger. Very few things worry me anymore. I've already lost so much, what else can be taken away?"

"Well, your life."

A bird flies above us, singing to the spring air. I stare at it, wishing I could be that bird. "Honestly, if I lost my life, that would be a relief. I'd have no more suffering. I'd have absolutely nothing to lose."

"That's true." He nods. "No more pain, but nothing accomplished either."

"What would I have to accomplish? I'm a woman who's lost everything I ever wanted. All I have left is to serve my country, and soon . . . you, as your wife." The words leave a terrible taste in my mouth as reality seeps into the cracks of the broken foundation of my life. Saying it aloud makes the situation so real, but it doesn't scare me like I thought it might. Instead, I feel numb. I feel detached. Since the annulment, I haven't felt anything. I'm a ghost drifting, yet stuck in the same place.

"Which I'm sure you will do well. Tell me the things you know about me then. I don't want to reiterate all that you are already aware of—to save time, of course."

I allow myself to smile. Even though I want to hate this man, I will soon be his wife. For a moment, I forget all the horrible things that have occurred for us to come to this point. For a moment, I become a bride who wants to know more about her husband. The more I know, the more leverage I have. Though, I'm almost certain we will never have anything to use against each other besides our countries.

A'zre

"I shall do my best, Your Majesty. You became king at age twenty-four. You contented with twenty-three siblings before successfully winning over the hearts of the people and ascending the throne—"

I almost scoff at this. I only became king because my father wanted me to. I won the hearts of the people because he already had many of them forced into submission, whether that was by money or fear.

"—ve six wives, and thirteen chil—"

"Fourteen," I correct. A light breeze skitters by, sending dark locks swirling around my face like the tattoos I've had since I was a child.

She glances at me, her purple eyes narrowing. "Forgive me. Fourteen." She tries to mask the venom in her voice, but she's already failed at hiding her obvious dislike over the situation, often challenging the norms of civil pleasantries. It's a welcome change since the last two women I married to secure an alliance bowed and scraped to my every breath in fear that I would punish them for not agreeing with me. The princess, however, is an extraordinary case. Usually, I'd be annoyed by her attitude, but I'm surprised to find it quite endearing.

It makes me excited for our impending nuptials. I don't think there will ever be a dull moment in Ren'R when she becomes my wife. I can already hear her talking back to my other brides. They won't appreciate it much. Ah, the complaints I'll receive. Of course, I won't 'receive' them, but I'll be made aware by gossip and under the breaths of my wives. They'll pretend to be okay with her, but Esther will become my first foreign wife, and that already will cause plenty of dissension. The princess has no idea what she's about to face. I hope it doesn't douse her fire. I doubt it will; she seems fairly set in her ways.

"From what I've heard, you enjoy experimenting with poisons, love your horse or horses in general, and you always attend every Sun'Arian festival, regardless of its insignificance."

Her knowledge is quite impressive.

"No festival is insignificant, that's why I attend every one."

A smile lights her face, and the action brightens her harsh violet eyes, turning them almost lavender in color. It's extremely beautiful, but something tells me she doesn't smile often. This is only the second time she's graced me with a genuine smile. The first appeared after I asked her to tell me about me. I almost match her smile at the thought, but I rarely give anyone a true smile either—and I'm not about to start.

"That's most of what I know, but I think it's your turn." Her purple eyes catch a pale yellow flower bud—the first of its kind.

"Most? What's left?"

"Assumptions."

How intriguing. "Oh, well in that case, I will state the facts I know and then we can test our assumptions." I throw her a sly smile—not a true one.

"Better make it fast. We are supposed to appear before a priest in a few hours." She waves a hand in the air, gesturing toward where the city of Morough lies over the hill.

"I'm a fast talker."

"Time's ticking."

This time I do smile, genuinely. It feels foreign, and some part of me is annoyed that my resolve crumbled so easily. Well done, Princess. Well done.

David

"Are you certain about this?" I ask my sister while we sit in the carriage headed to the chapel. Today we'll both get married. Peggy and I decided that we didn't want to wait. We always wanted a small ceremony anyway. Tomorrow, Esther will be headed to Sun'Ar, and I couldn't bear not having her at my wedding. Who knows if her new husband will even allow her to visit? This could be the last time we sit together; the last time we have a face-to-face conversation. I hope not, but nothing is certain anymore. I can't afford to be wrong.

I'm getting married first, then A'zre and Esther will follow. I hate that she's getting married to a tyrant. I hate that she had to leave the man she loved to do so. My eyes trail out the window as the city of Morough passes us by—quaint homes decorated with river stones, blue shutters, and sloped metal roofs in all colors. Citizens wave as we pass, while others shoot mournful glances. Even some hostile faces peak through the crowd. Many aren't happy that Esther is marrying the man who started this war and caused them to lose their loved ones.

I look away, trying to meet my twin's eyes, who seems to be watching the passing faces with interest. "Esther?"

She sighs, turning away from the window as if it was the hardest thing to do. A weight of cold fear hovers over her head like an intimidating shadow. I feel it pressing into my entire being, crushing the cerulean blue cushions and turning them into chunks of twisted fiction, like a mirror warped right in front of me, but it lied in the reflection.

I blink, and it's gone. Replaced instead by Esther's steady fingers on my knee.

She leans from her side of the carriage, reminding me that I'm safe, that she's safe. She shifts to sit beside me, taking my hands into hers. "I'm as certain as I can be. I have a duty to fulfill now. I will do all I can to save Casta."

She stares at our hands, but I watch the redness rimming her eyes, the tears she hasn't shed over Connan, Casta, and our family. The thought gnaws on my gut. She's leaving soon. What will I do without her here? We just reunited, and now I have to let her go. I have Peggy, but Esther and I share something special. A bond not many siblings have.

"It's okay to cry," I whisper, wrapping my arm over her shoulders and pulling her close. Her head falls against my shoulder. "Cry because I want to cry. Scream because I want to scream. If we never feel, how will we even remember we're alive?"

"If I cry, I'll never stop. If I give in, I won't continue. I won't go through with it." She lifts her head, swiping the two tears that managed to escape her swollen eyelids. "I have to go through with it."

"Esther." I take her hands again. "Promise me, you'll find time to feel. Promise me you'll find time to grieve. I couldn't take it if I knew you became a shell in my absence. We won't be there for you. I need to know that you will feel. I need to know my sister will still be there somewhere, and that when I see her again, I'll recognize her."

"David . . . I don't recognize myself anymore. How can you say you recognize me now? All I have is you and Dais and Mother and Casta. If I stop, if I feel, I'll never breathe again. I'll forget all I have left to fight for, but . . . I understand what you're trying to say. For you, I will try. When I'm safe, I will grieve, but I don't know when that will be. I will be watched at every moment in Sun'Ar. I can't afford to show weakness. I can't afford for it to reflect badly on Dais. I have to be careful."

"I know, but not at the cost of your sanity."

She nods, a ginger smile coming to her face, her purple eyes bright against the redness of her eyes.

"And you'll write every day? I—"

She smiles wider. "I don't know about every day, but every week, I promise."

I squeeze her hands. "I wish you didn't have to go to Sun'Ar." Tears appear in my eyes and I look away. I can't cry now. She's about to be married. How will I survive without her? I can't make this worse than it already is, but I feel the fear creeping in from my gift. The cold buries me in its icy depths. My gift takes others' fears until it freezes them to death. Peggy always holds it back because of her fire. What if Peggy isn't enough? What if I lose control? What if I destroy Casta with my gift? What if I can't be—

"David, you'll be okay without me. I'm not letting him take me away, but I will be his wife, and wives go with their husbands. You have Peggy, Mother, Dais . . . they won't let you give in. You're stronger than that. Just like I'm strong enough to marry him, you are strong enough to harness your gift and use it to help Casta." Her purple eyes blaze with conviction.

"You think so?" I raise my eyebrows, my heart palpitating with the possibility. "No. I can't use my gift for good. It's evil. Nothing but evil." Death. Fear. I see the monsters growing around the carriage, ready to use me for their ultimate demise.

"It's just lying to you. It's trying to make you think that it can't be used for good, that all it brings is death, but that's not true. Anything good can be used for evil just as anything evil can be used for good. I've seen it. This marriage looks evil, but it can be used for good. We always have a choice, David. Don't run out of time to choose. Don't lose."

I meet her gaze, ready to see the shadows, the cold; but in her eyes, I see light. I see hope. She believes in the good she can bring through this. I have to believe too. I can't give up because she's leaving. She's doing all she can to save Casta and end this war. So we can finally live in peace away from the constant fear of death.

"I believe you." I take a shaky breath. "I can fight. I can find a way to use this for good. While you're in Sun'Ar, that's what I'll do. I'll find a way. I know Peggy will help me. You're right. I have to choose. I can't choose to live like this anymore. If you can do it, I can too."

Tears appear in her eyes once again. She hugs me, even though I know she'll see the horrible monsters I see, but now I realize she isn't scared of them. I'm the one who's scared, and I've given it far too much power already.

"I love you, David."

"I love you too, Esther."

Connan

I stand in the back of the chapel, leaning against Maud. She holds me up with careful hands, concern lining her light pink eyes. I ignore her, keeping my gaze fixed on the front of the chapel. It feels like ages ago that I stood up there with the stained-glass window shining down on Esther and me. I remember their blue hue—like the ocean that calls my name louder and louder. I want to join it. Become it . . . but not yet. Not until I see the last bit of my heart torn apart.

I just witnessed David and Peggy get married, a quick ceremony of a beautiful promise. I hope they'll be stronger than Esther and me. I hope they never get torn apart by an evil war in a broken world.

"Are you sure you want to be here? We should just go," Maud

says as the chapel fills with Sun'Arian guards. He's here. Esther is next. "I have to see it, Maud. I have to see it end."

"I don't know why you want to torture yourself."

"It's not about torture. It's about saying goodbye. If I don't see this, I'll never see what my sacrifice bought. I'll never know what good Esther will do in Sun'Ar. I'm worried for her, and I hate that she has to go straight into a marriage with a man she doesn't know. A man I'm sure won't care for her, not like I cared for her." I lower my voice to a whisper, watching as Esther and King A'zre step from the side doors.

As I imagined him, the king looks prideful, like a man who believes he owns everything he lays eyes on. Right now his eyes are on my w— the woman who used to be my wife. My heart clenches before I remind myself that this is my fault. If I hadn't sacrificed my life, I would have saved her from this fate, but would we have been able to save Casta? Would we have been able to hold the waterfront? I think not. It would have been hopeless without the sirens.

The priest starts the ceremony, and I look away but don't move. I won't draw attention to myself by trying to leave now. I will endure, like I'm forcing Esther to. I catch sight of Rahuin in the first row, watching with a somber gaze. She looks haunted. When I first met her, I hated her. I hated that some random girl believed she was the chosen one who would help defeat the Darkness. I hated the confidence she had. Now she's nothing but a broken warrior whose sacrifice bought us some time.

I respect her now, because I understand what it's like to sacrifice yourself for those you love. I know she's not done paying for what she did. Mine was easy. I gave up the years left in my life, so I will never see the repercussions of what I did. It also means I'll never reap the reward, but maybe those who come after me will. With Rahuin, though, she will carry the burden of the lives she took, of the people she betrayed to accomplish it. Maybe she'll see the reward, but it will never outweigh the cost. Esther hates her for what she did, but I understand—and I wish I didn't. If I didn't, I wouldn't be watching the woman I love marry someone else.

Tears spill over my eyes as I watch King A'zre submerge Esther under the pool. As she reappears without her veil, I catch sight of her eyes. They burn with a thirst for vengeance, anger fuels the flame, sending shivers down my spine as she looks at the king. She tries to mask the darkness in her eyes by lifting the corners of her lips to make her appear sweeter, but I know Esther wears a disguise everywhere she goes. Her true feelings only show in her eyes. Unless you know her, you'd never know which feelings she keeps concealed, and you'd never know if they were true.

The emotions in her eyes give me hope—hope that she'll be okay. No matter what happens, she will do all she has to for Casta because she has nothing else.

Maud squeezes my hand. I look down at her as I hear the priest announce King A'zre and Esther married. My heart shatters in my chest, and I take a shaky breath, glancing up as they disappear through the doors again.

"Come on." Maud pulls me to the front entrance, forcing my gaze away from the altar. The thick air of late winter dredges along my skin as we step outside.

Maud starts toward the carriage we came in.

"Please tell the driver to take me back to the docks."

"Connan—" she starts as she opens the door.

"I want to get back on *The Grandier.* I can't spend another night in the castle."

She nods. "I'll tell him." She helps me in before speaking to the driver.

I stare out the little window, watching the sky as it darkens. I try not to think about how Esther will be spending her first night with her new husband. I try not to think about everything I've lost. Instead, I stare at the sky and think about sailing away in the wind. I think about letting my life fall into the sea. I think about dying, and finally . . . I feel at peace.

Esther

A'zre huffs as he paces the room. His red eyes dart around the space as if they can find a way to escape.

I smile a little at his antics before plopping myself onto the bed. The light blue and silver embroidered blankets swallow me in their embrace. I'm glad Mother moved us into a different room. I don't think I could have bedded my new husband in my old room. The decorations are less like Casta and more like how I imagine Sun'Arian décor to be—fleshed out with mosaics of setting suns and open oceans. Proud bronze lion statues line the front door and the glass doors that lead to the balcony. How fitting, because the big cats give me an idea. I smile up at A'zre.

He glances at me. "What? What's so funny?"

"Nothing." I quirk a brow. "I just find it amusing to watch you prance around the room like a disheveled cat."

A muscle in his jaw twitches as he stares at me like I'm the stupidest person he's ever met. "I'm not a cat."

"I'm aware," I quip with a roll of my eyes, before I pat the space beside me. "I mean you're making me nervous. I'm almost certain you're about to start meowing so someone will come get you."

"Is this funny to you? I'm not a cat. I don't meow!" he snaps, pacing some more.

"I find it immensely funny. If I can't poke some fun at you every once in a while, then this marriage is going to fail miserably."

"You know what?" he starts before closing his mouth and shaking his head. "Women don't talk down to me—especially a wife."

"Who said I was talking down to you? I was only trying to get you to loosen up. You look like you might snap from all the tension pulling your shoulders. At least try to relax." I pat beside me again.

He glares at my hand, his red eyes looking from me to the locked door and back to me. He huffs, spinning on his heels before walking over to the chaise and sitting on it instead.

Odd. I thought he would at least try something on our wedding night. I was preparing myself for it. Preparing myself for the night where I would absolutely betray the covenant Connan and I shared first. *It's technically not betrayal if you aren't married . . .* I glare at the voice in my head. It feels like it.

I've been in this position before. I've had to use my body to get close to men my father wanted me to read. This is nothing new. I shouldn't feel guilty. Connan and I are over. Maybe A'zre is so repulsed by me he can't physically touch me. No, that can't be true either. He said he found me beautiful when we first met. Maybe I should be glad he hasn't touched me, but I'm also a little put off by it. Shouldn't he?

Tampering down the swirling questions in my gut, I ask, "What's with you? Are you scared that I'll bite you or something?"

If question marks had faces, his would be it. "Is this another reference to a cat?"

Finally, we're getting somewhere. I shrug my shoulders. "It could be."

He narrows his eyes. "Like I said, 'I'm—'"

"I got it. You're not a cat. Can we move on? I just want to know why you're sitting over there and not over here."

"Does it scare you that I'm not sitting with you? I thought you would be happy. Sometimes sitting beside each other can lead to other things." A sly look prances across his face.

I glare at him. "I'm actually more than happy, just a little confused. You seem like someone who would want to cement our covenant as soon as possible, but you don't even seem the least bit interested."

"Under normal circumstances, I would be, but it's just that"—he clears his throat—"I don't have sexual relations with women I'm not married to."

What? I scoff. "You do realize we're married, right?"

He rolls his eyes. "With all due respect, Your Highness, I'm not married to you until we have our ceremony in Ren'R. I decided to sit over here so I don't want to sleep with you."

"Oh, and here I thought it was my looks."

"Dear gods above," he mutters, looking at the ceiling. "Women can be so self-centered."

"Really? I'm self-centered because I foolishly thought my husband didn't want to sleep with me over my appearance, or maybe it's because his wife is a foreigner—well, one of his wives because apparently he can't just have one."

He jumps to his feet. "That's enough! I should demand that I be let out of this room. Why should I be forced to stay here with you?"

"Meow, meow," I mock.

His nostrils flare and a vein bulges in his forehead. The sight only makes me want to laugh. Maybe I shouldn't provoke him. After all, I did give up my marriage to the man I loved just to marry him for the sake of my country, but I can't help that his reactions are hilarious.

"Do you have to act like such a child?"

"Now, I'm a child? First I'm self-centered, and now I'm a child? I think we're regressing. May—"

He holds a hand up. "Furthermore, Sun'Arian culture is different from Castian culture. A man is looked down upon if he doesn't have more than one wife."

"What's the point of that? How can you love them all?"

"I have my methods. I don't marry them for love. Most are alliances—like our matrimony will be."

"Do you love any of them?"

A sad smile flits across his face, but it's a welcome change to the anger that was there before. The same darkness I had seen on him time and again fills his features. He stands in front of me, looking straight into my eyes. "I'm not inclined to answer you."

I take a shaky breath. That means yes. "I'm sorry." I swallow. "I didn't mean to call you a whiny cat. I'm—this isn't exactly easy for me."

He sighs. "I'm sorry as well. I didn't mean to call you a child." He sits down on the other side of the bed, leaning into it slightly. "Hmm, this bed is rather comfortable."

I smile, leaning back to meet his eyes. "Indeed it is."

A grin tops his face, pulling at his tattoos, a mischievous look in his eyes. "Since we determined that I'm not sleeping with you tonight, I think it's rather fair I get the bed."

I sit up. "Excuse you? I'm perfectly fine with sleeping with you. If you're so worried about it, you should sleep elsewhere, and I'll take the bed."

"I'm an esteemed guest, so I'll take the bed." He sits up with a smirk. He thinks he's got me. Well, he's wrong.

"I'm the princess of Casta."

"I'm the king of Sun'Ar."

"Pulling rank on your wife?"

"We're not married. The bed is obviously mine."

"Over my dead body." I flop across the expanse of covers. I refuse to lose this argument—our first one. How quaint that it's on our wedding night.

"That can be arranged." He leans over me, his dark hair surrounding the space between us like a veil.

"Is that a threat?" My eyes trail the length of his face and land on his lips.

"No," he whispers before clenching his jaw and moving away from me.

What a shame. He has better resolve than I thought. *I thought you didn't want to sleep with him?* I don't, but I want to get it over with. I don't want to wait until we're back in Ren'R. That's going to be hell on my nerves, especially because I'll have to wait at least a month.

I turn over, patting the space beside me.

"I told you, I don't sleep with women I'm not married to."

"I never said anything about sleeping with me, I wanted to say that you should sleep beside me," I answer.

"That's the same thing."

I smirk. "I assure you, it's not."

"What game are you playing?"

"Nothing, I'm not willing to give up the bed, and you're not willing to give it up either. I don't want you sleeping on the chaise, so this is our only compromise. Sleep beside me tonight. That way we both get some rest before we leave tomorrow." My gut clenches at the thought. Right. I'm leaving the only home I've ever known, and who knows when I'll be back. I tamp the feeling down. I refuse to be the wife who cries and cries after she's taken away from her home.

He sighs, his chest huffing under the weight. "Are you always this persistent?"

"Not usually. In most circumstances, I get what I want fairly easily."

"This must be quite annoying for you then."

I ignore his comment as I sit up, propping my back against the pillows. "Sit down and tell me about Sun'Ar from your perspective, all I've ever had were books to tell me."

He sits down. "You've never been?"

I shake my head. "I've never been anywhere." Besides a black hole I was forced to live in for eight months . . . I shove the thought aside. That wasn't exactly going anywhere because I couldn't see or feel anything besides darkness.

"Books can hardly describe Sun'Ar."

"Then give me your best shot, Your Majesty."

He smirks, and I fall asleep listening to him talk about the beauty of his country.

Thesa

The dark night swallows us, and the full moon's light illuminates my puffy breaths as we wait in the clearing. To our right, steam rises to the sky from a little hot spring that splits the ground in two and provides the ceremony with a warm pool for the baptisms. A blue-clad priest stands next to Wen by a fire just to the left of the pool, warming himself as he waits for the bride and groom to appear.

Tonight, my son gets married. Married. I can't believe how quickly time went for him. From not being able to have the love of his life and denying himself the right, to taking the harder steps forward to marry her, stay by her side, and love her forever. My hands warmed in fleece lined gloves squeeze Jet's. His dark eyes meet mine in the silver light, shining with tears that he'll never let anyone but me see.

In his other hand, he holds a shimmering *heln*. When Jarret told me he was getting married, I immediately messaged Kyira and told her I needed two stones—one for Jarret and one for Renell. She sent them with one of the Treían scouts still reporting to Dais. I hold the other stone, the one intended for Renell. They are having a traditional Lan combined with a Castian wedding. Since Jarret doesn't know much of his Garon heritage from being raised in Casta, and Renell is the princess of Lanckest.

Though it's a sad thing for a princess to not have her country behind her on her wedding day—or her father. So, Jet and I will be parents to both of them. After all, Renell will soon be a part of our family. The stones, in Garon tradition, represent an unbreakable bond, as *helns* are tethered to each other due to an enchantment and are only given in pairs to a couple about to be mated. Once a Garon pair has mated, they are mated for life and cannot reverse the bond—they are tethered forever, just like these stones.

My mate and I would have gotten a pair if I hadn't defied my father. Unlike other Garons, I never had the privilege to choose my mate. My Father decided to betroth me to Erix, but I couldn't stand him because I knew he was a power-hungry *rlébe* . . . So I chose my own mate, and he chose me. Even though we tried to fight it for the sake of obeying the king, his will meant nothing when it came to our love. It was short-lived, and I didn't even get to revel in Jet's arms for longer than one night.

A shaky breath escapes my lips, sending puffy clouds into the air.

"Are you thinking about—"

"Yes," I cut Jet off. "I was. At the time, I was so angry about everything that happened, but now I wish we had been more careful."

"It wouldn't have mattered anyway," he says, frosty clouds nipping at his beard, leaving little crystals in his black hair. I smile because it only makes him look more handsome. "If your father hadn't found out that morning, he would have made you mate with someone else, destroying our bond and creating a world of pain for us both."

I nod, the past lurking over my shoulders at the thought. I remember that day so clearly—that day, and the day I gave Jarret away so he would be safe too. My screams still echo around the hollow of my cave, the dim rainbow stones glowing like lost sentries that couldn't do anything to stop the pain of two young lovers being separated.

"You're right." My hands shake in his, but he grips them tightly.

"They should be ready for us." He walks toward the tent we set up to give Renell privacy before the ceremony.

I slip a hand through the slit in the tent. "Renell? If you're ready, Jet and I are here."

"I'm ready," her thin voice calls from behind the fabric.

I lift the flap, and in the faint light from the lantern beside the entrance, my eyes light on Renell. Black hair is pinned on top of her head, upholding the metal headpiece that looks like the moon cycles revolving around Partin. Her moon face tattoos seem to glow in the dimness, creating an ethereal look. Her silver and dark green dress hangs off her shoulders in glorious tiers.

She smiles nervously at me. "What do you think?"

I let go of Jet and take her hands into my own. "You look beautiful." Tears appear in my eyes. "You are perfect."

"Don't tear up, you're going to make me cry too. I—" she chokes, blinking dark green eyes. "Truly, your kindness means everything to me, especially because my own mother and father are—" A tear falls onto her tattooed cheek.

I wipe it away with the tip of my thumb. "I know, dear."

She grabs my hand. "Thank you."

I lift my hand, showing her the stone. "This is for you. Jarret will get one too. They are for communication. You can write a message on it and the other stone will receive it. It can only send the message to that particular stone because of the way they are enchanted. You and Jarret will never be more than a stone's inscription away." I smile, handing her the gift. She hugs it to herself before setting it on a little overturned box.

Jet steps forward. "And we have this for you," he says, his stone for Jarret deposited elsewhere as he unravels a silver veil that's accented with dark forest green thread, matching her eyes.

She studies it, breath hitching with emotion. "Oh, it's gorgeous."

"I'm glad you think so," I take the end Jet gives me and help him drape it over her headpiece. Her eyes meet mine through the thin fabric.

"We're going to get Jarret ready, and when the priest calls you out, go and meet him," Jet says.

She nods, before wrapping us in a hug.

Soon, we stand outside Jarret's tent.

"Jarret," Jet calls, before our son appears in the tent's doorway. His dark green garments are tied in a skewed manner, bunching oddly around his waist.

His helpless brown eyes meet mine. "I don't know why this is so hard. I thought I could get it by myself but—"

We shuffle into the tent, and I immediately busy myself with fixing the clothes. Jet grabs the outer silver jacket hanging over a taunt tent line, helping Jarret into the sleeves.

I'm misty eyed again, once we've stepped back to look at his completed outfit—well, not quite complete. I reach into the satchel at my side, pulling the dark green and silver trimmed veil out. Instead of giving them matching veils, Jet and I decided to have them made opposite of one another, only to be completed when they came together in the pool, or hot spring. I hand one end to Jet, and we drape the cloth over our son's dark hair.

Tears spill down my cheeks as Jet pulls me into his side.

"Mother, don't cry." Jarret smirks.

I wave a hand in my face. "You just don't understand. Sometimes a mother just has to cry, especially when her son is about to make one of the biggest commitments of his life. I'm so happy I get to witness this."

He hugs me. "I'm glad you're here too."

It all seems so wrong though. It feels like only yesterday since we reconnected and came to terms with the past. We've been trying to make up for all the lost time since, but no matter how hard we try, it will never come back.

"I love you."

"I love you too, Mother." He pulls Jet in. "You too, Father."

Renell

I stare at him through the shimmer of my veil. Thesa's kindness overwhelmed my heart, and I almost cried more when I saw Jarret in his opposite matching veil. It's perfect. Even though everything hasn't gone according to what I had planned, this moment is perfect for us. Our two sides coming together as one. The darkness we carried, and the light we tried to shine through each other . . . all culminating in this moment. From here on out, we'll share each other's darkness, each other's light. I hope it won't consume us, but rather, help us grow and build each other up through difficult times so we can cherish the simple moments. It's a vow I make now for him, that no matter how deep our darkness, the light will always be found. No matter what, we will make that light thrive, even if it hurts.

His brown eyes meet mine, shimmering in the firelight behind our beautiful veils. We're standing in the middle of the waist-deep hot spring now, warm mud seeping into my toes. I wiggle them, loving the softness against my feet.

Jarret moves forward as the priest recites the ceremony. He takes me into his arms. He's not supposed to speak, but I hear the words anyway.

Are you ready for this?

Yes . . . I answer back. Because after all this time, after watching Jarret deny our feelings for the sake of the kingdom, after I pushed him away again, and after watching the darkness inside us feed our monsters, I am finally ready to be his wife. I won't hide behind the fear of what could happen, but rather, relish in the time I have with him—however long or short that may be.

"Jarret D'Arvent Organsi–Ganai, take your wife to be, Princess Renell Oslehan, and submerge her beneath the water, as a symbol of two hearts becoming one," the priest, who stands on the bank of the hot pool, says.

Jarret dips me in the warm water, and as I emerge into the frosty air, by Castian law, I am now his wife. Even though I grew up in Lanckest, I always loved Castain weddings. The symbolism of the water making us one always moved my heart. A tether that can never be broken, just like Thesa said with the stones—irreversible, unbreakable. I switch places with Jarret, so I am the one holding him above the warm water. As the priest utters the words that will forever make Jarret my husband, I can't help the nervous flutter that settles in my stomach.

Forever mine. His love, his pain. His light, his darkness—forever mine to carry as well, or as the tradition goes, not carry but share. I pray it will always be that way. He shares the hurt, the pain, the fear, the hope, the love.

He shakes the water off his dark hair, his veil lost to the bottom of the pool, flicking droplets over my skin.

I swat his arm, before he draws me in for a kiss.

He smiles as he pulls away. "Ready for the next phase?"

"I don't think you know what you're getting into here. A *Reiis* isn't exactly painless." I smirk.

"I'll endure it for you."

"Wooing me even though we're married? I like it."

"What husband would I be if I didn't woo my wife?" He leans in for another kiss.

"Hmm, I like you better as a married man."

"You better, because you're mine forever." He kisses me before a throat clears outside the pool. Jarret pulls away, the glare he had perfected for Wen etched into his face.

"Hurry up, lovebirds. It's getting cold out here." Wen reaches a hand to help Jarret out.

"You really have a way of killing a mood, you know that?" Jarret asks, before pulling him into the hot spring.

Wen gasps, hitting the water with a yelp. His tattoos light up as the water buries him, illuminating the pool in its eerie light.

Jarret helps me up. "Let's get out of here before he turns into some angry sea monster."

I swat him again. "Be nice. It's our wedding day."

"He started it."

Thesa and Jet wait with blankets and boots for both of us as we step onto the snow-covered ground.

"I'm so proud of you," Thesa whispers, wrapping me tightly into a hug. I'm not very cold, but her presence warms me more than she'll ever know, especially since I don't have my parents here.

Wen resurfaces with our veils in his hands. "Thought you might want these for the *Reiis*," he says, handing us the veils. He flicks water on Jarret as he passes, just for extra measure, and I don't hear the words they exchange as Thesa leads me back to the tent to help me change into my white gown. The white lace and gossamer skirt flares out into a long train. The tight bodice hugs my chest and little pieces of the lace reach up to my neck, giving off the illusion of stars. I don't know if it really looks like the night sky, but my father once explained that lace on Lan wedding gowns symbolizes the stars. So the bride is the starry night, and the groom is the moon, forever suspended in her sky.

Before I know it, Jarret and I are standing in front of each other again. His suit doesn't have any lace, but it's shaded with light gray and white in an effort to make him look like the moon. Short sleeves reveal his bare arms to accommodate what we are about to do. We're standing in one of the other big tents Jet and Thesa set up for this particular part of the ceremony. A little fire in the center dances to light up the room. They stand off to the side with Wen, as the priest appears in the tent again. In his hands, he carries two bowls and sets them on little tables before Jarret and me. A porcelain knife and several little bobbles fill the bowls.

Jarret inspects the new additions to the room, before glancing at me. Here is the part he isn't familiar with, so I will have to start.

"Take the knife, and with it create the *Reiis*. You have an equal amount of pieces, you may use all of them, or just a few, but make sure the incision fits all the pieces before the clay is set to hold it in place. Speak your vows out loud as you do so," the priest says, gesturing for us to start.

I take the knife before reaching for Jarret's right arm. At the top of his wrist, I cut a thin incision about three inches long. He gasps as blood drips onto the dirt at our feet. With my other hand, I grab some pieces. They are little things that Jarret and I have contributed—a dark blue scale he shed, a piece of gold from a bracelet I used to wear, a piece of both of our veils, a few precious stones in various shades of black, white, and silver. Each piece gets inserted into the skin, making the incision wider and wider.

"With these pieces, I claim you as my own. They will forever show that you and I are one in representation of our love. No one else will have these colors or items put together—they will always represent us, and our shared darkness, or shared light. It's a reminder that no matter how much happens, you will always be mine.

"I love you, Jarret. Even though you have three last names and your temper gets the best of you, you are loyal to a fault, and I will always cherish that side of you. You want a lot of kids, and I hope one day, we can fulfill that dream. I'm forever grateful that you will be the one to stand by my side in times of highs and lows. For you are my first love, my best friend, and the one who holds me together. I vow to be the same for you—your first love, best friend, and the one who holds you together. I promise to lift you up through the darkest nights and dance in the sweetest days. Forever, I will love you," I say, finishing up his *Reiis*.

Jarret's face is pale by the time I slip the last piece into his skin. The priest comes forward, smoothing black clay into the wound to hold the pieces in place. Under normal circumstances, this would heal on its own, but after the priest is done with Jarret, Wen moves forward, healing the wound and solidifying the *Reiis* in stone—literally. Jarret seems to breathe easier once the process is over. He studies the incision on his arm before starting on mine. The blood feels too warm as it flows over my skin and the foreign feeling of things being stuck into my wound sends shudders down my spine.

"Renell, you don't know this, but the first time I saw you racing through the woods in your cursed form, I fell in love with you. I didn't know it until a few days later, but then rationality took over, and I realized I could never have you. It broke my heart until you chose me too. Then things changed again. I thought I would have to let you go and hate you forever so I could forget you, but then you came back. You have no idea how much it meant to me when you let me come with you.

"My purpose from now on will be to stand by your side, lift you up when you fall, carry you when you can't move further, and love you at your lowest. I will protect you through the darkest nights and hold you on your loneliest days. Because you have my heart, and I can't go anywhere without it," he vows.

As he speaks, tears fall down my cheeks. I know his words aren't rehearsed or thought out—they're spoken straight from his heart. He loves me so much, yet I almost lost him forever because of it.

Once Wen has healed mine in place, Jet and Thesa wash our symbols free of excess clay and blood until our Reiis shine like they were polished so brightly you could see your reflection in them. With that, the ceremony is finished. Normally, we would have a feast and dancing afterward, but with our little group, Jet and Thesa lead Jarret and me to the tent they had repurposed for us.

A little feast awaits as we step inside, along with piled furs and blankets for our wedding bed. I blush a little at the thought. Tonight will be my first night with him, and I can't help but feel a little nervous. Suddenly, the food doesn't seem so appetizing. I rub fingers over my bumpy *Reiis* before Jarret takes my hand and pulls me into his arms.

"There's nothing to be worried about. Now, we're just officially married. If it scares you, it doesn't have to change yet. I'll just hold you until you tell me to let go." I can hear the smile in his voice.

"I don't ever want you to let go," I whisper, breathing in his scent. It's clear and fresh like the cold night sky.

"Good," he whispers, before lifting my chin for a kiss.

Esther

I stand in the courtyard of the castle, staring at my family as they descend the grand staircase to bid me goodbye. Soldiers and servants mill across the paved stone, going about their business as they head from the castle to the stables, to the warehouses, to the training grounds. I breathe in the salty air, filling my lungs with its nostalgic scent and trying my hardest to remember the way it tastes. I know Ren'R borders the sea, but I have a feeling that it will smell different.

A'zre stands beside me with his guards surrounding us, his red gaze following every glare cast his way. They know who he is, and none of them have tried to hide their disdain. He doesn't seem to care as he holds his head high so they never forget his face. I would do the same in his position. I'd want them to remember the face of the man who almost took everything from them. The man who could still do so if he wished.

The thought strikes me, nearly knocking the breath from my lungs. He can still take Casta if he wants. Even if it's in a few years, he can still decide to break the alliance. He doesn't strike me as a man who breaks his commitments very easily, but he's fueled by greed. I see it in his red eyes. I see it in the way he holds himself. He wants it all, even though it will never be enough.

I swallow the lump in my throat, hoping he won't decide to break the alliance and try to take Casta again. I don't want everything my family—I—have been through to be in vain. We've sacrificed too much to fight against this greedy man, and now I'm married to him.

My family reaches the bottom of the stairs, and Mother immediately pulls me into a hug, tears already shining in her eyes.

"Please be safe. Write whenever you can, and—" She chokes, squeezing me until I can't breathe.

"I will." I hold her just as tight I don't want to say goodbye. I don't want to go.

"I love you so much, and . . . and no matter what, i—it's too late to say this, but your life is more important than Casta. We've already lost too much in trying to keep this country safe, and I can't keep watching my family die for this. I feel so heartbroken that I forced you all into this. If I could do it all agai—"

"It's my choice, Mother." I pull away, holding her shaking hands, they're colder than I remember, and the fearful images that flash through my head help me understand. "What's done is done. I love Casta more than anything. I would never give it up over my life. Besides, what else do I have? I have my family and Casta, so I will serve them both this way, even if it kills me."

She nods, blinking away tears in her purple eyes. "I pray it never comes to that."

"Me too," I whisper, but I honestly don't care. If I die serving my country, then it will be a worthy death. Otherwise, I would have stayed here and sank into madness before inevitably ending my life. At least, I have something to live for right now.

Dais replaces Mother. He hugs me and the weight of all his decisions suffocates me. I see all the grim futures he envisions—everything he doesn't want to come true. Everything that can be prevented if we play our cards right. "Be careful. Learn what you can, and when you have enough . . ." He trails off. "I'll miss you."

"I'll miss you too, stay strong, and I'll be watchful. I don't want to be put into any position that could compromise our alliance."

He pulls away, glancing at A'zre with a hesitant eye before continuing, "That may happen whether we want it or not."

"You don't think he'll keep it either?"

His mouth forms a grim line. "No, he's too impatient for that. Just be careful, and when he slips up—which he will—then we'll make a move."

I notice that he says the words *'we'll'* when we both know that any move *'we'* make will inevitably be up to me. If A'zre slips up, I won't have time to contact Dais and wait for a reply, I'll have to take the opportunity into my own hands and pray that I'm right.

"I'll do my best, for you and for Casta."

"I love you, Esther."

"I love you too."

He moves on so David can say goodbye. My twin looks me in the eye, his swirling eyes of dark amethyst study mine. His light brown hair falls over his eyes, and for a moment, I wonder when he got to be so tall—just like Dais.

He breathes in shakily before pulling me into a hug. "I hate that you're going away. After all that we've been through, I thought this would never happen again. I . . . I don't want to say goodbye."

Tears smart in my eyes, but I blink them away, not just because of his words, but because of the scenes that flash in my head as my gift reaches into his memories. I don't know how he can stand to live with them. They're horrible delusions of fears that he's forced to know. His gift is so much like my own, but broken in a way that he can only perceive people's fears—never truth.

"I don't want to say goodbye either. I don't want to go, but I have a duty to fulfill. I've made a promise to Dais and to my new husband. I must go."

"I know. I love you, Esther. If he lets you, please come visit . . . and don't forget to write." He steps back with a sad smile.

"I will come visit and I promise I'll write. I have a feeling I'll be quite homesick. I love you too." I pull him in for another hug even though I know I'll see his memories. I don't care, I'll live with them for a small second if it means I get to hold him one more time before I go. I step back, clearing the tears from my eyes as I smile at my family.

"Goodbye," I tell them before turning on my heels and stepping toward the carriage. It's decorated with pale pink sides and red and white trim. It looks like a wedding cake, and I can't help but wonder if it was intentional.

With the help of a footman, A'zre steps in first, and then I follow, sitting across from him. The door closes, and I take a deep breath now that I'm away from my family. I hear their shouts of goodbye, but I make no motion to look out the window and return their farewells. If I do, I'll just start crying, and I don't want to look like a sobbing mess in front of A'zre.

The carriage starts moving, jostling us forward.

"Will you miss it here?" he asks, glancing out the window.

"Would you miss your homeland?"

"That's not an answer."

"Just answer the question." I meet his gaze, and he doesn't look away.

"Yes, I miss it already."

"Well, there you go, now you know my answer." I shift in my seat, wishing that the bench was more comfortable. I pick at the light pink appliques that decorate the red cushion. It's ugly, and I shudder at the thought that this will be my prison cell for the next month.

"I want to set one thing straight before we get to Sun'Ar." His words draw my gaze back to him, and the look in his eyes fills my heart with fear. "You will be my wife. You will come when I call on you. You will not speak unless spoken too. I cannot have you speaking freely in my presence, especially among my other wives. You will be treated just like them, even though you are a princess of another nation. You agreed to this marriage, so you will do as I say, since I'm your husband, and"—he leans in—"if you try anything, everyone will know it was you. The alliance will be broken, and they will come for you and your family. I don't play around with what's mine. I don't waste it. Everything I do is for my kingdom, so that is all we are, a means to an end. Do you understand?"

A fire rages in my chest, growing steadily with his words. He's basically saying he'll break the alliance if he can get Casta. Maybe he'll slip before we even get to Sun'Ar . . . No, I can't do anything to him here. They'll definitely figure out that I did it and have me hung. I don't mind portraying a dutiful wife. Of course, I'll have a hard time holding my tongue, but maybe that will be an advantage. He won't notice me if I don't speak.

Right now is not one of those times. "Everything you do is for yourself. It's your curse to be controlled by your greed. I understand you perfectly, and I will comply once we get to Sun'Ar. But as I am not your wife yet—your words, not mine—I am still a Castian princess. I will speak when I want to, however I want to. Due to your cultural standards, you don't own me yet, and my culture says I can speak my mind. So enjoy hearing all my thoughts until we arrive in Sun'Ar. Deal?"

"This isn't a negotiation. You're my—"

"What? Your wife? You already made it perfectly clear that I'm not. If I'm not, then I don't have to do as you say, but once we are—as I'm sure you'll have the ceremony as soon as possible—I will do all you say." I look out the window, watching the Castian countryside. I can practically feel the steam coming out of his ears. This next month is going to be so much fun.

"You will not look away from me when we're speaking!" he screams, pounding his fist against his knee like a pouting child.

"Oh, so I do have permission to speak? I'm sorry. I thought I had to wait." I roll my eyes. I know I'm poking the bear, but he can't hurt me without breaking the alliance we just created. I can't wait to see how long he'll hold out. I look back at him, and his glare is sharp enough to slice me in two.

He sighs then, leaning back as he closes his eyes. He's silent for a moment before he looks back at me. "You're right. You're not my wife yet, and I can't deny the freedoms you exhibit in your own country. So . . . deal."

I raise my eyebrows, upset that he could calm himself so easily. He's going to be harder to crack than I thought. I guess I'll just have to keep provoking him. "Now we're getting somewhere."

Chapter 12

Onward

1 Month Later

Wen

"Will you two just listen to me? The only way you're going to get a challenge from the High Chief is if you prove you're worthy of one. You can't just march in there and demand a challenge, they'll kill you on the spot. You have to prove that you're a threat, then it's all fair game from there," I say, running a hand down my face.

A cool spring breeze blows through our little camp, and in the dim evening light, a chill races across my skin. I look back at Renell and Jarret. They have to understand that taking over Cay-Llek isn't going to be a leisurely stroll; it'll be a gruesome fight to the death.

We just made it across the border into Cay-Llek. Traveling has gone a bit slow as the lovebirds decided to celebrate some of their honeymoon along the way. I try not to gag at the thought as I survey the gruesome landscape. Cay-Llek is brown on top of brown with more brown on the side. It's all rocky terrain and dry grass. Not even the white snow decided to fall here, just misty rain every afternoon and foggy mornings.

Renell rolls her eyes. "I know how it works. I just need to know how we make it happen."

I sigh, knowing she's not going to like this. "You start taking over villages. You show the High Chief that you are ruthless. Diplomacy doesn't work here, so you have to use force. You have to scare them into following you."

Renell stands up. "That's ridiculous. What's the point of gaining an army if they can just turn right around and take it from you? Doesn't admiration go much farther than fear?"

"Not to these people. You have to keep that in mind. Cay-Llekians aren't like Lan. They respect someone who can strike fear into others' hearts," I counter.

Our little fire in front of us smolders as Jarret throws another Kön chip on it. Yuck.

"So I'll have to fight chieftains?" she asks.

Jarret sighs from where he sits, holding his tongue, I'm sure. He's made it clear how much he hates this idea, and that was only when he thought she was going to be fighting one chieftain.

"Several."

"How many?" Jarret interrupts.

I glance at him. "At least ten. When the High Chief sees the trouble you're causing, he will call all of the chieftains together in Cizarrél. At that point, you can challenge him. He will, however, try to split a deal with you, and allow you to become the ruling chieftain over your conquered villages. That's how it's been done in the past, but I can't vouch for this new leader."

"What do you mean?" Jarret asks. "Why would she do this if there is no guarantee?"

"Jarret," Renell starts. "There is never a guarantee that this is going to work, but—"

"You have to try, I know. I just want to understand." He looks at me again, his dark eyes reflecting the orange, pink, and yellow rays from the setting sun behind me—the only vestige of beauty in this miserable land.

"Well, then it's a good thing I took the liberty of finding out all the important stuff while you two were enjoying your honeymoon." I gag for extra effect.

Jarret groans. "We weren't just enjoying our honeymoon. We did some training in the middle." He nudges Renell, shooting her a wink.

She giggles, her green eyes shining as she looks at him. Disgusting. I don't even want to know what kind of 'training' they're talking about.

"Anyway. Cay-Llek gained a new High Chief after the previous one was killed in battle against Casta. He's had many challenges since he successfully led the remaining troops home after retreating from the naval battles. From what I've heard, he's ruthless, and with Cay-Llek having no rules or laws, he can easily change any tradition. We have to be careful. Most Cay-Llek challenges for High Chief will use rules agreed upon by the participating parties before the fight begins. Though, anything can be changed at the last minute—especially if it comes from the High Chief himself."

"His word is law?" Renell asks.

I nod. "While Renell is gaining allies; Jarret, you and I must learn everything we can about this new chief. If we know all the ins and outs of his mind—the way he fights, the way he thinks—that will inevitably help Renell in her fight against him. In a similar situation, we must protect Renell's actions at all costs and help her change them. Because if anyone watches close enough, they will understand how she fights and in turn, tell the chief for whatever compensation they can garner." I lean back, watching the expressions shift across their faces. Doubt, fear, worry, hope, strength.

Jarret stands up. "I will do what you suggest. I don't want to leave Renell to fight alone, but"—he glances at her—"she's not going to give me much choice."

She meets his gaze, her eyes filling with determination. "Of course I'm not." She cracks a smile. "Well, I guess we get to conquering tomorrow. I want to make sure we don't cause too many casualties. If I have to—"

Jarret takes her arm, gently caressing it. "I'll be there. I promise."

I look away from them with a cough. "*Sev*, you two."

Jarret glares at me before Renell draws a big kiss from him.

I gag as I stand. "I'm going to get dinner started, but let's be careful, we don't need any more scouts to find us."

"You got it, *Jerè*," Renell says.

"How come he's the overseer?" Jarret pouts.

I roll my eyes as I start to walk away.

"Because you're my mighty protector . . ."

I think I'm going to throw up.

A'zre

A jolt from the carriage wakes me from my stupor. I look around the space, blinking to remove the sleep from my eyes. It's twilight outside, which means we'll be stopping soon. But the sound of the wheels moving underneath has changed, we're not traveling on the hardened roads anymore. Pavement means we're getting close to Ren'R.

I look beside me to find Esther dozing away, the back of her head leaning against the baseboard. Her mouth half-open in a gentle snore. I smile, before I carefully lean her head against my shoulder. I hate that she seems uncomfortable. Plus, if we're close to Ren'R, we won't be stopping till we make it to the palace. She sighs against me, and for a moment, I think she's awake, but I know if she was, she would have pushed me away.

It's been interesting getting to know the princess these last few weeks. I know she's been trying to weasel her way past my defenses since we met. I feel her gift trying to access my memories. Sometimes I think it's intentional, other times, I think she doesn't realize she's doing it. She has no control over her gift, which is quite a pity. She would be extremely powerful if she knew how to use it properly. Her lack of knowledge is useful for me because she'll never gain access to my darkest thoughts or memories. If she was any stronger, I wouldn't be able to keep her out of my mind with my simple tricks . . . and I still might not.

She's wearing on me. Her gift is involuntary and draws no energy from her veins, while my defense takes significant mental focus. I've almost slipped a few times during our trip, growing weary in the comfort of her presence, and I hate admitting that she has become a comfort. I hate becoming attached to someone so easily. Maybe I would have withstood my father better if I didn't care so much. No, I refuse to believe I care at all, because I don't. I won't. Maybe she's counting on my mishaps, but not for much longer.

When we get to Ren'R, it will be easy to avoid her since we won't be stuck in a four-foot proximity. *But you know you'll miss her . . .* I sigh, looking down at her relaxed face. No, I won't miss her. *Denial.* I want to tell my thoughts to be silent, but unlike impeding Esther's gift, I can't stop my thoughts—just like I can't make my feelings go away. I'll deny them all I want. I'll force myself not to care. I'll do everything to become the heartless ruler my father wanted me to be. I'll do it because I don't want him to come for me. I'll never let him come for me. I'll never let him destroy what I built. *What if he already is?* I gently push a strand of Esther's blonde hair from her face.

Then I played right into his hands. Then I became what he wanted, but isn't that the same thing I want? If that's the truth, then I will deny my feelings until I feel nothing at all. It hasn't worked yet, so maybe I'm already failing him. *But you haven't acted on your feelings...* No, not yet, but more than likely my desire will get the better of me one day. I'll fight it to the very end because power is more important than any other desire I might have. I just have to keep believing that.

Lights flicker outside the wagon, drawing random colors across the inside of the carriage. My heart lifts with the little rainbows refracting along the walls. We're here.

I nudge Esther. "Esther, wake up."

She startles, pushing against me as she cowers toward the edge of the carriage. *Interesting.* I didn't think I scared her that much. It must have been a nightmare. She sighs when she notices me. "Sorry, nightmare."

"You get those a lot, I've noticed," I say in Sun'Arian. Her knowledge of my language wasn't as extensive as her brother's so we'd been practicing since we left Casta, and now, I'm almost certain she can speak better than any native. I glance out the window, coming face to face with the outskirts of Ren'R. The poorer of my people live in these smaller homes, but they aren't impoverished by any means.

"As do you," she mutters in Sun'Arian after a yawn. I want to be surprised by her comment, but it's inevitable that she would have seen me sleep once in a while on this trip. But did she touch me during it? Was she able to see any of my memories? Most likely not, she has a hard time hiding her emotions, and if she had seen inside my head, her pity would've been very hard to hide—or perhaps, she wasn't surprised by it at all. I have a feeling her memories aren't delightful either, and if that's true, she has more leverage over me than I do her.

"I bet I don't look as pretty when I'm asleep."

She glares. "I can assure you you do." She glances around. "If I'm so fascinating to watch while I'm asleep, why did you wake me up?"

"We're here," I say. She immediately looks out the window, her eyes growing wide and I know she sees the castle in the distance. I smile at her wonder.

"I'll admit," she starts after a moment. "Ren'R is beautiful."

"I could have told you that," I mutter, ignoring the glare she sends my way.

"Do the different colors of stained-glass lamps mean something?"

"Somewhat, the more intricate ones mean you are more prosperous. The larger lamps mean that too, but if it's a large lamp with one whole color—that family is more middle-class, and so on. The more lamps you have, the more respect. Light, especially in darkness, means a lot in our culture. The winter months are darker than the rest of the year, so if you have plenty of light shining around your house, it means you will have good luck in the new year. If a lamp breaks, either through overuse or just a mistake, it means you're cursed for the new year."

"Or if someone just broke them . . ."

I smirk at her comment. "That can happen, yes, but Sun'Arians are very respectful of each other's things. If one person started destroying someone else's things, then their actions would be reaped tenfold. They would indefinitely lose more than the person they took from. It's self-cursing, and we believe wholeheartedly in it. It's the same if they gifted someone a new thing, it would be more of a self-blessing. They would eventually gain more than they gave."

"Who pays the favors?" she asks, her eyes glimmer like luminescent fireflies dancing along the wind as they reflect the lights from the city. *Belemè*. I look away from her, refusing to believe I find her beautiful. I have many beautiful wives; she is no different.

"In my culture, it's the gods. We believe that we are the chosen people, blessed by the gods if we pay our blessings forward. Ultimately, we are cursed by the gods if we do something evil."

She narrows her eyes, looking at me like I'm an enigma, and I know what her question will be even before she asks it. "Interesting, then why did you think you could take all of Partin?"

I smile. "Partin doesn't belong to your people or Lanckest or anyone else . . . my people, based on history, were given Partin. Then war brought on by greed caused its current division. I'm only taking it to give it back to my people."

"An odd way of looking at it, or maybe you're just lying to yourself. What if the gods don't want you to take Partin?"

The carriage jostles at her words, which is odd, because our roads shouldn't have any holes. Then again, I was gone for two months.

I scoff. "I see what you're trying to say, but the gods haven't exactly blessed Sun'Ar. We are a dying country. Our crops haven't been performing well. Our small forests have burned over the last few years, leaving us with little. Our mines are drying up. Our resources aren't what they should be for a country the size of Sun'Ar. I have to protect my people, and before you say we didn't steward it well, I assure you that Sun'Arian's take very careful measure of all that we use. The same will be expected of you."

"I have no doubts. I'm sure all your ways will be taught in due time." She looks back out the window.

I sigh. "I don't expect you to understand when you weren't born in this country. Our pride has taken care of us for this long, and every Sun'Arian believes that our diligence is the reason for our prosperity."

"No, I don't think I'll ever understand pride, but I understand someone who loves their country—and you obviously do."

I study her. At least I look like someone who cares for my country. I'm not sure I entirely believe her, but who's to say?

Peggy

"It's useless," David says, slumping back against his chair, his light brown hair sticking upside down as he groans. Rows of books in an array of colorful spines line the walls to our right. Servants move around the royal library putting titles away and dusting shelves to keep everything immaculate. The nook we'd chosen boasts of orange and yellow cushions with a circle window to our left, and gorgeous hanging baskets full of sunflowers and marigolds.

We've come here every day for the past two weeks trying to find answers regarding his gift, but so far, we've come up with nothing about a gift of fear or freezing for that matter. Plenty of scripts have been written about fire, lucky me, but none about his. I'd even found some interesting passages about witch curses and shapeshifters that I saved to tell my brother, Frobin, about later.

I set my elbow on our table, leaning my chin on my fist as I stare at my husband. "You're adorable. You know that."

He opens a purple eye, glancing at me sideways. "You're supposed to say something about it not being useless, or we'll find it eventually, or—what are you doing?"

I stand up and skirt around the table between us, my stiff right leg dragging a bit. I flop down on his lap. He grunts, and I kiss him before he can protest. My fingers run through his disheveled dirty blond hair, trailing down his jawline. He sighs, his hands crawling up my spine, drawing me closer.

"Let's get out of here. I'm tired of this," I whisper as his lips trail down my chin.

He groans, pulling away. "But we haven't solved anything." His fingers run small circles on my hips.

"You're the one who said it's useless."

"You're not helping. I only said that so you'd tell me to keep looking."

"What can I say? I'm a bad influence." I stare at his lips and don't miss the blush that flushes his cheeks.

He shifts me off him gently. "We need to focus." He leans over the thousand page volume of curses and cures he'd been studying for the last few days.

"You're no fun." I sit back in my chair with a sigh and try to concentrate on the scroll of ballads I'd chosen. Many of them had themes of fear, but none talked about someone who could see fears let alone kill people with them.

"Peg." I look at him, but he doesn't take his eyes off the page. "Do you ever think about going back?"

My heart sinks. "What do you mean?" He can't possibly be talking about going back to where we were held captive . . . right?

He finally meets my gaze, a war I'd seen on far too many occasions in his eyes. Fear and hope clashing with uncertainty and ideas—an endless cycle he can't escape from. "I'm starting to wonder if we should go back. Find the answers there. Why were we chosen? Were there other camps? Were they studying us? If they were studying us, they might have answers."

He's thought about this for a while now. My stomach clenches, and the hairs on my arms stand up. "What? No. I never want to go back there. I was imprisoned there for years, David. Longer than you. I was a child. I—" I was four years old when they took me. For fifteen years, they kept me a prisoner in that awful place. I still hear the screams and cries of my fellow cell mates. I still hear the guttural speech of the nymphs who held us captive. The fear, the pain, wondering if we'd see another day. David was only there for two years.

"I know. I just . . . I think I have to go back. What if I never find the answers? What if they've never been written? I should go there and see." He points toward the window like that would prove his point.

"What if you don't find the answers there?"

"Then I come back and keep searching. I just think that if there were answers here, we would have found something already, right?"

"David." I sigh. Why can't I make him see? Why should we go back to the hell that took so long to escape from? Has he forgotten that? It took us weeks to find an opening to leave. What if we get caught again? I can't go back. "Fine, but what if we can't find the nymphs or the place where we were held? You were barely conscious when we escaped. We should just stay here and search."

"I didn't say you had to come with me." He looks away, glaring at the marigolds lining the window.

The words feel like a knife in my heart. He doesn't want me to come? I glare at him. "Fine, you can find out all the answers on your own then." I stand. "If you get caught, don't expect me to come save you." My throat clenches and I hate that my voice cracks on the last word as I step out of our nook, heading down a winding staircase that leads to the ground floor of the library.

"Peggy! Wait! That's not what I meant. I just meant that if you don't want to go, you don't have to. I don't want to make you feel like you have to go back there just because I want to go. I know what that place means to you."

I whirl around. "Then why suggest it at all? You and I both know you can't go without me. What if you have an episode? Who might you harm if that happens? What if you get captured? What if we both get captured? I can't go through it again."

He steps down, placing his hands on my shoulders. "I'm sorry. I just . . . I have to go. I believe there is a reason, and yes, I want you to come with me because I can't control this yet. I just wanted you to have a choice. You never get to choose anything because you always have to be with me, and I . . . you're right. I can't go without you, but I will try if you don't want to go."

"Either way you'll go, so it doesn't matter what I want." I shrug his hands off me, glaring at the faded volumes of books surrounding us.

"Peggy—"

"I'll go with you." I turn my eyes on him. "Only because I don't want you harming innocents if you lose control. If you think this is the only way to learn, then you have to go. That doesn't mean I have to like it. But we have to put a plan together and train a bit more and . . ."

"We will. I'm not saying let's leave tomorrow. We've come a long way, but I agree, we have to be careful."

Since we arrived in Morough last year, we'd been training with the regiments any chance we could, but we're not skilled enough to take on the nymphs if we find them.

I try to hide the quiver in my voice. "We'll go then. For your sake,

I hope we find the answer, but I also hope there is nothing to find."

Esther

A'zre was right. Sun'Ar is beautiful, and not in the way I was expecting. I'd heard the tradition regarding their lamps, but I had never seen so much color surrounding a city. Every lamp is adorned with numerous shades clashing like vibrant rainbows, and my heart swells in the face of the beauty.

A'zre stares at me from across the carriage. He hasn't stopped studying me since we arrived, and I often wonder what goes through his mind. It's odd that I can't read his memories, because there is no way we were meant for each other like Connan and I were—at least that's my only reasoning for why I couldn't see Connan's memories. I have no idea how foresight works, nor do I have any desire to learn. I've hated my gift since it manifested. It's caused me nothing but pain. The beautiful colors outside the window are lost on me for a moment as horrible memories grip my throat—memories where I'd forced myself into alarming situations with my father's advisers so I could get close enough to understand their motives.

I still feel their groping hands, their hot breath on my skin. I still hear the echo of their sinister laughs. The blood drains from my face as goosebumps line my skin. I try to keep myself from shaking, wishing I could purge the feelings suffocating me. My fingers grip the cushion below me, but it does little to bring me back to the present. They're still there. They're still *touching* me.

"I think you'll like the palace. It's different from Casta's, of course, but no less extravagant."

I meet A'zre's gaze, his red eyes filled with soft understanding. Is he trying to distract me? I hate that it's working. I hate that he saw a vulnerable side I'm usually so good at hiding. Granted, I've seen some of his own dark past, but not because of my gift, because my soul recognizes that kind of suffering. I hate that I'm grateful for his comment. I hate everything about this, and I haven't missed an opportunity over the last month to remind him.

This time, I have no retort to offer as I nod. His eyes shimmer, and it's like an unspoken agreement—a treaty only we share. Special to our suffering. I hate that we now have something connecting us so intimately. I look out the window, refusing to acknowledge the kindness in his gaze. I shouldn't find anything about him safe or comforting. Because of his war, I can't find comfort in Connan's arms anymore. Because of his war, I'm forced to become a slave in a country I will never call home.

We're heading into the castle courtyard. My heart spikes as I look at it. It's extravagant all right. Some of the largest lamps I'd seen since we entered the city illuminate the sandstone courtyard in red, yellow, and white. Beautiful fountains and pools surrounded by exotic plants and palm trees decorate the inner area of the courtyard. Large vaulted open balconies lined with turquoise blue, red, yellow, and white tiles decorate the sandstone walls. Huge turquoise and silver domes surrounded by smaller spires reach into the midnight skies.

The carriage stops in front of large red-wood doors where guards line the path toward us. Our footman, Hi'z, opens the carriage door and helps us out.

A'zre offers me his arm as we start toward the castle. The tiles above the main doors are arranged in a pattern to look like the sun, and underneath it, the words *'Cola Sorenta de Nu'* are inscribed.

"What do you think?" he asks.

"It's beautiful, like you said."

He seems pleased by my answer because he smirks. "Good."

The cedar doors open before us without a sound. In a grand foyer decorated with garnet and gold floors, a single older woman stands, which surprises me. A'zre seems like someone who'd have a whole entourage ready to receive him. Long gray hair coils around her head in a braid, her dark red and bright orange shawl drapes gracefully over her shoulder, extending to the floor where I'm surprised to see her wearing pants. They match her shawl in perfect correspondence. Her golden eyes warm me like a mother's embrace as she smiles, her crow's feet crinkling.

She bows her head to me. "Welcome to Sun'Ar, Your Highness," she says in Sun'Arian, and her voice, although soft, seems to bring a certain comfort into the large foyer, almost like she's trying to make it feel like home.

I bow my head back. "Thank you . . ." I trail off since I'm not sure of her name or title.

"Lami, *Hidá*. I'm part of King A'zre's closest council."

"You mean my only council." A'zre smiles as he looks her over. "How was everything?"

"Everything went well, Your Majesty. There were a few small town skirmishes over some fishing spots and a length of yarn"—she pauses—"it's best not to get into it. Um . . . it was a rather uneventful two months, but you have plenty of messages to attend in your office. And . . ." She trails off, glancing at me, and I get the feeling that she doesn't want me to hear the next bit of information.

"And?" A'zre furrows a brow.

"Well, it's—"

"Speak, Lami. Esther will probably hear it soon enough."

"And Clis lost the baby. I haven't been able to calm her since," Lami says.

My heart sinks, and all my fears over losing my own son well up like an overflowing bucket. I remember his warmth, his smell, then his absence when I realized he was gone. When I realized they took him from me. A heart broken like that doesn't heal, no matter how much time has passed.

A'zre's expression softens, his face becoming solemn. "When was this?"

"About two weeks ago. She hardly eats, and I fear . . . she thinks you'll be disappointed."

At Lami's words, I realize we're talking about one of A'zre's other wives. Right. Over the last month together, I'd forgotten that he has other wives. I didn't ask about them, and he didn't offer any information, which I can respect.

A'zre shifts, leaning back as he taps his foot against the gold and red stone. "Ah, well, I'll have to see her tonight. Please assure her that I'm not upset."

"I will, Your Majesty." She bows her head to him and then looks at me, setting a wrinkled hand on my shoulder. "Well, *Hidá*. Let's get you settled. I already have a room prepared for you. I hope it's to your liking."

"I'm sure it will be." I look at A'zre. "I guess this is goodbye for a little while."

"Are you saying you're going to miss me?" He smirks.

"Absolutely not," I say and hear Lami inhale, *loudly*. I ignore it, keeping my gaze on A'zre and his annoyingly perfect brows.

"Well, then it's hardly goodbye." His eyes don't leave mine as he asks, "Lami, when is our wedding?"

"P—preparations have been set for the solstice," she answers.

Four days. I'm getting Sun'Arian married to this man in four days, and that means we'll be legally married in his eyes. Part of it makes me sad because I enjoyed our playful banter over the last few weeks, and when I'm his wife, we won't be able to share that camaraderie. I'll only get the serious side of him. *What does it matter, Esther? You're here to learn his weakness. You're here to save Casta.* My stomach rolls at the thought. Of course. I shouldn't be sad or happy or have any emotions regarding this man. He's done too much against my country to deserve my affections. I just have to keep reminding myself.

"Ah, perfect timing then." His gaze devours mine, and oddly enough, I don't feel exposed under his scrutiny. I feel . . . hopeful, for whatever reason. "I'll see you in four days. Lami will tell you all you need to know—where you're allowed to go and what you're allowed to do. Under no circumstances will you be able to leave this castle, unless you're with me. I can't have anyone seeing you on the streets, especially because you're foreign. You'd catch quite a price in international waters."

My blood grows cold at the mention of slavery, but I nod all the same. I don't like my freedom taken away, but it's not like I have much choice. I don't want to be sold into slavery either. I agreed to this marriage, so I must live with it.

"Good. I must attend—"

"No, you'll rest first. Go see Clis and attend to your messages later. I'm sure matters of the country can wait until you've properly rested," Lami admonishes.

A'zre shoots her a hard look, but sighs before nodding. "I can't deny your logic." He looks at me, taking my hand into his and kissing the top of my hand. "Goodnight, Esther." And then he's gone, floating down one of the domed hallways to my right.

"Come, *Hidá*." Lami takes my hand, images of smiling faces, squealing babies, and A'zre's gentle red eyes flash through my mind. After a month traveling with A'zre, the flood of memories overwhelms my mind, and I hesitate a moment before stumbling after her as she pulls me down the hallway. She reminds me a little of my mother and a pang of heartsickness pulls on me. "I can't believe he let you speak to him like that."

"Excuse me?" I rush to keep up with her quick stride. She's not a tall woman by any means, but boy can she hurry.

She slows, looking back at me for a moment. "A'zre has quite a temper, yet you spoke to him so informally. Usually, that results in a beheading or worse."

My jaw drops. I'd never thought of A'zre as petty, but I guess it makes sense. My stomach turns once again. What if he was only tolerating my insolence because of the alliance? Why didn't he say anything? Will he? What will happen after we're married?

"I—I didn't know," I gasp, waiting for her serious expression to fade—it doesn't.

"Well, then it's not your fault, but now that you are here, you should be careful of what you say to him. You will be a king's wife soon, and he doesn't need his other wives to get any ideas." She starts walking down the hall again.

"He mentioned something like that . . ." I trail off, thinking of our first day on the way to Sun'Ar.

"Good, I would take his advice to heart now. There will be no familiarity between you and A'zre, even though you will be his wife."

"I'm already his wife."

She chuckles. "Not by Sun'Arian standards, *Hidá*."

I want to roll my eyes, but I'm almost certain this woman will berate me for it. "I'm not sure I understand all that yet. Married is married. Whether it's in one country or another."

"Yes, but one is blessed and one is not. The gods won't bless a union that is not properly attributed."

I want to tell her I don't believe in the gods. I believe in only One. Of course, I'm not as devout as my mother, but I believe in Him all the same. "I see what you're saying. I'm sorry for the disrespect, all of this is a little overwhelming." We stop at a door, and she opens it, ushering me inside.

"I understand. It's not easy coming to another country and be forced to understand it. In all honesty, I wasn't expecting you to be quite so eager to learn. Already, your Sun'Arian is elegant."

"Thank you," I whisper as I look over my room. A domed honeycomb ceiling with a skylight allows a hint of starlight into the room. Indigo, cerulean, and pale blue tiles decorate the walls in what looks like waves. Lucious plants hang from giant urns placed around the room or drape from the ceiling. Some even sport little white and yellow flowers. A four-poster bed with yellow sheer curtains stands to my right. On the other side of the room, a gentle breeze flows from open doors leading to a terrace. A little reading nook with bookshelves extending to the ceiling lies to the left, and my heart soars at the thought of devouring Sun'Arian literature in my free time.

I gasp. "It's beautiful." I look at Lami. "Thank you."

"Don't thank me, A'zre had it designed for you. He gave me explicit instructions in the messages he sent before he left Casta."

I nod. Despite his supposed aloofness, he seems to be a kind man to his wives by trying to make them feel at home—at least in my experience. He appears to act like he doesn't care, but really, he cares the most. "I'll tell him then."

"Good. I'll leave you to get ready for bed. If you ever need me, the bell by your bed will let me know. I attend to all matters of the castle. If anything is wrong, or you don't know what to do, just call me."

"I will." I shiver at the almost cold breeze that flutters in.

"Good. The servants will be here soon with new clothes for you and some hot nighttime tea. I will be here in the morning to escort you to breakfast."

"Thank you, Lami."

"Of course, *Hidá*. Get some rest."

Chapter 13
Promises

Carrie

ÄLBRECT CASTLE, KÄS

"How did you become compromised? You had him in the palm of your hand!" King Rave shouts, his angular face leaning close to mine, enough so I can feel his warm breath on my skin.

I cringe, swallowing at his closeness. "It means exactly what I said. I was compromised. The traitors Commander Li sent us after were Walks. We didn't know. We were severely underprepared. I fell victim to two of their abilities and passed out. The guards called the nearest medic they could find, and wouldn't you know, it was our dear Lifewalker. What was I supposed to do? I was unconscious!"

He slaps me against my cheek, snapping my head to the side. My vision blurs as stars dance across what used to be gold-gilded white walls. His dark, almost black eyes, appear in my hazy gaze, like a monster crawling from the shadows of my mind. "You don't ever talk back to me. I'm your king, not an insubordinate comrade," he spits, saliva landing on my face.

I hold back a gag, and nod my head, refusing to touch my burning

176

cheek. If he sees a crack in my exterior, he might punish me more just for the fun of it. "Forgive me, Your Majesty."

"Good." He leans back, sliding his silk green robe strings around his fingers before twirling them in the space between us like a baton. He turns toward me, nearly whacking me in the face with the silk ribbons. "Well, you'll just have to continue your mission in stealth. I hoped you would snare him as . . ." he trails off as a light glints in his dark eyes. A sinister, mischievous smile settles against his lips. "Never mind. I have a new plan."

My face blanches as an unsettling feeling lands in my stomach. He watches me squirm for a moment, satisfaction glistening in his gaze. He makes me sick. I hate that he was cunning enough to become king. I hate that I have to serve him. I hate that he holds my life in his hands.

"I'm cutting you off."

My jaw drops slightly. "What?"

"You resent me so much, I've decided to cut you off. Without my power keeping your disease at bay, you will die. Unless . . . you run to the only person who can keep you alive."

No.

I start to shake my head. "What if Aiden can't sustain me? What then? You'll just let me die?"

"You're dispensable, Carrie. You should know that by now. I can find a million more like you. Even if they don't have a debilitating disease, holding someone's life in my hands is usually enough incentive to get anyone to do my bidding."

My heart starts to pound, and I can feel the blood rushing to my ears, making my face hot. "You're sick," I gasp, as tears start to appear. I look away from his dark, frozen eyes, but it's too late to hide my weakness. I don't want to die.

"Actually, that would be you, my dear. I know you will do anything to get him to help you, because I know you don't want to die."

No. No. Anything but this. I refuse to be his puppet, but I don't want to die. Maybe I could find someone else to sustain me, maybe I could . . . But then I remember that Lifewalkers are the rarest of Walks—one out of every one thousand. A knot crawls up my throat, and I swallow so I don't throw up on the obsidian and quartz flooring. Not that I care, I just don't want to be forced to clean that up too.

I flinch when King Rave speaks again because his lips are suddenly brushing my ear, shivers break along my skin. I try not to recoil. "Infiltrate him, figure out his ability, and report to me. If you succeed, I will sustain you for as long as I live, and I will give you a promotion. Finally, you'll be able to live quietly, just like you've always wanted. If you don't do as I've asked, you will die either way. It's your choice. I don't think it's a very difficult one."

He steps away, and as soon as he does, my heart clenches painfully inside my chest, sending me to my knees.

I gasp, gripping a hand against the cage that traps my most vital organ as if the gesture would stop the pain.

"Better hurry. You don't have much time."

Aiden

CITY OF PËR, KÄS

The sound of knuckles rapping on my door wakes me out of a fitful sleep. I glance up with a groan, but only darkness meets my eyes. Twice in one day—night? I guess it's still night, but why am I being bothered out of my sleep again? Yes, I know it wasn't exactly a restful sleep, but sleep is still sleep. I roll out of bed, stumbling over my Medic jacket that I'd thrown on the floor after helping Carrie a few hours ago. Was it only a few hours ago? I feel like it's been a lifetime. I still see her brown eyes consuming my world, and I wish they would stop. I don't want anything to do with her. I can't afford to.

I shift my jacket over my shoulders, blindly stumbling to the front door of my small flat. If only being in the king's favor as a Lifewalker actually got me some benefits, I wouldn't have to live in this dump. It's a single room with a small kitchenette and the occasional rat to keep me company. Lovely, I know.

I unlock the bolted door and shift it open just a crack. What I see sends my heart into a frenzy. Carrie stands on the other side of my door, all the blood drained from her face. Her dark hair is matted to her head with a sheen of sweat.

"H—help . . ." she gasps before falling forward into the door.

I scramble to catch her. I feel what is happening to her the minute I touch her. Her heart. It's dying. I feel it fluttering to survive, fighting for a way to live, but it's being forced to die. Tremors race along my skin, begging me to help her.

I set Carrie on the floor and race to shut the door before anyone sees an unconscious woman lying in my flat.

Her eyes flicker along the ceiling once I've gotten a kerosene lamp lit. Tears stream down her face, and for a second, I think she may already be gone, but I would have felt if she died. An amazing side effect to my ability—I feel it when a life dies near me. It's like a part of me passes on with them, leaving me debilitated for a few minutes.

I drop down beside her. What happened for her to come here in this state with an ailment she said Rave was controlling? He's just letting her die? Bile rises in my throat as a new thought strikes. He sent her here. He wants me to save her. No. He wouldn't do that, right? *Rave sent me to follow you, he wants to know more about your ability . . .* Carrie's words ring in my head. He would do anything to figure out if I'm valuable enough to carry out his sinister plans. Too bad he can't do them himself. It must be a shame.

It's probably a good thing he can't do them himself, Aiden. If he could, he would have already destroyed all Walks in his way. He would be unstoppable, not that he isn't already.

"You're wasting time," I tell myself before placing my hands on Carrie's chest, close to her neck so that when she wakes up, she doesn't think I've been doing something inappropriate as if that's her biggest worry. A thought crosses my mind, and I sit back contemplating. I've never dealt with a life threatening disease like Carrie's. What if I can't shoulder it? What if my ability isn't strong enough to save her and it kills me instead? Or worse, kills us both in my attempt to save her?

You don't have time to think about it, Aiden. If you do nothing, she'll die. I refuse to let anyone die on my watch. Rave may have sent her to me, but it's all on me if she dies right here. My life isn't worth hers. If this kills me, then Rave can't use me and I have nothing to worry about. I set my hands on her chest again. My ability flares in my skin, the white light racing along my veins. Pain pulses in my chest as my own heart starts to bear the weight of Carrie's disease. I gasp as the ache intensifies. *Release her, Aiden. She's going to kill you. Release.* My mind begs, but I can't. My limbs are frozen, my heart is frozen. I can't . . . I can't ho—

Rahuin

Dais whispered sweet promises. Promises of a better time. Promises we could build a future on but promises alone can't become a foundation. I realize now that promises are too fragile. Promises are upheld by spoken word that is easily manipulated. I hate promises now, just like I hate the way my dress doesn't exactly fit. I want to cry. I should cry, but a bride can't cry on her wedding day. I'm glad that finally our promises will become reality. In front of the world, our marriage will become a binding covenant—one that can't be manipulated or warped. I mean, it already was a binding promise, but only to a few witnesses. This promise will be so much more, because everyone will know.

I just wish my dress would fit. They took the dimensions for it a month ago, but my four month pregnancy is starting to show. The aquamarine fabric keeps bunching around my hips in weird pools, making me feel ugly and not ready to stand in front of hundreds of people while I declare my undying love to Dais. It seems like such a trivial thing to be sad about, but I can't help it. I want this day to be perfect, especially after all the turmoil recently.

I glance around the disheveled dressing room that is connected to Dais's and my room. Dark wood wardrobes line the wall behind me, a vanity and jewelry cabinet sit to the right, and a quadrilateral mirror waves my insecurities in my face where I stand on the platform in front of it. Several discarded lace chemises and corsets litter the mica flooring. A domed glass ceiling allows natural light to permeate the room, but it does little to quell the dark thoughts plaguing my mind.

Even though Dais released all of Timothy's known letters to the people, there were still a lot of people very upset over what I did to King Timothy. Some didn't even know I murdered him before the letters were published, so maybe by trying to clear the motives up, we only made things worse.

I shake the thought away before it brings more tears. We revealed all the evidence to tell the people the truth. It's their choice if they don't want to accept it. That's why this day has to be perfect. I have to show them how sincere my love is for Dais—that everything I did was for my country and family.

I don't think they would be against the wedding if it didn't mean I would become Casta's queen. By Castian law, once I marry the king, I become the queen—equals in marriage and rule, but if Dais dies, the line goes to the next bloodline heir—David, unless Dais writes a clause in his will that states me as his successor, but almost no king in Castian history has done that, unless they didn't have an heir to succeed them. I think they wrote the laws that way to keep power-hungry wives or husbands from killing their spouse to become the sole ruler. What a terrifying notion . . . and now I'm thinking about murderous spouses. The wedding is in two hours, and I am by no means prepared.

Thesa and Mother are arguing in the next room. My mother, Queen Aleetha, is here from Färrin for the wedding. They're supposed to be helping me get ready but haven't stopped bickering enough to actually do so. Instead, I'm hiding in my dressing room about to cry over a dress that should have been tailored perfectly for my wedding day. Usually, Thesa overhears my thoughts by this point and comes to help, but I'm sure she's so wrapped up in her dispute, she's not listening.

I grimace, rubbing my temples. If this dress doesn't make me cry, they most certainly will. Most times, they aren't that bad around one another. Let me rephrase that, they aren't that bad when Ellenora is around. For some reason she can get them to see eye to eye, but Ellenora is busy helping Jet get Dais ready.

I never thought Thesa wouldn't get along with someone, she's always amiable to everyone. But when it comes to my mother, it's like a frosty wind blows in, steals their manners, and replaces them with terrible ice queens bent on making each other look bad. The funniest thing is that they are almost completely alike—both are princesses, both have lost a child, and both are overly protective of me. If only their similarities would bring them together instead of tear them apart.

Glaring at the honest mirror, I huff, walking over to the door and wrenching it open. The bickering immediately stops, and the two women sitting at the table glaring at each other over cold tea glance at me like two frightened animals.

"Rahuin!" Thesa exclaims, looking me up and down. I know she's taking in my half-buttoned corset and aquamarine strips that are haphazardly pinned to my skirt. Her face pales as she stands. "How come you aren't dressed yet?"

I sigh, willing stupid tears not to come, but just like everything in my life, they don't obey me. "Because the dress won't fit, and no one is in here helping me. I've gained too much w—weight. I'm not a beautiful bride. You two keep bickering, and—and—" I know I shouldn't say what I say next, but I do because I'm tired, and I just want this day to be perfect. It has to be perfect. Dais and I need a perfect day. "I want Ellenora!" I retreat back into my dressing room, slamming the door before either can respond. I lock it behind me. *That wasn't childish at all . . .* I dissolve into sobs.

I don't know how much time passes before a gentle knock taps against the door. I lift my head, wiping the tears away before I shuffle toward it. I don't really want to open it, but I'm getting married soon. I can't afford to be irresponsible about this, unless I really want to look like an ugly, disheveled bride—because that's the picture I want to paint as Dais's wife and the future queen of Casta.

I open the door, peaking through the crack.

Ellenora smiles warmly at me. "I sent Thesa to get more tea, and Aleetha to help Dais for a little while. She will be back to finish the final touches, but I knew you needed someone to separate them."

I open the door wider and pull her into a hug. "Thank you. I tried not to do this, but it's so frustrating, and they were getting on my nerves, and this dress won—"

"I know." She gently grabs my shoulders. "Thesa told me. Don't worry. We're going to make you into an irresistible bride. However, you should apologize to your mother and Thesa. They want to be here for you. Yes, they should do better at getting along for your sake, but they're both so stubborn and too much alike to really understand each other."

I nod, feeling like a scolded child. The irony that on my wedding day I feel more childish than I ever have before. "I will. I know I shouldn't have said it. I just—needed you to work your magic." I gesture to my attire.

Her dimpled smile is back, her bright eyes shining like lavender flowers. "Yes. We better get to work, because now your face is all puffy too."

"It's not entirely my fault," I grumble as she helps me to the platform in the middle of the room so she can adjust my dress. I stare into the mirror as I pat my stomach that has a small bump. Not big enough that anyone can immediately tell I'm pregnant, but enough for those who do know to see the evidence.

"You can't blame all your emotions on Sira, even though I know exactly what you mean."

"She's a spitfire, this one. I think she's going to be a gentle soul, like Dais, but maybe for her to be that way she has to purge all her big emotions out for me to process."

Ellenora chuckles, shaking her head. "I don't think that's how it works."

I shrug. "Probably not, but that's my story and I'm sticking to it."

The door opens, ushering Thesa in with tea. "I'm glad to hear that your voice is chipper now," she says with a smile, but her eyes betray her remorse.

I chew on the inside of my cheek as I meet her jade eyes. "I'm sorry for my outburst, I was just—"

"I know. Aleetha and I should have been more attentive. I'm sorry, but you said you wanted to get dressed first and then adjust. We just assumed you could get it on your own. I should have checked." She walks over to us with a cups of tea.

I sip my drink as Ellenora continues to pin and clip my dress in all the right places, moving like a graceful fairy working her magic.

"I'm sorry she puts me all out of sorts, but we finally came to an agreement. I will be back later when your parents give you the veil they had created for you because I have a little something for you as well." Her smile reaches her cheeks now, lighting up her entire face like a proud mother.

I smile back, tears forming again.

Ellenora notices, waving a hand in front of my face. "That won't do. We need your face to clear up before I put the paint on." She giggles, and I hastily blink away the tears as Thesa leaves the room.

Dais and I will have mirroring symbols painted on our faces since we are both from different countries and royalty from both countries. He will have the Castian crest of crashing waves on his right cheek with it on my left, and I will have the Färrin Silfräs tree painted on my right cheek and his left. So that when we are baptized, our countries essentially become one with us. Not officially, of course, because the elven council has to approve of me becoming the crown princess, but something along those lines.

"All done," Ellenora states, helping me down from the platform.

I step down as carefully as I can so as not to trip on the beautiful skirt that now looks absolutely perfect. I'm convinced Ellenora is a fairy of fashion, even though she would never admit that. Because there's no way she can always make me look perfect every time she helps. I stare at myself in the mirror. I don't look like I've gained weight, in fact, she somehow made me look skinnier than I was before the pregnancy. I look gorgeous, regal—like a princess about to wed her prince, or a queen about to wed her king.

The thought strikes a nerve in my stomach—a queen. A queen to a people who hate me. I shake the thought away. I've pondered it enough, and now isn't the time for such things. Now is the time to focus on paint and hair.

Ellenora pulls me to the side, setting me in front of a vanity so she can work on my hair. It reminds me of the first time she helped me get ready over a year ago for a ball welcoming a different princess as Dais's betrothed. I smile at the thought of it all—that somehow, we ended up together. After all we've been through, we finally get to have the fancy wedding he promised me. I just wish so many terrible things hadn't happened before we could.

Now I'm a tainted bride. Someone who broke her sacred covenant with her husband by allowing someone else into her bed. I swallow the sick feeling that climbs up my throat. Again, thoughts that I have given too much weight to dwell on. Dais has forgiven me, and I'm slowly forgiving myself. My heart is overjoyed that he thinks I'm still worthy enough to uphold a marriage with, because I wouldn't have come home if it wasn't for him. Even though I haven't fully forgiven myself, I would have immediately given up if he didn't forgive me first and allowed me back into his heart.

So while this wedding is to show the people I mean no harm and am Dais's chosen wife, it also marks a starting over point—a renewing of the covenants broken between us. Maybe it will help me find some forgiveness in myself. I hope so. We've been through too much to give up now.

"You're overthinking again," Ellenora states, pinning red curls into place and meeting my eyes through the vanity's mirror, as if she can see my thoughts written there like words in a book.

"I don't know how you and Thesa do it." I smile.

"Mother's intuition." She gently grips my shoulder. "Plus, you're so silent. You have been since I got here. I know it's a little nerve wracking, especially after all that's happened. I understand. Most brides are worried about their first night with their new husband, while you and I . . . well, we worry that we'll never be good enough for them."

I meet her pale purple eyes again, seeing her past inscribed in them. Queen Ellenora was previously married to an abusive man before King Timothy chose her as his bride. Apparently, there was an uproar when she became queen, too. Many council members and nobles thought she was too blemished to be his wife, but she proved them all wrong.

"I want to encourage you that it won't always be that way. People who don't know you will always see you as something else. The people used to see me as tainted and unworthy, but Timothy saw me differently. He saw me as the woman he loved enough to marry. He saw me as perfect, and that's all that mattered."

"Was it hard to stand before all of Casta and declare your love to him?"

She nods. "It was. I was terrified. I kept thinking someone from the crowd was going to accuse me of not being able to marry the king and throw rotten food or something at me"—she chuckles—"but I was wrong. There were some angry glares in the crowd, but if I remember correctly, they were rejected prospects—girls who didn't get the chance to become queen." She smiles. "In reality, no one really cared, and now, several years later, no one cares to remember it. They won't remember what you did. The history books will say he died valiantly in battle saving his country, which is true. The people will see it that way one day, but I know that doesn't quell your fear for now."

"It doesn't, because I fear my sins are greater. They see me as someone who murdered a king to turn around and marry one. Dais has gotten endless messages from the people who wish to make him understand or paint me as a master manipulator. What if they do something drastic in the name of protecting him?" The sound of hairpins falling against the cup in the vanity leaves little clinks echoing around the room and draws me back to the present before my mind slips away into the despair I had been trying so hard not to fall into today.

"So what? What would it change? What would it matter? If they try to harm you or Dais, if that's what they really want, you can't stop them. So, are you going to let it stop you—"

"No, I'm not going to let it stop me. I'm going to marry Dais for all to see. He could have easily said we are already married, or made it a smaller ceremony, but I believe this is right. We have to show them we're not cowards. We're not going to run away because the people refuse to see the truth. If we cower in fear, that only solidifies what they think of me. Standing up shows what we said is the truth, and I hope this helps them see it that way." I clench my fists, digging my nails into my palm.

"I hope you are right too. I understand why you both want to do it, but I honestly still don't think it's wise. I'm afraid the loyal people of Casta will do anything to protect their king. They love him. I know many won't bear the thought of someone unworthy marrying their beloved ruler. But . . . I am moved by your courage, by my son's courage. If I were you, I would cower and hide where it's safe—where no one could have the chance to harm me, but you're not like me." Her fingers freeze in my hair momentarily as her eyes grow distant. I raise my eyebrows. I've always thought she's stronger than me. I wish she knew how much I look up to her. I open my mouth to speak, but she seems to snap out of her thoughts as she resumes,

"You are strong. I believe your strength will win over the people. What matters most is Dais loves you. People can try to twist the truth of your love all they want, but you know the truth. I know the truth. You are a part of my family too now, Rahuin, and if anyone comes against you, I won't hesitate to tell them that." She smiles at me in the mirror, holding her empty hands up. "All done."

I sit up, not even caring to inspect my hair. I know it's gorgeous. I wrap my arms around her, pulling her into an embrace. "I'm so glad, I'm a part of your family. A little over a year ago, I lost the woman who was my mother, but through it, I've gained three mothers—you, Thesa, and Mother. I don't think I would be courageous without you. I would never be able to brave this wedding without you three." I pull away, wiping the tears that decided to appear at my blubbering. So much has happened since I fled Castlehaven, it feels like a lifetime ago, not a little over a year.

Ellenora blinks away tears of her own. "I love you, my dear daughter-in-law. I should be off. Aleetha and Thesa will be here soon. Try not to despair too much until they arrive." She pats my cheek, lilac eyes shining.

"I won't."

Dais

"You should wake up, King Dais."

"She'll only destroy you."

"I don't know why you think this is a good idea."

"Didn't she murder King Timothy? How can you marry a mur-

derer?"

"Do you really love her, or did she force you to say those things?"

The notes never seem to end as they replay in my mind. I want the words to be blotted from my memory, a clean slate so I don't have to think about them. I just want this to be over. I'm so tired of receiving letters and messages from my people. Many were in celebration and congratulations. Some were letters of apology from those who hated Rahuin until they read the letters. The last of them were the ones that dug into my skull, decided to pour a foundation, and build a home there. They never leave—constant reminders that there are people who will never accept Rahuin.

It hurts because I only want them to love her as much as I do. Yes, it's not important that a handful of people don't approve of her, but like someone once said, a handful of united people can be dangerous. Who knows what they could be scheming if they decide to do something about their fears? I doubt any of them would be stupid enough to try anything at a royal wedding, but passion and common sense rarely fit hand in hand.

Aunt Aleetha swats my hand for the third time as I lean back in my chair. "Sit still! I'm never going to finish this if you keep moving!" she exclaims, eyes meticulously studying every angle of the glue she paints on my hand before she presses a white petal to the adhesive. She's assembling a flower on my skin—the *Elüh*. A flower that grows in the deepest parts of the Slifräs Forest. It symbolizes love, trust, and the perseverance it takes to uphold a relationship. Rahuin will get one too. I hope she's doing better now that Mother is there to calm her.

"I'm being as still as I can for a man about to be married."

She shoots a glare at me, bright blue eyes shining. "You're already married, so that's no excuse. I'm still mad about that. I can't believe Henry and Timothy deceived me. *Eoth*, even Ellenora was present! I didn't get a chance to see my only daughter married. My only daughter whom I had just reconnected with, I might add—"

"Aunt Aleetha, I know the story," I cut her off, trying not to smile at her distress. Her behavior right now is the exact reason why we didn't tell her about the elopement at the time. She would have made a huge fuss about it. Aunt Aleetha isn't really my aunt, but she's married to a man whom my father considered a brother since they grew up together.

"Of course you know the story, you were there!" She presses another petal to my hand, her thumbnail digging into my palm.

"Ow, you don't have to be so mean about it," I grumble as she turns for more adhesive, flexing my hand to take away the tightness caused by the drying glue.

"Excuse me? You think I'm the bully here? Nobody told me what was going on until it was too late—not Henry, not Timothy, not you, not even my daughter!"

"I don't think I'm the only person you should be angry at."

"Yeah? Well, no one else is here to listen to my distress, so you get to hear the brunt of it first." She lifts my hand to her face, inspecting the design.

"Should I get you a spectacle to magnify it?"

She glares, dropping my hand. "I'm blind now, is that it? I don't remember your being such a *xeh rer*."

"I'm just in a good mood." I smile, and the paint from the symbols drawn on my cheeks earlier tightens around my skin.

"And good moods mean torturing your mother-in-law?" she asks, packing up her materials. "You're all done. Go find someone else to pester on your wedding day."

I stand up, placing a kiss on her cheek. "According to you, it's not my wedding day."

She waves me off. "I guess it is your wedding day. I just wish I had been able to see the first one."

"You'll at least get to see this one."

She starts toward the door. "It just won't be the same. You won't understand. You're not a mother." She looks back before stepping over the threshold. "With all the wedding planning, I don't think I said this either. *Hevakseni.*"

My heart swells with a sense of pride at her words. It's a feeling I get when anyone says congratulations to Rahuin and me regarding our baby. I'm a father, and the reality has slowly started to settle. I will soon have a baby girl to uplift, grow, and nurture. "Thank you."

She nods and then is gone. I stare up at the ceiling, studying the designs of pastel pink and orange clouds that shroud tall, snowy mountain peaks glowing in the same brilliant colors. Soon, I will be married for the second time, not to someone else, but sometimes it feels that way. Rahuin and I have changed so much since our first wedding only a few short months ago. Today will be a renewing of our promises to each other.

At least, I'm hoping it will feel that way, but another ceremony won't wash away all the sins between us. I love Rahuin and forgive her, but I know it's hard for her to forgive herself for what she did. To me, it's not detrimental because I didn't see it. I didn't experience it. It's easier for me to forgive her and hope that we can move on past this—that it won't define us for the rest of our lives. I have a feeling she fears it will last forever, haunt us forever.

"I'm sure the ceiling isn't that fascinating. You've only seen it over a hundred times in your life." Jet enters the room wearing a black jacket with light blue and silver embroidery. His salt and pepper hair has been combed down and his beard and mustache have been trimmed. I stare at him for a second because I've never seen him look so . . . regal. "You can close your mouth now, Your Majesty. I do know how to clean up sometimes." He smiles, pulling me into a hug.

"Really? No chainmail, no leather, no swor—" I stop the words, cause he still has a sword sheathed at his side.

His eyebrows raise. "Aleetha was right when she said you were being a *xeh rer*."

"You can't listen to anything she says. I'm just glad this day has finally come."

He smiles. "I know."

"So am I." Mother breezes into the room in a haze of lilac. "After all that preparation, we can finally reap the rewards of our perseverance."

"Is she better?" I ask, referring to Rahuin.

Mother nods, purple eyes shining. "Yes, she's ready to go."

"Was she—"

"No, she wasn't getting cold feet, just worried that nothing was going to be enough, but I managed to talk her out of her panic. She is a perfect bride now."

"I never asked for a perfect bride."

"She only wants it for you." Mother walks further into the room, coming to stand beside Jet.

"I know," I say as Jet pulls a folded ocean blue veil out of his inside jacket pocket, unraveling and handing a side to Mother.

She takes it with sad movements, her purple eyes filling with tears for a moment. Father should be doing this with her. We disregarded the tradition of the ceremonial veils when we eloped, but now I wish I hadn't. He should have been here to do this with her.

I reach out, touching her shoulder, and she gasps, looking up at me. "I know. I miss him too," I whisper around the knot in my throat.

"I wish he was here"—she swallows—"but he's not. He would be so proud of you." Her lips quirk into a sad smile.

"I know." I nod as she and Jet place the veil over my head.

Thesa

Tears glisten in my eyes as I step into the room. I tried so hard not to get emotional, but I can't help myself. With Jarret getting married only a few weeks ago, and now, Rahuin . . . It just seems like too much. She's still so young to me. Yes, I know she's already married, but this just makes it more real. I'm so proud of how far she's come.

Has it really only been a year since we got her out of Castlehaven? It seems like centuries ago, yet Rahuin hasn't changed much in my mind. She's still the scared girl we pulled away from everything she knew. But as I look at her now, I realize that girl is gone—replaced by a young woman who carries too many burdens, too many worries.

She smiles, her green eyes blazing brighter than normal because of her aquamarine dress. The painted crests on her face stretch oddly. Aleetha and Henry are nowhere to be found, for which I'm grateful. I need this little moment with Rahuin. I know I'm not her mother, but through all this, she has become the daughter I never had.

"You look so beautiful." I bring a hand to my face.

"Thank you. I can't believe this is happening again . . . It's more official, so it feels different." She breathes in, as nervous as a flighty bird ready to take to the skies at the slightest commotion. I walk further into the room, holding my hands out to her. She pulls me into a hug instead.

"That's not all it is . . . and it's okay to be afraid," I say, because I feel her panic. I hear the thoughts, the lies telling her she will never be accepted—she will never be forgiven for what she did.

"I'm terrified."

"I know." I rub her back, hoping my presence can bring her some comfort.

She relaxes slightly in my embrace. "It feels wrong to be scared after all I've faced to be here. The Darkness didn't scare me nearly half as much as facing those people today—but like Ellenora explained, I can't let it stop me. I have to show them that I mean what I say."

"You will. You are one of the bravest people I know, and you wouldn't be that way if you didn't stand up to the most terrifying odds time and time again." Tears appear in my eyes once more. "You were stolen from the only home you knew, taught how to fight, sent into battle, lost everyone you cared about to save someone you love, resisted the Darkness alone, and came home to face a husband who had every reason to let you go. You will stand this and you will come out stronger for it, just like always."

She joins me in a teary-eyed state as I pull away. "Thank you," she whispers before forcing a smile and waving a hand in front of her face to dispel the waterworks. "I can't have it ruining the paint."

I smile, reaching into the satchel I have hanging off my hip. "I almost forgot this." I pull out a headdress made with small chips of *greint* and silver. The stones glow in a faint light as I lift the piece up to her head. Ellenora had braided and coiled Rahuin's red locks so that it could hold the Treían gift without falling off.

"I love it," she says, gingerly touching it.

I sigh. "Are you ready?"

"Now that's something *I* ask as we put her veil on," Aleetha's sharp voice cuts through the air, and I can't help the annoying tick settles on my chest. Maybe it's because Aleetha is Rahuin's real mother, or maybe it's because I've been able to spend more time around her—but there is something about our love for Rahuin that grates on us like two stones rubbing against each other.

"I thought we agreed I could say it too." I turn to stare at her, not missing the slump that appears in Rahuin's shoulders as I meet Aleetha's gaze. *Not now, Aleetha!* I want to scream, but I hold my tongue.

She saunters into the room with Henry on her heels. She smiles. "I know. I'm just teasing."

I almost sigh in relief. The last thing Rahuin needs is more bickering between the two of us.

Her blue eyes alight on Rahuin and they fill with tears just as mine did. "She looks beautiful. Thank you for the headdress," Aleetha says to me, and I nearly fall over in shock. She thanked me?

I smile, nodding before I turn back to Rahuin. I hug her once more. "I'll see you out there. Congratulations."

"Thank you, Thesa." She pulls away, and I leave her with her mother and father.

Chapter 14

The Cost of Promises

Zenz

I stand at the front of the chapel, watching as people file into the large space. Morough's biggest chapel has become the witness to Rahuin and Dais's impending nuptials—plus several hundred people. Sunlight filters through stained glass windows creating an aura of blue ocean waves along the floor. The colors shimmer beneath trampling feet and dance across awestruck faces.

I glance at my generals waiting in the wings and outer halls—four guards per entrance, two in and two out. Two guards every three meters—sixty guards total in the atrium. Not to mention the extra fifty scattered in the outer halls. Every citizen is checked for weapons at the entrance, and the chapel was thoroughly inspected this morning before we let any guests inside. This wedding can't afford any mishaps, and I won't let it happen on my watch. Dais assigned me the overseeing general, and I don't intend to fail him or Rahuin. They've been through too much for this show of faith to go astray.

"Father, all the left quadrants have been checked. The King and his mother are enroute with a thirty-man company led by Jet," Glena says, standing beside me. Her left arm is still suspended in a sling, the bone not quite mended from the blow it received over a month ago.

"Thank you." I nod. "And the bride?"

"Thesa will be leading her company, but they haven't left the palace yet."

"Good. I'm going to meet the King." I gently brush her hand. "Take a rest. I want you patrolling the boxes with the remaining royal family. I'll be down here closest to Dais and Rahuin."

She nods, and I head toward the front doors. Just as my face breaks out into the late winter's sunshine, soldiers on horseback escorting a gold decorated cerulean carriage appear in the courtyard. All men atop their animals except for the front and rear guards dismount as Jet signals them. He moves to the King's carriage, all pomp and circumstance, and the other guards create a line facing each other all the way to where I stand on the chapel's front step. It's a show for the curious citizens standing by who have never seen their king up close.

The driver opens the carriage door, and Dais steps out with Ellenora, wearing an ocean blue coat with silvery embroidery. His wedding veil drips down his back like a waterfall as he walks forward with Ellenora, a smile on his painted cheeks.

Shouts of "It's the king!" and "Look! It's King Dais!" permeate the crowd standing around the courtyard.

Dais, noticing their words, turns his head and waves at them. Pride swells on his face, blue eyes shimmering. I recognize the look. He's a leader, just like me, and like me, his people mean the world to him. He loves them with more words than he can ever express. He will do anything to protect them. But when it all comes down to it, will they be willing to protect him? Will their reverence be enough to keep them from doing anything drastic at this wedding?

Some of the faces in the crowd tell me no. No, because of the fear I see written like words across cheeks and noses. No, because of the anger I find embedded in their eyes. These are the citizens I can't allow near him or Rahuin. They are notched arrows waiting to fly, waiting to pierce whoever they can with their ideas of peace. Peace that will unfortunately kill innocents. Enough blood has been shed, but maybe they don't realize that. Maybe they don't understand because they have never seen innocent lives cut short. But will it be too late once they do? Will it be too late to stop them once they realize that blood for blood will never satisfy the hurt?

Something tells me yes, and the thought twists a knot in my gut. I'm so sick of feeling afraid. It's not even fear for my life. It's fear over those I'm supposed to protect. Fear over the king and his soon to be queen. Fear over my pack. I can't afford to let the fear win. I won't.

Dais

Here I am again, waiting for my wife to appear from the side door of the chapel. Well, last time, she wasn't exactly my wife, but we can ignore those details. This time, my people sit behind me. I feel their eyes, their anticipation as they get to witness their king marrying the woman of his choice. Everything is so still. I'm convinced we're all frozen in time and that's the real reason why Rahuin hasn't appeared yet. I'd left my cane in the side room as I wanted to appear strong and capable on this day, plus it'll be hard to hold it once Rahuin and I make it to the pool.

The stained-glass windows rising high on both sides of the chapel cast flashes of multiple shades of white and blue across the marble floors. They depict the Castian ocean in colors similar to the crest. It reminds us that even though the winds and the waves might become harsh, we are a people who will weather the storm. I find myself believing in more and more every day. My people are strong. They have stood up to fight against insurmountable odds. We have defied the storm and come out victorious, and we will continue to do so for as long as we can stand.

Rahuin appears from the side door, her aquamarine dress is stunning as it flows around her curves in graceful waves. My heart almost stops in my chest. *Sev,* she's beautiful. Her presence quells the trembling in my soul. She's here, standing strong beside me like she promised she would. Her green eyes meet mine through our veils. Courage shines through them as if they are a well filling me up.

She stands beside me, and we turn to face the priest, her fingers reach over, gently nudging mine.

I twine our hands together, feeling the warmth of her skin.

"We gather together to witness the joining of King Dais Verne and Princess Rahuin of Färrin as one."

"Murderer!" someone screams in the crowd, and I turn to find the guards advancing on him. Someone else screams from the other side of the room.

"She's a witch!"

"She murdered King Timothy!"

"She'll kill King Dais next!"

Shouts rise up, and before I know it, guards are being overrun by angry citizens. My stomach sinks.

No.

No, this isn't happening. This can't be. My heart pounds in my chest as my worst nightmares become reality. *Move, Dais!* I tell myself as my eyes meet Rahuin's terrified green eyes before we break for the side doors as if pushed by some invisible force. My bad knee shakes, sending pain shooting up my leg into my back. I wish I had my cane.

I make the mistake of looking into the crowd. I catch flashes of armor and swords crashing amongst the din. Jet and Zenz stand closest to the stage trying desperately to keep the angry citizens away from us so we can make our escape. The large doors at the back of the church swing open, and more civilians pour in. In the commotion, I search wildly for my family in the upper balcony to my right. They're being hustled out the doors by Glena. I stumble, eyes focusing on Rahuin as we run to the side doors.

I hear the woosh of an arrow, the sharp twang as it's released. I catch a glimpse of it flying toward us, more specifically to Rahuin, who's ahead of me. I reach for her, grasping at the aquamarine fabric of her dress, but it slips through my fingers like sand through an hourglass.

No! Not here. Not now. Not after everything. I can't lose her. "Ra—"

Suddenly Zenz is in front of the arrow and blood splatters against us as it pierces the back of his skull, killing him instantly. My eyes widen as a heaviness spreads through my bones. I barely hear Rahuin's blood-curdling scream as she falls to her knees in front of him, her shaking hands caressing his frozen face.

I drop down, ignoring the shooting pain that courses through my leg as I pull myself around her. She's still here. She's alive. I fight the tears that crawl their way up my throat as I take deep breaths to calm my racing panic. The commotion from the crowd becomes a deafening roar as I wipe the blood from my face. We have to get out of here. "Rahuin!" I shout. "Rahuin, we have to go! We have to leave!"

I glance behind us. The guards are slowly getting the upper hand, but I can't really tell, and I refuse to leave Rahuin here. I refuse to let Zenz's sacrifice be in vain. He saved her life. He saved her when I failed to protect her. She hasn't moved, her eyes fixed on Zenz.

"Rahuin! We have to go!" I pull her up as Jet, with reinforcements, surround us both and lead us into the side doors of the chapel. We leave the devastation behind, and the pride I'd felt about my people weathering the storm becomes a twisted, gnarled beast of hate. I hate what they've done today. I hate to call myself their king.

Rahuin

Everything comes back in fragments. I don't even know who I am anymore. I don't even know what I've done. I can't fathom it. I can't tell if this is real or not. It doesn't feel real. It feels like a nightmare. I feel like a nightmare. There are people everywhere, shouts rising into a cacophony that I can't discern. Maybe they're yelling at me. Maybe they'll shoot another arrow and kill me next. It doesn't matter. All that matters is Zenz bleeding and dead in front of me. My hands caress his cold face as if it will bring him back. The metallic scent of blood burns my nose.

He blocked the blow to save me. Me. As if I deserve it. I never did. I never deserved any of this. He didn't deserve this. He's gone. He'll never get back up again . . . He'll never smile again. I'll never hear his secure voice. Never again. The blood staining my dress seems to start burning like it's on fire. My hands shake as I scrape my skin and garments. I have to get it off. He shed his blood to save mine. How is that fair? I deserve to die after what I did. I deserve it all, and I almost got away with it.

I almost won them over. I almost convinced them I did nothing wrong.

Dais wraps himself around me, but I hardly feel it. I just want him to go away. I just want . . . I don't know what I want. I want the hate to stop. I want the bloodshed to stop. I want everything to stop, but maybe it only stops if I'm dead. Maybe it'll never stop because I'm still here. I'm still alive after everything I've done.

"Rahuin!" he shouts. "Rahuin, we have to go! We have to leave!"

I barely hear him or the commotion behind him. I can't believe that it's over me. I can't move. I can't get up. I don't want to move—not anymore. Not after this.

"Rahuin! We have to go!" He lifts me up, shoving me with him toward the side door as guards swarm us.

"No! No!" I scream as we stumble into the hall. The doors start to close behind us, but I turn to stop them. No! Zenz. We can't leave him. I can't leave him. Dais blocks my way, grabbing my wrist gently and pulling me down the hall. He limps with every step. I did that to him, just like I killed Zenz. It's all my fault.

"Let me go!" I scream, pushing Dais away from me. I stumble, falling onto the sapphire velvet rug in the narrow hallway. I don't make any effort to get back up. Everything feels heavy. I feel like I'm being crushed.

He kneels beside me, grimacing, and I know it hurts him. His blue eyes are filled with a deep fire I've never seen before, burning my soul with their anger. He doesn't touch me, but his words feel like a slap across my cheek. "Rahuin, get up. We have to go. We can't stay here." He stands up with a limp, holding out his hands.

I don't want to move. I don't want to do what he says. I don't want everyone to continue protecting me. I don't deserve this . . . but then I remember that it's not about me. It's about them. It's about Sira. Despite their better judgment, they love me. They would die to protect me . . .

Tears slide down my cheeks as I take his hand, standing up and immediately hugging him.

He holds me, gripping me like I might dissipate in between his fingers.

"Get me out of here, Dais. Get me out . . ." I sob into his shoulder. "I can't do this anymore. We should have never done this. We should have just waited. He's gone. He's gone."

"Let's go." His voice is hoarse as he pulls me down the rest of the hall to the secret exit underneath the chapel. Jet carries a torch ahead of us, the shadows cling to the walls like monsters waiting to pounce. The nightmares return, and I see Zenz running to save me. I feel the hot blood coat my skin. I smell its metallic tone. My breaths come out ragged and raspy. This didn't happen. It couldn't have. It's just a dream. A horrible dream. This isn't real. It can't be.

"I'm going to wake up soon . . . I'm going to—"

"Rahuin, let's just get back to the castle. We have to keep moving." Dais lifts me up into his arms. He stumbles on his bad knee again, but he doesn't stop. He'll never stop. Not for me. Maybe that will be our downfall. I already see the fabric of our reality starting to unravel. Little by little, bit by bit. I'll watch it become our undoing. We'll be the end of each other.

Renell

"You *caldig*! You have no right!" the chieftain before me spits, his arms and shoulders held down by my men. His black hair is styled in braids decorated with bits of bones and blue paint, his dark eyes narrowed like a viper ready to lash out. He struggles, letting out a strangled cry that sends droplets of spit and blood onto my dress. Red soaks the ground below his knees, staining the men's boots. It makes me sick. I'm already tired of seeing blood coat the streets of Cay-Llek villages, but it's a necessary evil to get Lanckest back—at least, that's what I keep telling myself. It's the only way to fight Sun'Ar's men and take back the land that once was my homeland.

Z'mak is the third chief I've defeated, and so far, I have about 700 Cay-Llek fighters and about twice as many women and children. I left everyone in their respective villages but told the fighters to come with me. I don't need them mindlessly pillaging the people I left behind. If they're with me, they can't undermine my authority.

Fighting the first chieftain was a struggle. They didn't believe me when I walked into the village of Clutt to challenge their chief. After some taunting, he accepted the challenge, and I proved my sincerity. After I defeated him, others started to say they would never follow and challenged me themselves. I had to kill five men that night until they respected me. Wen was right. These men only respond to violence, and I hate it. I hate the power it gives me.

"I have every right. You have something of mine, and I intend to get it back," I state, watching the firelight from nearby sconces dance on his face like the demons that taunt me. *You're a murderer. That's all you'll ever be.*

"Anything that belongs to you can belong to anyone. It doesn't matter. Get your own!" His eyes start to roll back into his head, his breathing becomes labored.

"Finish him off." I turn my back so I don't see the final blow. I've been finding too much joy in watching the light leave men's veins lately. Maybe it's the creature of death I struggle to contain. Maybe it's my own darkness. Either way, it's not something I should indulge in, ever. Unless I want to find myself buried in the darkness with no escape. I've lived like that before and I refuse to return.

I take a hesitant breath and lift my head to address the villagers watching me like I'm a bad omen. Many of the men glare at me, but make no move to challenge, while the women look at me in awe, as if they could find strength after seeing me with an army. Or maybe it's their darkness that draws them to the edges of insanity, giving them ideas of a better future, but all they know is greed and death. That's not something you can change, and it's all too easily attained. I should know. My eyes meet Jarret's in the crowd, filling me with courage and dissipating the dark monster of greed gnawing my gut. Everything else falls away in his eyes, but unfortunately his gaze won't bring my people back, and I have to find a way to atone for my sins.

I meet the new villagers' eyes. "My name is Princess Renell Oslehan. From this day forward, I am your new chief. I am compiling an army so I need all able bodied men to follow me. Once I have attained all that I need, your fighting men will receive many riches. If you have any problem with this, then I suggest you step forward, but I won't be defeated easily."

No one moves. They shift on unsteady feet, some looking at the ground.

"All women and children will stay here unless you have medicinal knowledge. If there are any food stores you can spare, please talk to my cook, Gevl-les." I nod to the man, standing a few feet away. He had his own storage cart and two sturdy Y-Ak to pull it. The huge creatures low as I look at them, tossing their heads laden with long tan manes and twisted black horns.

"Gather what you'll need, but not more than you can carry on yourself. We travel by foot. Be ready to leave in two days!" I call, sheathing the sword I still held. For some reason, its weight gives me comfort when I have to face these people. I hate that I live in a world where holding a sword reminds me of who I am. Reminds me of the power I hold. Sometimes I relish it, other days, I'm disgusted by it.

The crowd comes to life at my words, starting toward their homes to pack.

Jarret walks up to me, taking my wrist gently and escorting me to the tent that had been set up as my headquarters. If I'm to be their leader, I have to look like it. The smell of smoke from cook fires stifles the air.

Once inside my tent, Jarret lights a lantern, illuminating our small bed of furs and the makeshift table covered in maps. I just want to collapse into sleep, but instead, I stand awkwardly with my thoughts consuming my soul.

Jarret shakes black and blue hair out of his eyes as he steps toward me again, running a hand down my arm and pulling me close. "I'm proud of you," he whispers. I wish he wouldn't think that. I wish he wouldn't be proud of this monster I feel myself becoming.

"I'm not. I feel it, Jarret. With every life I take, with every drop of blood I spill, with every violent gesture, I feel my humanity slipping away. I feel my heart disintegrating. I feel the darkness taking over, and I want it to take me away. I want it to destroy me, because maybe then this would be easier. I could enjoy my power and not be bound by the morality of my heart. It's the war that keeps me alive, that reminds me what I'm fighting for. If I lose myself now, I'll lose everything, and I—"

"I won't let that happen. I won't let you lose yourself. Just like you won't let me lose myself. We can both become monsters, but that will be the end of us. I refuse to give you up for the darkness I feel. I want you more than power, than greed." He kisses my head, pulling away, and I'm drawn back into the deepness of his eyes. They are the comfort I seek, and I know they'll hold me together through this.

"I love you."

"I love you too." He kisses me.

"Ah, I see you two finally found a room." Wen's voice breaks us apart as he steps past the tent flaps, his white tattoos reflecting in the lantern light.

Jarret glares at him. Somehow it's become a game for them. Wen will find us being affectionate, and Jarret will glare at him in annoyance. Some days I enjoy their antics, while other times, it irks me. Today, irritation must be written on my face, because Wen immediately starts relaying what he found out about the High Chief of Cay-Llek.

"His name is Clòz. He is built like a brick wall and keeps all the bones of his enemies." Wen smiles.

"Get to the point, Wen, I don't think I'm in the mood for teasing tonight," I growl, and Jarret places a hand on my shoulder, steadying me. Odd, normally it's the other way around.

"Someone has their hooves in a twist, heh, get it . . . hooves?" He clears his throat when neither Jarret nor I laugh. "Okay, most of his closest chiefs respect him immensely. Apparently, he kept a lot of them alive during the battles. They would gladly go to their graves for him, though I was able to find out that three of them could bring their own downfall through ambition. They scheme to kill him, but I think the others would be great candidates to overtake. We'll need at least one to gain Clòz's attention. These little village conquests are good, but unless you conquer every single one of them, Clòz won't care. If you kill one of his top generals, I think that will gain his attention faster.

"Once he calls you in, he'll want to negotiate with you. He's not a stupid man by any means. He wants to keep his position. For his safety, he avoids fights but doesn't hesitate to kill anyone who openly challenges him. He's a ruthless and skilled fighter. He won't be easy to defeat." Wen locks eyes with me, his face solemn.

Now I get why he was trying to lighten the mood earlier, his news isn't exactly good. I was hoping that this new chief was someone who randomly came back victorious in the war. A mindless brute who happened to be strong enough to control the kingdom this long, but I had a feeling it was all wishful thinking. Running a kingdom takes way more than just skill and violence. It takes negotiation, compromise— politics.

"We'll continue with these outer villages for now. The more I fight, the stronger I'll become. Plus, a bigger army wouldn't hurt," I say.

Wen nods. "I figured you'd say that. I'll continue to keep an eye on him. So far all I've found is a weak right knee that he has treated and wrapped every night after a fight. No family and no children."

The thought of using his family against him sours my stomach, but sometimes you have to do terrible things to win, right? So why doesn't it feel like winning? I feel like I'm losing, losing everything I stand for. I'm glad he doesn't have a family I might be able to use against him. I'm glad I haven't had to put anyone else in that situation—for now. But I hate that it's even an option, and one I might still have to use in the future.

"Thank you, Wen. Get some food and rest."

"You too. I'll bring a detailed report in the morning." He leaves.

Jarret turns to me, pulling me back into his arms.

"Don't say it," I whisper. "Please don't say it."

"Say what? I just want to hold you. I'm in this with you. I promised. I'm not backing out, and I'm not letting you back out. You've come too far to stop now."

I pull back, astonished by his answer. I thought I'd have to fight him as well today. "Thank you." I pull him in for a kiss. "Thank you for staying by my side, for supporting me even when I know you don't want to. Even when you're scared for me. I couldn't do this without you."

He kisses me again. "Me either."

Glena

"He's dead. It's anyone's free game, so take it while you can!" One of the Fenrir snarls at me, but I don't feel anything at his taunts. I don't care. He scratches the ground, black paws digging into the spring earth. Stars wink down above the branches of birch and evergreen trees in the little clearing outside Morough where the shapeshifters had made camp. Frobin and I came out here following my father's death.

I dig my nails into my palm, staring numbly at the black Fenrir who stands almost as tall as the trees, but I don't see him. Instead, I see my father jumping to save Rahuin, I see his blood splattering the inside of the church walls. Bile rises in my throat, but I can't shake the images away.

"Don't you have any sympathy?" Frobin screams, drawing me back to the present. "We've lost a great leader. Shouldn't there be a mourning period?"

"I don't know about you, but he hasn't been my leader for long! He led me and my brothers to war. I watched my kind succumb to slaughter!" He circles Frobin while the other shapeshifters and Fenrir look on.

"You would have been slaughtered anyway. You think the enemy would have allowed you to live free in the mountains forever? No, they would have come for you and enslaved your brothers. Zenz knew that. That's why he came, so we could fight for freedom." Frobin gets in front of the wolf, and for a second, my heart spikes, my vision blurring.

No, I can't lose another. I can't . . . I race over, grabbing Frobin and pulling him back. With one bat of his paw, the Fenrir could swat Frobin away like a pesky fly.

"This doesn't feel like freedom," the Fenrir speaks, and Frobin spins, pushing me behind him.

"What are you doing?" I can't hide the panic in my voice. The towering trees feed my nightmares, turning into unexpected spectators. No. This can't be happening.

Frobin glances at me, his gray eyes burning. "I have to fight him or it won't stop."

He's right, but that doesn't mean I care. "No, I couldn't bear it if I lost you too. I—"

"Glena, your arm is still broken. You're in no condition to fight him." His hand caresses my cheek.

"Frob—"

"It's a grim reality we have to face, my love." He kisses my forehead.

My love? My love? If he loves me so much, then why is he putting me through this? What if I lose him too? What if he dies trying to become the leader? I—I can't watch this. I watched my father die right in front of me. *Die.* The reality still chokes my throat like a vice I can't remove.

I turn around and start walking toward the edge of the trees. But if I stay close . . . If he gets injured, I can get him out of here, and maybe the other shifters will follow us. So I turn back and stand my ground as Frobin challenges the Fenrir.

The giant wolf laughs at him, but Frobin is undeterred. I can't help but think that Frobin looks like he belongs up there, like he'll arise victorious. Maybe he was meant for this all along. Maybe Frobin was supposed to lead the moment Zenz found him in the ashes after his sister burned down their cabin when he was a boy.

Tears spring to my eyes as the wolf lunges at Frobin. He shifts into a mouse, narrowly missing the Fenrir's jaws. While the wolf recovers, Frobin shifts into a Fenrir as well. His coat is a burnt orange with dark red undertones, his gray eyes shimmer like slivers of the moon. My heart spikes and the other Fenrir around us gasp.

He can't do that?

He's a shapeshifter right?

He's an imposter . . .

Their voices bombarde my head, and I'm just as perplexed as they are. No shifter can turn into a Fenrir. But then I remember that unlike most shifters, Frobin isn't a descendant of Fenrir, so his bloodline was never cursed. Shapeshifters are all descendants of Fenrir. After a witch cursed them for hunting on her land, they weren't allowed to change back into the Fenrir they once were, forcing them from their loved ones who didn't become cursed. But Frobin, as far as he knows, has human parents. He and Peggy are cursed children. He's not a descendant. I don't know how I didn't realize that before, and judging from those around me, no one else did either.

When the Fenrir turns to face Frobin again, he pauses, confusion swaying his stance.

I hear his thoughts. *What? That's impossible.*

Is it? Frobin growls. *You won't respect me either way. I'm too cursed for your kind and not cursed enough for my kind. So I will lead both. Fight me if you want it!*

It doesn't even sound like him . . . like the Frobin I know. Instead, he sounds like a leader, like my father. My heart starts to pound in my chest, my breath quickening.

The Fenrir howls before lunging at Frobin, who digs into the dry ground underneath him, leaping and throwing dirt as he meets his opponent halfway.

A snap of desperate jaws and it's over. Frobin lifts his head, blood dripping from his snout and a wound seeping red along his neck. He looks around, his breaths heavy. "Anyone else?"

The Fenrir and shifters glance around before their gazes settle on the ground, acknowledging him as leader.

I rush forward as he shifts back into my mate. I pull a cloth from my satchel at my side, wiping the blood from his neck.

He smirks down, and I swat his shoulder with the rag. "You idiot. You made me worry for nothing."

"I had to keep a few tricks up my sleeve. I knew it would throw him off." He rub my arms.

"Him and everyone. Maybe they could have accepted you without a fight. Maybe . . .” My breaths are shaky as I feel the dread of death looming over my shoulder. I shrink into his arms, sobbing into his shirt. “Don't scare me like that again please.”

“I can't promise that. I knew after . . . you wouldn't be strong enough to fight. I just want to keep you safe, and there is always risk that comes with that.”

Keep me safe? Keep me safe. I lost my father because he was trying to keep someone safe. Has anyone ever asked me what I want? Have they asked me if I want to watch them die protecting others or even the ones they love? Why do we have to protect each other at all?

I nod against him, lifting my lips for a kiss, but it doesn't make me feel safe. It doesn't stop the onslaught of thoughts bombarding my head. It doesn't stop the pain I feel—the grief I've had to endure.

Chapter 15
A Wedding for a War

Esther

"Here is your *heighle*," Lami says as she swoops into the room holding a beautiful gown. It has a long, flowing skirt with gold flourishes and accents in the red gossamer with a cropped top piece that has long strands of sheer fabric hanging down. A huge gold headpiece with ruby accents sits like a proud queen atop the cloth.

I stare at it, trying to keep my head still for the servant styling my blonde hair with gold and red glass beads. Already my head feels like it weighs nine hundred pounds, and then I have to put a head-piece on top of that. How am I supposed to uphold this whole thing during the ceremony? How long do Sun'Arian weddings usually last? I hope it's a short ceremony, but it doesn't seem like Sun'Arian's do anything in the short term.

"It's beautiful, Lami," I say, feeling like the tempestuous waves depicted on my walls. Nothing seems steady right now. Today, I'm getting married to King A'zre Re'San of Sun'Ar. Today is the day he will claim me as his own. The thought makes my skin crawl. I don't like the idea of being claimed, but then I remind myself that it's all for

Casta. Only for Casta. But then I think of A'zre. I think of his kindness, even when he pretends that word isn't in his vocabulary. I think of the person I've been able to see over the last month we spent together. I don't think he's had that kind of intimacy with any of his other wives, and I'm afraid everything I've learned about him will change the moment I *truly* become his wife.

The thought terrifies me, and I wish it wouldn't. I shouldn't care for him. I should hate him, but I realize he's not the monster he tries to be. He's haunted, and I'm drawn to that darkness, the same way I was drawn to Connan . . . and I hate myself for it. He took me away from my country and family. His war killed my father and destroyed Dais.

I'm conflicted because I've seen the human behind his horrible facade. He does everything like he's afraid someone will hurt him if he doesn't. He's a king, not a boy, and I'm afraid he's stuck in a mindset that was forced there by his own father. I know because I've seen the same pain in Connan's eyes. But Connan spent his entire life trying to run from it, while A'zre tries everything to become it, like he doesn't want his suffering to be in vain.

"Your Highness, did you hear me?" Lami's voice breaks through my thoughts, and I shake my head.

"No, I'm sorry, Lami."

"I understand a lot is on your mind, *Hidá*, but you have to focus." She points to five bowls laid out before her.

I glance at her, realizing that the servant is done with my hair. I stand to see what she has for me to learn.

For the last few days, Lami has been teaching me all things Sun'Arian-wife-etiquette—how to sit, how to stand, how to be the most perfect Sun'Arian wife I can be. I even got to spend lunch with his other six wives over the last four days. They didn't take too kindly to my presence, but I did make acquaintances with one of them—Clis, short for Aclistier. She's from northern Sun'Ar, and A'zre's most recent wife before me. She just lost her baby—a sweet little boy she had planned on naming Pi. We cried over our lost boys until lunchtime was finished and we had to return to our duties. She's one of the only few who's shown me any kindness.

I doubt it will last. I'm the odd one out—the only foreigner besides R'sha who is from an island off the coast of Sun'Ar, but she's not exactly foreign in my book since Sun'Ar still owns that archipelago. Myra, A'zre's first wife, hates my guts for some reason. She barely looked at me when Lami introduced me to all of them, and never came up to introduce herself. I had to learn who she was from Lami and Clis. She then proceeded to talk to the other wives, glaring at me the entire time. Since then, I've gotten the cold shoulder from everyone except Clis, but I have a feeling that Myra will get through to her soon enough, and then I won't have a friend in this already lonely place.

The door opens as Lami starts explaining the ceremonial bowls of Sun'Arian weddings. Clis walks into the room, her dark brown hair piled high atop her head, accentuating her swan-like neck. She smiles when she sees me. Well, at least Myra hasn't gotten to her yet, so I will have her warm company nearby for the wedding. Her presence seems like a breath of fresh air in the tortuous Sun'Arian heat.

"Esther, you look beautiful, and is that the *heighle*? It's red." She spots the dress Lami hung up on the wall beside the door. It blazes in fiery glory, reminding me of my impending doom.

I nod. "Is red a bad thing?"

Lami sighs in front of me, realizing I won't be paying attention to our lesson now that Clis is here.

"Not exactly. It just means you are divorced. I thought—"

"He was dying anyway. He told me to go through with it." I swallow, looking away from her soft brown eyes. "It wasn't—I didn't really have a choice." I stare at the tiled floor, wishing I could be swallowed up by the ocean under my feet.

"I see. I'm sorry to have made you feel uncomfortable."

I meet her warm brown eyes. "Do all the *heighle* colors have a meaning?"

"They do," Lami answers as Clis hesitates.

What a terrible notion to be a Sun'Arian bride so everyone knows what you have or haven't been through just by the color of your gown. It makes me sick. Everyone will know that I had to divorce Connan, but they won't know the reason behind it. It wasn't because I was unworthy. It was because he was already dying, and I had to save my country. The more I learn about Sun'Ar, the more I begin to hate it. For all the pride they give themselves for being a country of 'kind' or 'chosen' people, they certainly have a way of making sure everyone knows your situation.

"What color was yours?" I ask Clis.

Tears form in her eyes for a moment before she blinks them away. "Blue," she whisper, offering no explanation for what that means, but judging from her perspective, it's nothing good.

Lami continues for Clis. "Blue means you have been tainted and not married by the one who had intimate relations with you."

Mine should be blue too. If that's the case, my *heighle* should be brown because I've experienced too much to have just one color in my garment, and brown is a mix of them all. "I'm sorry. That must have been terrible."

"It was a long time ago, but my entire village was aware. My father offered my sister to A'zre first, but he didn't like her." A smile crosses her features at the memory. "They wasted no time telling A'zre what happened to me, and once he knew, he announced to my father that he wanted to marry me. I look back on that time, and I believe with all my heart that he married me because he knew no one else would. So I gladly bore the shame to become his wife."

Again, A'zre's kindness shines when it comes to his wives. Maybe I'm going about this wrong. Maybe I shouldn't learn his weaknesses and try to destroy him. Maybe I should help him overcome them and convince him to call off this war. He said Sun'Ar needs resources, but if we can start implementing . . . My mind starts to trail off with ideas on how we can improve Sun'Ar without a war. My heart begins to fill with hope, especially because I don't want to hate A'zre. He said everything he's done has been for his people, but is that really true? I have to understand his fears to the very core. Somehow, I have to figure out if what he told me is all true.

I stare at Lami. Surely Lami will know.

She wrinkles her brow at me. "*Hidá*, you're daydreaming again, and that should be enough talk about *heighles*. I need you to focus on the other aspects of the marriage." She gestures to the bowls.

Clis takes the cue. "I'll let you finish getting ready, Esther. I just wanted to see how you were doing. I'll be back later to see that heighle on you and offer congratulations before you go to the ceremony." She bows her head before leaving the room.

"I'm sorry, Lami, continue," I say, even though my mind is still plagued with thoughts about A'zre's true motives over the war. I have no reason to doubt him, but besides his kindness, I have no reason to trust him either. I try to focus on what she tells me about the ceremonial bowls, and somehow I pass the test when she tells me to repeat her teachings. Part of me doesn't know how, because I was hardly listening the entire time, or perhaps, she's just tired of me. She's seen too many anxious brides threatened with thoughts over their wedding day to adequately question my knowledge of the bowls, for which I'm grateful. Because I have too many things to think about in regard to A'zre, Casta, and Sun'Ar.

She walks over to the hanging *heighle*, gliding over the ocean of my room. "Now that's over with, let's get you dressed." She helps me into the *heighle* and the beautiful fabric falls over my body, caressing my curves. After fastening the top piece, she situates the streams of cloth over my shoulders and attaches them to bands on my wrist, creating sheer, striped sleeves.

When she's finished, I hardly recognize myself in the mirror. I look regal, beautiful, but the color red bleeds into my thoughts. Divorced. I think of Connan. I feel my fingers running through his hair. I remember his smile, the shine in his ice-blue eyes when he looked at me. My stomach twists and tears appear in my eyes when I can't remember the feeling of his hands on my skin. I blink them away. I promised I wouldn't shed any more tears over him. I see Connan's face in the mirror, and gasp, turning around to find him, even though I know it can't possibly be real. Of course he isn't there, but the hope lingers in my chest, reminding me of my broken promises.

Lami stares at me instead, her features pulled into worry. "Esther?" She moves toward me, gently touching my elbow. "What's wrong?"

"Nothing. It's just . . . seeing myself in the *heighle* has me thinking about my first wedding day. And I—I miss him, is all." I hate how hoarse my voice is.

"I can't imagine, but I admire your strength to come to an unfamiliar place with no one. I know it isn't easy. I wasn't sure if you would be good for A'zre at first, but over the last few days, I've grown quite fond of you, and I imagine A'zre feels the same way."

I find that hard to believe. "He seems to be quite fond of all his wives, Lami. I wasn't sure how things would be . . . to share a husband with other women, but he's kind to all of us."

She steps back to retrieve my headpiece. I'm not sure I'm ready to wear it yet. I'm afraid it will make my head heavier than it already is, plus the ceremony doesn't start for another hour . . . I think.

"Yes, but with you he's different. I see it, and I want to say it's love, but A'zre hasn't loved anyone for a long time," she whispers, her gold eyes growing hopeful as she starts to attach the metal pieces to my styled hair.

My interest is piqued. He hasn't loved? How can you not love? Surely he loves one of his wives, but maybe that's why he can be kind to all of us and do his best to give equal attention. "What do you mean?"

"I probably shouldn't tell you this, but I'm tired of seeing that boy so unhappy. He does everything he can to follow in his father's footsteps, but I've noticed that it's starting to burden him, bringing him to the edge of madness. A'zre loved his first wife so much . . ." she trails off with a sigh.

"What happened to his first wife?" If Myra wasn't his first wife then who had been?

"His father forced him to marry. A'zre didn't want to do it. His father was a horrible man to his wives, and the boy never wanted to be like that to anyone. He never wanted to have the temptation, but he did what his father told him, because he wanted his father's love. They were just two little young things when they got married and those kids fell in love, and when his father caught wind of A'zre's love for his wife, he threatened to murder her.

"Now at the time, she had just found out she was pregnant, and A'zre had to push her away. He pretended to hate her, because he could never show how much he loved her, or his father would take them away forever. His father told him that no king could be capable of love," she stops to catch her breath.

Murder his wife? His own father? And I thought my father was bad. If I was A'zre, I would have done the same, but then I remember how angry I was after I heard about Connan's sacrifice. He did it to protect me, just like A'zre left Myra to protect her. Maybe Myra and I aren't so different. At least Lami confirmed what I guessed to be true concerning A'zre's past—his father was abusive. I'd seen little glimpses when I touched Lami, but his father always appears as an angry gruff man in her memories.

Lami continues, "When she went into labor, that boy frequently came to her chamber to check on her. He wouldn't go in of course, but wait just outside. When I came out on the hunt for fresh water or towels, he'd stop me and beg me to tell him how she was doing. When that baby boy was born . . ." She smiles at the memory, crow's feet wrinkling further around her eyes.

"With his first cry, A'zre appeared in the room, almost as if that little sob had summoned him. The wet nurse handed him the baby, while Myra was being cleaned up, and as he stared at his son, his eyes teared up, before he gave the baby back to his mother. I know he wanted to kiss her and his son . . . just to show her how much he loved them, but all he did was manage a tight nod and a stone face. He left the room without so much as a word, and Myra . . . she cried and cried and cried, because she knew he was lost to her forever."

She looks at me, her eyes kind. "He allows so much more with you, and I don't think that it's just because of the alliance. Although, that's exactly what he said when I pointed it out and then spewed some things about how everything would change after your ceremony because you would be his wife, but I think he's lying. I think he's going to run again, and when he does, chase after him."

Birds singing outside the terrace doors remind me where I am, and what's about to happen. Lami's tale somehow pulled all of my thoughts off my impending marriage. I stare out toward the doors, even though I know I won't see the birds unless they appear on my balcony to preen their feathers.

"Why me? Why should I chase him? I don't want to fall in love again, Lami. I don't want to be given this task," I whisper, turning my head, and I feel the beads and the metal headdress's decorative chains gently wisp against my cheeks. It actually doesn't feel as heavy as I thought it would.

"Because of that fondness. He doesn't have that with any of his other wives. I used to think he did for Myra, but she became quite bitter after he was forced to let her be and then married another woman almost immediately after . . . Another decision of his father's, of course, but it drove the wedge further between them. She has no ambition to bring him back into her arms, and I understand why. So, I want him to love you, and I don't want him to fight it anymore. I want him to be happy."

Yes, but what about my happiness? Does it matter that I was forced to give up all I love to come here just to save what I have left? He said this war is over resources, but I'm starting to believe there's more to it. I think it has something to do with his father, and if that's the case, then how can I ever really love him? How can I forgive him for what he did to Casta—to my family? All to please a man who is already dead. I won't.

What about Myra? She loves him already, even though she doesn't want to admit it. I think that's why she didn't even acknowledge me. Somehow she believes I'm a threat, but what does it matter to her if she won't even bring herself to love him anymore? Does she believe that if she can't have him, no one can? Seems like an odd mindset to have when your husband has seven wives—well, almost seven. What if Lami is wrong? What if I try to get him to love me, and he doesn't because of his love for Myra? What if my heart gets broken in the process? Because I know once I go down this road, I will begin to care for him. I will begin to love him. I already feel myself drawn to him, and I'm not sure I'm ready to fall in love again . . . not with someone whose war took everything from me.

"Esther?" Lami's voice breaks my thoughts.

I look up at her, breathing in shakily as I watch the blue sheer curtains flutter in the breeze, the sun flashes like a dance with the fabric. "I'm just thinking, Lami."

"I know it's a lot I ask of you, but I think it would be good for you too. I understand that you haven't said goodbye to your first love yet—maybe you never will—but I see something between you two, and I think you can help him. Maybe it will help you too." She reaches a hand down to help me stand.

"Help me?" I ask as more images flutter through my mind—her love for A'zre being the crux of all of them. I see every time she's upheld him, cared for him, stood by his side. So many countless memories . . .

"*Hidá*, don't pretend to play the fool with me. There is only one reason you would divorce your husband to come here, and not just because of an alliance. Yes, you bought some time, but I don't think you believe that." She takes a deep breath, and the silence makes my heart race. If Lami figured it out, then surely A'zre already knows. I mean, he had to believe it was a possibility, but the alliance is in place to keep that from happening. "All I'm saying is . . . give him a chance," she finishes, her golden eyes shimmering with all the love I saw in her memories. He's like a son to her, someone she has watched grow up and change, and probably not always for the better. I hadn't asked, but now that I stare at her face, I'm reminded of A'zre's. I wonder if she is his mother. I didn't see it in her memories, but it could be true.

"I will, Lami. This day—all I've learned since I got here has helped me change my mind when it comes to A'zre. I had a very different plan from the start, which you guessed. I don't know if I'm willing to love him like you want me to, but I am here to change his mind and understand his reasoning for this war. I have people I want to protect too." I take a deep breath, and it feels like a weight has been taken off my chest. Someone knows why I'm here now, and if I can get my plan to work, I'll need her influence to help change A'zre's mind. He respects her.

The sunlight dancing across the ocean of my room fills my heart with hope of a brighter future—a future where I help end this war and allow my heart to love again. No. I shouldn't hope. I shouldn't dream. I know it'll hurt too much if it never becomes true.

"I understand. I did all I could to raise A'zre and keep him from becoming a monster like his father, but I couldn't protect him from the worst of it. This is my little way of keeping him safe and perhaps see him happy. That's all any mother wants," she smiles, taking my hands into hers and starting to put rings and bracelets onto me. Beautiful pieces of gold adorned with rubies. I wonder if I'll get to keep these jewels after the ceremony today. I doubt it.

"Are you his—" I start as more memories fill my mind. I see a young pregnant woman, her lips pale and her eyes dimmed with brokenness. Lami clenches her hand, and a sense of overwhelming sorrow sweeps over me.

"No, no, I was his, what you would call, a governess. I practically raised him. His mother died in childbirth with his younger sister when he was hardly a year old. We were close, and I couldn't save her. So as far as I'm concerned, he is my son. I would do anything to protect him, even if it's from himself. That's why I want you to love him. That's why I want you to help him feel again. I don't want him to become the heartless man his father was, and if he continues this way, I fear I will lose him to that horrible man for good. Because one day, he will do something irreversible to fix what he thinks he's lost." Her brow crinkles as the sound of clinking jewelry she's selecting fills the room.

"I see, then I will try. I will do my best to reach his heart." I can't believe the words as they leave my lips. I don't want to love him, but maybe I won't know until I get the chance to break his walls down and reach him. And maybe it will be easier to sway him once I do have his heart, but that also means it will be the most guarded part of him. Maybe that's why Lami asked me to do this. She believes I'm strong enough to save him, and maybe I am.

I don't have anything to lose except my heart as well. If that happens, then all I'll have left is to keep an eye on what he does against my country and report to Dais. Perhaps I can use him until I learn his motives just like I used to do for my father. I hate that I'll be falling back into my old ways—the ways I hated my father for forcing me into. But if it saves Casta, I will do it. Perhaps, in a way, my father prepared me for this day . . . We just didn't know it.

Someone knocks on the door. "Come in," Lami calls and turns, taking my arm into hers.

Clis re-enters in a beautiful two-piece gold gown, showing off her position in the castle. A delicate crown decorates her dark brown hair, and she smiles when she sees me in the *heighle*. "My, you look absolutely majestic, Your Highness." She takes my hand into hers as Lami leaves my side and starts gathering small things around my room. Sacrifices, I'm told, and what she was trying to get me to understand with the ceremonial bowls.

"Thank you, Clis. Is it already time?"

"Yes." Her brown eyes smile with warmth like hot tea on a cold night. I didn't think Lami and I talked for that long, but we must have.

I take a deep breath as Lami moves beside me, taking my arm once more, while Clis takes my other arm. We start out of the room and back down the hall to the grand foyer. A carriage awaits us in the courtyard, guards standing at attention beside it. I glance around, but A'zre is nowhere in sight. I didn't think he would be, I just wanted to check. To maybe catch a glimpse of him before he becomes my husband for real.

The black horses prance on the tiled ground, their ears flickering back and forth as they snort in anticipation. The driver opens the door of the redwood carriage, helping us onto the gold cushions.

"Are you ready?" Clis asks as we settle in.

"Yes, but by my Castian standards I'm already married to him, he just didn't want to acknowledge it."

Clis chuckles. "Tradition means everything to us. I believe it keeps us alive, and if the king doesn't uphold it, everything would descend into chaos."

"Isn't it funny how easily people follow?" I ask, glancing out the window as we descend upon the streets of Ren'R. People line the roads, waving banners with the Sun'Arian crest and throwing flower petals of all colors.

"That's why we have to be careful. You and I and the others, we uphold the whole of Sun'Arian culture. We're the embodiment of it, and we'll do it to show our support of the king. He relies on us as well as all the citizens, and we can't forget that." Clis's face grows solemn, her eyes narrowing and the gesture seems to freeze all the warmth I'd seen in them earlier.

"I won't forget, especially because I have my culture to uphold as well." I nod. Lami pats my hand, drawing my gaze. The carriage slows to a stop, and my heart starts to pick up speed, a cold sweat breaks out on my skin. I shouldn't be this nervous since I already consider myself married to him, but this will be the first time the Sun'Arian people catch a glimpse of the king's newest wife. A foreigner. A princess. Divorced . . . I bury my restless hands into the red and gold fabric. They'll assume everything about me, while I'll know nothing about them.

The carriage opens, and a footman guides me out into a temple courtyard. Plants and trees line a stone pathway that leads to arched double doors. Fountains interweave among the plants bubbling out water in beautiful archways. Birds and bugs flitter around, reveling in the sunshine. The temple itself has large ivory walls that lead to huge domes tiered in gold. My mouth goes dry as I stare at it.

Lami touches my shoulder gently. "This is where we leave you." She nods behind me, and I turn to find A'zre standing there. Lami kisses my cheek before she heads into the temple with Clis.

A'zre saunters up to me, his red eyes muddied into more of a brown in the sunlight. I hadn't seen him since we arrived in Ren'R. His beard has been trimmed with swirls that match the tattoos curving around his face. His long black hair has been braided in certain areas with glass red and gold beads. His *heighe* is opposite colors than mine—gold with red accents. I wonder if he has been married in the same garments every time, or does his change with each new bride? I also wonder what gold means as a color, since mine has it too. I guess I forgot to ask Lami.

He smiles. "You look beautiful."

"Do you say that to every bride before you get married?" I smirk, watching him fiddle with the rings on his fingers. They almost match mine exactly, but perhaps Lami knew that.

"I would be lying if I said I didn't. Would a different word be preferable?" He takes my hands, entwining our fingers together. I hate the intimacy of it, but it makes me recall Lami's words. *That's why I want you to love him* . . . I don't think it will be so hard to get myself to love him, but will he be able to love me back? Will I be able to reach into that hardened heart of his?

"Preferably, yes." Our rings clink together in the silence.

"Fine. You look radiant, exquisite, like the sun when it kisses the horizon," he whispers in Castian.

My heart almost stops, and I try to keep my smirk from appearing. "Who knew you were such a romantic," I answer in Castian.

"I'm not a romantic. I don't believe in it." He leans closer, and I find my gaze drawing up the length of his jawline to his eyes.

"Well, now you tell me. I was convinced." I chuckle. Since he doesn't believe in romance, that makes what he said all the more worthy. He didn't say it just to woo me.

Something passes over his eyes, but it's too fleeting for me to understand what it is. "Are you ready?" he asks in Sun'Arian.

"As ready as I'll ever be when a girl has to marry the same man for the second time."

He sighs. "There was never a first time." A breeze flutters between us, bringing the sweet scent of flower blossoms with it. It messes his hair, and I can't imagine how mine fairs.

I play with the rings on his fingers, twirling them around and around. "I'm never going to forget it, but I admire your tenacity."

"Sometimes it's good to have self-control." His eyes shine, but they look so foreign to me, I've never seen them in this light before. I was so used to the red, but here they look more inviting—more like a man ready to wed his bride.

Fanfare starts to play behind us. A'zre straightens. "It's time." He offers me his arm, and I take it, pulling my shoulders as we ready ourselves to walk down the path into the temple.

A Sun'Arian wedding runs differently from a Castian one in the regard that there is no baptismal pool and no incense burning. As A'zre and I walk into the temple, people on the outer rows lay down giant leaves and flower petals for us to walk on, creating a lush pathway that Lami said is supposed to signal abundance. At the end of the temple, two thrones sit with five ceremonial bowls on a low table spread out before them. Directly in front of the table, a platform has been set up.

Lami said there would be a stage where ceremonial dancers will perform. They practice for weeks leading up to a wedding and then perform five dances as tribute to the gods. In Sun'Ar, they believe in four lesser gods that control earth, wind, fire, and water who report to the main high god. After each dance, A'zre and I will go up to one of the bowls, they'll be marked for each god, and light the contents on fire. They put a sort of pitch on the inner edge of the bowl to make the flame burn longer.

A'zre leads me up to the throne on the right and helps me into it before he seats himself on the other.

I recognize Lami and the other wives in the first row. All of them are dressed in vibrant gold gowns with gorgeous sheer veils covering their faces. I can't imagine what it's like to watch your husband marry another woman, but maybe they think nothing of it since their culture praises it.

A priest comes up between the thrones, taking A'zre's and my wrists and twining them together with a white piece of cloth. He chants a little song as he does so, and the words are a lullaby.

> *Together as one*
> *Together forever*
> *May the sun bless*
> *As the gods smile*
> *For one and all*
> *May this union bear*

"With all authority of the gods, I now bless the union between Princess Esther Verne and King A'zre Re'San. Begin the ceremonial dances and burnings that will join these two together."

A song rises up behind us, and I wonder where the musicians are because I didn't see them when we came in. Five dancers take up position on the stage with ribbons of brown—earth. They step to the music in perfect synchronicity, making the air feel electric with their movements.

I watch in awe, knowing that soon I will lawfully be one of A'zre's wives. I think of all I have to do. The daunting task of reaching his heart and getting him to change his mind. The trauma I will have to break through to find the boy that Lami said loved. It seems more daunting the longer I think about it, but I can't afford to think like that now. Casta depends on me. What else do I have left to lose?

A'zre

The sun has long since disappeared over the horizon when I retire to my room. Lanterns have been lit, the warm glow drawing my tired eyes evermore closed. The ceremony was beautiful like all my weddings, but it's left me exhausted. Sometimes I wish I could do away with all the circumstance and just marry my next wife without the whole of Sun'Ar attending, but I know my people would be outraged. We take our weddings, funerals, births, and festivals very seriously.

A cold breeze rushes in from the balcony and I sigh as I move to close the doors. The servants should have already done so when they lit my lamps, but like everyone else, they retired early to enjoy the festivities. I wish I could have indulged. Very rarely, do I take actual enjoyment from a celebration. Ceremonies are the one time Sun'Arian governors, advisors, and generals all come together. I've spent almost all my weddings making connections and having conversations about sensitive information I can't risk sending through messages.

I roll my shoulders, beginning to take out the beads in my hair. Despite my exhaustion, my mind keeps recalling Esther and how absolutely stunning she looked today. I found myself admiring the way her *heighle* caressed her generous curves and exposed her waist. My fingers itched to touch her soft skin more than once. I close my eyes and shake my head, beads clinking into a bowl atop my dresser. My head feels much lighter once I've shaken all of them out. I shrug my *heighe* off, draping it against a red and gold chair. It's seen me through seven marriages now. Of course, the garment has been altered over the years since my first marriage was thirteen years ago. I was twenty-one.

I sigh as an onslaught of memories fill my head. I remember the light shining in Myra's eyes as we watched the ceremonial dances for our wedding. I remember the white and gold *heighle* she had. I remember the way her fingers caressed mine when we held each other during the festivities. I remember our first night together . . .

I swallow, running my fingers through my hair. No, no. I shouldn't care. I shouldn't remember, remembering only causes pain. I can't afford to remember all that I've done to be where I am now. *Love only causes weakness . . .* I hear my father's words, ingrained into my head like an etching in stone. He's right. How weak I really am because the thoughts won't stop.

I should be with Esther tonight, but I made a feeble excuse saying I was too tired. It won't last. I can't avoid her forever. I know if I let her in, if I allow myself to get close to her, I'll never stop. I won't be able to keep her gift from invading my mind. I won't stop her from consuming every part of me. My inadequate body wants that. I want her like I've never wanted anything before, and I hate it. I won't destroy everything I've worked for—everything I've sacrificed—over a single woman. I can't. I'll avoid her. I'll push her away. I'll deny myself like I've done for years. I'll prove how strong I really am.

I take my shirt off, throwing it on top of my *heighe*.

A knock sounds. "It's me," Lami's voice comes through the door.

"Come in."

The door creaks as she steps inside. I glare at it. I'll have to have the servants oil all the hinges. I can't have a creaking palace.

Lami's gold eyes meet mine, long gray hair spirals down her back like a snake. "Oh, you've already cleaned up." She grabs my shirt and *heighe*, draping them over her arms.

"I thought you already retired. You've done enough today." I take my clothes out of her hands, dropping them back on the chair.

"I thought I'd check on you before I do." She clasps her hands in front of her.

"This isn't my first wedding, Lami."

"It is the first one where you sent your wife off to sleep without you." She raises gray eyebrows, accentuating her gold eyes in the dim light.

I look away. "How is she?"

She sighs. "I think you should ask her yourself." She turns away, opening the door with another creak.

"Lami—" I start, but the words die on my tongue when Esther steps into the room in a silk crème robe, the fabric accentuating her curves and cleavage. I can't tear my eyes away.

"I'll leave you to it," Lami says, pulling me out of my stupor before she rushes out the door.

"Lami!" I yell, but she's already gone. I refuse to look directly at Esther again. I glance toward the balcony and the twinkling night sky beyond. "What are you doing here?"

"It is our wedding night, and according to you, our first official night. Unless you still believe we're not married."

I hear her shuffle closer. *Stay away. Stay away. Don't come near me,* I will with my thoughts, but Esther has never been one to listen. I feel her warm hand touch my bare shoulder, trailing down my arm. I inhale as shivers breakout on my skin. "I said I was tired." I feel her gift pressing against my mental barriers, knocking on the walls I've built.

I step away from her, heading toward the balcony before I remember that it's freezing out there and I don't have a shirt on. *Eid.* My hand grips the gold handle, and I growl before turning back toward Esther. Her long blonde hair falls down her shoulders in gentle waves. Her purple eyes shine in the orange light of my lamps. I can't stop my gaze from wandering over her silk-clad body again and imagine myself taking it off.

"We both know that's a lie." She lifts her chin, her hands clenched into fists at her sides. "Why won't you just get this over with? Why do you keep torturing me?"

I'm torturing her? Does she have any idea what *she's* doing to me? If I let her in, she'll know. She'll see all of me. I can't have that. Our alliance is fragile at best. I can't let her hold all the cards.

I step toward her, keeping eyes locked on hers. "Get this over with? Is that all you think of me? That I'll just take because you're my wife?" *Step away, A'zre. You're too close.* I feel my heart thudding violently like it might leap out of my chest and into her hands. *Love is weakness.* I can't allow her to have it. It will be used against me. That's what always happens. I won't lose what I've built. I won't let her destroy me.

"Isn't that what you do?" Her eyes blaze as she steps closer to me again.

I should move away. This shouldn't happen. I glare at her. "Get out!"

"No! You don't own me. I'm not spending our wedding night

alone."

I lean over her, but she doesn't shrink. It only makes me want her more. Perhaps she knows that. "Actually, that's the definition of being married in my culture . . . I. Own. You."

"Then take me." Her eyes trail down to my lips.

I kiss her then, my hands immediately reaching for the waist that teased me all day long and pulling her closer to me. *No. No. Stop!* My thoughts scream, but I can't. I've waited too long for this, and I can't stop myself from taking a hit of the intoxication that is Esther. Her robe loosens a little, revealing her collar bone, and my lips kiss along her neck and exposed skin.

Her fingers tangle in my hair, and she lets out a soft moan as I bring my lips back to hers. My knees go weak, and I push her backward gently until she's pressed against the wall. I just want to drown in her and never come up for air. I want her. I can have her.

Suddenly the mental barrier blocking my mind explodes and I feel her gift greedily snatch the unveiled memories.

She winces as everything I've held back floods into her mind, almost like it wanted her to know.

No!

I push away from her, taking in deep breaths as I glare. "You had no right!"

She holds her head, her eyes closed as she leans against the wall.

This is why she's dangerous. She knows now. She'll take everything. How could I have been so stupid? How could I have played right into her hands?

She groans, opening her eyes slightly. "You think I wanted to see that? I've never seen so many memories all at once."

She's been wanting to see that since she got here. I clench my fists, stepping farther away from her. "Get out!"

"Az—"

"I said, 'Get out!'" I point to the door, keeping my back to her.

"Fine."

I hear the door creak and slam. I glance toward where she'd been, but she's gone. Good. I don't need her anyway. I don't want her. I can't have her.

Chapter 16
Tenfold

Wen

I shift position, hearing clomping footfalls above my head. My knee hits a wall, and I hold back my wince. The space is barely big enough for me to fit into, but I keep telling myself it could be worse. At least from here, I can see and hear what's going on above me. There's a little hole above my head where I can see into the room, and the floorboards create perfect percussion. I found this nook under the main hall in Cizarrél a few days ago. I teleport into the space to spy on the conversations presented to High Chief Clòz. It's not exactly a comfortable job, but it keeps me busy—keeps my mind off overused thoughts.

"Move! Move out of the way! General Nidn has a message for the High Chief." A voice cuts through the heavy footsteps. Sz-Kar is a guttural language that hangs on the back of the throat like a bad cough. It's my least favorite language since it's all grunts and possession. I think a herd of lowing cattle sound more pleasant.

I place my eye to the crack. Several men enter, carrying a wounded man on a Kön hide. Blood stains the bottom of the canvas, and I know the general won't last long. Clòz, the High Chief, stands as the men near his seat at the front of the room.

"What happened?" Clòz's voice sounds like an avalanche, grinding stone on stone. He stands above everyone else, looking down on them like the king he thinks he is. His head is shaved on both sides, leaving long black hair braided with bones in the middle. Red tattoos swirl along the right side of his face, bleeding into his black beard that reaches to his stomach. Dark brown eyes glare at the men in front of him and reflect the crude candlelight overhead.

"High Chief," Chief Nidn on the cot rasps. "She took them . . . She sent me to you . . . message. She's . . . coming." He gasps and soon his raspy breaths subside.

Clòz looks at the men who brought him in. "What's he talking about?"

"A challenger, High Chief. She's been going to every village and conquering them one by one, slowly amassing an army. They call her the Princess of Death," one of the men speaks, his voice echoing across the cavernous hall of Cizarrél. It's not exactly a beautiful place, more like a tomb with as many bones as they have decorating the stone and wood walls. Even the chandeliers holding crude candles are made out of bones.

"How come I hadn't heard of this sooner?" Clòz rumbles, pacing in front of his throne.

"Scouts reported some activity, but they assumed that a villager had gotten restless and just wanted a bit of power or fun," another man says.

"How come the report never got to me so I could judge it and squash the little bug before she amassed an army and killed one of my most trusted generals!" he shouts, and the men in front of him wince. Actually, they reported the incidents to him several times, but the High Chief did nothing about them. Although, if I was in these men's positions, I wouldn't point that out either.

"We're sorry, High Chief. We'll send a contingent of men right—"

"No. Invite this death princess here. Tell her I accept the challenge and make her come. Whether she wants a fight with me or not, she's getting it." He falls into his chair, and I hear the floor creak in protest.

The men nod. "Of course, we'll send a messenger right away and get Nidn ready for incineration." They grab the canvas again, but blood has already stained the floor.

Clòz sighs once they're gone, taking in a deep breath that reminds me vaguely of a wolf howl. "Well, death princess, I have just the thing in mind for you." A sinister smile lights his face with whatever horrid scenes he begins to imagine.

I teleport from my hiding place before he decides to voice the rest of the 'things' he has in mind for Renell. I imagine the village about twenty miles from Cizarrél where we'd set up camp—the same place the dead general ruled. I have to know exactly where I'm going or see where I want to go before I can teleport. Otherwise I could be sent somewhere completely different or become trapped in a dimension I can't return from. It's one of the hardest forms of magic I learned when I was with the Darkness.

I arrive in the middle of a muddy street. Every Cay-Llek village looks the same and, I wrinkle my nose, smells the same—like bad body odor, mud, and manure. Most people live in thatched sod homes but a few stone and wood houses are scattered throughout the mismatched alleys. Every resident, however, has bones from animals or people decorating their windows and doors. I find it quite disturbing, but Cay-Llekians believe that bones have significant meaning and by displaying them, they are honoring whatever beast they got them from. Most even wear the bones from their deceased loved ones. Again, very disturbing, but it's what they've been taught so I can't blame them.

I find Renell in her tent, and as always, Jarret, since they never seem to leave each other's sides unless they're fighting. They're looking at a map when I enter and don't notice me. I sneak up to Jarret, slipping my knife from its sheath at my side. Quick as a flash, I grab a fist of his hair and wrench him backward, bringing the blade to his neck.

"You're dead," I whisper.

"Jarret!" Renell screams, eyes narrowing as she realizes it's just me. "Wen!"

I swear I see a vein pop out of her forehead. *Sev*, these two need to lighten up, or maybe they need to have better security. It was way too easy for me to sneak in here. I'm doing them a favor.

Jarret struggles but tries not to move his neck before I release him. He stumbles, turning to me as he pulls his dagger out.

I drop mine, putting my hands up. "I surrender. I just wanted to show you how easy it was to put a knife to your neck."

Jarret glares before sheathing his weapon and walking out of the tent with a huff.

"What's gotten into him?" I look at Renell. Usually, I get some form of retort, but I didn't even get an angry grunt this time.

"You really have to ask that? But I guess, thank you for your asinine way of showing us what we're missing." She rolls her eyes, looking back at the map. "I have guards posted outside. They only let you in because they know who you are. You think it's going to be that easy for anyone?"

"You're welcome, by the way, and yes, I do think it's going to be that easy for anyone, especially the guards. Renell, you have to understand that you can't trust anyone from Cay-Llek. They respect you for now, but if something goes wrong, they'll immediately turn on you. Anyone can come after you; there are no rules and no exceptions here."

She sighs. "I know, that's why the guards posted at my tent are from Lanckest, they were slaves that we freed."

"I stand corrected," I mutter, looking at the very interesting rug she has covering the dirt floor. Beautiful rug really, full of whimsical shapes and blue crescent moons.

"Wen?" Renell waves a hand in my face. "What did you need?"

"Ah, yes, Clòz will be sending a message to tell you that he accepts your challenge. I'm sure it will arrive by tomorrow."

Her face blanches and she averts her gaze. "The time has finally come then."

"Indeed, but with the knowledge we have, I think you can win. He's ruthless and twice your size, but you know his weaknesses and he knows nothing about you except the moniker others have given you." At her confused expression, I continue, "The Princess of Death." I smile.

"Interesting." She looks down at the map in front of her again, taking a deep breath. Her dark green eyes meet mine. "Thank you. I don't think I could have pulled this off without your knowledge and help."

Now she gets sappy on me.

"Thank you for saving my life, for giving me another chance to prove myself. I feel . . . freer than I ever have." Now I'm being sappy, but I am grateful for what she did. I'm grateful that I have something else to live for. Something else to fight for. I still have a lot of mistakes to make up for, but my life wouldn't be the same without Renell and Jarret, no matter how much I pester them.

She smiles. "Well, enough of that. We have a lot to prepare for. Can you help train me more?"

"I would be honored."

Dais

I watch Rahuin, waiting for her to say something, waiting for her to tell me she's okay, but how can she be okay? How is any of this okay? She's hardly spoken or eaten or cried since the wedding four days ago. I know she will never forget what happened, what Zenz did for her, but will she recognize his sacrifice? Will she accept that he believed her worthy enough to die for? Dark clouds hang from the sky with the ominous promise of spring rain. I hope it doesn't. The cold always makes my knee worse and it's already starting to ache. I lean against my cane to keep the pressure off as I walk beside Rahuin. The courtyard is sealed, and guards patrol the area to keep out unwanted visitors. Jet stands behind us a few paces. After the wedding, I can't be too careful. I can't let anything like that happen again.

The League stands ahead of us around a mountain of wood that will be Zenz's funeral pyre. I didn't know him that well, but his insight and willingness helped more times than I can count. I look back at Rahuin. Dark circles haunt her green eyes and her lips are downturned into a permanent frown. I don't know if she will ever smile again.

"Stop looking at me like I'm going to shatter into a million pieces," she whispers, red hair whipping over her pale face.

"Rahuin—"

"I'll be fine."

"You don't seem fine. You seem—"

"Broken? I am. He's dead because of me. He's dead because I love you. Because I tried to save you, because I tried to save them, because I came back. I'm holding it together, but only because of you and Sira. I'm terrified something else is going to happen, and this time, Zenz won't be here to protect me. How many more need to die just to keep me safe? I can't keep sacrificing them. I can't ju—"

"Let hate win?" I spit as anger blurs my vision. I still can't believe what my people attempted against my wife. My people. I can make excuses all I want for their actions—they did it for my father, they did it to protect me, they did it because they want someone to blame… but I can't forgive them. How could they think murder was the answer? When is murder ever good? If my father hadn't been murdered to get Rahuin to the Darkness, then this would have never happened. If she hadn't murdered thousands, Casta wouldn't be ours. Our freedom would be gone, but now she deals with the consequences of her actions. Murder is never right, no matter how much you intend it to be good.

"Dais—"

"No, the people who attacked you were in the wrong. We knew it was going to be a possibility when we decided to have a public wedding. We tried to prevent anything from happening and it's because of our preparation that we were able to keep you and Sira alive. Zenz knew what could happen when he jumped to save you. He was ready. He pledged to keep you safe and that's what he did." I guide Rahuin off toward the gardens so the others don't overhear. She's finally talking to me, and I want her to continue, even just for a little while. Lush emerald plants reach for the heavens all around us, waiting for the rain that will surely fall soon.

"What if I don't want them to die for me?" I know she's speaking of the League. "How is that okay?" She shakes my hand off, her eyes becoming more panicked with every second.

I shouldn't have pushed her, but I just needed to hear her voice. I needed to know she'd be okay. "I'm not saying it is, but they think you are worth it. Zenz loved you enough to sacrifice himself. Just like you loved them enough to fight." I point toward the gates, even though I know she knows who I'm talking about. She sacrificed herself to save them too, or did she forget because her power didn't destroy her like it could have?

"It doesn't feel like love. It feels like guilt. I know he cared for me, but the weight of his death will always be on my shoulders."

A breeze whistles among the trees around us, sounding like a lonely ghost wandering along the manicured plants and budding flowers.

"Is that all you care about? Because if it is, you are belittling his sacrifice. He didn't die for you to feel unworthy of what he did. He did it to give you a chance to live. Because he thought you were worth more himself. Don't belittle it. Grieve. Say goodbye. Cry over him, but don't believe you are unworthy of what he did, because he thought you were. He did it for you."

The mask that had replaced her face over the last four days shatters into a million pieces. I watch it break her features as she falls into my arms and starts to sob. I lean on my cane to keep myself steady, hating that I can't stand firm for her.

"I—I, it seems so—so unfair."

Tears smart in my eyes. "I know, but I just want to know you're okay. If you cry, if you grieve, I know you'll make it through this— we'll make it through this."

She pulls back, gasping as her fingers gently caress my cheek. "B—but should we make it through this? Are we meant to?"

"Rahuin—" What is she saying?

"I mean . . . is this right? Are we right? So much is against us, and I fear more will be against us. Why should we continue? Will it be the death of us both?"

"We've made it this far—"

"Yes, but at what cost? Why should you have to deal with my sins? Why should you have to suffer?" She starts crying again.

I hold her close. "Because I love you. No matter how much I suffer, I'm not letting you go. I won't. If I do, it will mean they won. It will mean hate and Darkness won, and I refuse to give them the satisfaction." Conviction settles in my chest like an anchor holding me to solid ground. A raindrop plops beside us, expanding onto the paved pathway.

"I'm just so scared, Dais. I'm so tired of fighting. I'm so tired of death, and I know it might get worse. As I fight, I find more people I love, and that means more people I can lose."

"So what will you do? Are you going to run like you did the first time? Are you going to leave me without you, without a reason to fight?" I ask, feeling my throat tighten. I don't want her to run again. I don't want her to think the only way she can protect me is to leave. She would just be trying to protect herself, a selfish desire to keep her heart intact. But I can't make her stay if she decides to leave. It would make me selfish to force her to face it.

"No . . . I—I'm not going to run. I just wanted you to know how I feel." She pulls away as the smell of rain caresses us.

I swallow the lump in my throat. "I'm sorry. I'm glad you told me, I—"

"You have every right to think I would run again. I don't want to keep fighting without you." She entwines my hand in hers, her broken, red eyes meeting mine.

"Are you ready?"

"No, but I will do my best to say goodbye." Her voice cracks on the last word. "I'm going to miss him so much. I'm going to miss his wisdom and the—the comfort his presence brought." She wipes at the salty streams that bleed down her face with the rain.

A guard moves over with an umbrella to shelter us from the sky's tears. "It's time, Your Majesty," he says.

I nod and grip Rahuin's hand tight as we head back to the courtyard.

Glena

It's not real. It can't be real. I'm staring at the wood that will soon become my father's funeral pyre, but I can't believe that it's even for him. He can't be gone. He can't. We didn't come all this way and survive this long just for him to be gone now. It was so sudden. I was up on the balcony making sure the rest of the royal family was safe. I saw the arrow. I screamed, but it was too late. He was already gone. Tears appear again, immediately falling down my cheeks. My eyes are so tired of crying they can't even well up anymore.

Frobin takes my hand, gripping my fingers like I might just vanish into thin air. That's what it feels like with my father gone. I've never been without him. He's always been here. What will I do without him? How will I make it through each day without his guidance? I swallow, squeezing Frobin's fingers back. I've exhausted all of these questions, but I have no answers. How can I, when I have no idea what this reality looks like? How can I say goodbye when I don't believe it? I'm frozen.

Rahuin and Dais appear, their faces solemn, their heads turned in whispers none of us can hear. Heat grips my stomach, crawling over my skin in wrath as I watch them. He's gone because of her. Because he saved her, and she doesn't even look sorry. She doesn't act sorry for taking him from me, but maybe that's what she does. She took Dais's father away from him too. How could he forgive her? How can he stand to be anywhere near her?

Why did my father save her? Because of a prophecy? Wasn't it already fulfilled when she destroyed the Darkness's army? Why did he believe her life was more important than his? How could he have been so reckless?

"Glena." Frobin shakes my arm as he weaves our hands together.

I look away from Rahuin, not even trying to soften my glare as I look up at him. "What?"

"Nothing, I just want you to be careful. You're looking at her like you might kill her."

"She took him away, Frobin. That's not easy to forgive." A breeze sends short strands of hair swirling around my vision, carrying the scent of rain with it. At least the sky will mourn for Father.

"She didn't do anything. Zenz would have died protecting anyone. Why do you think he fought?"

I look back toward Rahuin and Dais, but they've disappeared. "I don't care. Why were we fighting to begin with? She destroyed the Darkness's army, and the King of Light still hasn't come back. Is it all just a lie? Did we fight for nothing? Did I lose my father for nothing?" I screech, pointing at the pyre as my whole body shakes with the weight of my words. I'm so tired of all my thoughts. None of them make any sense, and yet, they make all the sense in the world. I just want someone to tell me the truth. What is all this for?

"Not for nothing! I don't think we're anywhere near the end of the fight. We can't give up after one victory. The war is still ongoing. The Darkness is still moving, and he won't stop until the King comes back and defeats him. Zenz believed in that. Why don't you? Why are you looking at Rahuin as if she had something to do with it? She loved Zenz as much as we did—"

"Not as much as I do! No one loves him as much as do! She took him away, so she must pay for what she did." I rip my hand out of his.

"Glena!" He grips my shoulders, forcing me to look into his gray eyes. "What are you saying? Do you want his sacrifice to be in vain? Because it will be if you do anything to harm her!"

I break down into sobs, my shoulders hunching under the burden of grief. I can't breathe. I can't move. I can't do this. She has to pay. She has to feel my pain. "I—I can't do this without him. I can't live without h—him." Rain starts to fall around us, but we make no effort to escape it. Good. Let it kill me. Let it be the end of me.

"Glena, this isn't you. You are strong and you are going to be okay. He wouldn't want you to fall apart. He knew what would happen when he jumped in front of the arrow. He knew he would die, and he knew if that happened, we would be okay. We're going to be okay. We're going to get through this together," he whispers, but his words sound meaningless to me. I don't feel like I'm strong enough.

Behind him, I catch a glimpse of Rahuin and Dais, hand in hand . . . alive. I wipe my face as servants appear with umbrellas to block the rain. I look up at Frobin, but I don't see him. Instead, I see red. I see hurt. I see blood. I wonder if he sees it on my face, but he's not looking at me. He's watching the pallbearers as they carry my father's body out on a handled pallet, setting it on top of the pyre. I don't see that either. I can't bear to look, and when Frobin hands me the torch to light the wood on fire—all I see are the flames.

Rahuin

I watch the flames lick Zenz's remains. Tears stream down my cheeks as I watch the orange tongues reach to the cloudy sky. Raindrops sizzle as they meet the flames and the smell of burning flesh permeates the cool tone of rain. I catch sight of Glena across from me, her eyes trained on me instead of her father's body. Her brow is drawn in a poisonous expression, drowning her blue gaze in darkness. White wisps of hair graze her face and stick to her skin where the rain has left its mark. Even against the warm flames, my blood runs cold. I've seen this before in a vision, then I didn't know who we were mourning.

"You are doomed. Doomed. Doomed . . ." The words ring through my head. *". . . you will always destroy . . ."*

Shivers trail down my skin. Dais notices and pulls me closer to him, but I don't feel his warmth. All I feel is the cold . . . the fear. I did this. I continue to destroy. I remember the rest of the vision—everyone I love kneeling in their own blood. I tremble, curling around Dais. They'll die because of me. They'll die, and everything I've done to keep them safe will be in vain.

I try to shake the images away, but they remain, replaying in an endless loop . . . *Dais's blue eyes dulled in defeat as his hand tries to hold back a stream of blood from his stomach. Tears stream down Thesa's face as she weeps over someone in her arms. Jarret stares at me with a dead expression on his face as flames billow behind him . . .* I forgot them after getting back from the Darkness. I thought my sacrifice—the men I killed—would save them from the fate I saw, but I was wrong. The fate continues. Nothing I did changed it. Zenz died after my sacrifice. If I'd changed anything, he wouldn't have died.

"Are you going to run like you did the first time?"

Dais's words ring through my head. No. No. I won't run. I can't. Not after all this. *But if you stay . . .* The visions will come true. If I stay, they will die. I want to scream. I want to silence my thoughts, but they keep coming. They keep feeding my fears, forcing me to fight or flee. I will fight. I won't flee. I won't let the Darkness win. I won't let the fear control me.

I look back at Glena, but she's disappeared.

"You took him from me. Now, I will make you feel the same," a voice whispers beside my ear. I don't have enough time to react as my eyes catch the flash of a metal blade, but it isn't aiming for me . . .

"No!" I scream, pushing Glena away as her dagger slashes Dais.

Her blue eyes are feral as they meet mine. "You must pay!" she howls, swinging the dagger from side to side as Jet jumps in front of me, knocking the weapon from her hands.

Guards rush at her, grabbing her from behind as she screams, kicking and trying to escape, but I don't wait to see what else happens. I turn to Dais, who lies on the ground, his cane thrown to the side.

Please no. Please not Dais.

"Dais!" I fall down beside him, and he lifts his head, his blue eyes clear and alert. He's fine. Tears start down my face without consent. He's alive!

Jet drops down beside me, his dark eyes observing the rest of the area.

"I'm fine. I'm fine," Dais gasps. "It was just a scratch." Blood covers his hand from a cut on his side, the red marring his blue tunic.

Flashes of my vision blur in my mind as I nod, reaching for his cane to help him up. He leans heavily against me before taking the prop with a wince. His looks at Glena, who has her hands tied behind her back now, knees in the mud, and white hair plastered against her face in wet strands.

"Take her to the dungeon," Dais tells the guards beside her.

"No!" Frobin, who is being held down by guards as well, yells. His wide eyes search mine. "Please."

Peggy kneels beside him. "Frobin, stop fighting. She attempted assassination on the king. They won't take it lightly."

"Let him go," I say, heading over to them.

They release him, and Frobin meets me in the middle. "Rahuin, please. She didn't mean it. She didn't—she's so blinded by her grief. She's not in her right mind. Please," he begs, raindrops falling off his red beard.

Thesa appears by my side, gently grabbing my wet sleeve. "Rahuin, we must go."

I nod before looking back at Frobin. "I'll see what I can do, but it's up to Dai—" I wince as pain stabs my lower abdomen.

"Rahuin?" Thesa's worried voice draws my gaze to hers.

I straighten my stance before another stabbing pain appears and I double over. No. Not Sira. "I—I'm okay . . ." I swallow. But is Sira?

Shallow breaths escape my lips as my heart palpitates. I have to remain calm. I can't lose her, not now. I look back to find Jet ushering Dais into the castle.

Thesa wraps her arms around me, her eyes speaking more words than she can voice. She knows I'm not okay. She knows Sira isn't okay. "Hurry." She rushes me inside, yelling at someone to call a physician and get some linens warmed and put immediately into my room. My legs feel as thick as mud as she practically drags me down the hall. Why do I feel so weak? Please no. No. No.

"What's happening? I—"

"Frobin," Thesa cuts him off, continuing down the hall. "I promise we'll help Glena. Please be patient. Rahuin's pregnant, but if we don't get her to lie down right now, she could lose the baby."

I catch a glimpse of Frobin's pale face as he freezes in the hall at Thesa's words. Peggy stands beside him, pulling him away. Thesa ushers me into my room where servants are already bustling around. They immediately strip me of my wet dress and underthings.

"Dais," I gasp, looking at Thesa.

"I'll get him. Don't worry."

The servants take my clothes away, but not before I see blood on them.

No.

Tears well in my eyes, blurring everything around me. The fear remains. She's gone. She can't be gone. *Please God, no.* The prayer embeds itself in my mind.

"Get Dais! Get King Dais now!" Thesa screams as I slump into her arms.

The darkness closes in.

"What did I tell you, Rahuin? All you do is destroy. You made a deal with me. You broke it, and I intend to make good on my promise. Don't you remember?" His gray fingers caress my neck, but I'm too broken to fight back.

"Ten times the suffering," I whisper, my voice ragged.

"That's right." He tightens his grip, and I gasp as the air disappears from my lungs. It feels like I'm drowning.

I look up into his black, soulless eyes. "Kill me." End it all. Let it be over now.

A sinister smile breaks his ghastly face. "Not yet. Suffering can't happen when you're dead."

He releases me, and I gasp, coughing as I try to breathe.

"I'll see you soon, Rahuin."

"Mother. Wake up. Look at me. Come on, you can't be that tired," a voice says, but it's one I don't recognize. Birds and insects chattering in the background accompany the cadence.

I open my eyes to find a young man staring at me. He has to be around seventeen or eighteen. Giant blue eyes and a mop of fiery red curls cascade over a freckled face. Sideburns reach down his jawline and he smiles as I look him over.

"Who are you?" I ask, sitting up. Evergreen and deciduous trees tower over us in a curtain of gorgeous foliage. Flowers and grasses sway beside us, filling the air with a sweet scent. I breathe deeply, wondering if I'm dead.

His smile widens. "Mother, don't be like that, you know who I am." He sits back, setting his elbows on his knees as he sticks a piece of grass in between his teeth.

Mother. He called me mother. My heart starts to pound and tears appear in my eyes. It's a dream, a vision, but why do I feel so sad?

So undeniably sad. This vision doesn't feel anything like the ones I've seen Sira in. Those are always warm, happy.

"Elrian?" I whisper the name, but I don't know where it came from. Somehow I know it's his name. I lean closer to him and lift my hand to his face, stroking his cheek. My son. A weight settles on my chest, and I finally realize why this vision isn't like Sira's. The pain. I blacked out. I miscarried. He's dead, and this is goodbye. He just doesn't know it.

"Why are you crying?" He wipes my cheek. His finger against my face feels so real, but I know it never will be.

"Oh, my son. My beautiful boy." I pull him into my arms, hugging him close like a baby even though he's bigger than me.

"Mother, what's going on?" His voice cracks. "You're acting strange."

"Nothing. I—just let me hold you for a moment," I whisper, and as I hold him, he starts to shrink until he's a little infant squealing in my arms with a face as red as his hair. My face flushes as heavy sobs rack my entire body. A shadow passes over me, and I look up to see him—the man who appeared when I was with the Darkness. Once again, light seems to emanate from him. His presence is warm, covering me like a blanket on a cold night. He kneels in front of me, tears in his swirling brown and blue eyes as he reaches for Elrian.

"No," I gasp. "No, please don't take him. You said—you said it would be over soon. Why am I in so much pain? Why am I still fighting? Why?" I hold Elrian to my chest, but his cries have stopped. No, no, no. Not again. I feel the pieces of my heart shattering. This isn't happening. He promised. Why did he lie?

"Let me have him, Rahuin. Let him be with me. I will take good care of him. I promise you will see him again. I promise." The man's words steady me, filling me with peace I can't explain. He didn't lie. It's not over yet. I still have to fight, but I can't take Elrian with me. I kiss Elrian's forehead.

"I love you," I whisper. "I'll miss you every day, and I . . . I know you'll be safe." I shakily hand my son over to the man.

He stands and starts to walk away. As he leaves, Elrian becomes the young man again, looking back at me with a smile. A contagious

grin that warms yet breaks my heart.
      "I'll see you soon, Mother."

I gasp awake, finding healers standing over me. They open their mouths to speak, but I already know what they're going to say.

Chapter 17
How to Keep Fighting

Thesa

"Thesa! What's going on?" Dais rushes into the room, cane tapping on the floor. Jet follows behind him, lips pressed in a firm line as he meets my gaze. Dais halts beside me. He wears a new green tunic and I'm sure a clean bandage on his wound.

"What happened?" His throat bobs as his eyes look past me to Rahuin. A physician, healer, and midwife surround her bed as they work to assess her condition.

"Dais . . ." I start, but I don't know how to tell him what happened. I can't bring myself to say it. He starts forward, but I jump to stop him. "Let them finish. She's unconscious anyway."

"Is it the Darkness?" he asks, his face pale.

I shake my head. "I—I . . . no. She's . . . she may have miscarried the baby."

He stumbles, leaning on his cane as both Jet and I move to catch him. He holds a hand up. "I'm okay," he rasps, sad eyes blurring as he looks at Rahuin. He starts to shake his head. "I can't. I—please not this too."

Jet reaches for him, pulling him into an embrace. "Let's step out. Let them work."

"I can't." Dais clings to Jet like he's a breath of air to starved lungs.

"Dais, you can't do anything for now. Let's pray for the best." Jet leads him toward the door, throwing a glance back at me, and I don't miss the stoop of his shoulders as they leave. I almost follow to assure my mate that what happened today wasn't his fault, but I know it won't be of use. Dais needs him right now, and Jet will do anything to make up for what happened today. My heart feels like it might shatter as I watch them work over Rahuin. The pale blue curtains over the bedframe wisp at the bustle of movement, reminding me of serpents ready to strangle me.

First Zenz, then Dais, now Rahuin . . . and all because of fear. My vision blurs as I think about Glena. I promised Frobin we'd get her out, but I don't know how. She did an unspeakable act, and I fear that if Rahuin loses the baby, there'll be nothing we can do to pardon her. I'm afraid Dais will never forgive her for lashing out in grief. How could so much happen in such a short time? Everything seemed to be resolving, moving toward peace. Why is there so much brokenness now?

I blink away my tears. This is what happens when the world is against you—when you decide to fight back. Rahuin fought back, and now she's paying the price. Dais is paying the price because he loves her, and Zenz paid the price for what the people think Rahuin did. It's an endless, vicious cycle.

The door opens behind me. "What's going on? Someone told me Rahuin is hurt. I—" Aleetha races into the room but stops when she sees me. Not her. I can't deal with her right now. "What happened, Thesa?" Tears materialize in her eyes.

I steel myself, taking a deep breath. "We're not sure yet, but they'll let us know soon."

"Don't lie to me. I saw Dais. Tell me what happened." Her brow wrinkles as she clenches her jaw.

This is why I can't deal with her. She's so demanding. Can't she see we're all grieving?

"Rahuin may have miscarried the baby," I whisper, and it's a wonder she even hears me.

Her mouth falls agape as a shuddering breath leaves her lips. "Are you sure?"

"I told you I'm not sure." I glance at Rahuin. "We must wait until they tell us."

Aleetha follows my gaze, but doesn't move, tears streaming down her face silently. "Please tell me what they say. I'm going to get Henry." She hides her quivering lips by pressing them into a firm, thin line.

I nod, and then she's gone. A gasp from the healers draws my attention, and I hurry toward them. Rahuin tries to lift her head, wide eyes focused on the midwife who starts to speak.

"Your Majesty, you—"

"I know," Rahuin rasps as moisture fills her gaze. "Please, leave me." She rolls onto her side, and the healers glance at one another before the midwife nods.

"Let's go. There is nothing more to do." They start to leave, but I reach for the midwife, gently touching her shoulder.

"What happened?"

She glances at Rahuin, sighing softly before she speaks. "I'm certain the queen had a miscarriage, but she didn't expel the child. I've seen this happen when a mother is pregnant with twins and loses one. I believe the other baby is fine, but we shall see when the time comes. For now, she needs rest. I will tell the king." She leaves, and I head to Rahuin's side. Tears and snot run down her face, gathering on her pillow. Her unfocused eyes stare at the curtains, but I'm certain she isn't seeing them.

"Thesa," she whispers, and I lean close. "Please leave. I'm sorry. I—I only want Dais."

I nod. "He'll be here soon." I touch her shoulder, hating to leave her when she's like this. All my motherly instincts tell me to stay, but that's not what she wants. I start for the door, meeting Dais just outside. His eyes are red from crying.

"She asked for you." My voice cracks as I pull him into a hug. "I'm so sorry."

He nods, releasing me as he heads into the room.

I stand in the hall for a while staring at Jet. He looks so broken, so tired. I rush toward him, pulling him into my arms. I just need someone to cling to, and I know he needs it too.

He says nothing and soon his tears meld with mine.

Dais

I wait till Rahuin falls asleep before slipping out of the room. I slump against the door once it's closed. A son. I had a son, and I'll never get to meet him—not until I've been borne to the Gateway of Light. Rahuin said his name was Elrian, and that he looked just like her. Tears well in my eyes again, but I blink them away. They never seem to end. They're always around, always ready to fall. Some see it as a weakness, but I see it as a release. Although, I don't have much more time for release.

I clench my fists, knocking the back of my head against the door with a hollow thud. I should go back in there, but I don't want to. I need time. I've lost a child before I even knew he would be here. Sira is still alive, at least Rahuin believes she is, and the midwife confirmed it with similar pregnancies she'd seen before. How quickly could we lose her too? My gut clenches. If we lose Sira too, I fear Rahuin will join them. Sira is one of the only things keeping her tethered to this world. She says that I anchor her too, but if Sira doesn't survive . . .

Footfalls resound down the amber hall, pulling me from my thoughts. Lit chandeliers above try to add a hint of light to the darkness surrounding me, but I hardly see it. The darkness is all I know now as the shadows have become more comforting than the light. Because the light has come at too high a cost to keep.

Aunt Aleetha turns into the corridor and stops when she sees me. "How is she?"

I step away from the door. "She's asleep. You can go in." I head along the opposite end of the hall.

"Dais." Her voice stops me as she moves beside me. "I hate to ask this of you, but with the recent scares, I—Henry and I have been thinking . . . Well, we'd like to take Rahuin back to Färrin with us. Just until she is recovered, until everything settles down here."

No. I want to say no, but I know she can't continue like this, and if she tries, Sira might pay the price. I can't lose them both. "I think that would be best." I nod, hoping it will convince me, hoping the sick feeling in my gut will go away, but it doesn't. "I don't want her to go, but this place . . . she's not safe here, and if she loses Sira on top of all this—" My voice cracks, and I look away from my aunt's hopeful eyes, drawing in a deep breath to compose myself. I still can't escape the tears.

Aunt Aleetha rubs my arm. "I know. I hate to take her away from you because I know you need her just as much as she needs you, but I wouldn't ask if it wasn't detrimental."

"I understand. Really, Aunt Aleetha, I do. Please take her to Färrin."

"I promise she'll be back before Sira is born, and hopefully by then, things will have calmed down."

I wish that will be the case, but I don't know now. The hope I had in my people's forgiveness died with Zenz. I nod, and Aunt Aleetha holds me. I don't even try to fight the tears this time.

"Promise me you'll lean on your family while she's gone. Promise me you'll be okay too. Otherwise I won't take her away from you."

"I—I promise. We'll both make it through this," I whisper, though I'm not sure the words are true. David, Mother, and Jet are all I have left, but I'm not sure how I'll lean on them. I don't want them to bear these burdens too, but I can't tell that to Aunt Aleetha. Rahuin needs this. Sira needs this. I can't afford to be selfish because I want them close.

She releases me, and the chandeliers overhead shine rainbow lights on her skin where the crystal meets the flames. "I'll send you updates."

"Thank you, Aunt Aleetha."

She nods and leaves, the steady click of her heels echoing down the hall. I sigh, my thoughts lingering on what I promised Aunt

Aleetha. We'll be all right. But then Rahuin's words come back to me . . . *how long do we keep fighting?* I close my eyes. We can't afford to stop. We've already lost too much . . . but will we lose more? Will we survive if we do?

David

It's all coming true. Can't you see. She'll destroy everything. We have to stop her. We can do it. We can make this suffering end . . .

Voices whisper in my mind, but I hardly hear them. The cold creeps in, and this time, I welcome it. I'm not scared of it anymore. It can't control me.

But what if we are? What if you've already lost control . . .

I refuse to believe it, but when I open my eyes, I find myself outside Dais's room. He's talking to Aunt Aleetha. She wants to take Rahuin away. Good. Maybe she'll keep Rahuin there forever and our family will finally be at peace. Dais will finally have peace.

Wait?

How did I get out here again? Why am I watching my brother? What's happening and why do I want Rahuin to leave?

Dais nearly died today because of her. It's an endless cycle. She should never come back. We should make sure she never comes back.

Dais almost died? Is that why I'm here? Surely, I just came to check on him, but a sinking feeling in my gut tells me that can't possibly be true. Something isn't right. Maybe this is just a dream. A sick reality born out of fear, but whose fear am I seeing? Dais's? Rahuin's? My own?

I stumble against the wall to my right, the teal color accenting amber filigree. My palm digs into a swirl of complicated flowers, but they come alive, wrapping around my hand and pulling me inside. Darkness blankets my vision, but maybe my eyes are just closed.

Why do I want to make sure Rahuin never comes back? Why do the voices always seem to be right? Didn't they tell me once that she would cause death and destruction to all of Casta? Is that what's happening? Why did Dais marry her then? Didn't I try to stop him?

Yes, you did . . . well, we did.

Thousands of sparkling white lights illuminate the darkness like the stars coming alive. They dance around me until they form a picture.

But how? How did I try to stop him? Clearly, we didn't succeed, or Rahuin wouldn't have almost killed him today.

I watch the lights fade and grow until I'm watching a scene playing out. I'm in the castle barracks talking to generals and the captain of the guard. The scene shifts, and now we're in the armory. What? When was this? Did this really happen or is it another dream?

No answers appear to counter my thoughts. Just like always . . . I can't get a straight, clear answer to anything I see or experience. The scene shifts again. It's dark, but I can tell that the generals and I are in the big chapel in Morough. My pulse quickens, but I don't understand why this is important. Why should this be important? Why can't I ever remember?

Maybe it's just another fear I've seen, another dream I've experienced from someone else. A vision that someone doesn't want to come true.

Don't you remember? We tried to stop him. We did what you told us to.

The stars shimmer until the scene vanishes and blinding light envelops me until I'm forced to close my eyes. But my eyes are already closed. I'm asleep. I'm dreaming. I can't wake up. I can't—

I wake with a gasp, cold sweat freezing my skin. The moonlight seeping from the windows illuminates the puffy white clouds I breathe out.

No!

My fingers fumble against my bed's comforter as I reach toward the other side. Peggy's skin is fire under my frozen fingertips, and I melt against her side.

"David?" Her voice is heavy with sleep, and she shivers against me. She turns, her fingers finding my cheek. They feel so cold, or maybe it's just me. Her eyes meet mine, her cheeks rosy in the chilly air. Warmth blankets us as her skin starts to glow orange with her gift, filling the hollow cavity of my frigid chest.

I wrap my arms around her, pulling her closer to me.

She kisses my neck. "You're safe. You're warm. It was just a dream."

For everyone's sake, I hope that's true. I hope what I saw was just a vision . . . just part of my gift. We're set to leave in a few days to start searching for the nymphs. We have a few leads and places where we can start. Frobin is sending a few Fenrir to accompany us and help us destroy any camps we find—if they're still there. I hope they are. I hope answers exist for my gift. I hope it can be used for good, but what if I'm wrong? What if it's nothing but evil? What if all I'm meant for is evil? No. That can't be true. Anything can be used for good or evil, I just have to prove it. But I'm terrified of finding out that it's all a lie. Maybe evil is all there is.

Carrie

CITY OF PËR, KÄS

Wake up. Wake up, Carrie. You have to find me. You're the only one who can. There is no way to you. The portals are closed. Find me before it's too late. Hurry . . .

My eyelids are heavy and it seems to take all my strength to open them. A flickering kerosene lamp lies to my right. My heart jolts. I gasp, sitting up when I don't recognize the place I'm in. The rush sends my head floating. I feel like I've started swimming in the ocean—more like drowning. Stars spot my visions, and I blink to push them away so I can see where I am.

It's not uncommon for me to wake up in unfamiliar places, but I usually have some vague memory of falling asleep in said unfamiliar place. I don't remember any of this . . . My thoughts trail off when I turn my head to find Aiden lying beside me. My breath elevates. Is he dead? Why is he here to begin with?

I move closer to him and set my finger against his neck, checking for a pulse. His skin isn't cold, so I'm certain he's okay. This reasoning is confirmed when I feel the faintest of movements under his skin. I release the breath I'm holding. He's alive, for now . . . *and so are you.* The thought sends a new wave of panic through my bones, and all the memories from the previous night come rushing back— King Rave's words, me somehow finding Aiden, the pain. I instinctively touch my heart, just to see if it's still there. *Of course it's there, Carrie. You wouldn't be alive right now if it wasn't.* I can't argue with the logic, but lately, I haven't been able to decipher what is real or not, especially since my run in with the Walks.

I lean back as I stare at Aiden. I'm alive. That means Rave was right. Aiden is very powerful. My heart clenches. Some part of me wishes he hadn't been strong enough to save me, but then he'd be dead too. He doesn't deserve that. No one deserves to die at the hands of someone else. King Rave almost killed me. He believed Aiden was strong enough to save me. Shivers race down my spine. He was willing to sacrifice me to find out. *"You're dispensable, Carrie . . ."*

My stomach churns while Aiden sleeps. I didn't get the chance to think about it because I was knocking on the gates of Astyria once Rave relinquished his gift over me, but I wish I hadn't come here. I wish I hadn't placed my life in Aiden's hands. I should have just quietly went to die, that way the decision of my life didn't fall on his doorstep, literally. As a medic, it's probably hard for him not to help anyone in need. The thought only makes me feel worse, that means he didn't have a choice. He had to help me.

I look around his flat, although it's hardly large enough to be called that, it's more like a room. A bed lies behind me, ruffled from sleep where I'm sure Aiden was resting when I so rudely barged in. A desk with dried herbs hanging above it sits to my right, and a small kitchen with a stove stands to my left a little bit away from where Aiden lies face-down beside me. I should probably move him. It's not good for him to lie like that. I lean over, gently shifting him onto his back.

He mumbles something before sweat beads on his brow and he starts to scream. Not like a gentle 'I'm still asleep' scream, no, more like a 'I'm falling to my death' scream. I wince, and my heart rate speeds up as I jump to my feet, facing the door as if danger's about to come crashing through. The hair raises on my skin, and I shudder before deciding nothing is coming to harm us and sink down to my knees.

Aiden is mumbling again when I place a hand across his forehead. His skin feels like an inferno. How do you heal a Lifewalker? That's literally they're ability. It must suck to have such a powerful ability that you can't even help yourself with.

His eyes fly open, and I freeze, feeling slightly embarrassed he caught me with my hand still on his forehead. I snap it back to my side, willing my cheeks not to blush.

He stares at me, blurry-eyed for a moment before he blinks and closes his eyes with a sigh. I watch his throat bob as he swallows before looking away, suddenly feeling like this scene is too intimate.

"Wa—Wa—"

I look back at him. "What am I doing here?" I lean over him.

"Wa—"

"What happened?"

He narrows his bright blue eyes, and suddenly I feel like a stupid kid being scolded by an angry parent. Who knew an unspeakable Aiden Brachus would look so menacing?

"Water," he gasps.

This time my face does flush, because now I feel completely embarrassed that I couldn't figure out what he wanted beforehand. I'm usually not this ditsy, but waking up in a strange place after your king just tried to kill you can make anyone a little ditsy. I stand up, rushing over to his little kitchen area. I hand crank water into a bucket by the faucet and grab a glass before heading back over to him.

He's sitting up now and takes the cup from me with a grunt. After a few sips, he sets it down, looking up at me. "Well, don't just stand there, help me up." He rolls his eyes, lifting his hand.

I take it, pulling him to his feet. He looks down at me. Huh, with him lying on the floor, I forgot how tall he is. Somehow, I'm staring at his throat again.

I meet his gaze. "Sorry, I'm a little—um, slow," I whisper, feeling the blush coming back. *Stop it Carrie, you're way more confident than this.* Yeah? Well, I nearly died. I don't know about most people but that kinda takes all your confidence and throws it out a window. Especially since I had to rely on someone I barely knew to save my life.

A smile quirks his upper lip, dimpling the left side of his cheek, and part of me hates that I notice. *I shouldn't have come here . . .*

"I was just teasing you. The other questions you came up with are entirely valid. I probably should be wondering how you got here and what happened, but I already know the answers to those, so the questions didn't quite seem relevant."

"Right." I nod. Now he's just rubbing it in. Is he always this cocky after saving someone's life? Or maybe it's just because he saved my life. I know he's not exactly my biggest fan after I revealed my deception, but then again, I haven't exactly thanked him.

"Thank you . . . for saving me." I force myself to stare into those blue eyes. I wish I had something I could compare them to. They don't remind me of the sea or the sky, but they are refreshing, like a cool drink of water, or a hot meal after a cold day. *Great Carrie, now you're comparing his eyes to a meal. I think you're just hungry.* That's probably true.

His refreshing gaze softens, and this time, he's the one who looks away. "I can't deny help to anyone. Even though I have an idea as to why you're here."

I nod. "Rave cut me off. He still wants me to infiltrate you, but…" I trail off. I can't. It's as simple as that. Rave can threaten me all he wants, but now that he's set me free, I don't have to report to him. I have nothing that he can hold over my head. Nothing he can use to motivate me, because everyone I used to love is already gone. "I'm not going back there. He can hunt me down all he wants. He can leave me to die or kill me himself. I don't care because I'm finally free!" I laugh before tears shine in my eyes and I smile. "I'm free!" I hug Aiden, and he tenses. I'm so excited, I don't care that he's the only person I know who I can share the news with.

"You wouldn't have come to me if you weren't scared of death."

His words feel like a punch to my gut, and I release him, taking a step back as my shoulders slump under the weight of conviction. "You're right. I do care if he comes after me. I do care if I die. So maybe you're right, I will continue to report back to him. I will sell you out. I will force you to do something you don't want to do," I whisper as I start for the door.

"Carrie." He grabs my wrist. "I didn't mean it like that. I just—"

"Does anybody really want to die, Aiden?" I whirl on him, finding those eyes. It infuriates me that they still seem calming. I wish they wouldn't. I wish they would appear sinister and cold, maybe then his words wouldn't hurt so much. "Even though I really have nothing to live for, a part of me longs to live, to see my life through, to find love and get married and start a family—all those fantasies that I know will never be mine. I still crave them, but I won't endanger you just to fulfill my selfishness. I'll leave. I'll keep walking until I drop de—" I stop as a new idea dawns on me. Dead. Rave sent me here with the hope that Aiden could heal me, but he doesn't actually know Aiden can. I might as well be dead to him.

I stare at Aiden with wide eyes. "I'm dead!"

Aiden scrunches his brow. "Carrie? You're not—"

"No, let me explain!" I shout, dancing around him in my excitement. "Rave sent me here to see if you could save me, but he doesn't actually know you can save me. So what if I—"

"Fake your death?" He lifts blond eyebrows.

"Yes! What if we make Rave believe I'm actually dead? Then I'll be free for good! I'll never have to report to him."

He nods, and I can see the gears grinding in his mind before he starts to shake his head. "It won't work."

My heart sinks. "What do you mean? Of course it wi—"

"Carrie, I don't think I healed you for good. What if you leave and a few days from now, your disease comes back worse? I mean I don't know for sure, but if you go away and I'm not there to save you . . ." he trails off, running a hand through his short hair.

"Then I most definitely will die. It doesn't matter. I still want to fake my death. I don't want Rave to get his hands on me again. If that means losing my freedom so I can stay alive by your side, then I will." It's only transferring me from one master to another, but I'd rather it be Aiden than Rave.

"That's assuming I'll let you stay by my side."

"You're the one who said you couldn't deny anyone help." I got him there.

He smiles, his blue eyes transforming as mischief overtakes them. "You think we can pull this off?"

I nod. "I know we can."

Aiden

ÄLBRECT CASTLE, KÄS

"Did you get my gift?" King Rave asks as I enter his office. A few generals stand in the corner, some shooting me condescending looks. Gold and black tapestries hang from the ceiling making the room look more like a dungeon than an office. Yikes. Rave's sense of style is always eccentric. I think it's to show off his wealth, but if anyone ever knew, he wouldn't survive one day out in the world. That's why he never leaves and has all his little minions come to him. I guess that makes me a minion, but what else am I really? A puppet on a string. Hopefully after today, he'll have no more strings to pull.

"Your Majesty?" I question, glancing at his generals who are still looking me over.

"Ah, right." He smiles, his dark eyes poised like a viper as he waves a hand at them. "Leave us."

They drag their feet toward the exit. Clearly, they want to stay and hear the gossip of an unconscious woman arriving on my doorstep. The door closes behind them with a satisfying click. I almost smirk, but then remember I can't show any joyful emotions in front of Rave. He likes fear. He feeds off it, like a leach.

"So . . . my gift?" His fingers tap against a gold and black painted teacup with depictions of ravens flying in the sky. He sure is full of himself with all the raven artwork. Maybe he should just become a raven, then I wouldn't have to put up with his endless mind games.

I swallow. *Sell the story, Aiden.* "She . . . I—she's gone, Your Majesty. I tried to save her, but . . . I've had her body taken to the morgue." I really did stash her in a morgue. "She—um—does she have a family? Anyone who should know?" I allow tears to well in my eyes. *Good job, Aiden, you are a doctor who has lost his patient you feel. You . . .*

"Really? You'd cry over someone you don't even know?" He lifts dark brows.

I blink away the tears. "I'm sorry, Your Majesty. For being someone who has empathy when someone dies. A life was lost. I don't think that's fair at all and the least I could do is shed a few tears in remembrance of someone whose life has been cut short."

"Hmm." He smirks. "I'll have to admit it, Brachus. You're quite the actor. I don't believe you. I know what your gift can do, even if you deny it or pretend."

I wrinkle my brows. *Another mind game, Aiden. He's reaching. He's trying to get you to fall into his trap.* "Your Majesty, I don't understand what you are saying. You sent me a young woman to heal, but I couldn't save her. Do you want to rub my failures into my face? Do you—"

He starts to laugh at me, the cadence becoming more maniacal. "You think I'm an idiot, Brachus? I'm tethered to Carrie. I've used my ability on her for years. I'll know when she's truly dead. I know what she's feeling all the time."

Great, the one time I offer to help fake someone's death, she's tethered to a psycho. A sick feeling worms its way into my stomach, stronger than my fear of him finding out I lied. Does Carrie know the extent of his perversion? Does she understand what he's done to her? I doubt she knows, otherwise, we wouldn't have tried.

He smiles at the look on my face.

"You're sick."

"No, you're sick for trying to lie to your king." I want to tell him he's not my king, that I will never see him as a voice of authority, but I'm in no position to retort, neither is Carrie. He continues, "But no matter, don't tell Carrie I know." Yeah, so you can continue your sick mind games. "Let her think she's free. I have no use for her now that I know what you can do. I'm excited for the future, Brachus. Now go home, and if you tell her, I will kill her. So be ready to obey when I call. You should never to lie to me again. I know all, and what I want will be achieved as I see fit."

I stand. "Then if you are finished, Your Majesty, I'd like to leave. I won't tell Carrie because I don't believe in wasting innocent lives. I will do as you ask."

"Good. We finally understand each other, Brachus." He takes another sip from his garish cup.

I head to the door. No, I don't understand you at all. I'll never understand a terrible tyrant. I'll never become like you, and I will do everything in my power to fight you and destroy your crooked empire.

Chapter 18
The Monster Under the Bed

Renell

I stare into the mirror, my gift glowing under my skin and lighting up my veins in an almost pink hue. My tent surrounds me with a homey warmth—a little solace created by thick furs stretched over wooden poles. Crude candles glow, creating light in the dark hovel. I should be outside overseeing the camp as we get ready to move a little farther north toward Cizarrél, but I had to confirm my suspicions.

I lift my shirt, following the flow of pink. My vision blurs as I watch the lights entwine and ball up in a very small circuit low in my belly. I gently touch my stomach. My heart soaring as I blink away tears. I'm pregnant. Shivers breakout on my skin, shooing away my newfound elation. I have to fight Clòz in a few days. What will happen to my baby? Will it survive the fight?

I take a deep breath. The baby is small enough. We'll be okay. Either way, I shouldn't let my fear destroy this wonderful news. Jarret is going to be so happy.

Light floods the tent as Jarret moves aside the thick furs and steps inside.

"Were your ears burning?" I ask.

"Were you thinking about me?" He narrows his eyes. "While you admire yourself in the mirror?" He moves over to me and plants a kiss on my forehead. "You should. Beauty should be admired." He tosses his black and blue hair, winking at his reflection.

I scoff. "Yes, especially your exceptional beauty."

He turns, looking down into my eyes. "Hmm, look at that, she's even more beautiful when I'm not looking in the mirror. Mirrors obviously tell lies. You can't trust them."

I nod, blushing. "Definitely."

He kisses me then, drawing me closer.

I sigh, melting into his embrace before I pull away. "I have something to tell you." My lips brush against his.

A smile teases his face, drawing his eyes down. "What?"

I lean close, whispering in his ear. "I'm pregnant."

His jaw drops, eyes widening. "Really?"

"Really. I haven't been feeling well in the mornings and I had an inkling that something was different, so I checked. That's why I was staring at the mirror." My fingers entwine in his long hair.

His hand cups my stomach and tears flood his eyes. "Really? We're—"

I smile, my own tears shining once again. "Yes."

A chuckle escapes his lips as he hugs me to him, lifting me gently off the ground. "I love you. I'm so happy. I—" His words fall short as he sets me back down, a flicker of fear crossing his face. "What about the fight?"

His question is something I'd tried to ignore because I'm not sure. I believe I can still fight and use my gift without harming our baby, but that's just speculation.

"I have no choice, Jarret. He already accepted the challenge. I must fight him. I believe we'll be fine. The baby is little enough right now." The tent seems to shrink around us as if coming to stifle our joy. Maybe I should have waited to tell him after the challenge.

"But—"

"Please don't fight me on this. I'm going to do it, so please don't use this as another reason to stop me." I skirt around him, suddenly feeling like I need to get out of here.

"But I'm the baby's father. Don't I have any say in this?" He grabs my hand as I retreat, pulling me back toward him. I try to wrench my hand out of his, but he doesn't budge. I wince as a sick feeling overtakes my stomach.

"And I said the baby will be okay," I state, believing the statement as I try to pry his fingers away. He finally loosens his grip, and I stumble away.

"But you don't know for sure. How can you risk their life too? Please just—"

"It doesn't matter now. The challenge is already accepted, he'll come for me one way or another. I have to hope that our baby will be safe, because if I don't, we'll both die anyway."

A'zre

Madness. It's all madness! That's what I wanted to yell at the Darkness. His grand plan to help me seize all of Partin seems to be slipping through both our fingers. He's losing ground, and I heard Cay-Llek is in an uproar. *Eid*, Renell. I should have dealt with her when I had the chance. I never should have let her escape.

I shouldn't have listened to the Darkness when he told me to train her, because now she is using her 'gift' against me, which is exactly what I told him she would do. I'm not sure why I trust him. It's not like he's delivered me anything, only more losses and death. My people are starting to mistrust me. They're starting to question my motive for the wars. They don't believe I'm on their side . . . and maybe I'm not.

My steps echo along the hall as I thunder to my chambers. The mosaics of yellow suns in a sky of turquoise blue feel too cheery for my mood. I clench my fists at my sides. Maybe I should go to the sparring grounds, but I want to rest.

I open the door and growl when I find Esther lounging on the chaise with a book in her hands. "What are you doing here?"

She shoves something in the book before closing it and standing. Long silky strands of blonde hair frame her face, and my fingers have a sudden desire to run through them. *No! You know what happened last time . . .* "Lami invited me."

I huff. That insufferable woman. She can't mind her own *eiden* business. I step back into the hall. "Lami!" I seethe before stepping back into my room and ringing the bell that's supposed to summon her. I know she won't come, not when she's already heard my shout. This is all her doing. I look back at Esther.

She lifts her head, her purple gaze meeting mine. "Why do you want nothing to do with me?" She clenches her jaw, hardening her delicate features. She looks so fierce and beautiful.

I want everything to do with you, and that is the problem. I can't give in. If I do, then everything I've denied myself in the past will be in vain. I won't allow her the chance to see my memories again. I can't control my mental barrier when she's around.

"You've come here every night since we got married." *Since the night I couldn't deny you.* "I do have other wives to attend to," I mock, expecting anger or even jealousy to cross her features, but it never does. Why won't she leave me alone? Does she want another taste of my memories? Of course she does, that's all she wants . . . to bring me down. Destroy me.

"Lami told me to come, so I expected you wanted me. I'll go." She moves toward the door.

I grab her wrist. "I didn't say you could leave." *What are you doing? Don't you want her out of here?*

She glares and tries to free herself. "What's the point, A'zre? You won't touch me. You won't treat me like your wife."

"Fine! You want me to treat you like a wife?" My hand grabs the back of her neck as I kiss her until she bites my lip—hard. I pull back, and she slaps me. I stumble as my head snaps to the side. She did not just do that. "You witch! I could have your head for that!" I scream, forgetting to check my anger. I feel him. I feel his will pressing in as I look at her. No. He would do this. I'm not like him. I won't do this. I won't hurt her.

"So take it!" she yells, moving closer to my face.

I raise my hand, ready to slap her. Yes. It would be so easy. It would be so easy to do what I want with her but I feel the war within myself. I feel Lami's kind influence as it fights with my father's greedy monster. I feel everything telling me to choose and use it. I feel the Darkness—*she won't trust you.*

I lower my hand. "Leave me!" I turn away as I head to the balcony.

"A'z—"

"Esther." I whirl around. "I don't want this. If you stay, I will hurt you. I will destroy you. I will break you." I feel the war . . . *Just take her, she's your wife after all.*

"I'm already broken, and I don't think it's you who wants to hurt me. I know it's not you." Her voice softens, her eyes flickering with something I can't place.

I step up to her, my hand gripping her neck. "Just because you saw into my memoires once doesn't mean you know me. You'll never know me."

Her eyes flash. "You're right. Who would possibly want to know you?" She wrenches out of my grasp. "Even if you call for me, I won't come." She heads to the exit.

I step toward her, slamming the door shut before she can leave. "You wouldn't dare defy me."

"And you won't touch me, so I guess we're both liars."

Are you going to let her speak to you like that? Are you going to let her leave after this?

I seize her wrists, pulling her away from the door and shoving her toward the bed. I won't let her do this.

"Then I will break you," I say, twisting her wrists to keep her from fighting back. Her face pales, her purple eyes widening. In my mind's eye, I see my face. I see my father's anger. I see him hurting his wives in front of me—doing what I'm about to do to Esther. Me. I freeze, pushing away from her as I release her.

She falls against the bed, shaking. Tears streak her purple eyes, and my stomach roils at the look on her face. I hate myself. I hate that I almost hurt her. I've never done that to any of my wives, but none of them have ever defied me like Esther. I step back, heading to the door and telling my guards to take Esther back to her room, with an order that she's not allowed to leave.

They come in and grab her. Her broken eyes meet mine as they usher her past me. I avert my gaze. *I said I would hurt you. I told you to leave. Why didn't you leave? Why did you have to provoke me?*

Esther

"I can't do it, Lami. I can't reach him. I can—" Tears choke my throat, but I swallow them down. I refuse to cry over this situation. He doesn't deserve my tears. He didn't harm me, but I know if I continue to provoke him, he will.

Lami shakes, her mouth drawn in a firm line before she snaps, "That fool. I'll speak to him." She starts for the door. I called her in immediately after the guards brought me back to my room the blue colors dragging me down to the depths of despair. Normally the pallet makes my heart happy, but now it only make me think of melancholy, of cold and dark, of pain and hurt. I feel his fingers gripping my wrists. I see the malice on his face. I see the war within him. The war he tried to hide. The war he never wanted me to see.

"Lami, don't. Maybe we're not supposed to reach him. Maybe we're not supposed to help him." I hate the words as soon as I speak them, because no one with that much darkness can possibly defeat it on their own—least of all A'zre.

"How can you say that?" she scolds, stepping away from the door. "A'zre is good. You know that. You've seen into his heart. The monster who attacked you wasn't him."

She's right, but how can I continue to put myself in danger? What if I can't defeat the monster and instead, it defeats me? "Yes, Lami, but I have to beat his darkness and what if I can't? I should just keep my head down and do what I have to do." *A coward's way out, really . . .* I can practically see the words written above Lami's head as she thinks.

She narrows her golden eyes. "What you have to do? He won't

even treat you like a wife and that's because he's afraid. He's afraid of hurting you. He's afraid of losing you—afraid that you will be taken away."

"Then he's letting the monster control him and there is no way I can get to him unless he defeats it himself. I can't do that for him." I step up to Lami, pleading for her to understand. I don't want to do this. I can't be the only person who can reach him. He has several other wives, so what good will I do?

"Yes, but you might be able to show him the right way. You—"

"The right way? Lami, he's locked me in my room. He'll never call upon me again, and I'll never get to reach him. I want to reach him. Believe me, I do. I see the good in his heart. I've seen him . . ." I stop because Lami doesn't know about my visions. She doesn't know the things I've seen about A'zre. I've seen . . . us. I've seen him love me, cherish me like Lami wants him too, but I also saw the struggles it took to get there. I saw so much pain and hurt, but I saw love. I saw perseverance. I saw hope . . . but I don't know if it's because of my presence, or something else.

"Esther," she pauses. "I'll speak to him. Surely something set him off before he saw you, and I'm so sorry. I never thought he'd take his anger out on you. I did—"

A knock slams against the door, and Lami and I watch the wood shake with the force. I glance at her, my heart racing before a voice speaks, "Esther."

It's him. I silently plead with Lami. *Please don't open the door. Please don't make me face him.*

She sighs, shaking her head because she knows she can't disobey her king, and I hate myself for wanting her to. I'm sure he knows she's here. I glance at my desk as she opens the door. I slide out a dagger I'd brought from Casta and slip it into my palm, using the sleeves from my white dress to hide the weapon.

"May I speak to her?" I hear his voice on the other side.

Lami nods and steps away, leaving the door open for my husband. Although, it's hardly easy to call him my husband—not when I have to share him with so many other women. Marriage, to me, is an exclusive ordeal, and not something that should be so flippantly thrown into the wind.

He enters, looking me over. The last time I saw those eyes, they held so much malice. They scared me. They reminded me of who he could become, of who I never want to see again. The dagger is a welcome weight in my palm as I take careful strides toward him.

He sighs, lifting his hands to caress my chin or comfort me, but he drops them back to his sides as if remembering what those hands tried to do to me.

"Please, forgive me," he whispers, casting his gaze to the floor. "I didn't mean to—" He looks back at me, and I can see the war—the monster and the man—fighting for a chance to live and thrive.

"How can I forgive someone who's battling a monster? How can I trust you?" I cross my arms over my chest, taking a deep breath. "You fight this war with yourself. You fight against this beast you want nothing to do with, yet you can't change who you are. You can't make the wrong things right." I glare at him. "So how can I forgive you?"

"Esther." He steps toward me slowly, and I can't help but think of a hunter stalking prey.

I rip my dagger from its sheath hidden in my sleeve, pointing the blade at his chest. "Don't come near me. You said you could hurt me, well . . . I can hurt you too."

He glares at the knife, his nostrils flaring like they were before. "You would threaten me?" His voice seems to rip my heart out like that's all he wants to do, steal my heart and crush it.

"I would protect myself. I would do anything to protect myself from the monster under my bed, but unfortunately, the nightmares are a little too real."

A vein in his forehead looks like it's about to explode. "I'm your husband! Have you forgotten about the alliance—the alliance you so willingly agreed to?"

"And I'm your wife! Our alliance doesn't seem to be very valid when my husband won't touch me aside to show his force!" I shout, keeping my dagger steady.

He seethes, and I can tell he's deciding whether or not he should call the guards in to escort me to the dungeons and then hang me for all to see my treason.

I take a shaky breath. "I know you're not a monster. I've seen the good in you, but you make it very hard to hold onto that hope. You're at war and sometimes you let it have control." I swallow. What am I saying? Two seconds ago, I was ready to gut him.

He looks away briefly. "You're right. I am a monster—full of greed and spite! Is that what you want to hear?" His voice is hardened by years of abuse and pain.

"No, it's not what I want to hear! I just want you to . . ." The dagger starts to shake.

"You want me to do what?" He throws his arms wide, pacing in front of me. "To care? Well, I can't, and if that makes me a monster then so be it."

"But you're not. You don't have to be," I say, even though I'm still clenching the knife in my fist. His eyes glaze over it and he scoffs. I put it back into its sheath. "You abuse the status given to you, but you're not a monster."

"You called me the monster under your bed. How can you not see me as that? Everyone else sees it . . . I see it, and it's true." His eyes glint darkly in the dim light.

"I didn't call you the monster under my bed, I just told you that my monsters are real too, but I don't war with them. I don't let them have the chance. The monster isn't you . . . it's who you were forced to be."

"You don't know anything! You don't know me! You've only been here the last few weeks. How could you possibly know me!?" he screams, sparking my own anger.

"Would you stop telling me I don't know anything! I know you because I'm just like you! I am a greedy monster too, only I don't give into my greed!" I yell at his furious face. "I've lost everything I cared about! My child, my husband, my family, my country—all gone in the blink of an eye, and I would give anything—anything to have them all back! But I didn't choose that route. I didn't have the luxury of being selfish. Instead I came here to protect my country—to protect my people! So do not tell me I don't know anything! Do not tell me you know what I have sacrificed, when I haven't seen you sacrifice anything. All you do is take, and that is your monster, but it is not who you are!" I glare at him.

My voice falls low, "it's not who you have to be . . ." Tears clog my eyes over the words.

He watches me, his face rough with anger and pain—a sadness that can't be stripped away by me shouting at him.

I sniffle, glancing up at the blue tiles on my roof. I hate that they remind me of Casta. I hate that he's put me in this prison. That he took me away from my home but won't treat me like his wife.

"This is who I am." His voice sounds strained as his shoulders slump. "It's all I've ever known. How can I be any different?" He falls into a chair by the door, hunching over his knees as his head falls into his hands.

I start toward him even though I know what he could do, even though I know the threat he poses. I crouch in front of him, forcing him to look me in the eye. "What if I show you? Show you what it feels like to fight? What if we do it together?" This is what Lami wants me to do. If I can just reach him . . .

His red-brown eyes take me in. "I wouldn't know where to start."

"Right where you are is usually a good place."

"And what happens if all I prove to be is a monster? What can you do for me then?" His voice reveals a challenge but his eyes try to conceal so much sadness.

"Nothing . . . I can't save you. It's not up to me. It's not me who has to change. I just believe you can change."

He leans forward, taking my chin gently with his hand.

I grip the hilt of my dagger, ready to use it if I have to.

"Fine then, show me." His face is so close to mine now, but I know he won't kiss me. He won't because he's terrified. I don't have to read his memories to know. The fear is plain as day in his eyes. He wants me, but he doesn't want to fall in love with me. Already his heart bleeds for mine, already it feels too much. If he pushes it even farther, he'll never let me go, and then his war will continue. How can he love me and still watch over his other wives? He's already been forced to ruin a covenant of love and marriage . . . Why would he want to do it again?

"First, don't be scared."

"Why would I be scared?"

"Because . . ." I lean closer and kiss his lips.

He pulls back, the war reappearing in his eyes, desire burning under the surface. I can admire him for holding it in, but he's only giving into his fear.

"I'm not scared," he says, his fingers gently touching my cheek once more.

"Then—"

He kisses me again, cutting off the next words, as he sighs within our embrace.

Frobin

"Why did you do it? Why did you go after the king?" I ask, and in the dim light, I see Glena lift her head of white hair. It's stringy and muddy from the storm earlier. The sling on her arm has loosened too and doesn't even appear to be supporting her shoulder like it should.

She looks at me through the bars of her cell, blue-green eyes diminished, broken. How come I hadn't been fast enough to stop her? What if she can't be pardoned? What if I've lost her for good? My throat tightens. I just got her back. I don't want to lose her . . . not like this.

"I wanted her to hurt as much as I hurt. I wanted her to feel how I feel." Her voice sounds like broken glass, raw and emotionless.

"Glena—"

"He died protecting her, Frobin. He died—"

"He would have done that to protect any one of us, Glena. He cared for all of us, and unfortunately, her life was in dire stake before any of ours." I swallow the lump in my throat.

"Stop! I don't want to hear it. I don't—" Her voice cracks and she starts to sob.

It hurts my heart because I can't be there to hold her, to tell her that it will be okay. In fact, this is the first time she's actually cried since Zenz's death. I hadn't seen her break before this moment. I reach my hands through the bars. The sound of dripping water somewhere behind me reminds me that I'm still in a dungeon, too close, yet too far away to comfort her.

She scoots closer, sobbing as she takes my hands. "I'm sorry. I'm so sorry. I've destroyed us again. I've put an actual cage between us. I wanted . . . I just wanted someone else to feel my pain. It hurts so much, Frobin. I don't know what to do. I—I don't know how to make this right. I didn't want to hurt Dais. I just—I couldn't see past my hurt. I couldn't . . . I couldn't see Father again. So I did what I—" Her milky face leans against the metal bars as tears stream down.

I caress her chin, gently wiping her cold cheek. I wish I had something warm to give her. "I'm sorry. I should have made sure you were okay. I should have told you to cry, to mourn, to grieve, but . . ." I trail off. Even though I'm the pack leader now, it shouldn't be an excuse for the way I neglected her. I thought she would grieve. I thought she would never do something like this.

"No, I never should have let it get that far. I'll—I'll pay the penance for what I did. I will take whatever punishment he gives me." She swallows, her entire body shaking under my fingers.

My heart sinks at her words. Any punishment could mean death if the king so desires. I don't think Dais is like that, but she attacked him, and most people who have been attacked would probably not be lenient, even if they are a kind person. I don't want her to die. I don't want to lose someone else I love. I don't think I'd make it through.

Tears appear in my eyes, and I feel Glena's cold fingers touch my skin, wiping away the salty trails. "Don't cry for me."

I almost laugh. "Cry for you? No, these are selfish tears. I'm crying because I could lose you, and I'm not ready to lose you. Why did this—why did . . ." *Why did you have to do it? Why do I finally allow myself to love you and then you leave me again? Do you like breaking my heart?* Though, I don't say any of those things. I can't bear to see the pain in her eyes again—the pain I put there when I wouldn't forgive her.

"That's crying for me, you idiot."

"No, it's crying for us." I lean my forehead against the frozen bars even though it doesn't bring us any closer together. The metallic scent of the iron tingles my nose and reminds me that I can't set her free. I hate that she's caged in here, not free under the stars she loves so much. I hate that instead of soft grass and the sweet scent of mountain flowers, she's buried in the sludge of a dark dungeon laced with the putrid scent of human excrement.

"I'm sorry I made you cry. I've broken your heart one too many times, and I wish I could take it back. I didn't truly want to hurt him or Rahuin. I was . . . it doesn't matter, there's no excuse." Her bottom lip quivers in the dim light, and my thumb gently caresses it.

The sound of a door closing followed by echoing footsteps draws our attention to the entrance. Other inmates look on as well, some of them jeer at the newcomer who is being escorted in by two guards.

Thesa stands between them, her pale face drawn in exhaustion. Her black and purple hair escapes a braided updo in hazardous waves. Glena and I release each other to stand as she approaches.

She puts her hands through the bars, taking Glena's fingers. "My dear, I just wanted to give you an update. I don't know when the trial is, but it should be soon. Rahuin and Dais are both fine and resting, although Rahuin miscarried a child."

Pains tabs my heart. No. Dais will never forgive Glena now. I saw it when Rahuin gasped in—when Thesa led her away as soon as possible. That's what happened.

"No," Glena breathes. "Thesa, please, you have to tell Dais that I didn't mean it at all. I didn't mean to hurt him. I didn't mean to hurt Rahuin. I didn't mean to hurt their . . ." she trails off in desperate sobs.

"Rahuin was pregnant with twins. She miscarried one, but the other is alive. She will be going to Färrin soon to recover. I will try to get Dais to understand, but you might have to give me a few days. Neither of them are in a good place right now, and they could direct their anger solely on you, just as you had done." Thesa wipes Glena's tears. "I know you wouldn't intentionally hurt someone. I know you were in pain, but I'm afraid there is no excuse."

Glena hangs her head. "I know." She glances at me. "Please take care of Frobin. Please forgive me for what I have done."

"I'll always take care of him. I love you, Glena, and I will do my best to persuade Dais to keep you from death. I just wanted to let you know." Thesa squeezes her hands before turning away and leaving with the guards on her heels.

"I told you there is no excuse. I can't believe—I never thought I would kill an innocent. I never—" She breaks down into sobs, falling onto her knees as she leans against the bars.

I drop down beside her and wrap my arms through the bars as far as I can so I can hold her close. It's not ideal, but it works.

"I know. I'm so sorry, Glena. I won't leave you here. I won't let you be alone again."

She cries until she falls asleep in my arms.

Chapter 19

Living in a Nightmare

Jarret

The ominous halls of Cizarrél creep over us like reapers awaiting our demise as the boat we're in lulls gently through the canal. My heartbeat quickens, telling me to run, to flee, but I will not. Not when my wife is ready to face this madness with courage—no, not courage, necessity.

Renell wouldn't do this if she had another way to save Lanckest, but I still think this is a fool's errand. Why don't we use our forces to fight the High Chief? Why does she have to face him one on one? What if she fails? I can't shake the thoughts that keep poisoning my mind. I believe she can do it. I believe she can win, but what if she doesn't? What if all of this was in vain? What if I lose her? I can't bear to lose her, not when she's pregnant with our child. Not when it's my duty to protect her.

Her hand slips into mine as the gondola nears the main hall—the Hall of Chiefs. Cizarrél is a dark city with a constant cloud souring the air. It doesn't help that most of the buildings and towers are crafted with black stone. It was built on a river many years ago so most of the city is accessible by boats unless you find yourself on a bridge or one of the interconnecting dams. A network of bridges branch out like a spider's web from every building surrounding us.

Citizens cast disapproving glances as our boat moves gently over the water. I keep waiting for some terrible monster to arrive from its depths, but in the surprisingly clear canal, I find metal pipes. Interesting. I wonder what they're for. Other boats pass by, loaded with nets and cages for fishing as they head toward the open archipelago just past the city. I've heard it's Cizarrél's biggest import.

A dock waits before us, and our skipper lifts his oars to slow the vessel. Three men draped in dark cloaks and necklaces of bones wait for us. Two of them hold flickering torches, while the middle one stands with his arms crossed. They're faces don't exactly look welcoming. Will we even make it to meet the chief? The boat creaks as it hits the side, and the middle man helps Renell out first.

"Princess of Death?" he asks, gripping her arm like he might throw her into the water.

Wen and I stand, but the boat rocks underneath us as the other two guards take steps toward us. Whether to stop us or help us, I'm not sure because they freeze when Renell speaks.

"If that's what you wish to call me," she says, her dark green eyes boring into him.

He sighs, releasing her. I step onto the dock, but it still feels like I'm sitting in the swaying gondola. Good thing I can fly and don't have to rely on water for travel.

"And with you?" the guard casts one dark eye over Wen and me.

"My guards. I go nowhere without them."

He huffs, turning toward the huge hall behind him. "Follow me. I will take you to the High Chief."

We follow him toward the dark double doors of the building. Gargoyles and other stone statues of hideous beasts line pillars just outside the entrance. Metal tips protrude from the walls and strings of bones hang from them like grotesque banners. I glare at their choice of decor. Nothing about Cay-Llek makes me want to come back. They're people are highly superstitious, and their glorification of bones proves it.

The large metal doors groan as we walk into the building, and I have to stop for a second to adjust my eyes to the dim light. And here I thought it was dark outside. Finally I catch a glimpse of light coming from crude candles above. Lifeless skulls and empty sockets arranged with other bones cover the walls. A fireplace stands at the far end of the room behind a little platform and what looks like a throne. Hundreds of men clad in leather jerkins and plates of bone armor stand around us. An army. Maybe the High Chief won't be as honorable as Wen thought. Maybe he will silence Renell before she can fight.

Renell holds her head high, following our escort to the throne. A man I assume to be Clòz stands as she nears. My heart sinks. He's twice the size of her with arms thicker than her head. His black hair is shaved on the sides, showing pale skin and the top is braided all the way down his back. His thick, full beard styled like his hair reaches to his stomach. Red tattoos swirl around the right side of his face and enhance dark eyes. No wonder he's the high chief. I grip my sword as if that would calm my racing heart. How does she expect to win against him? How can she?

"Are you the princess who has come to challenge me?" he asks and his voice sounds like stones crashing against stone as he speaks in crude Lan.

"I am." Her eyes never waver as she glares at him.

My stomach sours and I have to force my bile down.

"Since I am the one challenged, I will set the rules for our fight." Clóz pauses, glancing at his men. I grip my sword's hilt tighter. If he bends the rules to have his men fight alongside him, I will not hesitate to kill every last one of them. "Swords will only be used in this fight. The first to cause a mortal wound or death wins . . . and there will be no use of inhuman gifts, oh Princess of Death." He smiles.

My insides twist like a hurricane. What? No. There is no way Renell will be able to defeat him without her gift.

"I a—"

"I volunteer to take her place!" I shout before I can overthink what my interjection might mean. Some of his men jeer and chuckle. Wen told us the rules. Anyone can take the place of the challenger before the fight begins—not many ever do it though, especially against the High Chief.

"Jarret!" Renell spins around, her eyes narrow. "Are you mad?"

I step forward, staring into Clòz's dark eyes—they're filled with intrigue and bloodlust. He's not afraid, not like we are. "I challenge you." I'm glad my voice doesn't shake.

"A volunteer! My, this is an exciting turn of events. The rules will stay the same." He chuckles, rubbing hands the size of my head together.

"I accept." I nod, my sword's hilt is a welcome warmth in the palm of my hand.

Renell jumps in front of me. "What are you doing? Get back now." She shoves me.

"No." I meet her eyes. "I will not. I will not sacrifice you." I take her shoulders into my hands. "I've trained too. I've learned. I won't let you kill yourself." I push her behind me.

"You liar! You said you would let me do this. I have to do this! Take it back!" She reaches for me, her fingers digging into the cloak around my shoulders.

I grab her hands. "That was before you couldn't use your gift. Renell, you cannot atone for Lanckest if you're dead. You can't unite them if there is no queen. Let me do this. Let me protect you like I promised. You can't stop me. It's too late." I shove her against Wen, who immediately holds her back, and turn to face Clòz.

A smirk lights his face as he stares at Renell with a suggestive gaze. "A feisty woman you have there."

My neck flushes. "You'll never touch her." I pull my sword from its sheath.

He does the same. "We'll see about that. If you win, you get Cay-Llek. If I win, I get her. Killing you will just be fun for me."

I hear Renell shout behind me, but I don't take my eyes off Clòz. "Deal."

He smiles. "Let's begin."

A horn blows from somewhere behind me, and Clòz immediately advances, sending his men into a hearty cheer.

I block, my feet sliding backwards at the force of his blow. I parry, spinning as my sword swings toward his side.

He sidesteps, his free hand reaching for my jerkin and pulling me close to him. He slams his head against mine, and I stumble backward in confusion. He laughs. "I thought you'd put up a better fight than that. Can't you wield a sword correctly?"

I rush at him, my sword crashing against his as my other hand reaches for the knife strapped to my chest. I slam against him, falling to my knees as I slice the knife against his calf. Blood splatters around me as he howls, giving me just a second to brace myself for the next blow.

"That was just a scratch, boy. You'll have to do much better than that." He grunts, lifting his foot and kicking me in the chest.

I stumble, having to tuck and roll to avoid his blade slicing where my head used to be.

We fight for what feels like an eternity with my limbs growing stiffer with every counterattack. I try to keep my blows quick because his size doesn't allow him to move as fast. After a while, he forces my sword out of my hands. It clashes to the stone ground in a clang of steel as I fall backward in my haste to retrieve it. Sharp pain shoots up my side, and I scream, turning to dislodge the blade from my back. I roll, reaching for my weapon, but I know it's too late. His boot comes into contact with my chest, and I gasp as the air leaves my lungs.

He leans over me. "You will die now. Pity, I didn't even learn your name, but I'm sure she'll scream it the second I plunge my sword into your chest."

The scream that leaves my lips and reverberates around the dismal hall becomes the last witness to my death.

Renell

"Jarret!" I scream as Wen and I rush toward him. Blood pools out underneath him.

So much blood.

Tears saturate my eyes as I stroke his already pale cheek. The cheers of men fall into a cadence of hushed murmurs. They don't matter to me, and I don't care who sees.

"Why did you do it?" I gasp. "Why?"

"You ca—can't marry him." Blood coats his lips.

"I have to. I have to fix this."

"But—"

"Jarret, you tried and I love you so much for it, but I have to finish this now. I should have never . . ."

"But you're—"

"I know, but you have to go. I'll find a way, before . . ." *you die.* I leave the words out. I start to stand, but Jarret grips my wrist that is decorated with the *Reiis*, thumbing the scale and swirl of moonstone dust. His brown eyes met mine. "I love you," I whisper. "Please be safe." I push his hand off me and stand. I turn to Wen. "Get him out of here. Do whatever you have to do just get him to safety."

Wen nods, gray eyes hardened in determination. "I will."

Clòz takes my arm and pulls me away from Jarret and Wen. Other men grab them, and Jarret screams as they make him stand. My new fiancé smiles gleefully at Jarret's pain.

Bile rises in my throat, and I look away to keep from throwing up.

"Lock them up. There will be a beheading ceremony tomorrow, but first"—he looks at me—"a wedding must take place." He shoves me toward an older woman who stands behind us. She catches me. "Take my bride to be made ready. We will hold the ceremony tonight."

The woman pulls me off to the side, and I desperately search the crowd for Jarret and Wen once more, but there are too many bodies smashed into the hall. My throat clenches and everything in me screams to run, to fight, but it's no use now. It's over. We lost.

I can't fight now. I'll have no control over my gift. Even though I would gladly destroy all of these men for Jarret, I need their armies. If I start killing them now, there'll be nothing left. I will destroy the whole world if it means I can reverse what happened.

The woman leads me to a side door, pulling me down a corridor and into a room filled with tons of furs hanging on racks of bones. She has graying black hair braided into a bun above her head and her dark eyes convey warmth that seems foreign in this horrible place.

As the woman moves around the room gathering bundles of furs, other people filter in with jars of water, fill a bath, strip me of my clothes, and start to pull on my hair. Part of me wants to speak to them, but I'm afraid that if I talk, I'll just start crying. The thought that Wen will get Jarret out of here is the only thing keeping me together. They will be safe.

Once I'm out of the bath, they braid my hair with little chunks of crushed bone and then place a crown made of it onto my head. The older woman brings a dress made of Y-Ak hide and ties it to me in a way that keeps my heart exposed. The others leave as the woman adds more strings of bones to adorn my dress. She sees the *Reiis* on my wrist and takes my hand into hers, studying the design.

"Don't let him see it before the ceremony," she says in Sz-Kar, covering my wrist with an armlet of fur.

I study her—her facial structure, her pronunciation. "You're from Lanckest."

Her warm expression meets mine as she gently touches my cheek, before bowing her head in reverence. "Yes, my Queen." Her tongue changes to Lan. "I know you've come here to save us. Many of us were sold into slavery to Cay-Llek and Sun'Ar, some even to Onar before the fighting started in Lanckest."

That early? Tears form in my eyes again. "I'm sorry it has taken so long. I'm trying to save you all."

"We know. When the others find out you are here, we will stand by your side. Some are angry, but many of us understand that you and your father had no time to prepare. The war came so suddenly and we realize that Casta did all they could as well." She puts blood red paint on my cheeks, creating designs with her fingers. "We will try to save your friends."

"Help Wen find a window. It's the only way he'll be able to save… Jarret." My voice chokes, and I do my best not to think of the blood surrounding him earlier, but it clouds my mind until it's all I see.

"Your husband?" she whispers, and tears stream down my cheeks. "Clòz will know if he sees the *Reiis*. Don't let him see until after the wedding. By that time, your friends will be safe."

"All I care about is that they both get out safely. They should have never followed me here, but I couldn't stop them."

"He loves you, especially since he gave himself to save you from this fate." She stops for a moment. "You know how a Cay-Llek wedding works."

I nod, and she continues. "Clòz will change the words. So make sure you understand and repeat them exactly. Hopefully the binding will not be as detrimental since you have already given yourself to another, but if it does, I will make sure we find a way to break it."

"Thank you," I whisper. "And your name?"

"Nella, my Queen. I will do everything to get us ready. You are here now, and we will do all we can to bring our country back—our people back."

I hug her. "Thank you, Nella. For your kindness. For your understanding."

"Be strong my Queen. We are with you."

Drums start to pound outside the door, sending my heart to the driving beat. This is it.

Nella looks up. "It's time for you to meet your groom. We will save your friends during the ceremony. Clòz won't know they're gone until the morning." I nod, and Nella leads me out of the room.

Wen

I hear drums pounding above us, and shiver in the dark prison we'd been shoved into. Cold sludge soaks through the bottom of my feet and the smell chokes my lungs.

Jarret leans against the metal bars of the cell, breathing heavily. I did my best to heal his wound, but his body needs rest. We have to get out of here.

The guards just outside our cell jeer at Jarret, calling him terrible names in their mother tongue. I don't think he understands what they're saying. Otherwise, I believe he would have spit the blood in his mouth at them, but all he does is let it dribble over his chin and onto the disgusting floor.

I grimace. He's losing too much blood. Renell is going to kill me if I don't get him out of here soon. I don't really want to face the brunt of her wrath. The guards just have to leave us alone so I can find a way to teleport into the city. I'll need a window since I don't know Cizarrél well enough to just jump us to safety, and I can only travel so far with a passenger.

Something scurries across my foot, and I don't dare look down. I don't want to know. A guard smacks Jarret's hands, and he grimaces, falling away from the bars. I catch him. The last thing I need is for him to get infected by the muck on the ground. I drape his arm over my shoulder.

"Stay with me, Jarret. I can't lose you. You know she'll kill me."

His pale face falls against my arm. "Now that . . . I'd like to see."

Even when he's in pain, he's still a *dir flak*. How does Renell stand him? I guess people tolerate crazy things when they love someone, just like this idiot. Why did he think he was going to defeat Clòz? Now we're in this situation, and I have to figure out how to get him out of here safely.

A commotion at the front of the prison draws my attention to the metal double doors. Someone is screaming. They're saying that all guards must report to the High Chief immediately because they're under attack upstairs. Attack? Is this part of Renell's plan? She never said anything about an attack . . . unless she kept it a secret for this exact moment.

The guards in front of our cell hurry through the sludge, their armor clamoring with every step. Once they're gone, a middle-aged woman picks her way over to us. She glances between the bars, staring at us.

Jarret's fainted against me and his sweat is soaking through my shirt. He's sick—too sick.

The woman pulls out a key and unlocks the door, ushering me forward.

I drag Jarret with me. *It'd be easier to just leave him here. Save yourself. You can't save him. You can't save anyone. They'll never trust you. You'll never be anything to them.* I shake the voice away, staring at the woman.

"Come with me." She hurries back the way she came.

Jarret stirs beside me, taking stumbling steps—at least I won't have to entirely drag him the entire way, but I continue to support his weight. He's in no condition to walk on his own.

"The queen sent me," she whispers, taking us down several winding corridors. They're decorated like everything else in this cursed city, with bones and broken metal. The woman takes us up a set of stairs until we stop at a floor-to-ceiling window.

"She said that you just needed a window and this was the only one I could think of." Her brave gaze catches a flickering sconce overhead.

"Thank you," I whisper. "Tell her I'll keep him safe."

She nods. Plodding steps pull our gazes toward the bottom of the stairs where shadows bounce off the walls. "Quickly," she says.

I look out the window, holding Jarret close. If he lives, he'll never let me forget this. I fix my gaze on a spot about three blocks away. I can see fishing nets and piled crates in perfect detail. Everything falls away from my thoughts as I close my eyes and feel the magic erupt in my veins.

Teleporting feels like squeezing my body through a pinhole, but the feeling intensifies with a passenger because I have to guide him through safely too. Thank goodness he's mostly unconscious. It's usually harder to teleport a second person since they won't know exactly where we're headed. It has to be clear, or we could end up in another dimension. From the few, very brief times I'd been in the wrong place . . . I never want to go back.

I feel solid ground under my feet and open my eyes. My glowing tattoos shine against crates and fishing nets before diminishing to darkness. I carefully pull Jarret behind a few boxes before I notice a golden light shining around us. Not good. It'll give us away. I follow its source to Jarret's wrist. Where the sleeve of his black shirt doesn't fully cover his arm, the shape of a crown embedded in his blue scales glows like a proud beacon.

I quickly cover it up. Definitely not good. The crown on a Garon's wrist only shines for one reason and one reason alone . . . the king is dead, and Jarret is being summoned to appear as a royal.

Thesa

"Are you ready for tomorrow?" Jet asks, his hands rubbing my arms as he stands behind me.

I'm out on the balcony, overlooking the sea. Lights flicker from the docks down below us as a spring breeze whispers loose hair against my neck. I lean back against him. "Yes."

Rahuin, her parents, and I leave for Färrin tomorrow. Part of me wants to stay for Jet and Dais, but I know they'll be okay without me. I just hate that we have to be separated. I haven't been away from him since we found each other again over a year ago, and the thought of leaving him sours my stomach.

"It won't be too long. Just until Rahuin is . . ." *healed*, I want to say, but I know what she's been through can't be healed like a wound. All she can do is find the strength to continue onward.

"Sounds like you're trying to convince yourself, not me." He kisses my cheek.

"We just—" Pain rips through my side and I grunt, grabbing the space and trying to rub it away.

"Thesa?" Jet's brow furrows.

I feel the blood drain from my cheeks. Something isn't right. Jarret's face appears in my mind. No. Is something wrong with him? Why would he be . . .

Jet's hand grabs mine, holding it tightly. I look up, and his face says it all. "Jarret?"

"You feel it too?"

"No, but I believe something terrible has happened."

Tears well in my eyes, blurring my mate's face. I stumble into our room, uncovering my *heln* before I remember that it won't communicate with Jarret's. My insides twist as I start to grab things I'll need. The cream and gold walls seem to mock me with their sweetness. First Rahuin, and now Jarret. I don't think my heart can take it if something happened to him as well.

Jet takes my hands again. "Thesa . . ." His brown eyes plead with mine.

"We need to find him."

"Let's not act rashly."

"But he could be . . ." I trail off, holding back a sob. I can't stand this. I have to know. "What if he's hurt and there is no one there to help him? What if their plan backfired and they're both dead?" Rahuin strikes my thoughts. I'm supposed to leave with her tomorrow. I shake my head. If I tell her it's Jarret, she'll understand. She'll be with her parents.

Jet nods. "Then find him. I—I can't leave Dais . . . not after what happened so recently. The country is in too much turmoil to leave him unprotected, but I—" I watch the conflict rage in his eyes.

"I know. I'll find him." I continue grabbing my things. "I'll bring him home. I'll . . ." I trail off, noticing a golden glow shining from my left wrist.

No.

My heart sinks.

It can't be. Maybe it wasn't Jarret at all. No, Jet knew something was off as well. I look up at him, tears streaming down my cheeks.

"No," I whimper. "No, he can't be gone. He . . ." I rush to the stone that is still uncovered. A message is there now. It's from Kyira.

Dear Thesa,

I regret to inform you that your father has passed on to the Gateway of Light. I'm sure you already know this, but I had to write to you. I had to let you know he went painlessly. He was thinking about you and Jarret the entire time. He said he was glad to have made amends. I'm so sorry. Please come soon.

Love, Kyira

No. No. What should I do? Jarret, my father, Rahuin, Zenz . . . this can't be happening. All of this isn't happening, right? I'm stuck in a nightmare. These are just my fears and worries that have manifested into a horrible dream. This isn't happening.

I start to sob.

Jet pulls me into his embrace.

"This isn't real, Jet." My fingers bunch into his shirt. "Just tell me what to do. I don't know what to do."

He pulls away, steadying me in his arms. "Kyira can track the stones correct?"

I nod, staring into his eyes that fill my aching heart with strength.

He continues, "Get to Treía. You can have her tell you where Jarret is and then go get him. Thesa, you are one of the strongest people I know. You can do this. They won't do the Enflaming Ceremony until you're all there anyway. Besides, maybe we're wrong. Maybe nothing is wrong with Jarret. Maybe he's on his way to Treía."

"You're right. I have to . . . but what if I get chos—" I can't bear the thought of being separated from him again, and he has to stay here with Dais.

"Don't think about that right now, just find our son." His dark eyes are like solid ground under my feet.

I nod, blinking away the tears and stealing my resolve.

He wipes the trails on my cheeks.

"I love you," I say. "I need to tell Dais and Rahuin, and then I'll be on my way."

"I love you too." He pulls me into his embrace, and I sigh into his warmth. I fear I'll be away from him for too long, but we've been separated before. We'll make it through this time too.

Chapter 20

Bent Until You're Broken

Renell

Nella leads me back into the main hall, her warm fingers pushing me onward and steadying me all at once. Clòz's men have been shoved to both sides to create a little pathway for me to walk to my new husband. More candles and lamps hang from the macabre ceiling, illuminating the room in a ghastly golden glow. My legs shake with every step as Nella leaves me at the end of the line, taking the warmth with her. I look back at her. No, she can't leave me to walk up there on my own. I'll collapse.

"There is my bride!" Clòz shouts, liquid sloshing out of a huge cup in his meaty fist. He takes a swig, laughing heartily as spittle flies from his mouth. His men join in his jubilee. I stare at him. Red tattoos bleed along the right side of his face. His dark eyes meet mine, and I notice that one is larger than the other.

How did it come to this? I was ready to destroy him a few hours ago. Why did Jarret have to be so foolish?

You can still destroy him. You can burn this entire city down—make them pay. The monster inside me begs.

No, I can't. If I release my curse now, there is no turning back. Everyone will die without Jarret around to steady me. My people are here too. I can't risk their lives for my revenge. I have to protect them.

I will marry Clòz, and then I will find a way to get him to make an alliance with Onar. Once everything is secured, I'll figure out how to break the Cay-Llek marriage curse. Cay-Llekian's marry one person, and one person forever. They are bound together as one. If one gets harmed, so does the other. If one dies, so does the other. It can't be reversed unless the curse is broken. But like Nella warned, Clòz might change the words so our marriage is unbreakable, though, nothing is unbreakable . . . least of all this man.

I force myself forward, ignoring the leering glances of Clòz's generals. He notices some of their stares and a throwing knife wizzes past me, hitting a man to my right square in the forehead. I gasp, falling over in the aisle as blood splatters onto me.

The drumming stops and the hall settles into silence.

"The same will happen to the rest of you lot if any of you dares to look at my wife like he just did," Clòz says, heading over to me and wrenching me off the ground.

Pain shoots up my shoulder, and I hold back a wince. The men around us avert their gazes as we pass. They don't want any looks to be interpreted as desirable. I shake under his grasp. He releases me as we arrive at the front. His hot breath whispers against my neck, and I nearly gag at the liquor on his breath. It smells like rotting carcasses.

"You shiver like you're afraid. I wouldn't . . . it only makes me want you more." Flames flicker in his eyes, picking me apart.

I swallow, taking a deep breath. "You'll be the one who is afraid once I'm done with you."

"Really, you must not know how our weddings work." He stands in front of me, pulling my wrists into his, and I nearly fall against him. I step back even though he still holds onto me.

"I know perfectly well."

"Then you're disillusioned. You won't break this. You'll be mine, and instead, it is I who will continue to break that fiery spirit of yours." He's handed a ribbon from a servant and starts to tie our hands together—his left hand in my right one.

"With these bindings, I bind Princess"—he spits—"Renell Os-lehan to me, High Chief Clòz, forever in marriage. Nothing on this land or any other will be able to break it—not death, nor curses, or... love." He smirks. "Now repeat it."

The words are poison in my mouth as I utter them.

Once I'm finished, he releases our bindings and drags a knife across his palm. Sharp pain sparks against my hand, and when I turn it over, a line of red appears.

He laughs in glee, taking our bloodied hands and lifting them to the ceiling for all to witness our covenant. The men cheer, pouring more drinks and hailing Clòz. He's offered drinks and congratulations but ignores them as he drags me away. I hope the distraction of a wedding was enough. I hope Jarret and Wen are safe. I hope . . .

A sick feeling permeates my stomach as Clòz takes me to his chambers. I try to remember this is my fault while he takes my clothes off. I try to remember this is all for my people. I try not to think of Jarret while he has his way with me. I try to believe I will succeed, but I realize I don't believe in anything anymore . . .

Rahuin

"Look at you destroying everything around you. What did I say? Didn't I tell you that you would never succeed. You will destroy. You will be the end of them. You're losing them." He smiles, his gray skin pulling in odd angles. His black eyes are bottomless pits of evil. As usual, darkness surrounds us. I think we're in the plane of existence he showed me once, but this nightmare has become all too familiar. It doesn't even scare me anymore. Little orbs of light shine down, but they're dim—too dim for me to continue believing that the light in this world will become stronger. What if it doesn't? What if the light doesn't succeed? What if it's not supposed to?

I stare at him and try to keep my knees from shaking. I'm not even scared, I'm just tired.

"You promised me that you would cause them all pain, but you

lied. Now I will collect my dues, because I don't forget like you do. Tenfold. Remember? Don't you see how easy it'll be to destroy them? Of course, you won't be harmed. I can't hurt you if you're already dead." He says the words like we're talking about the weather, but I'm not sure we're really talking about anything. Usually, I try to fight back, but the determination in my bones has disappeared. I don't believe in the fight anymore, and he's already taken so much. Maybe it's true. Maybe it's me. Maybe the tenfold punishment comes from my own hand. Maybe he has nothing to do with it at all. Maybe I'm giving him too much credit.

"Leave me alone. You're getting what you wanted." My voice sounds like a stranger's, like I'm a puppet being forced to speak, but who's commanding me? The Darkness, my fear, my will, Dais, numbness?

"What I want is you. I want you to come with me. We'll be unstoppable, and I will end all this pain, if you just come with me, if you just give in to me." His voice sounds so soothing, but I can feel the poison dripping on the end of each word. It's all lies.

"You'll never have me. Let the pain continue. It's what I've chosen." And with those words, he disappears in a vein of black smoke, choking the light with darkness.

When I finally have the strength to open my eyes again, I'm back in my room. A servant is already here, drawing back the pale blue blinds. A tray of tea with pewter utensils sits at the foot of my bed, a pale stream of steam rises from the spout of the main pitcher. I watch it swirl up and up until it dissipates. I feel like the steam, lifting up until it's all gone—like it never existed.

Is that all my fate should be? Up and up until I vanish. Maybe everyone would be better off if that happened. Maybe then, they'll be safe. I want to kick the tray off the end of the bed. I want the sheets to stop strangling me, or maybe, I want them to strangle me. I'm not sure, and I'm already tired of these thoughts. I don't want to die. I don't want Sira to die. She doesn't deserve the same fate as her brother. She deserves to smile. She deserves to play with flowers in the castle gardens. She deserves to grow up and be the shining light I know she will be.

The servant comes over and helps prop me up with pillows before handing me a full tea cup. I stare at the porcelain, seeing little depictions of Casta's beaches against the background of a cerulean sea. I find it oddly calming. I look to my right, but Dais is already gone, the evidence that he even slept beside me gets swept up as the servant makes his side of the bed.

He seems to be avoiding me. I guess, if I were him, I'd be avoiding me too. I wouldn't know what to do either. I don't know how to comfort myself, so how can I expect it of him? Or maybe he's trying to distance himself so it hurts less when I leave for Färrin today. If he doesn't want me to go, he should just tell me. I'll stay if he asks me to, but if he doesn't, I'll go. I'll heal in Färrin, then I'll return, refreshed and ready to be the supportive queen Dais needs.

The servant leaves, saying something about coming back to help me get dressed, but I don't care. I just lean back and settle for the warm tea against my tongue. It's sweet with hints of a bitter undertone. I hate it. It's like they doused it in sugar, but I'm fairly certain that it's just my enhanced taste buds.

Dais has done nothing but support me, while I feel that I haven't done enough, or forgiven enough, or loved enough to make up for what I did to keep Sira safe. He doesn't say it, but I know my infidelity leaves a black cloud in his mind. It haunts him with the possibility that it could happen again, and how can I reassure him when I've already proven myself to be untrustworthy? Nothing I say will ever make this right. Maybe that's why he doesn't want me leave. Maybe he's worried I'll do it again. Maybe he thinks it's too easy for me now that I've already broken his heart.

Well, it's not. I never wanted to break his heart. That's why it feels wrong for me to leave, but I can't risk Sira's safety. I can't lose her too. Besides saving Casta, all I've ever done is keep my daughter safe, especially from the Darkness, especially from me. If I have to go to Färrin to continue that, I will.

The door to my right opens as I take another sip from the beach cup. Thesa walks in, dark circles underline her red-rimmed jade eyes.

My heart clenches. I've been numb for so long now that the twinge of worry brings me back to life for a moment. What's happened?

"Good, you're awake," Thesa starts, approaching my bed. Her fingers fiddle with the light blue comforter's amber appliques. I notice a distant glow coming from her left hand, a small shimmer that seems to bathe her in an eerie light. She looks up with a sigh, meeting my eyes. "I can't come with you to Färrin." She lifts her wrist, showing me the glowing crown. "I must go to Treía. I have to find Jarret as well, for I believe something terrible has happened to him."

My heart sinks. No. Not Jarret too. I see his brown eyes in my mind. I see his smile. I see his anger and regret. I hear the bass of his voice when he told me he'd always stay by my side after we fled Castlehaven. It can't be true. He has to be okay.

"I'm going with you," I blurt without thinking as I toss the covers off.

"No, you're not." Thesa shakes her head, standing up and lifting her hands. "You're pregnant. I can't risk . . ." She swallows. "I promise I will find him. I just wanted to tell you that you must go to Färrin without me. I will let you know about Jarret as soon as I have news." She moves to my side of the bed and kisses my forehead. "Get better and hurry back. I'll do my best to join you, but I have no idea what the future holds." She looks down, staring at her wrist.

Right. She could be chosen as the next monarch of Treía. I might not see her for a very long time. The thought strikes me like a lightning bolt. How will I go on without her? She's always been here, making sure I'm okay and pulling me together when I only see my pain.

I wrap my arms around her. "I'm so sorry, Thesa. You don't deserve this. You deserved to rejoin your father in Treía. You deserve to know that Jarret is okay. I will be okay. I will get better, but I will miss you every day. You've become another mother to me, and I couldn't have made it this far without you. I love you."

"I love you too, Rahuin." She stands, pulling out of my embrace. "I will see you soon." She smiles and leaves the room with tears streaking her eyes.

I allow my own tears to fall. I hate this. I hate feeling helpless. I hate that I've lost so much already. I hate that others have lost because of me. *Tenfold* . . . It's too late now. I've already made my choice.

Dais

"I promised Glena I'd try to get her out. She wasn't in her right mind when she attacked you. She apologized and wishes you'll be tolerant in your punishment," Thesa says, after she's told me the news regarding Treía.

Rahuin's leaving. She's leaving. Why does it feel like everyone is leaving me behind? I shake the thoughts away. I can't blame them. It's not in their control. My office comes back into focus, a dark wood door with a gold handle to my left, light green wallpaper with brown accents that compliments the map of Partin behind me.

It heightens the green in Thesa's eyes. I want to be angry at Glena, but truly, if my anger ever got the better of me, I would have done the same in her position. I can't blame her for what happened, nor can I completely absolve her. I've heard plenty of whispers around the castle already, and it hasn't even been that long. I've heard them talking about how they think Rahuin and Glena were lovers and she was angry about the marriage. Some guessed that Glena was just upset about her father. Some were even more outrageous, because people's assumptions can be awful sometimes.

More and more, I'm finding the behavior of my countrymen hard to tolerate. How do I keep them on the right track? How did other kings accomplish it? How do I lead them and set the best example? What even is the best example? How can they have so much hate in their hearts? I feel like I've fought them more than any enemy that has come against me and my family. Does that make them the real villains?

I focus on Thesa. I need to stop getting lost in my endless thoughts. "I'll see what I can do. She still needs to be punished, but I don't believe she needs to die for what happened. After all, I'm—we're . . ." I trail off because none of this is all right. I've lost a child. And Rahuin . . . Rahuin isn't fine. She hasn't been since she got back from the Darkness, and the attack only pushed her off the edge. If only I'd been strong enough to pull her away sooner, but it's too late now, and our son has paid the price.

A light breeze flutters in through the doors to my left that lead out to a garden veranda. I hear birds singing in the morning sunrise, and I can't believe it's that early. I'd come to the office because the room brings me comfort when the world is in turmoil. I feel closest to my father here, and every day I wish he was still here to guide me.

"Thank you, Your Majesty. I'll keep you updated, and let you know who gets selected. Hopefully I can persuade them to keep the alliance." Thesa nods, black and purple hair falling into her face.

"Thank you, Thesa." I move forward, offering a hug.

She obliges. "Take care of yourself, please. Don't make it too hard on Jet. I don't need him force feeding you and knocking you out to get you to sleep. Remember, your health comes first."

"What if I like giving him a hard time?" I step away.

She shoots me a look that only mothers can. "Please, promise me. Rahuin is leaving to get better. I won't be here, and Jet will wear himself thin taking care of you."

I nod, feeling a little guilty, especially after what I put them through last time. "I promise. If things get bad, I'll . . . tell Aunt Aleetha I need her home, but she has to heal for both our sakes, and for Sira." I swallow the lump forming in my throat. I'm a liar. I know I won't be fine. I know I don't want Rahuin to go because the last time she left me… I don't want to think about it. I don't want to think about how she betrayed our marriage. I don't want to believe she'd do it again, but it still hurts, and I can't stop the way it plagues me. I've forgiven her because I understand why she did it, but what if some part of her enjoyed it? What if she does it again?

That idea scares me the most. She could do it again in a heartbeat if she wanted to. She could break my heart, destroy me in an instant. I hate that she has so much power over me, but if anyone's to blame, it's me. Love doesn't come without risks. When you love, it tears you apart because you put so much trust and faith into another person. You give your all, and when they fail you, it hurts the most.

"Dais?" Thesa waves a hand in my face.

She comes back into focus as I find a way out of the maze in my head. I wish I could snuff the thoughts out like a flame, but they continue to burn.

"I'll be fine." I nod to assure her, but it must not look convincing because she stares at me skeptically. "I've been thinking too much, but I'll take sleeping draughts and try to keep the thoughts at bay. I'll do what I have to while she recovers." I'm glad my voice stays steady.

She still doesn't look persuaded, but nods anyway. "Fine. I can't say I believe you, but I don't have a choice. I will come back as soon as everything settles in Treía. I'll be devastated if anything happens to you or Rahuin."

"I know . . ." I trail off because I want to tell her that I'll be fine again. I want to assure her until the worry leaves her expression, but any more promises I make will just be a lie. I can't afford to lie to her. I've made enough promises already, and I have every intention to keep them . . . I just don't know how long I'll be able to hold on. I'm hoping I can until Rahuin is recovered, but if she takes longer than my strength, then all my promises will be broken.

Connan

My hands shake as I bring the cup of hot tea to my mouth. The liquid sloshes out and burns my lip before dribbling down my chin and onto my shirt. Getting old is terrible. If I had the strength, I would have already heaved myself over the edge of *The Grandier* and been done with it, but Maud would just pull me back in and lock me up to prevent any more future escapes. It's not worth it.

I sip the tea, but it doesn't taste like it used to—the smooth, earthy notes fall flat. Everything is tasteless. I set the cup on my navy blue desk. I'd had it made out of the finest wood when I became admiral. Finishing it with brass handled drawers and clips to hold documents down. A few nicks and scrapes decorate the top even though I've only been in the position for three years.

Three years.

Has it only been that long? I feel like an old man who has lived seventy years . . . well, I look like one anyway. I hardly recognized my reflection yesterday. I cast a spiteful look toward the mirror that stands on the left side of my quarters. It reflects the light of the windows behind me and catches a reverse image of the map to my right. Thank goodness it doesn't catch my face. I'm glad it doesn't show the wrinkles and droopy skin that have now become mine or my white hair that falls out in droves.

Funny. I never pictured myself having white hair as an old man. I lift a hand to my chin, stroking the whiskers that cover my face. At least I can still grow a good beard and it looks a lot nicer in its gray tones than my snowy hair. Now I just have to shave my head and keep the beard. I almost laugh at the thought. It doesn't matter. I'll be dead soon anyway.

The door in front of my desk opens, allowing sunlight from the deck to flood onto the hardwood floors. Maud steps in, the light glittering behind her pale pink wings and causing them to sparkle. Her eyes narrow on the spot where the tea stained my shirt.

"Will I have to get you a bib every time you eat or drink now?" she asks, moving toward me.

I glare at her. "If I have to be confined by wearing a bib like a baby, then please kill me first. I'd never want to stoop that low."

"I don't know. I think it'd be entertaining." Her wings flutter a little as she chuckles.

"You're evil." I rub my thumb against the warm porcelain of my cup.

"I have a message for you. It's from the king." She holds a note with the Castian seal of a crashing wave. The blue wax shimmers in the light flooding the room.

"Read it for me." I wave a hand at her.

She raises an eyebrow but doesn't make any snarky comments on how bad my eyes are getting as she breaks the seal. "Dear Connan, this is a most urgent matter. Glena, suffocated under her grief regarding her father's death, attempted to harm me, and because of it, Rahuin and the baby have been threatened. Glena wasn't in her right mind and has apologized. I don't want to take her life over this matter and don't want her imprisoned. I would like to punish her for a year and have her come assist you on *The Grandier*. I know the fairies can conjure a barrier to keep a close eye on her. I want to know if it would be plausible and if you'd be willing to help. Please respond as soon as you are able, King Dais."

I look up at Maud. "Can you do what he asks?"

Maud nods. "It shouldn't be a problem. It doesn't sound like Dais has particularly had it very easy since he became king. Tell him we will fulfill the punishment."

I notice how she says 'we' because she knows I won't live for a whole year. I'll be lucky if I have two more months. I'm ready for whenever I do leave. I've appointed my first mate, Alaster, as the new captain of *The Grandier* and have already recommended him for the admiralty.

The fairies said they'd help Dais if he calls on them, but they are going to go back to Is'Er. I guess Maud will hold them back until Glena's punishment has been finished.

"As long as it's all right with you." I sigh, reaching for parchment and ink.

"Oh, don't sound so gloomy about it. It already seems gloomy enough around here. The crew have stopped singing and dancing after dinner, and instead, just drink themselves into a stupor. For which, we have to pick them up and try to get them to a cot or a bucket." She shudders.

I smile. "I'll stop. I'm ready for when the time comes, just don't put a bib on me or I'll go sooner."

"I promise nothing." She winks. "Get a reply together and I'll send the message back to the castle." She shuffles to the door once more, glancing back. "What if it was a nice, fancy bib?"

I look up, glaring at her.

"Just a suggestion." She smirks before exiting my quarters.

Jarret

Everything is blurry when I open my eyes. A sharp spike of pain shoots through my head, and I close my lids shut again, giving into the dark.

"Wake up, Jarret. Wake up and face me," a voice speaks, but it's

not one I recognize.

What? I open my eyes again, and this time they focus on a hazy outline of a man standing over me. I blink, focusing on his features and my brow scrunches when I see myself reflected back at me. What the . . . ?

"Finally. I was beginning to think you'd given up and gone to the Gateway of Light." My twin smirks, quirking his face in a sinister manner. His eyes glint with malicious intent as they become completely black.

I stare my mouth agape. What is this? Who is this? This can't be me. My stomach churns as sounds of distant screams start to plague my head. I remember those screams, the screams I heard when I . . . I close my eyes, but images race across my vision instead—faces filled with horror, blood pooling in the streets, fire licking humble huts.

I open my eyes again, but not-me is still there. He laughs, a sound that makes my skin crawl. He's crazy, or I am, but he's not me. He'll never be me.

"Oh, but I am you. You just don't have the courage to face me. I will take everything you love away from you, just like I did to Renell..."

I gasp awake, taking in a sky full of winking stars. I groan, trying to turn my head, but pain spikes along my spine.

"Jarret?" This time I recognize the voice—Wen.

My vision blurs then focuses as he leans over me. His white tattoos glow eerily in the moonlight, white hair falling over his forehead.

"What—" I start, but my tongue feels thick and heavy.

"Do you remember what happened? Renell is"—his gray eyes study mine—"Renell is in Cizarrél. She . . ." he trails off, and I think he wants me to fill in the blanks, but am I supposed to? I don't remember what happened. Why is she in Cizarrél? Last I remember, we were headed to Cizarrél. She was going to challenge the . . . Everything comes rushing back.

I lost. Renell made sure we got out. A mysterious woman helped us. Renell is——

"No," I gasp. "No, she can't marry him." My hand grips Wen's arm, and I ignore the pain that shoots across my shoulders.

He leans back, pulling out of my grip. "It's too late, Jarret. She made her choice."

No . . . The plea embeds itself, but I don't have the strength to shout it. She's my wife. She can't become his. She can't . . .

I'll take everything from you. No. This is a nightmare I can't escape. This is— this never should have happened. I should have won. No, I shouldn't have fought at all. Why did I fight him? Why did I have to destroy everything?

The memory of Renell's smiling face when she told me about the baby plays in my thoughts. That's why I couldn't let her fight. Clòz changed the rules. She couldn't use her gift. That's why I tried to win instead, but it was all for nothing. I still lost her. I lost them both. She could have defeated him, so why did I step in? Why did I ruin it? Now, I've lost her, and she promised—she promised she would always put her country first. But maybe in this case, she had to, to keep me safe, to get Wen and I out of there. I'm such an idiot. Why did I do this to her? Why did I do this to us?

"I've healed your wounds as best as I could, but your body is still in shock. You almost died." He runs a hand through his hair. "I still don't understand why you did it. She was ready. She could have won, but you couldn't accept that." The venom in his voice poisons me.

I glare at him. "Don't tell me what I could and couldn't accept. She is pregnant. I was scared I would lose them both, and now I have!" I try to lift myself up, but all it does is send more pain down my body. I fall back onto my cot as tremors ripple through me. I hate this. I hate that I can't move. My evil twin was right. I will lose everything.

Wen's eyes widen. "She's pregnant?"

I clench my jaw against the pain. "Yes. She told me a few days before the fight. I tried to convince her to wait . . . When he said she couldn't use her gift, I was so afraid. I didn't want to lose them. I thought I could win. I thought I could protect them." My voice breaks and I hate it. "I realize how foolish that was."

Wen sighs. "We do stupid things when we're afraid."

"This was beyond stupid. Now they're both gone, and who knows when I'll be able to get them back. Maybe she can just . . . Maybe she can kill her new husband." My throat clenches as I utter the words, but that was what we were planning all along—kill the chief, take the land.

"She can't," Wen utters, a sharp edge poisoning his voice as he surveys the landscape surrounding us.

"What? What do you mean?"

"They are bound by blood. Cay-Llekians bind marriage. If she were to kill him, she'd die too. It's a curse to keep spouses faithful, so they don't kill for power since Cay-Llek has no true law."

I really am an idiot. She can't kill him. Is it too late? No, I'm in a nightmare. This is all just a nightmare. I'll wake up soon and realize this is all a fabrication . . . But I'm not going to wake up. I feel like I've been punched in the gut. I can't breathe.

"Please leave me," I gasp. "Please just let me . . . go."

Wen looks back at me. "Absolutely not. I promised her I would keep you safe."

"Why does it matter? I can't be with her anyway. If he dies . . . I'll never get her back!" The hand of terror grips my throat, and I try to take a breath, but I can't.

Wen takes my shoulders into his hands, his gray eyes bore deep into mine. "If we can find a way to break the curse, you'll get her back, but until then, I'm not leaving you alone. Besides, you have enough of your own problems to worry about."

"What do you mean?"

He lifts my left wrist, shooting pain down my shoulder, but my retort about his roughness immediately disappears when I see the glowing crown embedded in my scales. No. Not this on top of everything else. I can't go to Treía. I can't— I have to find a way to break Renell's curse. I have to . . . My mind whirs. This is too much. It's all too much. I have hope that I can save Renell, but what if I'm chosen? How will I ever reach her and the baby again? How will I be able to make any of this right?

"I'm taking you to Treía. You must report first, and then we'll save Renell." Conviction lights his gray eyes. I never thought I'd find an ally in him, but he's all I have now, and he's willing to help.

I swallow, trying to loosen the chokehold on my neck, but it doesn't help. "Fine. Take me to Treía."

Chapter 21
To Fool a King

Renell

Clòz glares at me, but I hold his gaze. I won't cower in fear. I won't show him how much power he has over me. He'll never know how scared I am. The scar along his face contorts as he lifts his chin in amusement, the red tattoos twist in a horrific nightmare I'd seen far too often over the last few days. "How can I indulge my bride?"

"I have a request that I feel would be of utmost importance to you, my chief."

"And?" He slinks closer.

I resist the urge to step back, the walls decorated with the bones of his enemies seem to draw closer. "We should make our own alliance with Onar."

His brow quirks. "An alliance with Onar? What do you mean?"

"They were united with Sun'Ar like you, but you've fought and still don't have what was promised yet. What if we ally with Onar, so if Sun'Ar fails again, we can take it ourselves?" I lean closer to him even though everything in me screams to run away. I've done this to myself. I have to keep fighting. I can't allow myself to fail.

The flickering tallow candles cast orange light over his features, making his snaking scar evermore prominent as the shadows cause it to slither across his face. It makes my skin crawl.

His dark eyes glint with desire and a meaty hand reaches for my face. His fingers caress my cheek, and I swallow to keep from spitting in his face. "How do you know that wasn't my plan all along?"

"Then it's a brilliant plan, my chief."

He leans back, not even questioning why I'm telling him what he wants to hear. He's clever, so he's more than likely aware of my own motives, but hopefully he won't call them out yet.

"I knew you'd be a great asset to me, Princess." He smirks, his face leaning closer to mine. "Don't even think about trying something. If you do, I will find it out, and I will destroy everything you hold dear. I will break your spirit, so you will never go against me again."

"I wouldn't imagine going against you, my chief, but do what you will with me. For I live to serve you. I am your wife." I almost choke on the words. I've only been his wife for a grand total of three days. I inhale musty air.

"Good." His other hand snakes up my side, his fingers loosening the strings that hold my dress together. It takes everything within me not to tap into my gift and destroy him. His hot breath assaults my skin as he kisses my neck. "We'll go to Onar." His voice is thick with pleasure.

"As you wish, my chief," I whisper and clench my teeth to tamper the monster brewing under my skin.

Thesa

"Looks like your little bastard isn't here yet. He might have to forfeit the crown even though your old man already affirmed him. How stupid would that make him look? Oh well, at least he won't have to revel in the embarrassment," Erix goads, his gold eyes blazing like fire, but I hardly hear him.

My mind is stuck on what he said—Jarret isn't here yet. My heart sinks. Perhaps I'll have to go find him after all. What if something terrible has happened to him? I shouldn't have come here first . . . I shouldn't— Kyira will be able to track his stone. She'll find him.

"I knew you had no respect for your king, but this is low, even for you." My nails dig into my palm as I catch a glimpse of the shining crown in his wrist of green scales. "Speaking ill of the previous king. I know the stones will not look kindly on you."

"How would you know? Are you a stone seeker? Do they listen to your will?" He smirks, leaning against a glowing wall, the rainbow colors washing over his face.

"No, but they listen to yours, and I'm sure they don't like what they hear."

His sharp eyes narrow as he steps close.

I glare at him, hating that he's taller than me.

"A disgrace like you will never be chosen, and don't even think about trying to steal it from a true heir." His face flushes as he lifts his chin, staring down his nose.

"Who would call you a rightful heir? Your bloodline is tainted deeper than mine, but this was a good chat, Erix. I always enjoy them." I turn on my heels, ignoring his insults as they step with me down the cave. Somehow he always finds me, and I don't even know how or why. I'm starting to believe he searches and waits since he didn't get his chance to scare me off the first time I came back with Jarret a few months ago. My heart clenches at the thought. Both Jarret and my father aren't here now. What if Jarret never arrives? What if I lost him for good by coming here? No, I can't afford to think like that. If I do, I'll never find the strength to get back to Jet and Rahuin.

I steal a breath as I pass under Prism Arch and head to my father's quarters.

Kyira stands in front of the altar on the other side of the council table. The room still holds all the signature things my father left—his maps, his chair decorated with golden scales, a sheathed sword hanging from the back of it.

I hold back the sob that lingers in my throat.

Beside Kyira, a pile of shimmering stones covers my father's body. They will preserve it until everyone arrives for his Enflaming Ceremony. All Garons are called to attend and witness the choosing of a new monarch. I stare at the assemblage, afraid to move farther into the room.

It's said that the ghost of the deceased lingers until the Enflaming Ceremony is complete. I don't know if I believe in ghosts, but I feel my father's presence here. Perhaps it's just the memories that we made the last few times I'd seen him. The memories of forgiveness and reconciliation. The memories where I hugged him and stood in his presence without our conversation ending in a fight.

I'm so grateful Kyira told me to come back last time, or rather, he did. I meet Kyira's milky white eyes, as if she can truly see me. Her sweet demeanor envelops me as she pulls me into an embrace, and I can't help the sob that escapes. The weight of the last few weeks falls from my shoulders and onto her. "It's all too much, Kyira. It all happened at once. I can't breathe. I can't continue on."

Her fingers run through my hair as she shushes me. "It's all right, child. Everything will be all right."

"It doesn't feel all right," I whisper. "And there has been no sign of Jarret?"

"Ah, that's what worries you the most. The stones say that he's safe. He's on his way." She pulls back, and I find her milky gaze drifting to the ceiling as they grow wide.

My heart lifts. I knew Kyira would know. She has a special way with the stones because she's a stone seeker—a prophet of sorts. I think they even help her 'see' since she was born blind. Because of her attachment, she tethers helns for Garon couples.

"He is? Where is he? I have to go—"

"Stay. The stones say stay. He's moving slowly, at least his *heln* is, but he's been separated from Renell. Hers is still in Cay-Llek. He's currently in Lanckest, skirting around the mountains. I'm sure the snow is still deep in the upper valleys. At his pace, he'll be here in a week."

A week? Why isn't he flying? He'd be here much sooner if that were the case. "Is he hurt?"

"I'm not sure. His pace would say yes, but you can't head after him. You won't find him, they say. You must stay." Her voice echoes among the cavern and her eyes finally relax as she sighs.

"I can't just stay here, Kyira. He's my son. I've left him too much already." I hate the way my voice shakes.

"I understand, but I urge you to stay. He will be all right." She takes my hand, squeezing it. "We have much to prepare for while we wait anyway." She starts walking with my hand still in hers.

"Kyira, do you kno—"

"I don't, child. The stones tell me a great deal, but so much can happen before an Enflaming Ceremony. Sometimes I think they don't know who they'll choose until the time has come."

So it's not set in stone like I always thought it was. Perhaps the chosen heir could still have misfortune befall them. My stomach prickles. I pray Jarret gets here soon.

Glena

The door to my cell opens, and I stand. Frobin rushes in, pulling me into his arms even though I smell like a pigsty.

"Frobin," I whisper, burying my face in his shoulder. He smells like the night air, like how my father used to. My heart clenches as I swallow the lump that forms. This isn't the time to cry.

I start to pull away, but he tugs me closer. "Wait. Just let me hold you for a second."

My stomach churns with the force of an avalanche. Oh, no. Dais has made his decision. I'll die now. I hold in a sob because I knew this was coming. There is no way Dais will forgive me after what I did. I still can't forgive myself. I killed a child.

A child.

Shivers break out on my skin as bile rises in my throat. I cling to Frobin as I start to shake. I hate myself. I hate what I've done. I hate that my stupidity has pushed Frobin away from me again. If I could take it all back . . .

Rahuin was my friend. I never meant to hurt her, so why did I do it? Why was I so blinded by my own grief? My father would have never wanted this. He died to protect her, and I tried to kill her husband. How is that right?

Frobin starts to lean away, but I know if he lets me go, I will collapse. Somehow, he understands my unsaid plea and leaves a steady arm around me so I can see his face. Tears stream down his cheeks, marring his orange beard, but he doesn't look sad, instead he looks relieved.

"Glena." His thumbs caress my cheek. "You've been pardoned. You . . ." he continues, but my mind is stuck on one word—pardoned. Dais has forgiven me. Frobin is still talking, but I'm not listening. He steps back, so I can see that we aren't alone.

King Dais stands in the door to my cell. His pale blue eyes aren't filled with anger like I thought they'd be, they're filled with compassion. He steps forward, and Frobin must think I'm strong enough to stand before the king because he releases me.

"Glena," Dais speaks. "Do you understand what Frobin said?"

I blink and glance helplessly at Frobin because I'd completely blocked out the explanation.

"He said I was pardoned?" I swallow. My voice sounds so quiet.

Dais smiles warmly. "Partially pardoned. I can't pardon you completely because fanatics think you deserve death."

I glance away because I believe them. I do deserve to die.

"But I don't. I believe you have so much more to offer. I want to give you a chance, but there has to be a punishment. I've spoken with Admiral Connan, whom I know you are acquainted with, and he will have you work on *The Grandier* for a year. The fairies who accompany him will monitor your punishment. Once you have fulfilled the sentence, you are free to come home."

Tears fill my eyes as I bow my head. "Thank you, Your Majesty. I'm deeply sorry for what happened. I don't deserve this second chance, but I will use the rest of my life proving how thankful I am." I lift my head. "Your forgiveness means the world to me."

"I'll let you in on a little secret. If I hadn't had my family and the responsibility of this kingdom I would have done the same."

I meet his eyes, and a sadness has overcome them. Right. He lost his father too.

"I'm not above you because I'm a king. I'm human too, and my emotions could have influenced my actions as well. I'm glad I never acted on them, but I have no right to judge you and neither does anyone else. That's why I'm not giving you a real trial, and it's why we have to steal you away now and leave you on *The Grandier.*" He glances back toward the dungeon entrance as if someone will come and stop us at any second, but who would deny their king's wishes? "We should get going. You can say your goodbyes then."

Dais

"You shouldn't trust her, Your Majesty," Lord Gervios says, brown eyes deep pools of concern. He runs a hand through short gray hair.

The sage green walls of my office are starting to look more and more like a prison cell every day. Rahuin left three days ago, and I haven't even had a moment's reprieve from this room. I need sleep, but what would be the point? I had a meeting with Lord Rhëtt, Lord Morrlok, and Lord Gervios early this morning, but I'm not exactly comprehending anything they're saying.

"Lord Gervios is right. For the sake of the monarchy, you should divorce her," Lord Rhëtt states, blue eyes shifting as his throat bobs.

"Divorce?" I stare at my father's three most trusted council members—three he advised me to keep close.

"The people are still restless, Your Majesty. They demand that she be . . ." Lord Gervios trails off. He waves a hand around the room as if all of Casta is present.

"Sacrificed?" I spit. "Do they even recognize what she's done for them?" I sigh because the question is stupid. Of course they don't. If they did, they wouldn't have staged an attack on our wedding day. We'd found and captured a few of the traitors, questioning them as to who their leader is, but so far, they've revealed nothing. It doesn't help that I'm running out of time for answers, especially if I keep having this conversation with my closest council.

"Your Majesty—"

"No, I refuse to listen to any advice saying I have to divorce my wife. She's been through too much. I've been through too much to give her up. She's pregnant with my daughter. I won't divorce the woman I love because my people think she did something awful. I wish they would transfer their anger to the real enemy, the enemy trying to take their home from them. Can't they see war is still on the horizon? We've won battles, but the end isn't here yet, even with the ceasefire. I need them trained. I need them ready. I don't need this pettiness that seems to be going deeper and deeper. Someone is spreading lies, and they are believing it. I just need to know who . . ." I trial off as I contemplate the new idea.

This has to be more than mere pettiness. They can clearly see that Rahuin has caused no other harm to me or my family.

"I agree," Lord Morrlok declares. He's a man of few words, so when he does speaks, his wisdom outshines the rest. "King Dais is right. Something is amiss here. You all saw how the people accepted her explanation and the letters long before the wedding, but on the day of, suddenly there are weapons in the temple and a vendetta that needs an answer? People's lives were lost, and a day that should have been merry was covered in blood. They're using it as justification that our king is in danger, and that his wife is the cause. Our two captured traitors aren't being very informative, but I have a hunch this was an inside occurrence. Someone has power among the guards and that someone told them to either plant the weapons or overlook them."

Lord Morrlok looks at me, his dark brown eyes imbue me with strength. "Many of the guards became loyal to Zenz once he started training them. They respected him because of his eloquence and achievements in battle. I think we need to find the ones who were loyal to him and have them tell us if anyone was against Zenz or was acting odd in the last few weeks."

"You think we should make it seem like we're trying to find who killed him? Instead of who went after my wife?"

Lord Morrlok nods. "Precisely. If we tell them we're looking for traitors, they'll turn tail and run. We have to be delicate with this matter, and since they could potentially be a part of the royal guard, they could easily try another attempt, especially once Rahuin gets back."

"But why would they go after Rahuin? Why not just go after the king outright?" Lord Rhëtt asks, stroking his brown beard.

"I didn't say they'd go after her. I insinuated that they would use her against him. Since King Dais insists on staying married to her, they can kill him and blame it on her. Or, if the king decides to divorce her, they can still kill him and blame it on her."

"And how did you draw this conclusion, Lord Morrlok? It seems you've had plenty of time to come up with a plan like this. How do we know you're not behind the attacks?" Lord Gervios asks. Usually, his skepticism is a terrible pain in my side, but this time, I agree with him.

"It's what I would do if I wanted the monarchy. Though, I would initially go after Esther and David first. If I truly wanted power, I would make sure everyone is taken care of so I could even be considered. Which makes me think that whoever is behind this, isn't after the throne."

"What do you mean?" Lord Rhëtt asks.

Lord Morrlok smiles, his gray goatee quirking upward. "You both certainly have a lot of questions today. Do I need to spell it out? Or can one of you understand why the monarchy wouldn't be important if a certain power won?"

Lord Gervios clamps his mouth shut while Lord Rhëtt opens and closes his like a fish out of water.

"The Darkness. Whoever is doing this has struck a deal with him, or it is him," I say as Lord Morrlok nods.

"Precisely, now we just have to figure out who is in league with the Darkness, and what he might be gaining from this. Maybe he is trying to spread turmoil so we aren't prepared when the time comes, while also getting rid of a formidable foe—someone who destroyed his armies already."

"Rahuin," Lord Gervios says, brown eyes twinkling with realization.

"Yes, I suggest we start convincing the people that there is a greater enemy and sway their opinions. During that time, we should start questioning the guards, in accordance with the other captured men to see if we can draw the same conclusion. Maybe then we will find our traitor." Lord Morrlok nods at me.

"I agree. I will start the interviews today." I stand. "Thank you, gentlemen. You are dismissed."

They start for the door.

I circle around my desk, patting Lord Morrlok's shoulder. "As always, thank you for your wisdom."

He bows his head. "May I speak plainly?"

I nod. "Of course."

"Dais, King Timothy asked me to watch over you. When he told me his plan, I thought he was insane. I thought you weren't ready, but every day, you show me that your father was right. You are an excellent king, and I've vowed to serve my king until my last breath. It is my job to think of every scenario and warn you what could happen. It is your decision whether you accept my conclusion or not. I hope you don't find it ambitious. I know my thoughts can sound . . . extreme, but sometimes that is what you might be dealing with. I don't want anything to happen to Casta, and you love this country as much as I do. It is my duty to see you through this, and every challenge to come."

I mull over his words, his prior conclusion had me a little skeptical of his motives. "I'll admit that I held you back to be sure that—"

His brown eyes twinkle. "I'm not opposed if you keep a close eye on me. If I were in your position, I wouldn't know who to trust either. I pray that I will be found trustworthy. For a loyal man without a king or country to serve, well . . . it would feel like death itself." He smiles warmly, in a way that reminds me of my father. I can tell why Father told me to keep him close. He's a good man, a loyal man, and I can see that now.

"Thank you, Lord Morrlok. You are dismissed."

"Your Majesty." He bows out of the room, and Jet securely closes the door behind him.

"Do you think you can trust him?"

"I do. He's the only one I feel truly cares about Casta. No one else drew that conclusion because they aren't worried about what's coming. At least he believes in the Darkness. I can't get anyone else to understand what could happen if the Darkness wins, and we're running out of time to get prepared. I have to put an end to this madness. If Lord Morrlok proves to be someone I can't trust, then it's a risk I took. That's why I have you." I clap him on the shoulder.

He sighs. "I fear I've been failing you too, Dais. What if I can't keep you safe?" He casts his gaze downward. He's apologized more than once over what happened at Zenz's funeral, but I have a feeling he's having a hard time forgiving himself.

"If you lack confidence, Jet, then you won't, but if you say you will keep me safe, then I trust you without a doubt."

He grips my arm. "I will keep you safe. I will not fail."

"I know."

Carrie

CITY OF PËR, KÄS

The door creaks open, and my heart jumps at the sound. Stupid heart. Why do you get so easily attached? Is it because he saved your life? Do you just fall in love with anyone who shows you an ounce of kindness? Well, what he showed was more than an ounce since he almost killed himself to save me.

Aiden closes the hardwood door behind him, his pale blue eyes meeting mine from where I stand in the kitchen cutting the stew meat I'd bought in the market. We'd hid my body in the mortuary in case someone came to check on Aiden's story. I say my body, because Aiden put me into a deep sleep with his ability. A sleep that would seem like I was dead, and no, no kisses would be involved to wake me up, sadly.

I woke up about an hour ago. Aiden said it would only last as long as he allowed, something to do with the connections of his ability. I couldn't question it. I don't know anything about Walk abilities but I wish I had more knowledge. I hunted them for years without regard to who they actually were or what they do. I was taught to hate all Walks because of their cursed blood, but they are just human, like me. They still feel and breathe and have compassion.

"Well?" I ask, hoping that I'm finally free of the king's chains.

Although, I didn't think through that I'd have to be locked up in this house most of the time, but maybe we can find a way to alter my appearance and change my name. It's possible . . . until I see the look on his face. The king didn't buy it. He knows I'm still alive.

"I'm sorry. You know, but I can't say it because . . ." He looks away, studying the stone walls.

I feel the air rush from my lungs. He can't say it because Rave will know. He will kill me or Aiden or both of us if he tells me the truth. "It doesn't matter. I can guess what happened. It's okay. It was a long-shot anyway. I thought—I thought I could be free," I whisper, starting to grab my things. We'd even set up a cot beside his bed for me to sleep in.

Aiden walks further into the room, taking my shoulders into his hands. I lean into his touch. *Stupid heart! You can't feel comfort from him. You can never have him.* But I don't move. I need the comfort to steady me, if only for a moment. "You don't have to leave. You shouldn't know. You can't go back."

Right. If I leave and report to Rave, he'll think Aiden told me. He didn't, but King Rave won't really know that. He can't read minds, but he does have spies everywhere. Any one of them can embellish the truth.

I sigh. "He'll use me against you. If I stay . . ." I trail off because we both know I'm not brave enough to leave. I don't want to die. I want to live, but can I call this living if I have to hide my very existence from the world anyway? If I have to continue to be a pawn in Rave's sick games? For Aiden's sake, I should just leave and die quietly like I should have done to begin with.

Aiden studies me, his blue eyes flickering like flames. "You don't have to leave. Yes, he will probably use you against me, but what other choice do you have? I'm not going to let you die. I just—"

"You just what?" I ask, escaping his hands that are still on my shoulders. It feels too intimate. I should keep my distance in case he starts to care more than he already does, but maybe it's too late for that as well. I stare out the small window where I watch shadows from the outside world shift over the sunlight. If I could reach up there, I'm sure I'd see hundreds of people and transport shuffling past since the little window looks out onto the bustling street.

"I should just keep my distance, but it won't matter. I already care too much about your life. I'll never sacrifice anyone just for my sake. Every life is precious, and I will do anything to preserve it. So please, don't leave."

He cares for me. He doesn't want to distance himself. My heart soars. I know that's not exactly what he said, but my foolish head can't help but focus solely on that. I draw my gaze back to his. "I won't. I'll stay. If you want, I'll help at the clinic. I'll go anywhere with you, just not to the palace unless we can come up with a clever disguise to keep Rave in the dark about my knowing."

He nods. "I'll put you to work. You seem like someone who'd go crazy if she had to sit down here all day." He runs a hand over his shorn locks, sighing as his eyes light on the forgotten dinner I was working on. "Dinner?" he asks, but I hardly hear him cause I'm watching the way his throat bobs, the way his fingers slide against his hair . . . He does that when he's nervous, look how much I've learned about him already. I shake my head. *Get a grip, Carrie!*

"Y—yes, I'm still going to make it for you . . . as a thank you!" I smile, heading back to my forgotten vegetables. I continue to dice carrots.

"Are you a good cook? That could be a dealbreaker. Because if you can't pull your weight and make dinner . . ." he trails off leaning over my shoulder.

My heart speeds up at his closeness. "If you're going to be noisy, I should put you to work." Proud of myself for being able to say it without a stutter. I almost wave the knife at him before grabbing an onion from the sack I'd left on the counter. I toss it to him.

"Of course, you leave me with the onion. I don't think I'd like you to see my manly tears." He grabs another knife.

"What makes you assume I see any of you as manly?"

"Shots fired!" He grabs his chest, falling over. "C—call a Lifewalker, our other Lifewalker is in critical condition. A pretty girl had the audacity to question his manliness."

I poke him with my foot. "You called me pretty." I can't contain my smile as I set my knife down and face him.

He sits up. "Okay, I've called you pretty before, it can't come as that much of a shock."

I hold a hand out to him. "Well, it does," I whisper, pulling him up until he's towering over me once more.

I look up into those gorgeous blue eyes. They look as open and as free as clear skies without one cloud to darken the horizon. My gaze trails down to his lips. I know I shouldn't be so obvious because we shouldn't do this. We shouldn't let these feelings come between us, but we can't stop it. It's too late.

He looks down at me and swallows as his fingers gently touch my cheek. "Is this—is this okay?"

I nod, touching his face with my hand. "I don't see why not."

"What about distance?" We're so close to each other now, there's no turning back.

"To hell with distance. It's too late already."

His lips touch mine, and I melt into his arms, leaving no space between us. My heart flies into the expanse of his blue skies, and I never want to come down. I don't want to think about distance or death. I don't want to worry about the future or what any of this could mean. I just want him to be mine without a crazy king suggesting it. I just want us to be like every other couple, we found something common, we had a little attraction, and we built off it.

He pulls back slightly. "We should—"

"Just one more." I giggle, starting to wonder why I feel a little bit like clay in his arms.

He smiles. "Was that a giggle?"

"Shut up." I smack his arm, and he laughs before obliging me one more.

Aiden

CITY OF PËR, KÄS

"Why are you in the service of King Rave anyway?" Carrie asks over a steaming bowl of soup. It smells heavenly. She made it with some chicken meat and fresh vegetables. My mouth waters as I take a sip. Flavors burst in my mouth, warming my heart. Her cooking is delectable, and it only makes me like her more. Who am I kidding? I liked her from the first second I laid eyes on her. Now that we're tethered, my attraction has only grown. Especially in lieu of her hidden talents like cooking. I haven't discovered anything she can't do yet. I bet it's singing. I haven't heard her sing yet. Because there has got to be something.

"He found me after the rebellion. He sent me to that school. The one where they train special Walks."

"There's a school for that? I thought that was a rumor."

"Oh my word, you didn't even know there was a school where Rave tried to train us to be his mindless followers? Yikes, I've got a lot to teach you. I mean it's not your fault you're arrogant, you're not a Walk after all." I take another sip of soup.

She whacks me playfully. "I didn't know. What did they try to teach you?"

"That Rave was perfect, and everyone else was horrible and needed to be put to death. Of course, they used more words than that, twisting it in a manipulative way, but you get the idea. Rave wanted to keep a special eye on me because my parents were a huge part of the rebellion. I was nine when they died, and Rave's guards took me to that place. He had us all watched until we developed our powers.

"Once he found which of us were useful to his campaign and which weren't, he separated us. Some went to the arena to die while the rest continued our mind-numbing education. How he decided which were useful and which weren't is a mystery to me, but I don't claim to understand what goes on in that foul mind of his."

"You're telling me." She rolls her eyes, grabbing a bun she'd made and slathering it with butter. I grab one too, reaching for the butter so our hands touch. She blushes and practically throws the knife into my hand. I try to burry my smirk. I love flustering her.

She hides behind the roll. "You did that on purpose."

My smile breaks through. "Of course."

"Okay, don't change the subject. Who were your parents?"

The question sends my heart sinking as I set the knife down. "I don't like to talk about it."

"Oh, I'm sorry. I just—I—you said they were important to the rebellion so I just was curious."

"Curiosity killed the cat." I wink. "I'm messing with you. They were Esther and Connan. Esther was—"

"The sister to the rebellion leader, Dais," she finishes.

"You know that, but you don't know that Rave imprisoned little kids into a horrible school?"

"If you've known about the school for so long, why haven't you done something about it?"

"Because Rave watches my every move. I don't need his scrutiny on this, especially now that you're here. I can't do anything." I take another bite of soup.

"But what if we could do something?"

I meet her eyes. "Carrie, we can't. I hate to let those kids suffer, but there is nothing I can do."

A light shines in her eyes, and I can tell that she's got an idea. "But what if there is? Here me out"—her hands splayed out in front of her. I've noticed when she's really excited, her hands start to do all the talking for her—"What if there was a way to get in there and adopt or help the children he's training? What if you could use your credentials as a prominent member of Rave's confidence and help get kids out of there, even if it's for a little while? I'm sure he'd put a limit on it, but it would be helpful for someone. If we get to save one kid from a horrible fate, won't that be worth it?"

Her words fill me with hope of the possibility. Could we really do it? I've been wanting to find a subtle way to rebel against Rave, but I couldn't figure out how. "Okay, I think you're onto something."

"Yes!" She pumps her fists in the air, her enthusiasm contagious.

"But"—I hold up a finger—"we have to be careful about this. Most adoptions can't happen unless there are two parents." I hold up two fingers. "And Rave will recognize you if I just randomly appear with a wife and proposition." I don't mention that he already knows, because I would break my promise of not telling her.

She blushes, coughing on the spoonful of soup she just ate. "Your wife? I mean—I didn't."

"Relax, I didn't ask you to marry me . . . yet."

"That means you're thinking about it. That's not what I was going for, but if you're sincere, I mean—"

"Carrie." I reach over the table, grabbing her shoulders. "Breathe. I'm just saying that you'd have to pose as my wife, but since he's watching my every move and you're not supposed to know the truth. Unless . . ." I trail off, thinking.

"Unless what?" Desperation clings to her big brown eyes. "Unless what? Tell me now!"

I start to laugh. "Unless, we change how you look."

"Huh?"

"It wouldn't be hard. We'd just have to find a Walk with that ability. Wait, I know someone from the school who could do it. He makes masks for theater with his ability and often works with spies. Hey, you maybe even used one of his designs working for Rave."

She nods. "I remember. His name is Mr. Kampf. He's a bit eccentric, but he could do the job."

"Exactly! Then, we have to let things take a natural course. I'll post a job offering for an assistant with no ability, and you can apply for the job and viola! Then it looks like I fell in love with and got married to my assistant instead of some random person I just posed as my wife." I stand, spinning around the room.

"Yes, and Rave will already know who I am, but it'll make it look like we tried to hide from him." She stands as well, taking my hands and spinning with me.

"See? It's perfect. He might not even let us do this, but it's worth a shot. Plus, it gives him more to use against me," I hum.

"You think that's a good thing?" She stops spinning, and I nearly collide with her.

I take her shoulders steadying us in our head-spinning state. "We've got to stop ending up like this." I smirk at her, staring at her lips because now I just want to kiss her again.

"You're right. I shouldn't put you in any more position to choose. I shouldn't have suggested it. I . . ."

"Carrie." My thumb brushes her cheek. "I said let's do it. If we play our cards right, we'll be able to save more Walks or at least wake them from the brainwashing before Rave decides to do whatever he wants with my ability."

"But what if we condemn others?"

"At least we tried. I've been wanting to make a difference like this for so long, so let's do it."

She smiles, throwing her arms around my neck, squealing in happiness. "Better get on a job posting."

"You better be ready to apply." I lift her slightly, looking at her lips again.

"Trust me, I am." She blushes and kisses me.

Chapter 22

How the Broken Bleed

Wen

It takes a week to get close to Treía, and even then, I'm not entirely certain how to get into the fabled Garon city. Jarret slips in and out of consciousness, so he's about as useful as a rock in a shoe. Mostly, he's just an annoying burden I have to carry most of the way. He should have come out of his delirium by now, but infection has set into his wound, and I couldn't find enough astringent herbs to reduce the swelling.

If only I can get into Treía so he can become their burden. Whispers of doubt nag the back of my mind. *Will they really help him? If other royals get a hold of him, they could end his misery quickly to keep him from getting chosen.* I grumble to the chorus of my thoughts. They're right. I can't leave him defenseless and alone here . . . that is, if I can find here.

Mountains surround us on all sides, and I feel their scrutiny as I hustle to a cliff face. The valley is covered in partial snow drifts and brown leftover grass pokes through the murky white. I'm tired of the snow already. Why does Treía have to be so high in the mountains?

317

It's impossible to get to and there are no green plants within a ten-meter radius. *Because Garons can fly . . .*

Ugh, if only I'd known where we were going, I could have teleported us there and saved myself the seven day trek. I think they do this to keep unwanted visitors out. What if they see me as an unwanted visitor? I don't exactly look like a Garon.

I study the blue streaks running through Jarret's long black hair. Suddenly I wish I had white streaks running through my hair instead of a full head of white. Or, perhaps streaks of black against the white? I think I'd like that.

Jarret groans, his head tilting as he stumbles against a rock and nearly sends us both into a bank of ice.

I counteract his weight by shifting my arms around his shoulders to pull him back against my side. I could sleep for a week after this journey, and honestly, that doesn't sound like a bad idea. Then I remember I still have to protect him while he recovers . . . *if he recovers.*

I banish the idea. He has to recover. I refuse to become Renell's personal vendetta. She'd destroy me in all of two seconds if he dies. *So, live, you idiot, live. You saved my life once. Do me this one favor, or second favor, and live so I can too. I promise I won't waste the second, er, third chance,* I will to him, refusing to voice my concerns. I don't want him to think I care about him. He's like an annoying cramp, like after you've run too far and long.

"We're almost there," he mumbles, and I look forward to find a wall of solid stone blocking our way. We only have a few feet before we crash into it.

"Well, we better be, because there is nowhere else to go. Unless we climb up a sheer cliff face, and there is no way I'm dragging your *flak* up that." I point at the granite that will soon end our journey, but my finger falls as I feel a presence begin to close in on us. It crawls over my skin, leaving chills. Someone's watching us. They're here, or more specifically, they know we're here.

The mountain in front of us seems to move. Garons of all sizes and colors appear around us, flapping their leathery wings and snorting huffs of fire.

A Garon covered in orange and black scales that make him look like a glowing ember moves forward. "State your business."

I release Jarret as he straightens to his full height, his pale face layered with sweat.

"I'm here for . . ." He shakily lifts his wrist, but his weakness causes him to stumble against me again.

This time, I realize how warm he is. He shouldn't be this warm in the chilly mountain air. I hold his wrist toward them, revealing the shining crown. "Please, he's very weak."

"Jarret!" A call rises above the sea of rainbow scales surrounding us, and some Garons turn their heads to the newcomer.

Thesa pushes through her brethren, jade eyes locked on her son, black and purple wisps of hair whipping around her face. Her features fall when she realizes his weakened state. "My son," she gasps, moving toward us. She looks at me. "Thank you." She strokes his sweat soaked hair. "Follow me. I'll get Kyira to make him a tincture immediately." She starts toward the stone face, the other Garons slinking back to their hiding places.

I drag Jarret with me, apprehension staring me down as we move toward the mountain. Thesa slips into the stone, and I halt for a second. Ah, a hidden passage. Very clever. Not sure why I didn't think of that before. I pull Jarret through the entrance, my eyes taking a second to adjust to the sudden dark, and when they do, a breath of awe escapes me.

Rainbow stones of all shapes and colors shine down from the huge cavern littered with hundreds of orifices and passages. Garons, both in human and dragon form, wander around the paths. Several narrow their eyes at me, and I can't help but feel like a mouse trapped by a cat. I shouldn't have come here. They might not let me leave. No, once Jarret gets better, he'll vouch for me . . . I hope.

Thesa starts up a spiral stone staircase to my right, leaning back to help me coax Jarret up them. She heads down a hall until we arrive at a door surrounded by a rainbow archway. She ushers us into a private cave, which has a huge round table in the center and what looks like an altar on the far wall. To my left, a fireplace sits with some meager furniture, but a comfortable looking chaise stands out among the other chair and little table.

I help Jarret onto the chaise, and his brown eyes light on me and Thesa before they roll into his head.

Thesa sighs, her fingers brushing against his forehead. "What happened?"

I fall into the chair beside them, warming my hands by the crackling fire. I meet her gaze and tell her what happened in Cay-Llek. Tears shine in her eyes once I'm through, and she looks down at Jarret.

"You foolish boy. Why did you risk so much? How could you have done that to me?" She wipes her face, before looking at me again. "Thank you for bringing him all the way here. I—I'll never be able to repay you."

"A hot meal would be nice."

She nods. "Of course, and I'll have a bed made up for you. Rest as long as you need. You're welcome to stay."

"Thank you." I lean my head against the back of the chair, closing my eyes and giving away to exhaustion.

Rahuin

We've been traveling for two weeks and we still haven't reached Silfras, the capital of Färrin. Once we crossed the border, it felt like I entered a magical world that I'd only ever read about in books. Lush foliage and trees taller than mountains canopied the skies, creating dark shadows on the ground, but the forest wasn't as ominous as I thought it would be. Instead, rich, vibrant flowers and glowing plants filled the area with ethereal light. Birds of all shapes, colors, and sizes often flashed through the foliage and add even more pigment to the gorgeous landscape.

As we near the city, which my mother describes as a giant tree palace, smaller homes appear around us. Each home looks like it's made with pure silver, and most are built in the crown of a tree with tall spires reaching for the sky. Slender windows often reveal curious elven faces, who appear in silent greeting of the royal entourage.

My heart fills with wonder and I feel like a child exploring the world for the first time. I shift on the purple seat in my parent's carriage, gently caressing my stomach that seems to have grown twice its size. I still have several more months of this . . . at least four, my mother thought. How do women do it? I haven't even moved all that much, just traveled, but maybe that's worse than actually exercising my stiff muscles.

I glance at my parents, who both have their noses stuffed in books. I've read as much as I cared to already, but now I wish I could read more. If only to provide a distraction from my creeping thoughts. . . I still see Elrian's smile. I still feel Zenz's blood coating my skin. I still hear the screams.

I glance out the window again, but this time the forest looks darker. The shadows seem to come alive and head straight for me as if they'll devour me whole. Part of me wants them to, just so I don't have to keep seeing the same things over and over again.

My fingers caress the sapphire necklace at the nape of my neck. Dais gave it to me before I left, reassuring me in my decision to go. I lift it to my face, admiring its heart shape. It looks just like his eyes. My heart fills with warmth as I recall his teasing smile and the visions of him holding Sira. Elrian's bright green eyes flash across my mind, and now I'm deliberating over what I've lost again. I take a deep breath, dropping the necklace back to its place. I hate my circling thoughts. All they do is loop around and around until I'm driven into insanity. I hardly sleep, even though we stop traveling at night so we can get a proper rest. Every time I close my eyes, I see it happening again.

My parents do their best to keep my mind off the images, but there are only so many times they can tell me about Färrin until I feel like I've heard it all. Apparently, the *Suvitaas*, the eleven teachers who keep the balance of the forest, have a remedy for my broken mind. Mother said training will help me focus and be able to grieve the recent events, but I'm not sure I want to grieve. To me, grieving says I'm letting go, and I'm not sure I want to say goodbye. Doesn't goodbye mean leaving it behind? I can't leave them behind.

My eyes drift around the interior of the carriage. White trees with curly leaves branch from the four corners as their canopies merge on the ceiling. A royal purple background cushions the velvet seats which I run my fingers over as I try to ignore the thoughts.

"You will destroy. You will be the end of them." A shiver breaks out along my skin. How many will die because of me? Maybe I shouldn't have come here. Maybe I'll bring the end of my parents, of Dais, of the League. Thesa was called to Treía, to Jarret, who could be hurt, and I still haven't heard any updates. What if those sudden occurrences have to do with the Darkness? What if he's right? What if I could end their pain . . . *No.* If I give into the Darkness's demands then he'll just use me to destroy them. Of course I'll feel no pain because I won't care about them anymore. I'll feel nothing. I'll become nothing.

"Aihha." Mother's soft voice pulls me from the void. "You're slipping. You can't give in, that's what he wants." She shifts until she sits next to me, her slender, soft hands taking mine.

I hate the callouses she finds, callouses from a year spent fighting for all I love and care for, but was it really worth it? Have I accomplished anything in my attempts to battle the dark? It doesn't feel like it. The reward outweighs the cost, and I fear that I'll be paying for the rest of my life.

"I know. I'm not going to give in. I'm just . . . I hope the *Suvita-as* can help me. I can't stop thinking about it, no matter how hard I try. The fear never leaves, and then I wish for it to end, but that would mean death. The fear reminds me I'm alive, but I can't help wondering if maybe I can end everyone else's suffering too."

She wrinkles her brow. "End our suffering, how? Do you think you're the only cause of all that's happened? It seems a bit vain of you. No one is the sole cause of someone's suffering. Sure, maybe the Darkness makes you think that it's all your fault, that all the evil in the world was done by your hand. That all—"

"No." I shake my head. "I just—I know the Darkness is the cause, but if I was no longer here, then he couldn't use me against the ones I love anymore." My voice is a soft breath that barely escapes my clenched throat.

"Then you wouldn't be the chosen one and all that you've fought for, all that you suffered for, would be in vain." Her striking blue eyes bore into mine, crashing like a tempestuous ocean drowning me in her gaze.

What is she talking about? Of course I'm the chosen one. Why else would the Darkness want me? Why else would my power nearly be the end of me?

At my confused expression, she continues, "The chosen one is supposed to bring back the King of Light, and if you die before He comes back, then you aren't the chosen one. Someone else will take your place. Perhaps they will be the correct chosen one, but will they fight for the dark or the light?"

Chills rush down my spine. She's right. How come I never considered it before?

"The Darkness won't kill you because he believes you are the one prophesied about," Father speaks up, his green eyes meeting mine with a silent conviction that runs as sharp as a blade. "The prophecies clearly state that you either choose the dark or the light. If you choose the light, then you're fighting until the King is back, and if you choose the dark, then you end everything for the Darkness. There is no in between. So if you die or kill yourself, it won't end our suffering. It might even create a new hell."

I take a deep breath, staring at both of them before I cast my gaze to the purple floor.

"We're not saying these things to scare you, Rahuin. We're just telling you the truth. When you claimed to be the chosen one, we were scared because we knew what it would mean for you and for us. Because you fight for the light, the dark will never stop coming against you and all you love until the King of Light returns. When He comes with a host of armies, He will vanquish the Darkness and all our suffering will end. That is the hope we cling to, and we're here now to help you face the next fight until the prophecies have been fulfilled," Father continues as Mother nods, her fingers squeezing mine until it feels like she's drained the blood from them.

I flex my hand to loosen her grip, and she does. "But what if I lose you all in the end?" Tears appear in my eyes. "What if I keep fighting and you keep supporting me until everyone I love is gone and the

King of Light still hasn't returned? What will happen then?" I whisper, because I already know what they're going to say and I can't bring myself to make my voice louder.

"Then it was all in vain, and you really weren't the chosen one, but I don't believe it will ever come to that. I believe He'll be here soon. Perhaps, sooner than we think. You can't allow those thoughts when you still have battles to face. We're here now, and we won't let you fail. If you're constantly focused on what you might lose, then you'll never succeed. The fight will be lost before you've even begun." Mother's words echo around the carriage, and I lean against her, falling into her embrace as I let my tears fall.

"You're right. I—I don't believe any of this is in vain, because the King of Light has spoken to me. He's told me to keep fighting, and that He will be there even if my strength runs low."

I feel Mother's fingers stroking my hair. "Good. You have the assurance, so it cannot be wasted. You will succeed, and the Darkness will be defeated."

Jarret

I stare at the blinking rainbow rocks, the light refracts around the dark stone walls. It's so beautiful and soothing, unlike the turmoil in my heart. It's been two weeks since Wen got me to Treía. He saved my life. Kyira said I wouldn't have made it one more day.

My grandfather's enflaming ceremony is today. Now that every Garon of royal blood is present, we can finally send him onward. I look at the ground as I shift into my scales. Mother's supposed to come get me before the ceremony starts.

She said there are thirty-nine in the descendant bloodline competing for the crown, and nine already had 'misfortunate' accidents befall them. I can only imagine who might have been behind them. Since arriving, I've had several curious Garons come to my grandfather's old chambers just to catch a glimpse. Many of them know who I am, they just don't know me, and I don't believe they ever will. I don't even know me.

Renell.

I see her dark green eyes, her bright smile that lit up my days. Will I ever see it again? It feels like someone's left claw marks on my insides. I just need to get this ceremony over with so I can continue finding a way to break her curse. I will see her smile again. I will kiss her lips once more. I will hold our child. Everything will be okay.

Wen enters the room, staring up at me. "You know, you should count yourself lucky to be able to do that. I wish I could become a dragon, but alas, I was cursed with white tattoos that light up when I use magic. Ooh, so terrifying." He shrugs his shoulders.

I glare at him.

He points up. "See, even that death glare is ten times scarier in your dragon form."

I roll my eyes, but I'm not sure how it comes across as a Garon. Wen is still an annoying pain in my side, but he hasn't left since he brought me here. In fact, Mother said he kept watch every night while I recovered, and for that, I don't know how I'll ever repay him.

Thank you, Wen, for everything you did for me. You didn't have to stay, but I'm grateful you did, I say in his head.

He grimaces. "Look, stop getting sappy on me. I didn't do it for you. I did it because I knew Renell would kill me if you died. I saved you purely for selfish reasons."

Well, whatever the reason, you saved my life.

He looks away, his gray eyes flashing in the rainbow lights. "Fine, call it what you want. I wasn't planning on staying long, but whatever happens, I want to help you break Renell's curse."

You do?

He scoffs, a sad smile spreading over his face as he looks up at me. "Yeah, Renell saved my life once. I want to repay that."

I stare at him for a minute. I never would have thought I'd hear those words come out of Wen's mouth. *I could use all the help you offer.*

"I thought you might say something like that, though, I did believe you'd want to be rid of me as soon as possible." He smirks.

Well, I'm not exactly fond of you, but you're not as bad as I thought you were.

"Hmm, again, I acted on selfish reasons, but it's okay if you want to lie to yourself." He turns around, heading for the massive door he'd come through earlier. It opens, revealing my mother in her Garon form, her purple scales shimmering under the lights.

It's time, she says.

I follow her out into the main hall of Treía. Thousands of Garons in all colors and sizes appear from every crevice, all of them facing the heap of wood upholding my grandfather's body. His sallow skin has sunk around his bones, and his body looks so small in comparison to the armor he's surrounded in. Mother and I take our place at the forefront of his pyre, right alongside our other royal brethren.

Somewhere, a Garon speaks and his voice whispers inside my head like a stowaway.

Today, we release, King Grelik Organsi, 126th monarch to the Treían throne, onward to his next journey. We enflame him as a symbol of release.

A Garon at the head of our circle starts a steady stream of fire from his throat, the rest of us follow suit. Flames lick the wood, and as they touch my grandfather's exposed skin, golden smoke rises above the orange until the flames themselves turn into the unnatural hue. The fire burns for a while before my grandfather's body seems to vanish, his armor consumed with him. As the pyre reaches to the domed ceiling, Garons around me start to shift back into their human forms, the royals immediately checking their wrists.

I do the same and catch sight of the crown in my scales shining as bright as the sun. Gasps filter through those present. I'm blinded by the light emanating from me, but I can't tear my eyes away.

"Jarret," Mother gasps as the shine starts to fade, and I notice that every Garon around us is now bowing their heads to me. No. Anything but this. How will I save Renell? I can't be king.

Mother lifts her head, her jade eyes speaking the truth I want to run away from. "You've been chosen."

All hail, King Jarret Organsi, 127th monarch of the Treían throne.

Renell

The early morning shimmers under a fresh rain and the dark clouds above threaten to fall again. I stare up at them, wishing for a bird to flutter along the murkiness, but I'm starting to believe there are no birds in Cay-Llek. If I was a bird, I wouldn't want to live here either. I dig my fingers into the chestnut mane of my horse, Heefe. He's my only comfort on this dreary journey. Usually, the steady clomp of his hooves is a helpful distraction, but not today. Today, I fight a losing battle of keeping my breakfast in my stomach where it belongs.

I close my eyes, leaning over Heefe as my gloved fingers twist the reins. We've been traveling for over a week now, and I'd been successful in keeping Clòz unaware of my morning sickness. But I fear that my luck is about to run out. Is four weeks long enough to become pregnant? It should be. He claimed me as his own on our wedding night, and it only takes one time.

I glance beside me where Clòz rides on a gray gelding, but he hasn't paid me any attention. His dark eyes are focused on the rocky terrain ahead of us.

I lean over the other side of my steed, and my head swims as the ground blurs beneath us. I throw up, coating the muddy road. "I'm sorry, Heefe," I whisper, gently patting his side.

"Halt!" The call echoes down the entourage following behind.

My heart starts to pound as the nightmare of his voice calls for the healer to come inspect me. Heefe's ears flicker as if trying to assess the danger. I wish I could snap his reins and send us flying out of here, but I clench my fists. When I was in Cizarrél, I had a Lan healer check me after my first night with Clòz because I knew she would keep my secret. The baby was fine, and she attended to me until we left with a different healer I didn't know. This one surely won't keep my secret.

The healer now stands below Heefe and helps me down. Immediately, he goes about checking me over, and I try not to feel personally invaded while he does his job. I wish we could have at least gone toward the wagon to give me a little more privacy, but I'm realizing that there is no privacy in Cay-Llek.

"How long have you been throwing up in the mornings?" he asks.

I swallow. "Right after we left Cizarrél."

"And you didn't tell anyone?"

"I thought it was the dried meat we've been eating. I have a hard time with meat."

"Hmm." He heads over to Clòz, who has dismounted.

I can feel his eyes boring into the back of my head while the healer tells him my secret. I turn slightly, petting Heefe's neck, before I peer at Clòz. His glare causes my knees to knock, but I kick my legs out one by one to relieve the tension and keep them from shaking anymore.

He pushes the healer out of his way before he moves around Heefe and grabs my wrists. He could kill me if he wishes, but we both know where that will put him—in the grave, right beside me.

I glare at him, not even bothering to hide my disdain.

A guard holds our mounts steady.

"Tell me the truth." His hot breath assaults my face, and it takes everything in me not to shrink away. "Is the baby mine or his?" The scar on the side of his face seems to stab me as if it's the blade that left the mark. The heavens tear open and frozen droplets fall onto us.

"I'm certain it's yours, my chief," I whisper, my eyes never wavering, although my heart beats like running horse hooves. The chill sets in my bones, but I refuse to quake. I can't let him even think it's from fear.

His gaze bores into me, deciding if I'm telling the truth or not. He sighs, releasing my wrists. "You'll travel in the wagon then." He turns to his guards. "Make sure she stays there." He looks back at me as a guard takes my wrists. "Don't touch her!" he barks, pulling his sword from its sheath and lopping off the fingers of the guard on my right. He howls in pain, falling to his knees. The red mixes with the muddy ground. The cold rain soaks my wool cloak, suffocating me under the weight.

I bite down the scream that almost erupts from my throat. Bile chokes my breaths and I swallow to keep from throwing up again. *Come on, Renell. It's not the first time you've seen blood.* I can't believe Clòz just did that. No, I actually can. I just wasn't prepared. My mistake. I'll have to make sure he never surprises me again. Otherwise, I'll never make it out of this alive.

I meet his gaze as he flicks the crimson off his sword, flinging the droplets over the crumpled guard.

"Get him out of here!" he yells, water dripping from his brow as more guards carefully take away the wounded man. He steps toward me, raising his sword, and for a horrible, split-second, I fear he'll use it to cut my head off in one fatal blow. He leans the tip against my cheek, and I feel it dig into my skin. "I don't trust you, and if you lied to me, I can do things that will make you wish for death."

I shouldn't speak. I shouldn't say anything. That's what he wants—a complacent, quiet wife, who keeps her head down and wanders the halls of Cizarrél like a ghost. "We understand each other then."

He huffs, the sword drawing blood, and it appears on his own cheek.

I smell its coppery scent mingling with the rain, but I don't wince. I don't give him the satisfaction.

He removes the blade, opting to grip my neck with his free hand instead. He squeezes, and I feel tears make their way to the corners of my eyes as my lungs choke for air. He can't kill me. He can't kill me. He can't . . .

He releases me, and I gasp for breath as he sheathes his sword. "I told you I'll break that spirit of yours. It's a shame you haven't learned your lesson yet, but don't worry, I'm up to the challenge." His dark eyes glint with a lustful evil as he rubs his hands together. I'm starting to believe he likes feeling pain as much as inflicting it. "Get to the wagon. We're wasting time." He sniffs, looking around his company. "And get her something warm and dry. I can't have her catching a cold and killing my son."

He says it like he's so sure. I head to the wagon, hiding underneath the dry canopy, but it's no use now, I'm soaked to the bone. I probably won't be able to change until we stop to make camp. I finally allow myself to shiver as two younger guards with soft faces take up position to watch me. Their sympathetic eyes wander over me, but their gazes soon move on. They don't want Clòz catching them looking.

I curl up into a shivering ball. Now I don't even have Heefe to keep me company. Tears fall without warning as Jarret's brown eyes consume my mind. The fear Clòz has started to instill in me is nothing compared to what I felt when I read the message on my *heln* that appeared late last night. Jarret was chosen. He's King of Treía now.

How did this happen? Why him? Is it punishment because I broke our vow and married another to save my people? He promised he would find a way to break the curse Clóz and I share. I don't want him to. I want him to continue without me. I've already caused him so much heartache. He almost died trying to protect me. I just want him to be safe. I shouldn't have been so selfish. I shouldn't have allowed him to follow me.

But then I remember what happened when he had no one to care for and protect. He lost himself. Now he's responsible for an entire nation. He shouldn't try to save me. Maybe this is always how it was meant to be.

Chapter 23

Hope Is a Fleeting Thing

Peggy

Rocks skitter underneath my horse's hooves. The light brown mare's tail whips at flies and her muscles jitter as she works to keep the pests away. We'd left the main road several weeks ago, yet still haven't found any evidence of the camps where David and I were imprisoned. Part of me is relieved, while the other part of me is annoyed. David will never stop searching until he finds his answers, but I'm starting to wonder if the camps were a figment of our imagination. I'm not sure how we could have both dreamt the same nightmare, but maybe it's possible.

The sun beats down on us, and I fan myself with a hand. The leather armlets and jerkin David insisted I wear keep me surprisingly cool, but the humidity of the southern plains isn't something I'm used to. The land still carries scars from the Battle at Gra'Lore—boulders here, piles of ash there—even though we left the area where the pass used to be almost a week ago.

David and I don't remember much about where we were, but we know we didn't travel long before hitting the coastal city of Valorm.

That's where we met Connan before he took us to Morough.

David wipes his neck with a red handkerchief, his light brown hair darkened with sweat. I can't imagine how I look. Our Fenrir companions, Qlapus and Leyf keep pace behind us, they're massive snouts sniffing for any unwanted scents on the breeze. I'm glad my brother convinced them to come with us. I wish he was by my side, but he just became the leader of the shapeshifters and Fenrir.

I swallow the lump that forms in my throat at the thought of Zenz. I didn't get to know him for as long as I would have liked, but his death still leaves an ache in my heart. Frobin seemed to be fairing as well as he could after losing someone he considered his mentor. My chest tightens as I glare at the landscape. I can't even be in Morough comforting my brother or training for the battles surely to come. Instead, we're out here searching for something that may not exist.

"There is something different up ahead," Qlapus, the Fenrir behind me says, his deep voice rumbling over the plains. He stands about three times larger than my horse, towering over me in a menacing shadow.

"I agree." Leyf's voice is airier and as soothing as gentle waves lapping the shoreside. I stand corrected. Maybe they've finally found evidence of the camps. I don't remember if they smelled different, but when they imprison hundreds of children and teenagers, one can only imagine.

"What is it?" David perks up, sitting straighter on his roan gelding. He stretches his hands and turns his head toward Qlapus.

The silver wolf lifts his snout toward the skies. "I'm not sure. I smell humans, but there is something else, one I've never smelled before. It's just over this rise." Qlapus looks past us, orange eyes caught on the hill in front of us.

David looks at me, a hint of a smile lifting his features. We might have found it. "Race you." He flicks his reins, spurring his horse into a canter.

I can't even tell him that I have no interest in finding that horrible place any sooner. I hoped it didn't exist so I never had to live through those memories again, but he wants answers. He needs answers.

Despite my palpitating heart, I spur my horse onward, meeting him at the top of the rise. I expect to see my nightmare fulfilled. I expect to see a camp riddled with starved, dirty children being worked to the bone by ghastly nymphs, but when I crest the hill, I find nothing but more plains and a few clusters of trees. I barely restrain my sigh.

David glares into the valley. "There has to be something here. The Fenrir smelled something. Why . . ."

"Maybe it doesn't exist anymore, David. Maybe we're too late." My heart lifts. There's nothing here. We can finally go home. After this valley, we'll be in Valorm. It's finished.

"No. There has to be something. There's not even any evidence. It wasn't that long ago. We should have found something." His voice pitches upward, and I wish I could comfort him, but nothing I say will convince him to let this go. He hinged everything on the camp answering his questions.

He spurs his horse onward, racing down toward the valley.

"David!" I call, starting after him. I don't know what he thinks he's going to accomplish. Can't he see it's over?

Suddenly, he and his gelding disappear like they were never there.

I blink, but he doesn't reappear. My heart plummets.

No. No. No.

I didn't think about there being a barrier around the camp. I dig my heels into my mare's sides, forcing her to move faster. Qlapus jumps ahead of me, vanishing right before my eyes. I take a deep breath and try to swallow the lump in my throat as I clear the barrier.

David

The world warps around me, smearing like someone has run a hand over a freshly painted canvas. All the air leaves my lungs, and voices fill my head, muttering in low tones that I can't distinguish. I feel like my chest is collapsing as darkness blankets my vision. What's happening? Am I having an episode?

I look around and the world comes back into focus, but the green valley I was in a moment ago is gone. It's been replaced with ash and soot, choking my senses. I pull my horse to a stop. The sky is gray and smoke lingers over the ground like a fire still blazes, but I see no evidence of orange flames. I cough and slip off my horse, surprised the Fenrir couldn't smell smoke. Surely, they'd be able to identify it? My boots crunch on something. I look down, realizing what I'm standing on isn't ash.

I gasp, stumbling backwards as bile rises in my throat. I fall over in my haste and try not to gag. I'm surrounded by bones, thousands of human bones. I can't breathe. This isn't real. It's a dream. A nightmare. My entire body shakes as I try to stand up, but the sickening, hollow sound of bones tapping together curdles my stomach. I empty my insides, trying to force air back into my lungs.

"So weak. I thought he'd be stronger."

"He's perfect. He came all the way here for us."

"We're the only ones who can help him."

"We'll finally be back in the master's good graces."

"He won't sustain us."

"We'll give him the answers he seeks."

"We can finally finish what we started. He's perfect."

Voices bombard my head, but I don't know where they're coming from. An ear shattering crack reverberates around me and a ringing echoes in my head. I bury my head in my lap, placing my hands over my ears. My whole body shakes. This can't be real. This isn't happening. It's just another episode. Peggy will find me, and I'll wake up soon. All will be well.

"She can't save you now."

"All you need is us."

"We'll keep you safe."

My trembling stops and the ringing in my head silences until all I hear is howling wind. I open my eyes, finally able to breathe. I look around. The gray haze seems less ominous, but the ashes still swirl around me. What happened? My head no longer aches and I stand up, feeling stronger than I have in months. My mind is clearer too, the voices are gone. The silence is a little disconcerting. I'm so used to hearing fears and seeing visions, but the calm is strange.

"David!" Peggy appears to my left. Ash covers her skin and her gold eyes appear like glowing embers in the gray. Her red rimmed gaze meet mine over the destruction, and she spurs her mare faster. Bones and ash crumple under the horses hooves, and my stomach sours to think about everyone who lost a life here. If only we'd gotten here sooner, maybe we could have helped.

I take the bridle of her horse as she slows to a stop. Tears stream down her soot-covered cheeks, and she leaps into my arms. I grunt, barely catching her.

"Where were you? We looked for hours. The Fenrir could smell you, but we couldn't find you!"

"Hours? It's only been a few minutes . . . I didn't go far past the barrier. I—"

"What happened, David?" She pulls back a little, tear-streaked eyes meeting mine.

"I went past the barrier, and there were these voices, and I think I had an episode, but I made it out. I'm okay. Something happened, and I don't—I don't hear them anymore."

"What do you mean?" Her gold eyes search mine.

"I think—I think I'm free, but I don't know. Everything seems so clear. It's like the voices left. Maybe they've been set free." I set her down. "Maybe I can learn to control it now. Your fears . . . I don't feel them."

A breathy gasp leaves her lips, and she hugs me once more. "I was so worried. I hope that you're finally free. Let's get out of here."

I kiss the top of her head, believing I can finally leave the evil of my past behind . . .

Rahuin

I stare at *Suvitaas* Areis. Her long black hair extends to the small of her back, and unnatural orange eyes study me amidst a pale, high-cheekbone face. Lush foliage folds around us in dazzling emeralds and vibrant jades, complimenting blossoms in an infinite variety of colors. *Suvitaas* are teachers. They are the only elves who can harness all four elements—earth, wind, fire, and water. Other elves have magic all their own and can sometimes harness one element.

"To keep the balance of elements, you first have to understand the nature of them," she says as water droplets appear on her skin, running down into a pool in her open palm.

I want to tell her I don't want to control the elements. I just want to forget everything that's happened, but what's a better distraction than learning? Plus, any new understanding of magic or nature is good for me. I can always use it against the Darkness when the time comes, and the time will come, whether I like it or not. I don't want to think about facing him again, but what choice do I have? I'm sure he's already come up with ways to destroy me, or worse, my family. *Tenfold* . . .

Areis snaps her fingers, and I realize I hadn't been listening. I meet her gaze that doesn't seem upset like I thought it would. "I'm sorry. I just—"

"Once you open up your mind to the elements, they will tell you their nature, but you have to have a mind that's pure of thought. If you start to learn with a mindset of what you might gain, you'll never learn properly."

I scrunch my brow.

She adds, "The way you learn and open your mind will determine how you heal. Your damaged mind needs something to keep it occupied—to process what you experienced, but it's a thin line. If you learn to forget completely, you'll only suppress what you feel. Those emotions will just come back even worse than before, but if you use these new skills to heal, you'll be able to accept and function with the memories. It's up to you to decide how you'll use this instruction." She turns her hand over and the drops in her palm fall one by one to the loamy soil under our feet.

"I don't want to forget. I don't want to say goodbye. I want to heal."

"Remember that as we learn. You must harbor that desire deep in your heart to understand all the elements will show you."

"I will." I meet her fiery gaze.

"Good. Now, the four elements are water, earth, fire, and air. They all exist together and none of them can exist without the other."

I nod, as she forms a stream of water around us. Its pale complexion reflects the greenery as Areis creates a curtain out of it. "Water is gentle and calming." She lets it flow toward a tree. "Earth." She hovers her palm over the ground and it rises to caress her fingers. "Is peaceful and solid." The dirt falls back to our feet. "Fire." A blaze ignites between us, warming the air. "Is temperamental, but soothing." The flames vanish. "And air." A ferocious wind blows between us, nearly taking me with it. "Is mischievous, but adventurous. It'll take you anywhere." A smile lights her lips. "It's my favorite." She walks forward, her feet hovering over the ground.

I stare up at her.

"Come on." She beckons, pale hand outstretched to me.

"But—" I start.

She steps higher. "Feel the wind. Tell it where you want to go, what you want it to do. If you ask, it will obey, but be specific."

I close my eyes and take a deep breath, blocking the thoughts and memories flooding my mind as I feel the slight breeze whisper over my skin—literally, whisper. It giggles and whoops through the trees. "Come on, Rahuin. Hurry up and ask me. Don't be too shy. I won't bite."

"Yet." Another voice interjects, but I have no idea from where.

I take a deep breath. "Take me up there, take me to *Suvitaas* Areis."

"As you wish," the whistling voice says, and I shoot up into the air.

I scream as the wind tumbles me upside down. I squeeze my eyes shut. The ground suddenly looks so far away. "Not like that! Like *Suvitaas* Areis."

The sudden rush calms, helping me stand right-side up like Areis as it brings me face to face with her.

I try to soothe my racing heart as I utter a small thank you to the air.

Suvitaas Aries tries to cover the smile on her face with a hand.

"It's not funny." I narrow my eyes.

She drops her hand. "It's a little funny, but I probably shouldn't have laughed at you."

I smile and look away, thinking about my terrified scream. "It's all right. I would have laughed too." I peer at her, before caressing the leaves of a huge deciduous. Its green crown shimmers where the sun hits it.

Areis reaches with me, before glancing below us. "Now, look down. See the world from here. See the beauty and remember. Even in the midst of evil or turmoil or hate, the world continues to thrive. It continues to grow, even in the hardest spaces. Just like this forest, it grew over a silver mine, and that didn't stop it from trying to reach the sky."

I glance sideways at her, before taking in the scene below us. I see wild animals mingling among the foliage, birds flying among the canopies, and bugs fluttering around flowers.

I swallow. "Despite what my mother might have told you, I'm not giving up. I can't afford to." I caress my stomach.

Suvitaas Areis nods. "I know, but do you believe it? Do you truly believe you can make it through? That you can live and thrive, even with painful memories?"

Elrian and Zenz's faces flash before my eyes, along with countless other faces I've never seen. Shivers break out on my skin, and the air vanishes from my lungs. I know who these faces are, even if I've never seen them before. These are the people I killed before I came home. I murdered them. My vision blurs and I fall to the ground . . .

A'zre

From my balcony, I watch her walk down in the palace gardens. Two guards accompany her, and her nose is shoved into a book. How can she walk and read at the same time?

Esther is a mystery I still haven't figured out . . . not that I want to, but she does look quite endearing. I take a deep breath, as if I can inhale her scent from here. I remember the feeling of her skin under my fingers. Her lips against mine . . .

I close my eyes and sigh. I don't love her. *I don't love her.* The words circle around in my mind, but I'm not sure why I'm repeating them. The princess is an aching thorn in my side, and I'm starting to believe she's a punishment I can't escape.

I open my eyes and find that she's moved on.

Lami comes out on the balcony, leaning over the railing beside me. The warm breeze tousles her gray hair and sends the lanterns above us jingling on their chains. "Maybe she can help you. Maybe that's all she wants." Her gold eyes trail after Esther before she disappears around a bend.

How does this old woman always know what I'm thinking? Do I wear it like a veil on my head? *"Look here, the King of Sun'Ar is thinking about his seventh wife, and he can't stop thinking about her."*

I turn, glaring at Lami. "Or she's coming to steal everything from me."

Maybe the Darkness was wrong when he told me to marry the princess. Why did I trust him? Clearly, he hasn't done anything for me but cause pain and misery. He promised Partin, but all I have are defeated armies paired with a leftover headache. There is talk of rebellion in Lanckest. The Onarian and Cay-Llekian troops stationed there are starting to become restless, but I don't have enough manpower to seize Casta and Färrin yet. Not that I can capture them with the alliance anyway. So what's the point? To make me fall in love with the irresistible princess? Bring me down with the love of a woman? That's what my father warned me about, yet I fell into the trap anyway. What a fool I am.

"A'zre," she scolds.

"No, Lami! You keep saying you want me to love, you want me to feel, but that is the worst thing I could possibly do. I don't trust her, and you shouldn't either. She's here because of her people. Who knows how deep her loyalty runs. If the opportunity arises, who's to say she won't just kill me herself and blame it on something else? This is what my father warned me about. Love destroys, it doesn't protect!"

"Not if she loves you back! I've seen into her heart, A'zre. She wants to save you—"

I step closer, looking down at her. "Save me from what? Myself?

Is that what you're worried about? Well, you shouldn't be. You should be worried about yourself. Your position here is only allowed because of my mercy."

She lifts her chin. "Listen to yourself! You'll let your paranoia destroy all you have? Even the few people who have loved and cared for you all these years?" Tears shine in her gold eyes. "Because of your greed, your people are starting to mistrust you. Is that what you want? Do you want to become him?"

The last part feels like a slap to my face. "I am nothing like him."

"Then why do you act like him? Why do I see him more and more in you with each passing day?" Her voice trembles, but her eyes never leave mine.

I lift my hand ready to strike her, but I realize she's right. My father would do that. I step back, running my fingers through my hair. I swallow. "Pack your things, Lami. I never want to see you in this place again." I head back into my room.

"That's it then? Push me away. After all I've done?"

I hear the tears in her voice, but I ignore them. I ignore the way my heart tears. I see my father standing off to the side of my room with a smile on his face. It's like he's saying, *Well done, my son.*

No. Never. I'm not him.

"You fight against a monster you want nothing to do with, yet you can't change who you are. You can't make the wrong things right." Esther's words ring in my head. She was right. I can't win against this beast. It's what I am. I can't defeat it. It's too late for me.

"You already are him." I hear Lami's footsteps recede and the door slams as she leaves the room.

I glare at the door, refusing the tears that crawl their way up my throat. I should go after her. I should say I didn't mean it, but I don't move.

"You can't love, A'zre. Love will be the end of you. Let me show you why." Father's words ring in my head. I didn't understand him until now. I've tried so hard not to be like him, but I've failed. Lami is right. I am him. I will do everything I promised. I will make him proud. I will rule all of Partin, and no one will stand in my way.

Esther

"Lami?" I find her weeping in my quarters. The blue palette seems to drown her in sorrow, the ocean tiles sweeping over her in relentless waves.

She's sitting in the middle of the floor, swiping tears that keep falling.

My heart constricts. I've never seen her so upset. She's always so composed. What's broken her beyond repair? I kneel beside her, taking her shaking shoulders into my hands.

She gasps, lifting her head, before falling into my arms and clinging to me as if I'm oxygen. "Az—A'zre has—he wants me to leave. He told me t—to leave," she cries, her sobs muffled by the fabric of my dress. "Where will I—I go? I don't know anything besides this. Th— he's all I have."

I clench my jaw, glaring at the wall. How could he do this to her? Lami is the most loyal and kind person I've ever met. "I'll speak to him, Lami. Don't leave."

"No. No, child. You'll only make it worse. He's—"

"A coward. I know, but I won't be able to survive without you here, and I don't think he will either." I stand, extracting myself from her embrace.

"Esther, please." She whimpers.

"I won't let him do this to you, Lami. He's scared. That means he cares." I meet her golden eyes.

She nods, and I slip out the door, heading for A'zre's study.

I haven't been inside his office before. Bronze lions keep watch on either side of his dark wood desk. Skylights let in little bits of the sun rays, and a cool breeze sweeps in from a balcony directly in front of me. To my right, books line the walls, and in front of it, a huge table with a map of Partin and a small chess table sit.

A'zre stands there, hunched over the map as if all the land would become his if he just stared at it long enough. "I thought you'd come." He doesn't even cast me a sidelong glance.

"How could you do this to her?" I step closer to him, slapping my hand on the table and causing little wooden pawns to tremble.

He looks up, his red eyes as menacing as the day I confronted him about his greed. I feel the slap before I even see his hand. "You forget that I'm the king. I can do whatever I want."

I grab my cheek, feeling tears well up, but I blink them away, taking a deep breath. "Then tell me to leave instead. Please don't make Lami suffer. She's the most loyal person I've ever met. She would never do anything against you."

"You say she's loyal, but she didn't hesitate to tell you how you should love me—make me feel again," he spits into my face, degrading me with every word.

Moving my hand, I lift my chin. "Is that really such a bad thing? Do you even feel anything by sending her away?"

"No, I don't care. All I care about is—"

"Liar. You're such a liar, and you're making Lami pay for it." I know I shouldn't speak. I shouldn't defy him, but I don't care anymore.

"You have no right to call me a liar. The only liar I see here is you." He steps closer to me, lording his superiority, pressing me to cower.

But I'm not a coward. I'm not like him. "How am I the liar? When have I ever lied to you?"

"You lied to me about your motives! You're here to steal my crown, my kingdom!" His eyes change, becoming deranged like a frightened animal, and I realize he has no more control. He's letting the monster win. He's letting his paranoia get the best of him.

"A'zre, I've never lied to you. I told you from the very beginning that I would come here to save my people. I just want them to be safe. I want you to help me keep them safe by promising not to attack them. That's the only reason I'm here. Yes, I'll admit that I—I find you captivating." I can't believe the words coming from my mouth, but if I'm being honest, I've been drawn to his darkness since the very beginning. I'm still attracted to it. So much of A'zre begs me to unveil him, release him. I want to help him. I want to pull him out of his anger. I want to see the man behind the monster, and he's given me little glimpses, but not the full picture.

As long as this beast controls him, my people will never be safe. His greed will consume him, and no alliance will make him honor his agreement. I have my answer about his war. This isn't about Sun'Arian resources, it's about his greed, more specifically, his father's greed. "I just want to help you overcome the monster."

"There you go again with the monster! Is that all you really see? Is that all I am?" He throws his arms wide, as if the room encapsulates all he is instead.

"No, that's why I'm begging you not to send Lami away. I know that's not who you are. I've seen the good in you. I see it in the way you treat your wives, your children, the servants . . . I know you can overcome this—that's all I want. That's all Lami wants. We just want you to love and care for us by not giving in. This paranoid monster is not who you are, and we don't want you to stay that way." The war wages in his eyes. I can see it stirring. I take his hands, gripping them tightly and hoping he doesn't shove me away. "Please, don't send her away. She loves you so much. This will break her. She has nothing besides you."

He looks away. "I'm not weak."

"I never said that."

"Love makes you weak." He spits, ripping his hands from mine.

"No, it doesn't. I've loved and I've lost. Yes, the losing hurts, but it's never broken me. In fact, it's made me stronger because it's given me purpose to fight for what I love. You're wrong about love. Yes, it can be used against you, but only if you let it. Lami will never be used against you, she loves you too much for that."

He takes a deep breath, letting it out as he turns his back on me, walking toward his balcony. Rainbow colors from the floating lanterns above him shine over his face as the sun starts to disappear over the horizon.

"Tell Lami to stay. You will stay as well. I honor my agreements." He leans against the balcony, his arms spreading out over the railing.

"Thank you, Your Majesty."

"Make no mistake"—he spins around—"I'm not doing this for you. I'm doing it for her. You're right. She doesn't deserve this. She has been my most trusted and loyal adviser, but if you ever arrive in my study unannounced again, I will confine you to your room and never allow you to leave."

I nod, my heart hammering in my chest as I remember that his study is strictly off-limits to his wives. Apparently when you have so many, you need a safe space from them.

"It won't happen again." I bow my head, as I turn toward the door.

He says something else, but I'm too far away to hear it. It sounded something like, "I doubt it."

Chapter 24
How Far is too Far?

Wen

My vision blurs as I once again start to nod off. I blink, snorting awake as I try in vain to find where I'd been reading, but what's the point when I know I'll just drift off again? I need sleep. I can only stare at old text for so long until my head feels like it's been running in circles. I'm not sure I even remember what I've read in the last few hours. I gently roll up the scroll, mindful of the frayed edges worn away from years of countless other readers.

I grab the candle sitting next to me on the old desk. It's almost burned down to nothing. I should just blow it out because the rainbow stones scattered around Treía give off enough light to see me back to my quarters, but I kind of enjoy the little flicker.

I stand up, my gaze sweeping over the desk covered in scrolls and volumes bigger than me, towers of shelves filled with books ranging from anything about history to the studies of fish surround me. Almost five weeks of studying and I still haven't gotten any closer to finding a way to break Renell's curse. I'm almost finished with Treía's library, and I doubt I'll find the information I need here. I'll have to

345

search elsewhere, but I need to speak with Jarret first. He's indisposed at every moment. Which makes sense. He's the king now.

I've hardly seen him as he's rushed from one council meeting into studies over Treían lore and customs. Some mornings, we've been able to slip away to train so he can defeat Clòz once we break Renell's curse. I'll just have to get a message to him. He's due for another lesson anyway.

I've heard whispers from the other Garons, and most of them can't believe the stones chose him since he knows nothing about Treía. Some of them have even thought of removing him from position, but according to their lore, he'd have to die. No one else will be chosen while a king sits on the throne. Removing Jarret would be treason.

I run my fingers through my white locks before I shuffle out of the library. The musky, earthy air of Treía is starting to drive me insane, but it's too cold in the mountains for me to sleep outside. It seems like spring has finally arrived up here, but the chill lingers like a bad cough.

The halls are empty, aside from the occasional guard, and the silence makes me feel more alone than I have in weeks. I've been alone most of my life, but the weeks spent with Renell and Jarret have made me realize I don't want that anymore. I crave closeness, even if I don't want to admit it.

During these times, memories of Rahuin learning, smiling, and holding me often cross my thoughts. I knew the last time I saw her was nothing but fiction—a lie to make me believe she loved me, but I entrusted her with my heart again. I knew she still loved him, yet I tried to make her stay for me. I'm partly glad she didn't. I'm glad Renell and Jarret saved me, and the little time with them has made me yearn for the beauty found in this life. I no longer desire the Darkness or his acceptance.

I stare at the stone under my feet, thoughts slowing my stride as I study where the basalt has been worn smooth under hundreds of people and dragons alike.

I've been thinking of Rahuin more and more in the absence of Jarret and Renell's banter. It doesn't help that I have to go to Casta next to search their library, the second largest in comparison to Onar. I can't go to Onar because I don't want to ruin Renell's charade. Thesa said Rahuin's in Färrin, so I won't run into her. But I've been wanting to make everything right with her, and maybe just maybe, my search will cause our paths to cross. Of course, that means I'll most likely run into her husband, but based on what I've heard of Castian politics, I probably won't. I'll just have to get Thesa's blessing to search Morough's library. Hopefully, she'll grant the request.

And if I find a way to break the curse and Rahuin still isn't there, maybe I can take a quick detour to Färrin. I want to speak with her and apologize, tell her I forgive her for what happened between us. I don't know if it will be any consolation for her, but hopefully it'll be a step in the right direction.

We heard what she did to the Darkness's army a few weeks afterwards. Guilt choked my heart once I knew because I gave her the means to do that. I taught her how to slaughter thousands. I find it disheartening that I'll never know how many lives I took while I was with the Darkness. His influence often made me black out and forget what I'd done in the past. Like my consciousness had to hide the memories just so I could go on living with myself. No more. I refuse to be someone who murders to make the world mine, and the worst part is . . . I didn't even do it for myself.

I took the Darkness's oath because I felt like I belonged. I destroyed and killed because I wanted someone to care for me. How messed up is that? Now I know who I am. I know I can be accepted, even loved without destroying the livelihoods of others. That's why Rahuin left me. She thought I was blinded by the Darkness. I wish she would have tried to pull me out, but I understand that would have been hard for her. It was easier for her to leave me so she could choose Dais. It wasn't her place as another man's wife to save me, and I'm grateful Jarret and Renell believed in me enough to do it.

Renell

Arriving in Onar was like arriving in another world after being stuck in Cay-Llek for the last few weeks. I hated everything about Cay-Llek's wet climate and rocky terrain. The second we entered Onar, lush trees taller than any I've ever seen rose high into the sky. We passed several lumberjacks working in the dark forests as they tried to earn their wares, cutting logs and piling branches. The sweet smell of wood chips permeated the air, and I've done nothing but breathe in the fragrance since my lungs were tired of the stagnant, wet scent of Cay-Llek.

We reached the capital, Oberin, last night. The city sits just past the open plain of Gar-Ren. Most of it had been built into low sandstone hills with an acropolis in the middle and plenty of beautiful manicured gardens and open courtyards where many Onarian's gathered to study the arts—paintings, literature, and theater. The architecture consisted of sandstone columns upholding red or blue tiled roofs. The entire city is set in a spiral pattern, and each roof from the top of the acropolis looked like a chess set.

Onarian's seemed to boast about their knowledge of other cultures and classics. Almost every ceiling we'd seen depicted some ornate painting of a scene from the great literary poets like Hikilś or the horrible battles of the War of Races. They love beautiful, antique things, and I didn't miss the glances of disgust that were thrown our way as we went through the city yesterday.

Barbarians.

Filth.

The words were uttered in disdain from multiple lips.

If I were them, I would think the same. I feel like filth. Nothing about Cay-Llek made me think about beauty. I felt nothing but fear, death, and destruction. No wonder others see them as barbarians, and now I look just like them. All in the hopes that I can get my people back, but the long days of travel and the constant fear of Clòz's anger has made me forget why I'm truly here. He was right when he said he'd break me. I already feel like I'm breaking, and he's only been around me for five weeks.

Now, we're in the palace—a glorious building built just underneath the acropolis. Skylights filter sunshine down into a cavernous room. Gorgeous paintings created in the highest detail line the walls, telling of Partin history in chronological order. A smooth onyx floor echoes our every step. Ahead of us, the queen, Ruby, sits on a raised platform surrounded by a parliament of thirty men and women on tiered levels. They look down at us with wrinkled noses as Queen Ruby bursts into a sinister laugh at Clòz's appeal.

She's clothed in a grand red robe garnished with gold threading and diamonds that wink every time her arms stretch toward the sunshine in front of her platform. Her gray hair has been braided and coiled around a gawdy ruby crown that looks like it weighs more than I do.

"You think you can go against an alliance I've already formed?" Her words drip with disdain, talking down with a sneer.

Clòz's hands clench into fists, and I shuffle closer to him, brushing his knuckles with my fingers to calm him. He grabs my hand and squeezes it tightly, and I try not to wince.

"Your Majesty, what has Sun'Ar really given us? We entered an alliance where the rewards were promised indefinitely, but we've seen no evidence of these promises. Where has King A'zre been? Licking his wounds like the dog he is, I'm sure. Because of his arrogance, many of our men were slaughtered out on the plains of Ei-Kar. How is that rewarding to any of us? My men are thirsty for answers, and I've come to offer them a solution. If Sun'Ar doesn't deliver soon, I say we take what we were promised . . . Lan lands."

My heart clenches at the mention of my homeland. I hate A'zre for offering it as a bargaining piece in this awful war. It makes sense in relation to topography. What better way to get others to join you than by offering more land for future wars to be fought over? Though, King A'zre didn't seem like someone who wasn't fueled by greed. He wants to rule all of Partin, but I still can't figure out how he was going to oust Cay-Llek and Onar from his plans once he had Casta, Lanckest, and Färrin. It doesn't make sense, but then I remember his involvement with the Darkness. The Darkness probably promised that he would get all the lands if he cooperated, but what does that mean?

"And what if we help you? What is to stop you from taking the lands for yourself?" the Prime Minister sitting next to the queen asks. He's a rotund man with a hook nose and a crop of brown hair that reminds me of a bird's nest. His gray eyes glare at us like we're a stinking dung heap.

"We split it directly in half. You take one half and we take the other. Or if that isn't enough because of Saresh, we'll split it differently. I'm not asking you to make the alliance here and now. We'll be in Oberin for the week. I want this decision to be discussed thoroughly before a conclusion is made. Though, I don't think it will be difficult." Clòz oozes confidence, even with the impression of their obvious dislike.

Judging from their faces, there is no way they will enter an alliance with us.

"High Chief Clòz, we'll take your plan into consideration, but don't believe that we trust your motives. We'll have to keep some collateral as a measure of good faith." Queen Ruby quirks a gray brow, her gold eyes shining in delight. Although, I'm not sure why. What kind of collateral could we give that would satisfy a woman who has everything and hates us?

"I'm afraid I have nothing to offer, Your Majesty."

"Oh, but you do." Her vulturous eyes wander over me, and I flinch as a choking noise escapes my throat. I don't remember the queen being this straightforward when she visited Lanckest when I was younger, but maybe I was too innocent back then.

"My wife?" Clòz steps in front of me. "No one touches her but me."

The queen laughs again. "High Chief, you misunderstand me. I just want the pleasure of her presence for the week. She's quite beautiful. All I want is to have her sit with me for that time. I appreciate beautiful things."

I swallow, wanting to show her how deadly beautiful I can be if the situation calls for it, but I don't think that mindset will help me in this case. I can't just kill the queen of the nation I need help from, but the lines of morality are starting to blur too much for my comfort. How far is too far to get my people back?

Already, I've forsaken my vows and married another. My husband is abusive and never misses an opportunity to hurt me. Now, this crazy queen wants me to keep her company. Though, she assures it won't be the type of company I'm thinking of, that doesn't mean she'll keep her word, especially if Clòz never finds out. The familiar thread of panic slides down my stomach, and I close my eyes, taking a deep breath as Clòz consents to the queen's request.

"As long as she isn't touched—not by the guards, and definitely not by you."

She chuckles. "I can assure you, High Chief. A finger won't touch her skin."

How can he possibly agree? I open my eyes, glaring at his broad shoulders.

He turns to look at me, bending over so he can whisper in my ear. "If she touches you, I will burn this city to the ground." His dark eyes bore into mine.

I nod as guards come toward us, gesturing for me to follow them.

Clòz glares as they usher me out a side door and into an atrium with a glass ceiling that has lush plants closing in on every side. A bath with steaming water sits in the middle.

A servant rushes in from another door somewhere to the right and sets clothes, soaps, and oils on a side table just outside the tub.

A bath sounds heavenly after weeks of travel, but my weary heart is reluctant to accept the generosity. What acts will I have to perform if I indulge in something as simple as bathing?

The guards leave, and the servant gestures for me to undress and step into the water. She speaks two Cay-Llekian words. "No touch."

"I speak Onarian," I say in her language, and the tension in her shoulders eases a little.

"Most visitors don't, and your pronunciation is impeccable, High Chiefess."

"Please, my name is Renell. I refuse to use any title that loops me with my husband." I spit the words out like they're poison.

The servant shivers. "Of course, my lady. I—I didn't mean any offense."

"Forgive me. The journey was less than desirable. I'm pregnant, you see, and haven't had a bath in a very long time." I sigh, hoping the servant will gossip about my condition. Perhaps, the queen will hear it and prevent any unspeakable acts.

"Of course, you may undress when you're ready."

I nod as she disappears.

Once I'm finished with the glorious hot bath. I wrap myself into a provided robe and stare at the clothes that have been laid out for me, if you could even call them clothes. My face flushes as I bite my bottom lip. I knew this was going to happen. The sheer two piece hardly covers any skin, and even then, it leaves no room for modesty. There is no way I'm wearing this contraption.

The servant comes back in, staring at my hands that are gingerly holding the outfit.

"I'm sorry, my lady." She swallows. "The queen requested it."

Of course she did. "I'm not wearing it. I won't"

Her face pales. "I—I—"

"Please bring me something suitable to wear." I drop the clothes back onto the table.

The servant scurries away just as the door opens in front of her. The queen, the prime minister, and a few guards amble in.

I wrap the robe tighter around my skin, trying to disappear behind a flowering bush as I sneak toward the other door, but two more guards walk in from that direction and block my escape. I huff, turning back toward the other entourage.

The servant squeaks, dodging out of the way as the queen addresses her, "Is she ready?"

"Y—Your Majesty, I—she refused to wear—"

"You're dismissed." The queen waves her away, her venomous gold eyes pin me.

"A feisty one, your husband. Although, I'm not sure how you ended up by his side, Princess Renell Oslehan."

My heart clenches at the use of my full title.

"I thought you were in Casta, of all places. It's a shame what happened to your father."

I want to tell her she doesn't have the right to speak of my father, but I bite my tongue.

"Now, I suppose my generosity is lost on you since you've been living with those barbarians, but when someone offers you something to wear, I expect you to actually put them on."

"Those are hardly considered clothes." I lift my chin.

"Well, you'd be right, but I'm not going to stipulate the details. I promised I wouldn't touch you, but I can be very persuasive in other maneuvers." She smiles, nodding to the guards who immediately point their spears at me. "And if you'd have gotten dressed sooner, this wouldn't have been an issue."

I glare at the queen, but I still don't move. I don't want to indulge her sick fantasies, but besides my people, I have a child to protect. I've already compromised so much, what difference would it make now? Nothing about my modesty means anything if I lose my baby.

I hold my head high like my title implies, even though at this moment I feel as far from royalty as I could possibly be. I drop the robe from my shoulders and slip into the sheer two-piece. It doesn't even look like I'm wearing anything, so what was the point of trying to make it look like they want me to be modest?

All eyes are on me and I don't miss their leering glances as they ogle every inch of my skin. I've never felt so humiliated, but I try not to let it show on my face. I'll never give them the satisfaction.

"See? That wasn't so hard, and you look absolutely ravishing. Follow me," the queen says as she and her entourage head back the way they came.

My heart pounds in my chest, and the air grows thick with humidity, making me sweat. I don't want to move. Shouldn't this be enough to fulfill their promiscuity? But of course, greed is never fulfilled, and I've just become a piece to indulge their selfish desires. I'm not surprised when the queen takes me to another room where most of the other members of parliament are lounging on luxurious couches and cushions, drinking expensive wine and committing acts of debauchery in which I avert my gaze to, but it's hard to avoid.

Plants, fountains, and pools surround the lavish room. A floor to ceiling window spans the entire wall ahead, looking out to a large balcony with more of Onar's signature pillars. Lamps in red and blue line the outside where the sun has just started its descent, filling the room with the golden light.

"There." The queen points to a pedestal in the middle, and I notice other women and men on raised platforms dressed in the same scandalous outfit as me. The guests below sometimes reach up or join them. I look away, swallowing the bile that rises in my throat. I'm sure the other spectacles are prisoners, just like me. Their sad eyes wander around the room as if they could imagine an escape from this sick place. If I get the chance, I want to come back and free them. No one deserves this abuse.

The queen clinks a glass and makes a few remarks before announcing that I'm not to be touched, just admired.

I want to throw up, being admired is like being assaulted with someone's eyes, but I don't comment on the atrocities happening around me. I try to block them from my mind as the sun vanishes and leaves me to the obscenity of the night.

Jet

"A man named Wen will be coming to search the castle's library. He saved Jarret and is trying to find a way to save Renell. He's much changed from what I remember of him, but he was the sorcerer who tried to take Rahuin to the Darkness. He no longer serves his evil master, but I have to warn you. Keep a close eye on him. He has history with Rahuin, and I fear that he may try to talk to Dais or goad him. I believe he has had a change of heart, I'm just not certain of how much. I know Dais can't struggle with it now."

I reread the message more times than I'd like to count. My shimmering *heln* glows jade like her eyes. She got it for me after Jarret was named king so we could communicate since we didn't get one at our own mating ceremony. High skies, I miss her more every day. I'm glad that Jarret is all right . . . and he's a king. A king! My son. I wish I could be there with them, but Dais needs me too.

I'm still not welcome in Treía. King Grelik pardoned me, but I wasn't present for the ceremony, so I'm sure the other nobility wouldn't give two wits about the previous king's pardon. From what Thesa mentioned, they hardly even trust Jarret as the king, and even the most devout Garons are starting to question the stone's choice. Of course they are. They've always been skeptical—especially when it comes to outsiders.

I stare at the message again. Now I'm faced with a choice. Do I tell Dais he's coming? My heart aches. I think I shouldn't because I know Dais will be curious and want to meet him, but Thesa basically said they should stay separate. If I don't tell him and he finds out later that he was here . . .

I sigh. I should leave it up to Dais, but he's got his hands full trying to find the traitor while also keeping the people satisfied and aware of the true enemy. I don't need this consuming his thoughts as well, but in the same vein, he doesn't know who to trust right now. If I keep this from him, he may begin to suspect me too. I have to tell him.

I start for the door, the dark oak staring back at me as I reach for the gold handle. What if he won't let Wen come search the library once I tell him who is coming? An uneasy feeling tears at my insides. If I tell him why Wen is coming, I'm sure he'll understand and allow Wen to continue. Renell is in trouble, and Dais has always seen her as a friend. Hopefully their relationship will be enough to allow Dais to trust Wen.

I open the door, heading for Dais's study. Even though it's the crack of dawn, he's already at his desk, one hand writing decrees with his head in the other. A mass of golden curls fall over his stubble-covered face. I tap his desk, and he lifts his head. Dark half circles outline his blue eyes. Not again.

"You stayed up all night?" I ask, glancing at the stack of envelopes lying beside him. I have no doubt that he handwrote every single decree he needs to go out to the cities of Casta.

"Yes." He holds a hand up. "And before you tell me this isn't healthy and that I promised to take care of myself, I will go to sleep after this. I have nothing on the agenda today, so I will rest. I just need these ready for the couriers and criers."

"No interviews today?" I ask in regard to the soldiers we're questioning to find out who planned the attack.

"No, I have a good idea who it is. I will conduct more interviews tomorrow to confirm. Hopefully, he hasn't heard I'm looking for him and ran by then, but if he runs, then we'll know he's guilty." He dips his pen in the ink again, writing a few more words.

I take a deep breath. "Dais, I've heard from Thesa, and she's sending someone to Morough who will need full access to our library."

He looks up again, his brow furrowed as a maid scurries in with a cup of hot tea and a platter of steaming breakfast. She sets it on the edge of his desk and disappears. He grabs the tea. "And I need to know this, why?" He takes a sip, adding two cubes of sugar to it before stirring. The clinking porcelain grates on my ears.

"Because he's no ordinary guest, so I wanted you to be aware of him, especially since many around you refuse to tell the truth. I don't want to be another person added to your list."

He sets the cup down, running a finger across his chin. "Who is he?"

"His name is Wen."

Dais's curious brow shift as his eyes narrow and his jaw clenches. He knows who Wen is. Rahuin must have told him.

"No. Tell her he can't come." He stands, hobbling over to the window. His bad leg is another painful reminder of Rahuin's betrayal.

"I was afraid you'd say that, but Rahuin isn't here. He saved Jarret's life, and now, he's coming to look for a way to save Renell's."

He looks back at me. "Renell? What happened?"

"She was forced into a marriage curse in Cay-Llek to keep Jarret safe while they were trying to win back Lanckest. Her new husband is a horrible brute whom she can't kill without killing herself. Wen and Jarret are trying to find a way to break the curse so she can finish him off and take Cay-Llek."

Dais lets out a deep breath, and I can see the war fighting on his face. "Fine. Thank you for telling me he's coming." He limps back to his breakfast tray, taking a bun.

"Will you meet him?" I can't stop the curious question.

He sighs. "I don't know. I'm not sure I want to know, but it's all in the past. Rahuin assured me of that. I just . . ."

"It's hard to trust her?"

He nods, and then looks at the decrees on his desk. The Castian cerulean blue wax seal on their envelopes shimmers in the sunlight spilling from the terrace. "Have those sent out today. I'm going to get some rest, and then I'll eat some proper food." He tucks the breakfast bun in his mouth, shuffling to the door.

"I will, Your Majesty."

Wen

The ivory towers of Morough's castle mock me like leering mountains I can't climb. Last time I was here, the Darkness sent me. I'd taunted Jarret, and now I'm helping him. I smile at the thought. How odd life is. Then, I had been so certain I was right, and now I'm truly fighting for what is right. I want to keep Renell safe, and if I can't do that, then I'll fail her. I owe her my life. I can't sit around while she suffers in silence, and I know she's suffering, Clòz isn't a forgiving man. There has to be a way to break her curse. I will find it, even if it takes my entire life.

Once again, thoughts of Rahuin fill my heart, and even though I know she's not here, I still imagine running into her. I keep wondering what I'd say to her if I did, but I won't because she's not here. I have to keep reminding myself so my hopes don't climb higher than I can reach.

Before me, a grand staircase reaches up to a gorgeous terrace crawling with ivy and flowers spilling out of huge vases in an array of vibrant colors. To my left is a manicured garden where workers weave in and out. To my right, a courtyard leads to what looks like the training grounds, stables, and barracks. Men and soldiers run around the area as they continue their day—training in hand-to-hand combat, riding horses, and finishing chores.

A man steps down the staircase and extends his hand as he reaches me. He has shoulder-length black and gray hair that has been pulled back at the nape of his neck. Narrow brown eyes meet mine and a solemn face drags the corners of his lips into a frown, making his subtle wrinkles appear more prominent. "Wen, I assume?"

I take his hand with a nod. Ah, this must be Thesa's mate—Jarret's father. I can see the resemblance now. "Yes, and you must be

Jet."

"That's Sir Jet to you. Come, I'll show you the library, then take you to your quarters." He spins on his heel. It feels like he's dismissing me. I'm not surprised. I'm sure Thesa told him who I was before Renell and Jarret saved me. I'm sure his sole mission is to keep the peace between me and his king . . . not that I want anything to do with Dais. I just don't want to deal with the drama right now. At least he allowed me to come to Morough and search. Though, I'm sure that decision has more to do with Renell than me. Jarret said they're close friends.

The castle holds all the opulence and excellency I've always admired. I was born on a poor fishing island, but I'm certain I was made for the finer things. I love the gold filigree covered walls and two-story windows and crystal chandeliers. Maybe that's why I enjoyed being with the Darkness. His castle was as grand and beautiful as this— enticing and perfect, or maybe that's what he wanted me to see. Maybe it was just an illusion bred from my own imagination. I guess I'll never know, because I'm never going back. I won't know if my perception of it changed because my beliefs have.

Jet—excuse me—Sir Jet leads me through the corridors with gorgeous vaulted ceilings painted with epic battles of old or stories of folklore and fairytales.

I study them in awe, nearly breaking my neck to enjoy the artistry. I stumble against someone, almost sending us both to the quartz floor.

"Watch where you're walking, Sir," the man grumbles, straightening his jacket and casting me a nasty glare before continuing on.

"I suggest you keep your eyes ahead. I'm sure there will be plenty of times to see the ceiling when you aren't about to run into noblemen," Sir Jet quips, continuing down the hall with hardly a glance behind him.

I take long exaggerated strides to reach him before he turns down another corridor. It's improper to run down a castle's halls, you know.

He turns right, opening double mahogany doors that lead into one of the most opulent libraries I've ever laid eyes on. A huge domed roof made entirely of glass shines shimmering sunlight through its fragmented crystal texture, casting little rainbows on the rows of shelves lining the walls. It gives me flashbacks to Treía. Tall sliding ladders are centered around the room, and a few servants walk among the shelves, returning books or dusting volumes. Other people sit on balconies where comfortable nooks have been designed for cozy readings. I catch the title of a book on a servant's stack as he walks past. I wouldn't call the History of Gilded Textures a cozy read, perhaps boring. Maybe that's why they need comfy furniture, so they can sleep when prompted by the pages of some dragging monologue.

Plants hang from the certain outcroppings, filling the room with an earthy scent that mixes with the smell of ink and paper. It's delightful. I take in a deep breath, following Sir Jet as he moves toward the left of the room where cabinets with glass doors hold slots of scrolls. Gold genre titles adorn the top of each cabinet—History, Cay-Llek; History, Curses; History, Färrin; History, Herbs, History, Lanckest. . . and so on and so forth.

Sir Jet stops at one that reads History, Curses. "You should find what you're looking for here, hopefully. If not, the catagorium will be able to tell you what we have elsewhere." He points to a huge book in the center of the room that has its own gilded mahogany pedestal. How quaint, but I'm sure it will come in handy. Unlike Treía's library, where nothing was organized or even in the right area. If I get the chance to go back to Treía after we finish getting Renell to safety, I will work on cataloging that library. I'm sure the nobility will thank me, eventually. Although, I might just make it harder for them to find things. Maybe their chaotic setup is intentional. Who knows.

"Ah, my favorite . . . curses regarding frogs." I smile, reading the headers on each slot for the scrolls.

I swear I see Sir Jet roll his eyes out of the corner of my vision. I think I'm growing on him. He turns back toward the double doors. "Let me show you your quarters, then you can come and read about frogs as much as you like."

Is that sarcasm I hear? Amazing. Now I know where Jarret gets it from.

Chapter 25
Hope Remains

Dais

I step into the library, the huge double doors swinging out in front of me. I know I shouldn't be here, but I can't slate my curiosity. It seems stupid, wanting to meet the man my wife betrayed me with—the man she loved first. He'll always have that over me, and I hate that I can't let it go. I wish I could . . . for my own sake. I want to compare myself to him. I want to know that I'm the better man in every way. Due to Jet's careful diligence, he's kept our paths very separate as if we're children in need of a governess.

Though, if I told him my plan, I know he'd have stopped me, so I couldn't risk his involvement in this matter. He told me Thesa believes in the man's change of heart. I trust Thesa, but I don't trust this man . . . and I never will.

He's been in the castle for a few days now, so at least he hasn't caused any commotion I'm aware of, but that could also be Jet's influence. It'd be just like him to keep things quiet until I could devote attention to them. At least he didn't keep the secret of Wen coming here from me. I know it was hard for him to divulge the information

360

because of how I might react—like a jealous schoolboy who wants to know everything about his rival. I'm not sure I could call Wen my rival though. He's just a sorcerer, and I'm a king. I'm married to the woman we both love, and he isn't.

He still slept with her though. The thought poisons my mind. I hate that he stole something beautiful in my marriage, but if I'm being honest, it wasn't just his fault. It would be easier for me if it was. Then I wouldn't resent my wife for what she did. I know she had to protect the pregnancy, but the wound digs deep into my heart, leading me to the library on a fine afternoon.

Golden sunlight spills through the crystal domed ceiling. Servants wander around, lighting candles and chandeliers for the evening readers still packed in the room. I meander down the main section, finding a man buried under scrolls and a few books. He sits at one of the largest tables, and even then, parchments spill over the sides. He couldn't have read all that in such a short time, could he? He only arrived a few days ago. I couldn't have done that.

Comparison.

I glare at him. I wouldn't say he's more handsome than me, but he isn't ugly either. Long white hair falls to his shoulders, dark tanned skin with white tattoos snake up and down his arms, face, and neck. He's got squared features, unlike my chiseled face. If I'm honest, there isn't that much difference.

I lose myself in between some stacks of books, trying to loosen the tightness in my chest. I should go. I saw him. I don't have to meet him. Besides, what would I say? *Greetings, I'm the king of Casta, and you slept with my wife?* Yes, very tactful.

Embossed gold titles shimmer under flickering candlelight. I'm acting like a child. I should leave or meet him and prove that I'm the better man by not hiding like a curious cat lurking in the shadows. He didn't spy on me . . . that I know of.

I square my shoulders, marching out of the shelves. Jet would call me an idiot. Wen is a sorcerer and could probably do anything to me that he wants. All I have is a dagger strapped to the inside of my boot, but rarely does common sense make me listen. I head straight for the man. He doesn't look up as I approach, his nose buried deep in the book while his mouth whispers the text as he goes. I glance at the title.

"Curses in the art of Cay-Llekian culture? Interesting read. Old one, too," I say, and am surprised to find my voice clear and strong.

He lifts his head, gray eyes meeting mine. He stumbles when he sees me, standing with a bow of his head. "Your Majesty, thank you for allowing me to come."

"Wen, let's be honest with each other. We both know what's happened between us and we don't have to delude ourselves. At least, I don't like fooling others. Let's not pretend that we have to be polite."

He wrinkles white eyebrows. "If I'm one hundred percent honest, I'll most likely be thrown out of here. You have nothing to lose in this situation, and I don't like to play games." He crosses his arms over his chest, and I find myself comparing my muscles to his.

"I don't like games either. I promise you. You'll be able to stay no matter what you say. I appreciate what you're doing for Renell." I lean against another table, keeping his gaze steady.

"She saved my life. It's the least I can do." He relaxes slightly, glancing at the mess on the table beside him.

Now I really don't know what to say. *Honesty.* The word embeds itself in my heart. "I'll be honest. I didn't come here to talk. I was curious."

"Curious to see what tedious scrolls I'm reading? Now that must be a boring day for the Castian King." The remark seems to loosen him a bit more.

I chuckle. "It's never a boring day."

"I can only imagine, and I've never been in a place where people weren't curious about me. It's the hair." He flicks his head.

"Really, I would have thought the tattoos."

"Everybody else does too, but alas, it's the hair." He smirks.

I can't believe I'm getting along with this man. I actually enjoy his light-hearted presence. I don't know if I should be ashamed to admit that or not. I should hate him, but I can't find it in me to. He was a victim as much as I was, and I know that's why Renell saved him. She saw good in him, and I trust her. He can't be all bad, regardless of the infidelity my wife shared with him.

"Well, I hope you find what you're looking for, for Renell's sake.

Dinner will be served soon, if you'd like to partake. If not, stay as long as you need." I turn, starting for the door.

"I thought we were going to be completely honest?" he asks. "Don't you have anything else to say to me?"

I stop and look back at him. "I don't. I thought I did. I'm not happy about what happened. What husband would be? But I know why she did it, and you do too." He nods. "I've forgiven her, and I don't resent you or know you enough to have to forgive you. I wish I could hate you, but I know Rahuin hurt you too. Maybe you deserved it, maybe you didn't. I honestly don't think anyone who gets their heart ripped out deserves it."

He smirks. "I wanted to hate you too. I wanted to hate you because she chose you. I wanted to hate you because she used me to keep your child safe. I wanted to hate you for so many reasons, but you're right . . . I don't. She loves you and that will never change. I don't want to ever come between you again. I just want to make what I've done right. I knew it was wrong, but I gave in because it was the easiest way to serve my master. It was what he wanted all along. I'm sorry I took a piece of your union that you will never be able to get back. Maybe that is unforgivable, but I hope it's not, or my soul is damned." He keeps his eyes fixed on mine, but more than just his words pass between us. An array of hurt, loss, and grief connect our souls in a way only suffering can.

"Will you tell Rahuin that?"

He nods. "Yes, something along those lines. I want her to find forgiveness. I know that's why she's in Färrin. She can't forgive herself for all that happened, and I'm afraid she never will until I make things right with her too."

"So you'll go see her?"

"Only if I have your blessing. If not, I will wait until she's home in Casta."

"You have my blessing. I'm afraid if you don't go, she'll never return home." I look away briefly, running a hand over my curls.

"I will find Renell's cure first, but thank you."

"You seem like a good man, Wen. I can see why she saved you. I'm glad you had the courage to come."

He scoffs. "Don't act like you're proud of me now, Your Majesty. You hardly know me."

"That's right. Best to play it safe?" I chuckle.

"For now."

I hear the double doors open, the wood groaning under the weight.

"Dais, there you are. Why did you come here without telling me? Thesa is going to kill me. I really don't want to die that way because it'll be a hell of a way to go!" Jet rushes past shelves, his eyes taking in both Wen and I still in one piece and not bleeding from thrown fists. He glances all around the library, brow furrowed.

"Relax, Jet. I just came to greet our guest. Everything is fine. I'll tell Thesa it was my fault. I know she was just looking after me because of my anger issues." I smile. "But I'm getting better, as you can tell from his face."

"Yes . . ." Jet trails off. "And now you're getting some sarcasm from him." He rolls his eyes.

"It just oozes off me. Not much I can do about it really," Wen quips.

"Unbelievable," Jet mutters when I snicker. "Come, Your Majesty. You have to get prepared for dinner." He starts away.

"Of course." I nod at Wen. "Come join us if you'd like. If not, enjoy your evening."

"You too . . . Dais."

I don't feel the need to correct him as I follow my bodyguard out of the library.

Rahuin

I hear water dripping somewhere. The steady plunk, plunk, plunk invades my thoughts, disrupting sleep. I open my eyes, only to find the familiar darkness closing in. My heart starts to pound. I shouldn't be here. I can't do this right now. I close my eyes, curling up into a ball so I don't have to search for the light. I don't want to move. I don't want to try. I can't defeat this. I can't make the hurt end.

"Do you think hiding from me is going to make me go away? After all you've done, are you going to give up now?" The voice sends shivers along my skin. *How is he always here? Why does he always find me? Why can't I ever find peace?* Because you took so many lives . . . do you think they will ever find peace? *I came here to heal, but I can't even do that. I can't change what has happened.*

"Leave me," I whisper, but I doubt he hears. I can't even hear myself.

"I can make it stop, Rahuin. They always fail you. They say they can help, but they never do."

"Go away." I choke on a hopeless sob that appears in my throat even though I know I won't cry. I haven't cried in a long time.

"I'll stop your suffering. I'll make the pain go away. You won't have to pay tenfold. You can end it now. Just come with me." I feel his bony hand on my shoulder, and I jump, swinging my arm against his, but all I hit is air.

I hear him cackling from somewhere. I cover my ears, screaming to block the sound, but it echoes in my mind like crashing waves. *I can be free. I will be free. I will survive.*

"Will you?" The voice is in my head now, and then I see them again, the people I've killed. Every face that has met heartache and pain because of me—Dais, Thesa, Jarret, Connan, Glena, Wen . . .

No. I didn't hurt them. I didn't do this. I close my eyes tighter, but it doesn't make the images go away.

I hear a giggle and a voice saying, "Open your eyes, Rahuin." But I don't obey. *What if it's just another trick?*

"But you did, and you will continue to hurt them. You will destroy them. They will turn on you. They can't save you, and why would they want to? Everything would be better if you weren't with them." I feel his fingers parting my hair. I feel his hand lifting my chin. "Come with me. All this will be over . . ."

I hear the giggle again. "Now, Rahuin."

I open my eyes then, and fire ignites around us, illuminating the monster in his all-black wardrobe.

The Darkness lets me go, hissing as the blaze dances in between me and him. His black eyes reflect the flames as he glares. "What *have you done?"*

"It's not what she has done, but what you have done. The King is coming. Your time is almost up. Better enjoy it while you can." The fire surges as the voice titter.

"The King is gone. He will never return," the Darkness snaps, trying to reach me through the flames, but the wall between us blazes higher and brighter.

The voice changes to a deeper cadence, matching the inferno in front of me. "Your reign is almost over! He will destroy you once and for all! You've been warned!"

I gasp awake. Sweat coats my skin to the point where I can see it soaking through my nightgown. I shiver as a cool breeze flutters from the window to my left, and I hear it giggle. What?

A fire ignites in a hearth to my right, illuminating the room. I jump, scrambling closer to the wall where my bed presses against it.

"Rahuin." I hear the fire's voice.

I stare at the flames. It saved me. It fought for me. The King. The fire talked about the King. The prophecies come to mind. That's right. This entire time, we've been fighting to bring Him back. I'd forgotten that.

"I will be with you when you need more strength . . ." The words appear in my head. Him. He was the King. He had to be, and I saw Him again when He took Elrian. Why is He only appearing in my dreams though? The fire said He was coming, but coming when? Haven't we all suffered enough? Surely, I've done enough to bring about His return.

"You talked about the King. When is He coming?" I ask the flames.

"Soon," the voice responds. "The King has no set return date. He's just told me He will come soon."

"He's said the same to me, so why isn't He here yet? Why do I have to keep . . ." I trail off, feeling tears crawl to my throat.

"It's not time yet, but it's coming soon."

"What if it's not soon enough? Hope is dwindling, and I thought He couldn't come if the Darkness rules."

"Not all hearts have darkness in them. There is more hope than you think." The blaze rises and falls with the words.

"But the prophecy—my hope is almost gone."

"That's why we're here. We'll help you through it. You're almost there. That's what He said." The fire's sincere voice calms me a little, but the lingering images of my sins haunt my thoughts. How can I learn to live with them? How can I continue, knowing what I've done all in the King's name? Surely, I don't deserve to live after it all.

The door to my left opens, and I turn to find my mother rushing in with a pitcher of steaming water.

"I'm here to bring you calm, Rahuin. I'm sure you're frightened by that whole ordeal," the water says. Now the water's talking to me?

"I'm frightened by everything right now," I mutter.

"What, *Aihha*? I asked when you woke up." Mother sets the pitcher down on a bedside table, dipping a cloth into it. She glances behind her at the fire. "Hmm, I forgot to tell someone to light the hearth . . . Did someone come in?"

"She thinks I need someone to light me? I give them the opportunity to let me blaze," the flames huff.

"N—no, I mean, I'm not sure. I just woke up." *And I'm listening to flames talk* . . . I leave the words out. My mother already thinks I'm unstable. I don't need to give her more reason for it.

She touches my forehead. "You had a horrible fever and woke up screaming." She grabs a wet cloth, gently placing the rag on my head.

I sigh at its warmth. "Just a bad dream. I—um—I remember falling. What happened after that?"

The breeze giggles again. "I caught you."

"That's what you like to think, young one," a new voice speaks, but I'm not sure from where.

"*Suvitaas* Areis used her gift to catch you," Mother says, but I'm having a hard time trying to block the voices arguing in the background of my mind.

"I caught her, I did!" Air squeals.

"We grant *Suvitaas* Areis the power and even I feel offended."

"Oh the high and mighty *Earth* feels offended?" Fire chuckles.

"Will you please be quiet?" I call through the room and the voices fall silent.

Mother looks at me quizzically. "*Aihha*, I've hardly said any-thing."

Great, now I'll have to tell her. "It's not you. It's . . ."

"Us!" Wind exclaims and rushes through the room, tousling my hair and the fire.

"The elements?" Mother asks, astonishment on her face. "You can hear them?"

I stare at her. Perhaps I'm not crazy. "Yes. Mother, what's going on?"

"*Suvitaas* Areis said you could harness them, but she didn't say you could speak to them . . . Suvitaas are the only elves who can har-ness all four elements. Not everyone can do it, and fewer still, can hear them. Not even all *Suvitaas* can hear them." She smiles, check-ing my forehead again as I try to process her words. "I can only har-ness water."

"Well, that would explain why she didn't say anything about be-ing able to hear them," I mutter.

"What do they say?" She sits beside me, tucking my blanket around my shoulders and wrapping her arms around me.

I fall into her embrace.

I hear the wind scoff. "As if we'd say something profound."

"Nonsense, mostly. They chat about anything. They seem to have very distinct personalities," I whisper, despite what the fire told me about the King. I believe that news should be kept close to my heart for now.

"Well, not all people act the same, so why should we be the same?" Earth asks.

"I think we should all be quiet for now. Rahuin needs her rest," Water says.

"But the day is so close to beginning! I love new days!" Wind whoops.

"In this instance, I agree with water." Earth sighs.

"You always agree with water!" Air grumbles.

"I agree with water, and we never get along," Fire says.

"I would expect nothing less." Mother laughs.

My head is starting to hurt from trying to decipher all the conversation. I close my eyes as I lean against my mother. I wait for the horrible images to fill my head. I wait for the fear to consume me, but whatever the fire did against the Darkness, it must have worked.

Renell

"The queen is dead."

"Really? I'd heard a rumor but I wasn't sure. You're certain?"

"Positive. They're keeping it quiet so they can find the killer."

"Do you think—"

"Hush, she can probably hear us."

I step back from the door, holding my breath as I slowly let it close. I gasp for air once the barrier is between me and the gossiping servants. The sky lightens with the appearance of the sun, illuminating the forest painted on the walls. I don't think I slept at all last night. After the queen and a few of her parliament members disappeared with most of their clothes missing, a servant brought me to my room, which thankfully, was devoid of any more salacious human beings. They finally gave me a proper nightgown. Once I'd changed, I sat in the corner all night watching the door.

Now that I've finally opened said door, I wish I hadn't. The queen is dead. Not by my hand, thank goodness, though I wish I could have had a hand in it. The vile woman deserved it. *No, you shouldn't think that way. Death is never deserved by anyone, no matter how awful they are.* I wish I could say I agreed with my thoughts. I wonder if Clòz did it. No, he wouldn't dare. He would've come here first to find out if the queen laid a finger on me, and then he would've killed her. For once, his possessiveness saved me from roaming hands and perverse intentions. Though, I feel as if I need another bath after all the eyes had drunk their fill.

A knock at the door draws my attention, and a servant enters the room with something to eat. It's the same one from the bath last night. She bows her head. "My lady, I'm here to see you ready for the day." She flutters around the room, pulling garments from a chest along the far wall—dresses in gorgeous silks and corsets with the finest under-garments arise.

Should I really take more hospitality after last night's obsceni-ty? But the queen is dead . . . that is if the servants were telling the truth. What if it's another heinous act against me? A trick to see what I would do with the absence of Her Majesty?

"W—what shall I be doing today?"

"I don't— They just— I'm just supposed to see you ready."

I nod, stealing myself before I ask a question that could incrim-inate me. I know I shouldn't ask, but I have to know for certain. "I heard a whisper this morning that the queen was murdered last night. Is that true?"

The servant gasps and meets my gaze, her own light pink eyes fill with conviction. "I—It is true. Though they're not sure if it was . . . murder or if she accidentally k—killed herself."

My brow furrows. "Why would they assume it was accidental?"

"T—the queen, as you witnessed, i—is no stranger to alcohol an—and narcotics. They think she might have . . ."

"Taken too much?"

She nods, grabbing the undergarments I need and helping me into them.

"Thank you for being honest."

"It's the least I—I could, after . . . after last night."

At least someone in this wretched place has a heart. "Has my hus-band arrived?" I don't even know if he was going to come and see me this morning, or if they'd let him. I'm sure he would, while threaten-ing to destroy everyone if they didn't let him through.

"I'm—I'm not sure. Was he expected?"

"No," I whisper as she helps me into the garments, tightening a corset and helping me into a giant hoop skirt, before securing a gor-geous emerald green dress over it.

The door opens again as she's tightening the bodice, and Clòz walks in, his brown eyes squinting around the room. "I gather the queen didn't treat you too poorly." He sneers as if the room itself might come alive and strangle him.

"That's to be determined."

The servant hurries out.

"Oh? Do tell. I've been waiting for an opportunity to wring her neck." His features light up, the corners of lips lifting in a gleeful smile at the thought of a kill.

"It's too late for that, she's already dead."

Clòz raises his eyebrows. "Really?"

"Really. She might have had a little too much to drink, or she was murdered. You didn't, by chance, happen to kill her?" I ask as he steps closer to me, his fingers reaching for the soft silk of my dress.

"No, I don't kill without probable cause. I had to come check on my bride first. She didn't lay a hand on you then?" His fingers snake up my waist. "I heard there was quite a party last night."

"No, she didn't lay a hand on me, and the party you're talking of was a pigsty of debauchery. She made me become a living statue to be admired." I draw the words out, whispering them in his ear.

He draws back with a huff. "You were naked?" His dark eyes flash.

"Practically."

He scoffs. "Now I wish I would have been the one who killed her." His hands draw into fists.

"I wish I could have had a hand in it too, but unfortunately, we have bigger problems to worry over."

"And that would be?" he asks, falling into a chair next to my breakfast, popping a grape into his mouth, his black beard draping over his lap.

"If they determine that the queen didn't accidentally kill herself, then you or I could be a suspect. Did you stay somewhere in the palace last night?"

"No, they offered, but I declined. The outside air seemed much more inviting. I rode back to the caravan and stayed in my tent."

"Good, they can't blame it on you then, but they could blame it on me, especially after the queen's care of me yesterday.

"Hmm, what do you suggest?" His eyes bore into mine, his red tattoos swirling in dizzying circles.

I grip a side table beside me to curb the nausea that's suddenly appeared. "I suggest you make yourself scarce. You can come get me if they lock me up or find a way to help prove my innocence. It won't do much good if we're both stuck in a cell."

"Any guesses as to who the murderer could be?" he asks, munching on more of my breakfast.

I swallow bile. "The prime minister, unless he's dead too. The monarchy passes directly to him since the queen has no children."

He stands, sighing as his fingers reach for my arms and pull me closer to him. His lips crush against mine, and it takes all my will-power not to spit him out and throw up all over him.

"Goodbye, my bride." He smirks, sauntering out of my room.

I sigh once he leaves, stealing a glance at the breakfast he devoured. My stomach churns, so I take a deep breath and look away.

The door opens again, this time with an unwanted visitor—the prime minister and a few guards. I stare at each of them wearily. Oh, good, they've already come for me.

He smiles, his gray sideburns pulling oddly with the smile lines around his face. He looks like he purposefully drew extra lines there to make him look creepier. "Your Highness, how lovely it was for you to join us at the party last night."

"Yes, lovely is the word I'd use." I glare. "What can I help you with, Prime Minister?"

"I'm sure you've heard by now, but the queen is dead. We've determined that her death was . . . not an accident."

Of course they did. "What would that have to do with me?" I quirk an eyebrow, wishing I could destroy them all where they stand, but not yet. I still need their help, and I can't just kill everyone here and not risk the citizens retaliating. Clòz will get me out. I despise that I have to rely on my abusive husband to save me. We'll find the killer, and we'll get Onar's help.

"Surely, you aren't that daft, Your Highness."

"I didn't kill her if that's what you're asking." And since you're still standing before me, my guess is you killed her . . . but I leave my thoughts to myself.

"I'm afraid that's for a judge to determine, Your Highness." He nods and the guards move forward, restraining my arms behind my back with shackles.

"Is there evidence to support I'm the killer?" I ask as he steps up toward me, his eyes scouring every inch of my exposed skin. I scowl. Didn't he have his fill last night?

"Your presence alone is enough, Your Highness, and I've heard a rumor about you . . . the Princess of Death. Not a wonderful title for someone who claims to be innocent." His breath assaults my face as he leans close. He steps back, eyes set and nose upturned. "Lock her up."

Chapter 26
The Cost of Freedom

Jet

"Your Majesty, what an honor." The man bows. General Hike stands around six feet tall, his dark brown eyes reflecting the sunlight shining into Dais's office.

I stand behind my king, keeping watchful eyes on the man with thinning blond hair, his red beard needs a trim, and the way his tunic bulges over a protruding belly, tells me he enjoys a malted drink often.

According to other soldiers, this general never tried to hide his disdain for Zenz. Everyone knew he didn't respect Zenz, and many stories suggest he never followed Zenz's orders. That doesn't mean he's a traitor to the crown, but he could know who is. Even after Dais ordered me to glean some information from the men captured during the wedding, I hadn't been able to get anything useful.

Dais had them hung yesterday morning. The crowd was thirsty for blood—for someone to pay, but it wasn't the blood they wanted to see, and their actions made me sick . . . still make me sick. Their cries for Rahuin's death still cause my skin to crawl. I know it pained Dais to see. I watched his face go from pale to furious in an instant.

More and more I see him resenting the people he's charged with leading, and I understand. Who in their right mind would want more bloodshed when so many lives have already been lost? Doesn't that make them worse than the people who waged war against us? I know they're angry because they had to send their loved ones to lay down their lives for this kingdom, but hasn't there been enough loss? Hasn't enough blood been spilled?

What's worse is, we're nowhere near finished with this war. We might be in a ceasefire, but how long will it last? King A'zre made an alliance through Princess Esther, but who's to say if he will honor his agreement? Greed is never slated. It's a jealous monster that begs to be satisfied, and never is. Greed devours everything until there is nothing left but an empty shell.

We have to start preparing. We have to be ready. I know Dais feels that pressure too, but he can't satiate their thirst for vengeance. They want someone to pay, but they keep directing it at the wrong people. Maybe it's just another hunger that can't be satisfied. Maybe they'll never be appeased, because nothing can bring back the loved ones they've lost.

I know it's weighing on Dais, because he can't get them to focus on the real enemy. He can't get them prepared when they have no interest in it. Sure, they want the pain to end, they want someone to blame, but will they blame themselves when the enemy overruns our borders? Will they finally see their mistake when they have nothing left to fight for?

Maybe they have to learn the hard way, but if that happens, then Casta is lost, and the Darkness reigns. Everything we've fought for, every life lost, every sacrifice made, will all be in vain. What a horrible legacy to leave behind. I hope for Dais's and Casta's sake the people will come to understand who the real enemy is. I hope we can convince them in time, but the weight of despair has started to settle over us, and I'm not sure how long we'll be able to fight it.

Dais stands, his blue eyes boring into the General's. "General Hike, do you have any idea why you've been called here today?"

"No, Your Majesty." The man glances at me, twiddling his thumbs.

"General, did you have anything to do with the attack that killed General Zenz?"

"I beg your pardon, Your Majesty?" His brow knits. "I'm not sure why you would ask such a thing."

"I have captured informants who claimed you were the mastermind behind it all. I don't like to go around accusing innocent men, so I want to get to the bottom of it. I hope you are a man with enough morality to be honest with me. If you aren't, it is my duty to find the truth. I will not have anyone threaten the crown or my wife since General Zenz died protecting her."

"Maybe he shouldn't have gotten in the way," the general mutters.

I reach for the hilt of my sword, taking a step forward, but Dais slips a hand in front of me.

"So you admit to orchestrating an attack on my wedding day?"

Something within the man's face changes. His features harden, dark eyes narrowing.

"The world should be free of tyrants like you! You don't care about us. You never will! You never listen to us. We told you she deserves to die, but you wouldn't believe us. She's blinded you. We've gone to great lengths to make sure you finally see, and if you never do, then you don't deserve to be king." General Hike moves forward.

I glance at Dais, who wobbles against his desk, his gaze faltering and turning completely black. My heart clenches. No.

Dais faints, falling backward. I catch him, hauling him away from the crazed general.

"Look! Look what she's doing to him! We must cleanse the influence!" His wild eyes watch Dais as he reaches for something under his tunic. He shouldn't have weapons, but I'm not going to take any chances.

I pull my sword from its sheath and parry the blow from a nine-inch dagger he has. The weapon topples from his grip, and I point my sword at his neck to keep him from moving.

He smiles and the insanity in his expression twists his face like a mangled tree. "May my death bring the beginning of a new empire." He steps into my blade, blood splattering as he falls into it.

I rip my weapon away, but it's too late. He's already gone. What the *sev* just happened? I spin around, checking Dais's pulse. He's alive. I lift his eyelids, but the traces of darkness are gone. He's fine. I sigh before looking at the aftermath. General Hike didn't deserve to die. He wasn't in his right mind either. How many other soldiers are just as manipulated as he? When Dais wakes up, will there be anyone left who is loyal to him?

He wakes with a gasp, his blue eyes wildly taking in the scene before him. He pales.

"I'm sorry, Your Majesty. He walked into my blade. He wanted death."

He nods. "I know. I—"

I help him stand. "What happened?"

He looks at me. "The Darkness. He came for me. We're running out of time, and I fear the people won't be willing to follow me for much longer. We have to get them on the right side, Jet. If we lose them all, we'll lose everything for good." He starts forward but stumbles, even though he's got his cane in hand.

I reach to catch him, but he waves me away.

"I'm fine. We have more pressing matters to worry over beside my health. Call the generals together. Call the advisers. We have to test their loyalty. I have to know who I can trust."

I nod. "Of course, Your Majesty." I want to speak my mind. I want to tell him he should rest, but I know there is no point. He won't listen when his mind is made up. He won't stop until Casta is safe, but at that point, who will be left standing to rule it?

Dais

A cold feeling washes over the room.

"The world should be free of tyrants like you! You don't care about us, you never will! You ne—" The man slumps over, a gurgling sound echoing from his throat.

I stand up, rushing to his side, but it's no use, he's already gone.

No. Blood coats the floor where he'd fallen forward. He didn't deserve this. Sure, he stirred up trouble, but he didn't deserve death. He was just a disillusioned man fighting for the wrong things.

A dark figure steps over General Hike's body, and my skin crawls.

"You killed him. Why would you do that? He did nothing to you," I spit.

"Ah, King Dais. He's just a mouthpiece. You're the one who seems to keep getting in my way."

The Darkness . . . but what is he doing here? Why has he come to me? He usually appears to Rahuin. My stomach sinks. Is he done with her? Did he get to her and now he's after me? No. Surely if he had her, she would be here right by his side, sneering it in my face.

"I seem to keep getting in the way? I'm just trying to keep my country safe from your evil. My people never asked for this. They don't deserve this."

"No one ever asks for war, Your Majesty, but I get what I want, and I want this kingdom. So I will get this kingdom. I will destroy it from the inside out, and there will be nothing you can do." He steps closer, his all-black attire seems to darken the entire room, as if the chandeliers would snuff out under his cloak of ebony.

"You'll turn my people against me?"

"Precisely. I've already started. Can't you see? They already hate you for choosing her. For letting her kill your father. How does it feel, Dais, to be betrayed?"

"It hurts, but I'm sure you wouldn't know. I doubt you even feel anything at all."

"Trying to be defiant? I'm afraid it won't help in your case. Soon I will have all of Partin, then you will be nothing but a distant memory."

"You couldn't reach Rahuin, so you thought you'd try to get to me?"

"Bold of you to assume I see you as a threat. You're just an annoyance I need out of my way. I came here to show you that you can't win. You will never win. They will continue to turn on you until there is nothing left. They will destroy you. No, Dais, there is no getting to you. I just want you to know who's behind it all."

His words send the chill deeper into my bones.

"I'm not afraid of you, and I will never let you take them from me."

"Then this will be extremely fun. Good day, Your Majesty." With that, he vanishes. The darkness he brought immediately disappears.

I stumble against my desk, shivering. Now I understand why Rahuin struggled. She saw him all the time. He said horrible things to her too. No wonder she could barely keep it together or even decipher what was real. I hope she's okay. I hope his visit was just what he said and nothing more. Though, I doubt that's true. He'll never let me have a moment's peace. Partin is in his grasp. He'll never give up on it, not until the King Himself comes to claim it.

David

"You've done well. I thought I left you out there to die, but you had other plans." A deep voice takes command of the darkness in my mind, filling the void like I'm sinking in water. It surrounds me in a sinister embrace.

"We've only finished what you've started, Master. He's perfect. A product we worked so hard to achieve." The voices from before fill my head next, sounding like a cacophony of thousands talking all at once.

No. Not again.

I haven't had an episode in weeks. The voices were gone. I was safe. Everyone was safe.

"One out of thousands. I don't think those odds are particularly impressive." The deeper voice scoffs, but the dark doesn't dissipate.

"But he's powerful. You saw."

"Yes, I was particularly impressed with what you did at the wedding. He's gaining a following. That will benefit me in the long run."

"Then the deal is the same. We continue to run this little charade, convince him of his potential, and when we take the crown, you set us free . . . like you promised before we failed. Clearly, you can see we haven't failed. You can do whatever you want with him once we're free."

The deep voice chuckles. "It's a deal. Have fun."
"We will. Oh, we will."

Everything comes back into focus, and I realize I'm standing in my room. Cream and gold accented walls rise around me. Large murals of mountains and beautiful meadows fill spaces in between the accents. Peggy had them commissioned because she said they reminded her of home. Sunlight seeps through the three floor-to-ceiling windows and the doors leading out to our private terrace. They're open and I can hear the ocean crashing in the distance. I take a deep breath, looking around the room to see if Peg is here, and catch a glimpse of myself in the mirror.

I freeze as bile rises in my throat. Blood and ash coats my hands and green tunic. What? No. I step closer to the mirror, my heart palpitating. My purple eyes are wide, and I notice small cuts and abrasions all over my face. How did this happen? I didn't go anywhere. I never left the room. Right?

But the voices . . .

They were there. I heard them. Did they do this? No. That's impossible. The voices were gone. I was free. This isn't real. I must be in a dream. My stomach churns. I haven't had an episode since we got back from the camp over six weeks ago. Peg and I were so happy. I started taking on recruits and training more soldiers for Casta. I was finally able to start helping Dais by getting our people ready for the next phase.

My trembling hands reach up and touch my cheek, smearing flaky blood over my skin. A dark shadow overtakes half my face, pulling in a sinister smile. I gasp away from the mirror, nearly falling over in my haste to distance myself.

It's not real. Just a dream. It has to be.

"Why do you keep thinking we're nothing but a dream?" My reflection speaks to me, the darker shadow completely overtaking my face, but it's not my voice. It sounds like a thousand speaking all at once.

I look behind me, but there is nothing but the windows. This has to be a dream. I just have to get out of it.

"There's no leaving this, David. You are us and we are you. It's been that way for a while. We saved you. We enhanced that beautiful gift of yours."

Enhanced? What?

My heart sinks, and I swallow as I move closer to the mirror again, keeping my eyes on the shady version of me. "The camp. You did something to me."

"Before that, David. Unfortunately, we were separated. You kept rejecting us. Such a shame. But we're home now. You're safe. We're helping you control the fear. Don't you see? You haven't felt the cold in a while."

I look down at the blood on my hands, lifting my palms to show what I've done. My reflection mirrors me, but his skin is completely clear. "But this blood. How did I get this?"

"Just a game, David. We're helping you live up to your full potential."

"What do you mean?" Are they talking about how normal the last few weeks have felt? About my ability to train soldiers and not have Peggy constantly worrying about me going overboard? Was that them—him?—them?

"You'll see soon. We're creating a better world. Helping you keep what you love safe. That's all you want, right?"

A knot twists in my stomach, something about this isn't right, but I don't know why. Everything within me has felt right until today.

"Right," I find myself answering. The shadowy version of myself vanishes, and all I'm left with is my bloody, bruised reflection.

Renell

The cold of the Onarian dungeons seems to seep into my bones. I was surprised that they actually let me keep the dress I was wearing when they arrested me, but the beautiful material isn't known for warmth. My beheading ceremony is tomorrow, and no one will pardon me because the people in power are the ones who really killed the queen.

I haven't seen Clòz in weeks, or maybe it hasn't been weeks, it just feels like it. I can't tell time in the dark of Onar's dungeons.

I heard Onar was built on old catacombs. I wonder if the prison is part of it. Maybe I can escape if that's true. Musty smells of rotting bodies and wet feces have left me gagging more times than I can count, and the pregnancy doesn't help. The whimpering sounds of other inmates has become a cacophony of our grim reality.

At least no one has decided to do whatever they want with me, because if they did, I would kill them instantly. Then, they'd really have a reason to kill me. Not that I care anymore. I feel like I'm already dead, and the loneliness often has me thinking of Jarret, even though I know I shouldn't. Thinking about him only makes me hurt more. I'll never get back to him. He probably doesn't even think I'm alive. I haven't been able to contact him, since my *heln* is hiding within my saddlebags. I'm sure Clòz has already discovered it, and then he'll transfer me from one prison to the next.

Though, I'm sure he'll be less neglectful than my current captors . . . if he even comes for me. He must have abandoned me or gotten caught, and if that's the case, he'll die tomorrow too. The thought hardly brings any consolation. I rub my stomach for the thousandth time. A lump choking my throat. My baby will never see the light of day, and the realization devastates me.

"I'm sorry you chose me as your mother. I'm sorry I failed to keep you safe," I whisper to the little bump.

"I hear people say you're crazy once you start talking to yourself." The voice causes my skin to crawl, but it brings more hope than I'll ever admit.

I shakily stand. "You try being trapped down here for days on end and find out how you fair. I was talking to the baby, not myself."

Clòz's hand reaches through the bars, and I allow him to caress my cheek. "Let's go, my bride." Other Cay-Llekian men rush into the prison as quiet as mice, unlocking my cell. I fall into Clòz's arms, even though it's the last thing I want to do, but I'm too weak to support myself. It's not like they've given me the royal treatment.

He picks me up, and I can't even protest. At least he's getting me out of here.

A shout sounds behind us, before it's cut off with a squelching sound. I swallow the bile in my throat, even the sound nearly makes me gag. Sconces flicker against sandstone as Clòz and his men weave through the castle's underground.

"Thought you could run? Only the guilty run." The prime minister blocks the path with a slew of guards on either side of him, more rush into the halls from the other end.

"Only the condemned don't want to die," I gasp.

"Get them." He shuffles backward as the guards advance.

Clòz sets me down, placing my fingers around his waist. "Stay close." He brandishes his sword as they come after him, but they are no match for his strength and skill. His other men cut their opponents down like a knife in butter. I try to keep my eyes away from the splattering blood, but the smell invades my senses. I bury my head into Clòz's back.

"Get the Prime Minister. He's the one who murdered her. He touched me," I whisper the words closer to his ear, and I feel him start to move faster. There is no way he'll let the Prime Minister escape alive now. I'm not sure how it will help us gain Onar's support, but I'm certain we won't be able to reason with the Prime Minister. Hopefully, someone who isn't as corrupt will be placed on the throne instead.

More guards flood the halls. Funny how they'll fight us because they believe I killed their queen, when the true culprit stands behind them. We have to get a confession out of him, otherwise we'll never make it out alive.

I tell Clòz.

"No," he answers. "He must die." He grunts, hacking away at a soldier in front of him. Arrows fly through the air, and I hear something crash in the distance.

"And you'll get to kill him. We just need a confession so all these loyal soldiers know who really killed her. If they know, they'll turn on him and anyone else he's in league with. Then, if we reveal his true nature, we might have a better chance of gaining their support.

"Or"—he thrusts his sword, moving slightly away from me—"It was just the queen's war. What if her people don't want it?"

"More room for us. If Onar recalls their armies from Lan land then it's all ours and Sun'Ar's, or we get Lanckest and Sun'Ar gets Casta. Truly, it would be to our advantage if they decide to leave this war." Though, I know Onar won't stop fighting. If they do, then they'll become an immediate target. They won't have enough resources to hold their ground, and anyone could easily overtake them. It would be stupid for them not to fight, even in the midst of their queen's death. I'm not sure how she ruled, but clearly, her soldiers were loyal to her.

He huffs, an arrow narrowly missing his head and grazing his ear instead. He hisses. "Fine. We'll get him to confess. I'm not going to fight through this hell when we've got an entire city to get out of. We've memorized escape routes and cracks in their defenses, but we have to get to those places first." He marches forward, cutting men down in his path.

I stand behind him, trying to avoid stepping in the spots of blood. The beast inside me screams at all the lives dying around me. I feel each one down to my soul, as if they are a part of me, but I feel the bloodlust too. The hunger feeding Clòz's men, and the fear driving Onar's soldiers.

"Let's get him," he says. He reaches back, taking my hand into his as he attacks more men. I resist the urge to rip it from his grasp. "Now, my bride, it's time to show them your skill of death." He swings me forward, as I unleash the hungry monster inside. Black smoke swirls around me as I transform. A few brave soldiers try to attack, but they soon realize it's a foolish mistake.

Men fall like flies as I race into their offensive line. It's so easy— too easy to destroy them. I could annihilate this whole city if I want to, but I need them. *But if you destroy them now, they can't throw you in a dungeon again.* True, but it doesn't matter, I'll never see the inside of an Onarian jail again. I just have to expose the Prime Minister for the traitor he is, and luckily, Clòz is a master interrogator.

I reach the end of the hall where a huge door is closed. I bet it's barred and the Prime Minister stands just behind it. I let my curse slip away, trying to let the hunger fade, but it rushes just under my skin.

Clòz darts toward the door, and the monster inside me starts to speak, *"Kill him! Kill him! End it! End your suffering. He deserves death!"* I reach a hand toward him, possessed by this newfound thought of freedom.

No!

I freeze. If I kill him, I die too. Finally the hunger ceases, forcing my monster to disappear. I straighten my shoulders, realizing this is the first time I've been able to fully unleash my curse and pull it back without Jarret's help. I dig my fingers into my palm, feeling my heart sink. I miss him so much.

The rest of Clòz's men start to work on pushing the door open. I stand back, leaning against the wall as I scan the hall. My stomach curdles at the mass of bodies lying on the ground. I killed them. I destroyed them. I look away. It's too late to take it back.

The door splinters as swords thrust through the holes at Clòz's men. A shout bounces along the sandstone walls as the doors crumple and men rush forward. The fight against the Onarian guards doesn't take long. I ignore the stench of blood and littered bodies as I walk over the threshold to Clòz, who has the Prime Minister in a choke-hold.

"If I'm right, more guards and parliament members will be here soon. We need them to witness the confession if this is going to work," I whisper into Clòz's ear.

"You better be right, because this *gizzek* deserves to die." He glares at the Prime Minister, who struggles against Clòz's meaty fist, his face flushing with the lack of air.

Clòz turns toward his men. "Stand down when the others get here. We have a confession to hear."

He shakes the man in his grasp. I would like to say I'm happy to see the Prime Minister in this position, but I'm not. In fact, I'm sad that ambition and possession destroys men. I wonder who the Prime Minister would have been if he hadn't been blinded by greed. I often think the same of Clòz. Would he have been a decent man if he hadn't been raised like a barbarian and forced to kill for what he wants? I'm certain he would have been, but I'm not sure why I mull over these useless thoughts.

Men pour into the hall on the far end past the door. Several parliament members walk in between them with eyes taking in the carnage and hands raised to mouths in gasps of horror.

Clòz laughs as they near, shoving the Prime Minister in front of him with a blade to the man's neck. "Don't come any closer, or I'll kill him."

They stop just outside the door. The two leading the pack halt, their hands outward to prevent the rest of the group from moving. "High Chief Clòz, if this is about the alliance, I'm afraid that can never happen after all the terrible things you have done against this kingdom."

Clòz laughs again. "You think I'm only here for the alliance? No, I'm here to expose a traitor who wrongfully touched and imprisoned my wife." He tips the blade closer to the Prime Minister's neck, and the man whimpers like a chastised dog.

"What do you mean?" a woman on the left asks, her face stricken.

"Your beloved Prime Minister murdered the queen," I say, moving closer to Clòz.

"I would never do such a thing. I've been loyal to Queen Ruby. You know that," the Prime Minister says.

Clòz draws more blood. "Tell the truth, or I will gut you where you stand."

"If I confess, I die. If I don't, I die. Tell me which do you think I'll choose. I know your little plan. I know you want to use me to pardon you. I'm not a fool."

"Well, fools rarely get what they want anyway, and no fool would be able to think up a plan to take the crown. Wait until a stranger appears, tarry until they have a motive, and then blame the attack on them. It's a brilliant plan really, and it should be recognized," I taunt, turning circles around them, letting the train of my dirty silk green dress whip the Prime Minister. I stand before him, whispering close to his ear, "Genius shouldn't be wasted."

"Prime Minister, did you kill Queen Ruby?" the man at the threshold asks.

He glares at the man. "I didn't kill her, Viscount Fridensburgh." He lifts his chin, a smirk painting his lined face. "Did I set up the plan? Indeed."

"You admit it?" Viscount Fridensburgh gasps, as if it's the most appalling thing he's ever heard.

"Genius should be admitted." The Prime Minister cackles his eyes looking like a deranged wild animal. "Yes, genius should be appreciated. It should be recognized for the peace I will bring to this land as king!" He spits in my face.

"Guards, arrest the Prime Minister."

"Not so fast." I hold up a hand, transforming just enough so the guards see the dark smoke curling around my arm. They freeze. "We'll give the Prime Minister back if you let us leave peacefully."

Viscount Fridensburgh scoffs. "You murdered many of our men, we can't just let you walk out of here."

"Your Prime Minister framed me for a crime I didn't commit, and your queen paraded me naked like a painting to be admired."

Clòz grunts next to me.

The Viscount pales, his expression becoming solemn. "I'm truly sorry that happened to you. I wasn't present. The queen's perverse ideas of fun were never to my liking."

Finally, someone who speaks truth. I would have remembered him from that night because I wanted to rip the eyes out of everyone there.

"I agree. You have a choice to make, Viscount. We can leave peacefully, or we can kill our way out. Your men froze because they've seen what I can do. I will destroy this entire city and leave you with nothing."

The Viscount's brown eyes wink in the light of dancing sconces. "You mentioned an alliance apart from Sun'Ar when you came. Would the alliance still be on the table if we put the Prime Minister away and forget about this unfortunate ordeal?"

"Put me away? You can't silence me! You can't just—"

Clòz hits him with the handle of his dagger, knocking the man unconscious.

"Only if we're allowed to leave the city safely. If you break the deal, I will destroy you before your guards can even put cuffs on me. If you want part of Lan lands, you will get half. If Sun'Ar sees we are united, maybe they will take Casta, and we'll split Partin evenly."

"Or they'll retaliate."

"They haven't exactly given us what they've promised yet either.

We've sacrificed brave men for nothing in return. I say we negotiate for ourselves by becoming a force to be reckoned with." I know I'm manipulating them. I know Sun'Ar won't allow us to have Lanckest. I know they'll fight or send assassins to kill the figureheads, but it's the only way I can even gain a small chance at getting Lanckest back. The only way I can get my people home. Hopefully, Onar will be lost in the aftermath. If not, I'll find a way to appease them, but every day is only one step.

The Viscount turns to the other members of Parliament, conversing in the best course of action. Voices raise and lower. Some for it, some against.

He turns back around after a moment of intense whispering. "We accept." He meets my eyes and gestures to the Prime Minister lying prone on the sandstone black and blue tiles.

I release my curse, and the guards swoop in, taking the man away.

"We'll have a contract drawn up immediately, but for now, you are free to go."

Chapter 27
What We Fight For

Dais

I walk in the gardens beside Wen. I'd pulled him from his studies for a moment so we could both grab a breath of fresh air. Jet walks behind us, ever watchful and careful. My gaze lingers on the honeysuckles, snap dragons, and marigolds that burst in arrays befitting vibrant sunsets. Bees, hummingbirds, and butterflies swarm the blossoms, eager for a quick drink of nectar.

"I just love an afternoon stroll with a handsome king. You make me feel like a young damsel," Wen teases, winking at me.

I laugh, shaking my head. "I had you join me for purely selfish reasons."

"Oh, he's lonely, even better." Wen's fingers brush a day lily's red blossom, leaving a streak of golden pollen. I know I shouldn't have called Wen out here, but I'd be lying if I said we hadn't started to become good friends. Apparently, shared experiences over a broken heart do that to you.

I clear my throat. "I was visited by the Darkness for the first time. You were with him the longest. Can you tell me why he would be coming after me now?"

Wen lowers his head, stopping for a moment on the paved stones. "Because he wants to control you. He can only manipulate through fear. He tries to make it seem like it's your fault, or someone else's. Someone you can blame, but it doesn't always work." His gray eyes meet mine in serious contemplation.

A bird twitters overhead.

"Talking about some scandalous stuff, but then again, my hearing hasn't exactly been that great." Connan appears, rubbing the inside of his ear with a crooked pinky. Wrinkles and deep canyons adorn his face now, showing his false age. His hair is all white, sprouting from his head like the puffy clouds above us. Like me, he leans on a cane, with Glena supporting his other side. His metal left arm looks twice as big as him now since the rest of his body has shrunk in atrophy. His milky blue eyes shift over us.

"Connan, how are you?" I ask.

"How do you think I am? I look like an apricot, scratch that, a raisin. Who said growing old was a good thing? No one," he snaps, rubbing his crooked back for emphasis.

I smile. "You're still the same."

"Mhmm." He looks Wen up and down. "And who is this, young'un?"

"You know you're not that old right? You can't exactly call everyone a young'un." I lean back on my cane, straightening my spine with a crack at the movement. Now I'm starting to sound old.

"I look old. I might as well play the part, and I'm pretty sure this guy isn't Jet. Unless I'm losing my eyesight too." Connan squints, causing his already milky eyeballs to completely disappear under wrinkled skin.

"He's not. Jet's behind these two," Glena answers for him.

"Ah." He holds a hand to Wen. "And you are?"

"Wen. Just Wen."

They shake hands.

"Admiral Connan Brachs. Your name is familiar, but I'm not sure why . . ." Connan trails off, glancing at me. "I hear things aren't that great up here, Your Majesty. The people are still on edge, a loaded cannon pointed at the wrong person."

"That they are." I sigh. "I've been doing my best to appease them, while also keeping my sanity."

"Well, take it from this old geezer. You're doing a good job. The people are behind you as their king. They're just bored."

"Too bored. We're trying to get as many trained as possible so they can teach more. If we keep their hands busy, we'll keep their minds off all the gossip."

"The farmers have their crops in?" he asks. We play this game every few weeks. Connan makes a random appearance with Glena, claiming he wanted to smell the flowers. Then he asks me questions about random things until we eventually end up on Esther. She doesn't send him letters because she believes he's already dead. She always talks about him in the past tense. I've never corrected her.

"From the reports I've heard, yes. So, at least someone has been doing their jobs." I run a hand down my face, scratching the back of my neck. "I just needed some fresh air."

"So did I, it's good for my lungs. Any news from Esther?" His gaze wanders around the flowers at our ankles.

There it is.

"Not much. She's still trying to understand why he's waging the war. She wants to see if she can get him to change his mind, or something along those lines. She's fed us a few messages on movement in Lanckest for his troops, but not much since she's playing a long game."

"Yes, I understand all too well what role she plays in all this." He tries to mask the bitterness in his voice, but I hear the subtle sting nonetheless. "It doesn't matter. I'll be dead soon. Did you get my recommendation for the new admiral?"

I nod. "Judging from his exemplary record, I believe he'll be a good fit."

"Yes, I've been training him since my agreement with the sirens. He knows everything he should." He glances around. "Well, let's not annoy the king any longer, Glena." He pats her hand, and they move on.

"Connan Brachs . . ." Wen trails off, his eyes following the duo as they shuffle along the path.

"Yes, my sister's previous husband. She's married to the Sun'Arian king now. Though I'm not sure why I'm telling you. You probably already know that." I shake my head.

"Actually, I didn't. Everyone thinks I was so high in the Darkness's ranks, but I'm starting to see I didn't really know anything. I was more of an outcast with him than I ever realized. The world is much bigger than I thought, and I tried to compact it into something that revolved solely on how he saw me. I did anything to gain his favor." He starts to walk again, tattooed arms clasped behind his back.

"I can only imagine. Sometimes we do absurd things to feel accepted."

"Like you've ever felt like you don't belong, being a crown prince and all," he jests as a bee zooms past his face.

"That's what I mean. I always did what was expected because I didn't want anyone to think any less of me. I didn't want them to think I couldn't be a good king . . . one day." I look up at the sky, watching clouds pass overhead in strange shapes.

"Well, you seem like a good king, and I hope your sister is doing well in Sun'Ar. I remember the Darkness had plans for the king there. He never shared, but he was manipulating him just like everyone else. I believe he still is. Just tell her to be careful."

I suspected as much. "I will. Wen, why are you helping me? You could have ignored my question. You could have swept our brief mention of Esther away." I meet his gaze as he runs a sheepish hand through his white hair.

"I could have, but that's not who I am anymore. Helping people with my knowledge is all I have left, it's all I'm good for. I was with the Darkness for a long time, so why can't I share that knowledge . . . like with the Corrupted?" He plucks a marigold, smelling the blooming orange petals.

I consider him. Rahuin said he was a liar, a master manipulator. Are his words true, or just something I want to hear? Thesa said he's changed, and he saved Jarret, but what if he has a sinister motive? What if he wants to gain our trust and get close just to betray us? What if he's still working for the Darkness?

"Your silence says you don't like my answer." He twirls the flower.

I lean against my cane, reveling in the sunshine against my back. "It's not that I don't like your answer. It's just that I'm skeptical of your answer."

His gray eyes shift to mine, reflecting almost white in the sunlight. "It's too perfect for you?"

"Do you still work for the Darkness?"

"Is this how you interrogate people? You know, you're not supposed to ask them the question directly, right?" He raises white eyebrows.

"Just answer." Sometimes his antics irk me, like Connan. They'd be fast friends if Connan had the energy for it. Never mind, that might be a bad idea. They'd watch the world burn with their heaps of sarcasm.

"Whether or not I answer truthfully, you still won't believe me. I'm not working for the Darkness anymore. I was left to die. He didn't care to save me. I'm trying to make amends for what I've done. Besides, how would it benefit me to trick you? Why wouldn't I just kill you and get it over with so the Darkness can make his move right away?" He plucks petals off the marigold in his hands. "The Darkness can't physically harm anyone who is under the protection of the Light. If he tries . . . it doesn't bode well for him. So he has to use fear and manipulation to control people and make them destroy themselves or others. Yes, he taught me how to use those tactics, but I'm done with that. I just want to repay my debts. I want to live the life of a scholar when this war is over, but I will help fight in any way I can."

He's right. I still don't believe him, but sincerity shines in his eyes, a conviction that holds fast like an immovable mountain. Something that can't be easily faked, but he's a master of this sort of thing. I can hardly trust the people in my own parliament, let alone a stranger who has a history of deceit.

"You're right. I don't believe you, but you also haven't tried to kill me. I'm the one who came to you first and sought your thoughts on the Darkness. Thank you for answering me, even with my skepticism." I smile.

He chuckles, watching another duo approach us. "I'd be a skeptic in your position too."

David and Peggy amble toward us.

"Ah, I'd heard about our newcomer but hadn't had the pleasure of meeting yet. You've joined us for a few dinners now, and my brother-in-law didn't even have the courtesy to introduce us. I'm Peggy," Peggy says, holding a pale, freckled hand out to Wen. Orange bangs tease her face from the gentle breeze.

He smiles, placing a peck on her knuckles.

I ignore the side glance she throws at me.

She half turns to David. "And this is my husband, David."

David holds a hand out to Wen. "Dais's brother."

Wen shakes it. "Wen. I'm in Morough for a short while. Perhaps that's why Dais forgot introductions."

I nod. "We'll chalk it up to that. Not like I've haven't got a million other things on my mind."

Peggy pats my shoulder, aquamarine eyes shining. "And we don't know where we'd be without you."

"Darkness . . . Darkness. It surrounds you." The whisper from David draws my attention back to him. He's still holding, more like clenching, Wen's hand, his dark purple eyes frozen like his gift.

"Fear. Fear surrounds you like vice. You can't escape it. You never will." Wen's voice comes out like he's in a trance, as if David controls him. Frost travels up his arm where David grips it, nails digging into Wen's skin.

"David!" Peggy shouts, pulling David's hand off Wen, flickers of flame jumping from her fingers.

Wen stumbles backward, and I catch him. He falls against me, shaking, and I steady us with my cane. The tattoos on his arms and face glow faintly. His gray eyes are still pale and unfocused, his pupils dilating.

"Wen?" I shake him. "Wen, wake up."

"Who is he?" I hear Peggy's voice. "David hasn't had an episode like that in weeks."

David leans against her, staring at Wen. "Get away from him, Dais. Run. He'll destroy us all." He says it over and over again, getting quieter and quieter with every repetition.

"He's a scholar," I say.

Wen

I read the same sentence for the third time and groan, looking up toward the domed ceiling. Little rainbow lights refract off the crystal structure, and beautiful vines with light pink and blue flowers twirl around the rafters. I'd guess it's somewhere around early afternoon. Unfortunately, my head still throbs like someone slammed it with a mace. I've been here for six hours now and accomplished the mighty goal of reading one scroll. Wonderful.

Get a grip, Wen, you're never this distracted.

I rub my temples for the thousandth time and try to focus on the scroll of divorce and marriage customs, but my mind keeps wandering to what happened in the garden yesterday. I fainted like a damsel in distress. Unfortunately, I didn't have a knight in shining armor to save me, unless I count Dais. I almost laugh at the imagery. Apparently, he caught me. I feel so important.

But David . . .

Shivers break out on my skin, and the fear I felt when I shook his hand strikes my stomach once more. Something about him isn't right, but I can't put my finger on what. I knew he and his sister, Esther, have gifts. The Darkness used to collect cursed children. I believe he thought one of them would turn out to be the chosen one. I remember the nymphs, who were supposed to watch them, often asked if they could perform experiments.

Nymphs are elemental beings, and they've been around since the beginning of time, back when the King still ruled. Some scripts called them peaceful beings, whom the King cursed for a time. Other scripts portray the nymphs as deceivers, who became corrupted by the Darkness and started turning men's hearts away from the King, leading to the War of the Races. During which, the King cursed them to roam the world with no ending and stripped them of their powers.

Which is why cursed humans carrying the bloodline of their ancestors' sins become gifted with elemental powers. The nymphs want their power back so they can free themselves of their endless wandering.

I think David's power had something to do with ice, but they altered him when he was taken by the Darkness. I think they've possessed him somehow. I felt it when he touched me. They recoiled, recognizing the darkness I once carried. I'm not sure if it's possible for them to possess a human, but maybe because of the alterations… I'd have to find evidence to support this claim and warn Dais. Who knows what the nymphs can do in David's body? What they might have already done.

I stare at the scroll in front of me, running my fingers through my hair. First, I have to find the cure for Renell's curse. I can research David's predicament later, if Dais allows it. I sigh. Hopefully, after I make things right with Rahuin, I can come back to help them.

Once the sun has sunk low in the horizon and painted the sky with brilliant orange and pinks, I finally find the answer to Renell's curse. It's a procedure that will break all curses, including blood oaths. I stand, skirting around the large table and jumping like I was just handed the crown jewels. I'm not sure she'll agree to the operation because it will also break her birth curse, but maybe that won't be such a bad thing. I know she's struggled with it for years, but it's still a part of her.

I roll up the scroll and practically race out of the library and down the hall to Dais's study. I'm glad my headache is gone, because that means I can leave right away. Servants light the chandeliers out in the grand halls, and I take a second to once again admire the beautiful paintings on the ceiling. One day, when we're not in the middle of a war, I'll lay down in the hall and stare for hours. Beauty deserves to be appreciated, and I'm sure these ceilings have been neglected from admiring eyes for far too long.

"Halt!" Guards outside Dais's door stop me as I approach.

"Please inform His Majesty that Wen would like an audience with him," I say, realizing I could have avoided all this and just teleported into his study, but that might have scared the wits out of him. He's had too many brushes with death recently to welcome my teleportation with open arms, and I don't want to strain our newfound friendship.

They announce my presence then usher me inside. Dais hunches over his desk, scribbling like a madman. With his disheveled hair and stubble, he looks like one. He wasn't this unkempt yesterday.

"Someone needs a makeover, and fast. I'm surprised Jet let you go this long without a shave," I remark, winking at Jet, who rolls his eyes. He's so much fun to pick on.

Dais glances up with a glare. "Don't remind me, I'm well aware." He leans back, running a hand over his face. "What do you need, Wen?"

Ouch, someone is grumpy. I guess I would be too in his position. "I've come to say goodbye. I found the cure for Renell's curse. I'm leaving tonight. I've wasted too much time looking for this." I hold up the scroll I'd brought. "Oh, I'm hoping I can take this with me."

He nods as he grabs his cane, limping around his desk. His bloodshot blue eyes meet mine. "Well, I guess this is goodbye." He holds a hand out.

"Don't think you can get rid of me that easily. I've got to return the scroll." I take his hand, tossing my head to get the bangs out of my eyes.

"I wouldn't imagine. We all know that hair attracts way too much attention to be forgettable." He steps back.

I wink. "You know it."

He smiles, shaking his head. "Thank you for all that you're doing for Renell."

"You're not going to say you'll miss me?"

"That could be treason."

It's my turn to laugh. "Right. I better not get carried away." I start toward the door. "And Dais?" I turn before I can stop myself. He needs to know. "Your brother, David."

He furrows his brow. "What about him?"

"I know you don't know me well enough yet, and I'm sure you'll trust your brother over me. But you asked about the Darkness, and I was with him for a long time and . . . there's something about David that the Darkness is trying to take. It's strong around him. I just—I want you to be aware. Maybe try to keep a close eye on him."

"David would never let the Darkness win. He's fought it for too long to just give up." He crosses his arms over his chest, leaning back against his desk.

I nod. Of course he doesn't believe me. It was a long shot anyway. "Right. Take care of yourself, Dais."

He nods. "You too."

Rahuin

I close my eyes, listening to the clacking of tree leaves above as the wind giggles around them. It keeps calling me to come join, but I smile and shake my head, feeling the earth under my bare feet instead. It shifts a little, spinning me in its own slow methodical way. I take a deep breath, filling my lungs with the loamy scent of rain. I know it will be here soon. It makes the forest alive in anticipation. Birds fly along the wind, singing their own song of longing. Bugs chatter, landing on me and tickling my skin. Fire doesn't burn out here, but I can feel it blazing in my heart, warming me against the cool day.

A new presence breaks my concentration and it's not an element or an animal or a plant. It's a person—no—something far more powerful. For a second, I think it's the Darkness, but the presence isn't sinister.

"Don't lose your concentration, Rahuin," Fire says. "Who is it?"

The presence is familiar. Intimate in a way only I would know. I gasp with a smile, opening my eyes. It's Dais. It has to be, but when my eyes land on him, my heart sinks. It's not Dais. It's Wen. My smile fades as I rub my neck. I couldn't discern the two. The presence was powerful, and Dais wouldn't have powerful magic. I can't believe I forgot that. Dais holds a power all his own over my heart, so maybe that's why I was confused.

"Wen." His name escapes my lips in a breath, his gray eyes meeting mine over the lush foliage.

"Wen? What kind of name is Wen?" Air asks.

"Shh," Earth hushes. "Be quiet. This encounter is very important to Rahuin."

"How do you know?"

"Air, Rahuin needs to concentrate, so be silent," I hear Fire growl from within me, and the elements all quiet down.

"Rahuin." He moves closer, his eyes taking in my bulging stomach. A sad expression passes over his features for a moment, but he masks it quickly.

"What are you doing here?" Jarret told me he was alive. I just never thought I'd see him here in Färrin.

"Really? Is that all you have to ask after you left me for dead?"

"Wen—"

He holds up a hand. "No, I understand. I know why you did it, and I'm not here to—to berate you. I just wanted to see you and clear the air between us. I feel like I owe you that." He's so close now, his white hair tousled by the wind's gentle caresses. At least it's not giggling over it.

"You don't owe me anything. I left you to die, remember?"

He grimaces. "Don't remind me." He looks down, his eyes lighting on my belly once more. "Do you know how excited I was when I thought that child was mine? It was selfish, I know. I wasn't your husband, but that was all I wanted . . . to be yours."

My heart constricts under his words. "No, Wen, I didn't. I'm sorry I hurt you. I didn't want to. If things had been different, you would have been the only one in my heart, but you didn't fight for the right side. You lied to me. You used me. Then I had someone else to love, and I—I did the same thing to you," I say, but the words feel like gravel on my tongue. Hard to say, but true.

"Keep going, Rahuin. You're doing so well." I hear Fire's voice.

He nods. "I know, but I believe I'm fighting for the right side now. The Darkness . . . he never wanted me. He wanted you all along. It became evident when he didn't even try to get me back. I—"

"I know you're on the right side now, but we can't continue like this. You can't keep coming to me. You have to let me go." *I have to let you go.* I thought I did. Though, leaving someone for dead isn't letting them go. It's taking the easy way out. Even though it was anything but easy. I was so relieved when Jarret told me he was alive. I was glad his blood didn't stain my conscious too.

He runs a hand through white locks. "Rahuin, I'm sorry. I'm sorry for what I did to you. I'm sorry I taught you how to destroy the enemy. I'm sorry he almost made you use it against your own people. I wish I could have known before all this happened. I wish I could have been on the right side. Then maybe none of this would have happened between us."

My stomach churns. I never even tried to get him to join me. I didn't want to choose. I didn't think he'd ever want the light. I thought if I convinced him to come with me, he'd betray me, and I couldn't go through that again. My throat constricts with tears, and I look away from his intense eyes.

"You don't have to apologize. You were only doing what you were told. I'm sorry I never told you about the light. I'm sorry I left you for dead. I'm sorry for so much that I can never take back. I should have tried to save you, but I didn't because I already loved another." Tears stream down my cheeks now.

He reaches a hand out but stops because he knows he can't comfort me anymore. "I know. I—" He runs a hand down his face. "Though you left me for dead, you made me see everything differently, and if I had to go through it all again, I would. If I hadn't been there with the Darkness, who knows if you would have been able to keep your child safe. Think about it, if I wasn't there she wouldn't be here either.

"I'm not mad you didn't try to save me. If you had, I wouldn't have trusted you. I probably would have hated you and resented the light after what you did to me. Believe me, I wanted to, but because of my light, Renell saved me. The Darkness never came back. He never wanted me other than to use me." He shuffles around, sitting on a moss-covered log not far from me, slumping over it like the weight of his words are dragging him down.

I sit beside him, leaning backward for comfort. I shouldn't listen to more. I should tell him to go. What if Dais finds out? No, that's the wrong thought to have. I'll tell Dais Wen was here. I'll tell him everything we discussed—that we're two broken people who just want forgiveness for what we've done. Hope has started to weave it's way between us. His experience is something I understand. We were both manipulated and forced by the Darkness to do horrible things. Yes, I did it to protect the people I love, but if the Darkness had never waged his war, I wouldn't have had to go to such extremes. So many wouldn't have died.

"Why did you stay with him then?" I ask.

"I felt like I belonged. My entire life, I didn't belong anywhere. My mother gave birth to me and then she was sacrificed by the village people because they thought she consorted with sea monsters. I was to follow her fate, but an old healer saved me. He taught me until he died when I was twelve, then the Darkness came for me. He told me of my power.

"He thought I was the chosen one until you appeared with power even stronger than me. He sent me to collect you. All he wanted was you. He wanted you to fulfill the prophecies for his gain. I stayed because I had a purpose, but that purpose meant nothing when you left. Because at the end of the day, I had no one to hold, no one to love, no one to love me." He smiles sadly at me, and I look away.

I fiddle with Dais's necklace, the shape of the sapphire heart warm under my fingers. "I can't be that for you, Wen. I've made my choice."

"I know. I'm helping Renell and Jarret right now. I'm finding a place. I just wanted to make things right with you first, and . . . I've spoken to Dais." I snap my head up at his words. "You made the right choice." He smirks, gray eyes shining.

"You spoke to Dais? But—"

"Relax, we were both men about it. We spoke and understood each other. I just didn't want you to not know."

"But why were you in Casta?"

"Renell is in trouble. She was forced into a blood oath marriage with someone from Cay-Llek. It—It was the only way she could protect Jarret. Because—well—he did something stupid, and she had to pay for the mistake."

"Oh no," I whisper. Thesa sent me a message saying she found Jarret and told he was crowned king of Treía, but she didn't mention Renell. I assumed she was in Treía with them.

"Jarret and I have been trying to find a way to break her curse.

Treía didn't have an extensive library so I went to Casta with Dais's permission. I met him there, and we found out that we're not all bad. We became friends." He smiles.

I raise an eyebrow.

"Well, more like acquaintances, but we're getting there. I'm glad he let me look because I found the answer for Renell's curse. I decided to stop here before I headed back to Treía to get Jarret."

"You've changed a lot, Wen. I'm grateful you were there for him. Thesa told me you kept him alive and got him to Treía. I'll never forget that." I almost reach a hand to take his, instead, I clench it and hold it to my side.

"They saved my life. It's the least I could do."

A crack of thunder splits the sky, and we both look up at the gathering clouds.

"Yay! Water is here!" Air exclaims as droplets fall onto the leaves overhead.

I smile, breathing in the fresh scent as I carefully make my way off the log.

Wen joins me. "Rahuin, I have one last request to ask you."

I meet his gaze. "Yes?"

"Would you, um—would you be all right if I joined you in Casta after I help Renell and Jarret?"

"Wen, I—"

He holds up a hand. "I'm not finished. I want to help you and Dais in any way I can. I don't know anything else in this world, and Renell and Jarret won't need me after this. I want to come to Casta to help you and Dais fight the Darkness . . . to keep you both safe—well, all three of you." He nods to my belly.

A sickening feeling settles in my gut again, but it's not because of Wen's request. It's because he's reminded me that eventually, I will have to leave my peaceful paradise and fight the Darkness again. "Are you sure? Are you sure you can fight the Darkness? Go against him?"

"Renell asked me the same thing. Yes, I believe I can." He nods, conviction filling his gray gaze.

"Believing and doing are two different things, Wen. I'm sure Thesa told you why I'm here. Fighting against the Darkness is no easy task. It's the hardest thing I've ever done, and I'm terrified to go back." I feel the raindrops getting thicker around us, and I kindly ask Water to miss us with its rain.

It chuckles. "Of course."

He takes a step forward. "But we have to go back. We have to because we believe in what we fight for. I know what I fight for now. I have something to fight for."

"And what is that?" I ask. Because all I've ever fought for has led me to regret, to fear over what inexcusable act I will do next.

"Good. Beauty. Literature. All the things I've never been able to enjoy. It's as simple as that." His bright smile seems to take over the woods. "So, can I fight with you?"

"I'll have to speak with Dais first, but yes, you can," I say the words, but I don't hear them. Is it really okay to let him back into my life like this? Should I? I don't feel worried over what I'll do. I know where my heart is. I know it's with Dais, and that is where it will remain. How can I deny Wen this request when I left him to die? If he wants to stay by our side, he can. Though, I'm not sure what Dais will say.

"I'll await his response." He looks up. "Why isn't it raining on us?"

I laugh. "Because I asked it not to."

He raises white brows. "You speak to the elements?"

"Yes, they have a lot to say."

"Can I finally speak now?" Air whines.

"No!" Earth rumbles.

"But they're talking about us."

I smirk, lowering my head, and Wen notices. "Are they talking now?"

"Yes, but they were silent a few minutes ago. Now, I'll never get them to shut up." I smile as we start back toward the city.

He taps my shoulder. "Thank you for listening."

"You're welcome. Your words did me a lot of good. I'm not ready to leave yet, but I think I'm getting close. I'm understanding the role I play in all of this." I glance at the ground, mindful of my steps in the slippery mud. "You can stay for dinner. I'm sure the elves wouldn't mind."

"I think your mother would kill me if she found out who I was. I'm not fond of losing my head. I need to go. It won't take me long to get to Treía anyway."

"Right, teleporting. And she wouldn't decapitate your head, it's far too gruesome for her."

He laughs, stopping our stroll before we make it to Silfras's perimeter. "A hanging then?"

Trying to imagine my mother sanctioning any public death is a bit too absurd. I quirk my head. "Maybe." I take a deep breath, meeting his eyes. "Be safe."

"I will. Goodbye."

"Goodbye." And with that, he's gone.

Chapter 28

Striving in Vain

Dais

Jet steps into my office. "Dais, we have a situation."

I run a hand down my face. What now? I finally ousted most of the traitors. They are behind bars, but we can't seem to figure out if they're innocent or guilty. Men will say anything for a chance to spare their lives. If only they'd give me the names of the real traitors, then I wouldn't have to wonder. Perhaps if they haven't given me any names, that means they're the traitors, but I can't gamble with innocent lives. I have to be sure. Every life deserves a chance.

"They finally confessed?" I ask, leaning back in my chair. My throat tightens at the uneasy expression on his face. It's more than we thought, and I'll have to punish them all with death.

"Unfortunately, no. Something terrible has happened."

My stomach sinks. Terrible isn't a word I want to hear. Grabbing my cane, I stand. "What happened?"

"The village of Grayscale was raided and pillaged last night."

Grayscale sits just outside the Pass of Forough. It's a small sheep and goat herding community, but the border should be protected. I have men stationed there. "Cay-Llek?" Maybe they found a way past our defenses, and if so, we need to find out where immediately.

Jet's pale face once again tells me no. "It was Castian troops, Your Majesty."

My chest constricts, and I lean against my desk. "What?" It's not possible. Why would soldiers pillage a village in their own country? It doesn't make any sense. Could they have been Corrupted?

"There was a rebellion against the generals leading the squadrons along the pass's border. I'm not sure why they did it yet. Healers came with the generals who were still alive. Once they wake, we'll know more, but angry citizens arrived almost immediately after the generals. They request to see you."

I can't breathe. There is no reprieve. It's one thing after another, and there is no reason for this bloodshed. "But how is it even possible? It doesn't make sense. Could it be something with the Corrupted?" Of course, the one man who might know already left.

"It could be, but these people wa—"

"What am I supposed to say to them, Jet? I don't even have answers myself."

He takes a step forward, gripping my shoulder. "Just assure them that it wasn't on your orders. You have to do something. You don't have time to wait for answers."

I stare into his dark brown eyes. This has to do with the Darkness. He said he would make them turn against me. Maybe this is the next phase. I just have to convince my people of his demands.

I walk to the door. "Send them to the throne room and get a trusted contingent after the troops before this happens again." I step into the hall.

"Of course." He bows out of my presence.

My feet feel like lead as I hobble down the never-ending hallway. How can I do this? How can I make them see? I can't even convince them that my wife was fighting for Casta.

A servant meets me at the side door of the throne room with my crown and robe. I slip into the layered cerulean fabric, steeling myself before I step inside. The few bedraggled and disheveled-looking citizens bow their heads in my presence as I shuffle to the blue velvet throne, sweeping my robe as I sit and set my cane beside me.

They raise their heads, and I nod to the man standing in front. He steps forward, his face covered in soot, his shirt torn on his right arm where blood soaks through a bandage. He wipes a hand over his sun-tanned face, smearing soot into his wrinkles.

"Your Majesty, thank you for seeing us. My name is Wenel Rwit of Grayscale. I—we come regarding a matter of utmost importance."

"Tell me all that happened," I answer, surprised to find my voice steady.

The man swallows. "They came. They came in the middle of the night. Castian sentries. They were supposed to protect us, but they tormented us, burning our houses down and murdering and raping our women. They destroyed our food stores and poisoned our streams with the bodies of those they killed. We were the few who escaped. We hid in mountain caves until they were gone." Dark green eyes pierce my soul. He's lost so much.

"I'm truly sorry this happened. Mark my words, these men were not acting on my orders. They were supposed to watch the border in case the Darkness's armies became bold enough to cross. I'm waiting for the men recovered from the border to respond so I may give you a proper reason. I've sent men after the traitors, and they will get what they deserve. In the meantime, you are all welcome here." I look at one of the servants waiting off to the sidelines. "Please get them bathed and clothed. Give them a hot meal and set them in rooms to rest."

"Thank you, Your Majesty." The man bows his head. "But we would like to return to Grayscale as soon as possible with aid."

"Of course. I will make all the arrangements. Please get some rest." I nod at the group of people who meet my gaze with hopeful glances. Though, a sliver of darkness poisons their expression. They don't trust me. How can they after all that's happened? My reign has been nothing but uncertainty. I haven't been able to keep them safe. I haven't stopped the threat of Darkness. If anything, it's only become worse. Will it ever get better? Will all my striving finally have a reward, or am I just meant to lay down and die?

The townspeople follow the servant out of the hall, and Jet reappears by my side. I stand, leaning on my cane as I start for the door to get out of this ridiculous robe. I don't feel like a king worthy to wear it anyway.

"Didn't I say they'd turn on you? How long can you hold out, Dais?" The Darkness flickers in front of me, blocking the door.

I slump forward, feeling as if all my energy has suddenly left.

"Your Majesty." Jet holds me up.

My hand starts to shake and I lean both of them on my cane to ground myself, but it doesn't stop the trembling. "Leave me alone. You won't break me."

"I won't, but they will. Casta will be mine soon. It's futile to hold on. If you do, I'll be waiting." He vanishes.

"Was it the Darkness?" Jet asks, but I hardly hear.

I stare at him, but he seems so far away. My vision blurs, and everything fades to black.

"You're almost out of time, Dais. I said I'd be waiting." The Darkness's voice echoes around me, and I stumble in the dark space, wishing I could see. I feel like a drunken fool.

"Where am I? What have you done to me?"

"Nowhere. I've done nothing to you. You followed me. You think you can stop me?"

"No, I can't stop you alone, but I'm not alone. You will be defeated."

"That's just what you think. You think the prophecies are right. You think the King of Light will come to save you, but He's abandoned you. He'll never come."

"You're wrong. He will come."

He scoffs. "You've been lied to. You're out of time. Better go back, Dais. You don't have long . . ."

I blink open my eyes, feeling like I'm being crushed.

"I'll join you soon, Ehé," a voice says in the dark of my room, making my blood run cold. Someone is on top of me. I raise my arms as quickly as I can, catching the man's wrists.

"Jet!" I scream as I try to force the man off the side of the bed, but his grip is strong. If he pulls me off with him, I could easily land on the blade he has pointed at my chest.

Jet bursts through the hidden side door. I hear some struggling as the attacker's grip slackens before he's ripped off me. I hastily grab a candle and light it while the man struggles against Jet.

The warm flame reveals Jet half-dressed with his long black and gray hair whipping around his face as he brandishes a sword at the man's neck. My heart freezes when I look upon the face of my attacker—Wenel Rwit of Grayscale. The one who petitioned for aid.

I stand, leaning against my bed posts as I glare at the man. "You, why would you do this?"

"You don't care for us! You're letting us die endlessly for no reason. I lost my son to the war that you claim isn't over, and my wife…" His face contorts and tears appear in his green eyes. "My wife was brutally raped and murdered. What king allows his people to suffer like this? This never happened with your father. There has been nothing but uncertainty since you took the throne, and then you marry a witch. How can we take you seriously? You're a boy king who can't control his own soldiers." His words are poison injected into my veins.

I feel my blood boil, my hatred spreading and screaming to be unleashed. "What people want to murder their own king? All I want is to protect this nation so our posterity don't have to. So they can live in peace and not be enslaved by a king who could care less about them! I'm doing all I can, but it's never enough, is it?"

"No, not while you sit in your palace and do nothing to stop what's happening in this country. You used to be a great general. Now you're a scared king who offers aid and sends more men after the same soldiers who murdered and abused your civilians. It's an endless cycle where you have no authority." His face flushes, his brow drawn in harsh angles. Hate fills his eyes, but I know it's fueled by hurt—undeniable hurt he can't erase.

"And you thought killing me would help?"

Wenel's features fall. "Someone had to pay." His voice cracks as tears trail down his cheeks.

"Someone always pays, and it's never the ones you expect." I look at Jet. "Get him out of here."

Jet moves out of the hall as I sink onto the bed, catching a glimpse of two dead guards lying just inside my door. He murdered them too. Isn't that payment enough? Spilling innocent blood of men who were just doing their duty? I look away from them as Jet re-enters the room with more guards to clean up the bodies.

"Should we lock up the others as well?" Jet asks. It's an innocent enough question. If Wenel tried to kill me, the others could too.

"No, if they want me, they'll come for me."

"Dais—"

I lift a hand. "Don't. I'm done hiding like a coward. He was right. Tomorrow we ride after the traitors."

"Dais, you can't—"

"Jet!" I stand back up. "I am not helpless. I have to assert myself as their king. They see me as a hoax instead of their ruler. They're scared, and I've done nothing to assure them. I have to do something. If not for their sake, then for yours. They'll never stop if I don't try."

"Or you'll just make it easier for them to kill you. Please, Dais, we don't know who to trust, and I can't protect you out there."

"I can protect myself!" I shout. I sound like a whiny three-year-old and I hate it.

"No, you can't! You haven't fought since your injury, and you're the king."

"Exactly! Nothing will ever change unless I try. I'll train before we go, but I have to show them I'm not an incompetent *shiev*!"

Jet steps forward, dark brown eyes boring into me, nostrils flaring. "Fine. I know I will not change your mind. Try to get some rest." He sits into a chair by the fireplace hearth with a sigh, running a hand down his face before cracking his neck and glaring at the door.

I settle back under my covers, my eyes wandering to the empty place beside me. I'm glad Rahuin wasn't here. Who knows what Wenel would have done to her. I miss her. I want her here. I need her to ground me and help me fight against the Darkness. His taunts are starting to get to me, and no one else understands. I can't believe she has to deal with his lies constantly, and she never complained. Now I'm aware. I want to be there for her. I want her here with me, but I know that's selfish and dangerous. There are too many threats after us, and we can't afford to fall victim to them now.

Rahuin

"Save me, Rahuin. Save me!" His blue eyes drown me, becoming an endless ocean I find myself swimming in, swallowing the salty waves.

"Dais!" I scream as I'm berated by the tempest. He's nowhere to be found. I call for Water, but it doesn't respond. I'm abandoned. I'm going to drown. How can I save Dais when I can't escape myself?

The scenery changes. Now I'm walking through the Färrin forest, but it's dark and cruel, filled with gnarled branches and twisted roots. Leafless trees covered in black bark cut through the murky sky.

"Yes, save him, Rahuin. Do what you couldn't do for others. Keep him safe. Always him. No one else deserves it." The Darkness's twisted voice echoes around the dark wood.

"Come and face me, you coward," I shout, refusing to be daunted by his presence. I'm not afraid anymore..

He moves into my line of vision, floating around in a giant black cloud. "How can you save him? You can't save yourself. Not even your new little friends are here. They've abandoned you."

I glare at him.

"Maybe you can't save him because he doesn't want you to. He hasn't called you home yet. He must be better off without you."

I step toward him, feeling a gentle breeze on my back. I won't cower this time. I'm not abandoned. I never will be. I lift my palms, feeling the light coursing through my veins. "You don't scare me."

I wake up, calling upon Fire to chase away the lingering images of Dais's face filled with anguish. I see blood pooling around him. A nagging sense settles in my gut, but I know I have nothing to fear. The fire ignites in the stone hearth across my room.

I stare at the flames. Warmth spreads around me, but the fear doesn't dissipate. I still see him crying for help. I still feel his desperation deep in my soul. I reach for the necklace under my nightgown, drawing strength from its heart shape.

"It's not your fear that you're feeling. It's his," Fire says.

"How do you know?"

"I'm an element. I can see or hear what's happening all over the world in any fire. Dais isn't doing well. The Darkness is after him. He hasn't slept in days, and he's had an attack on his life."

"What?" I stand, moving closer to the hearth. This is why I shouldn't have left him alone. We should have stayed together and kept each other safe. "He's okay?"

"Yes, right now, he's with a squadron of soldiers. They've made camp for the night, but I'm not sure what the goal is."

Why is he with soldiers? He should be at the castle. He could get killed out there. He knows that. Does he want to die?

My heart jumps. "I have to get to him. He can't be alone out there."

"I don't think that would be a wise choice, Rahuin. If assassination attempts have been made on his life, yours is next. You're safer in Färrin." The flame creates dancing shadows along the wall. They seem to spin around in a dizzying frenzy as if they're taunting me.

"But I've been here long enough. I'm not afraid anymore. I know why I'm fighting."

"You may know why you're fighting, but you have to be smart about this. You can't just charge after him. You have a child to protect."

I touch my stomach. "I have a husband to worry about too. If it's his fear I feel, I should at least be there with him. I can't lose him as well, and you'll all be with me. I'm not alone."

"Then we will do our best to keep you safe," Earth speaks up outside my window.

"No, you're not alone," Fire concedes. "Wait till morning, at least. You have a long journey ahead of you."

"I'll get a message to Thesa. She can get me back to Dais quickly," I mutter, more to myself than to the elements present, while I pace around the room, rubbing circles around my belly. I know Thesa is in Treía with Jarret, but I just need her for a few days. I need to get to Dais. He and Sira are all that matters to me, and I will do anything to keep the Darkness from harming them. If he has decided to target

Dais, he'll soon regret it. I'm not scared of the Darkness anymore. He can't take what I've found. He won't harm those I love. He won't destroy them to get to me. He won't succeed, and I refuse to live in my guilt any longer.

Dais

Drip . . .

    Drip . . .

Blood drips from a cut on my arm, but I'm not sure where I got it. I stare at the pile of red on the dirt my boots are covered in. It's a puddle no bigger than my wrist, but I don't move to cauterize the wound. Memories of another time flash before my mind. I see men killed by my hand. I see the spray of their blood assaulting the sky in crimson. I see my father, red spilling on the battle-torn ground from his neck. I see Rahuin's ruby hair. It feels like a hand has seized my heart, crushing until it cracks under the pressure.

I'm on my knees with my palms pressed to the dirt floor inside my tent. A flickering candle on a makeshift desk made of crates casts ominous shadows that dance around me, taunting. Their sinister gazes become my worst nightmares, until I'm reliving the scenes over and over again. I can't escape them. They'll never leave me. They'll always haunt me. Failures I can never redeem. Blood I can never put back. Lives that will never be lived.

The wound on my arm seems to open wider and the blood mixes with the dirt. It's all over my hands, all over my skin. I start to scrape it away, but it only spreads the crimson around me.

"Dais?" Jet walks through the tent flap, his eyes widening when he sees me.

"Get it off!" I scream, digging my nails into my flesh.

Jet grabs my wrists, pulling my arms apart, but I hardly feel him. All I see is blood. All I smell is blood. It suffocates me until I can't breathe, my heart squeezing and squeezing.

"Dais! There is nothing there!"

I glare into his narrow, dark eyes. "Let go of me!" I fight against him, but the shadows are still dancing and my head feels too light. My vision blurs, and everything looks so far away, spinning and spinning.

Jet still holds my wrists. The tightness in my chest finally disappears, and I relax, my arms falling limp in his hands. The blood is gone. It was never there.

He lets me go.

I touch my arms, looking for the red, but it was just a figment of my imagination. What's happening to me? Why am I seeing things that aren't there? Why now? I can't afford to go insane. I have a kingdom to take care of. Traitors to stop. This can't be happening.

"Dais, what happened?" Jet's dark eyes beg for answers I can't give.

I run a hand down my face, feeling my beard. I should shave. That would make me feel less crazy . . . right? "I don't know." I shake my head.

"What did you see?"

"Nothing." I shrug, grabbing my discarded cane and getting off the ground. I head for the tent flap. I need to clear my head. There is no way I'll be able to sleep after that. I haven't slept in several days. The thought gives me some comfort. Maybe I'm not mad, maybe I'm just exhausted.

Jet stands, grabbing my shoulder. "Dais, please."

I ignore the worry in his voice. I can't assure him. I'm losing my grip on reality. I can't sleep. I can't eat. They want my blood. They want everything I stand for, but the lines of what I stand for are becoming blurred too easily. Who is 'they' anyway? I don't know.

With each passing day, I feel more lost than when I started. I thought I knew what I was fighting for. I thought I could be the king they all want me to be. Strong. Authoritative. Generous. Wise. But I'm none of those things, and the more I try to prove it, the more unraveled things become, the more my reality blurs. I'm so tired of sleeping with one eye open. I'm so tired of trying to get them to see reason.

If the nobles find out about this episode, they will question the soundness of my mind and then they will transfer the monarchy. Maybe it's what they wanted all along. Ultimately, it will go to David if that happens, and maybe it should. Maybe he's more fit to rule than I am. Even I know that's not true. David struggles with his own form of blurred reality. They'd quickly condemn him as well, and then who knows what would happen? Maybe he'd finally snap and consume us all in cold fear. What Wen mentioned about David's darkness prods me, but I push it to the back of my mind. It doesn't matter right now.

"What do you want me to say? I'm losing it, Jet. I'm seeing things that aren't there, and if they found out . . . No one can know."

"Dais, I've sent a message to Thesa. She's coming."

"What? Why—"

"Because I can't protect you on my own, and when I don't know who to trust to protect you, she's the person I call. I can't do this alone, and neither can you."

I push his hand off my shoulder. "I have to do this alone, Jet. I have to show them my strength."

"Show them your strength? How can you be strong when you can't even eat or sleep? The only thing you'll show them is that you're unfit to rule. You have to stop, Dais. This mission is madness. Let our guards hunt them down. Let this go."

"Let this go? It was my soldiers who pillaged and destroyed one of Casta's villages. I can't condone that! I can't let them get away with it! I can't trust my other soldiers to hunt them down! I have to do this!" I scream, pointing a shaking finger at the tent flap, but the motion makes my head spin again. I need food. I need sleep, but I don't have time. I have to stop them. I have to show my strength. I have to be the king they all want me to be, but who is 'they', anyway?

"You can't kill yourself over it either."

"You can't stop me, Jet. I will make them pay for the evil they did against Casta. I have to do this."

"I'm not going to try to stop you. I just want you to eat. You have to eat at least." He leaves the tent, his voice flat.

I know he wants me to stop. If not for the sake of my sanity, then for Casta, but I can't stop now. They'll never respect me if I don't end this. I'll never be a true king in their eyes. The care of my sanity won't matter because I'll rule over people who don't trust me, and trust is all

I have left to offer. Funny, when I can't trust anyone around me, it's the thing I crave most. Maybe that's why they won't respect me. Now I'm just thinking in circles.

"Trust. So easily lost and so hard to gain." The Darkness tsks in the corner of my tent, his shadowy form lingering like a cloud threatening an ominous storm.

"You don't have to tell me twice." I don't even have the strength to tell him to go away. "If I'm not a threat, why do you keep visiting me? Is it just to rub in your accomplishments? Well, you're winning!" I don't care who hears me outside the tent.

"I really thought you'd put up more of a fight, Your Majesty. I thought you were a magnificent commander, not this sniveling little rat I see before me."

"I don't have much fight left, and I'm certainly not going to waste my effort on you."

I hear the smirk in his voice. "You're right. I am winning." And then he's gone.

Thesa

Thesa, I need your help. Dais is in trouble. I want you to take me to him as soon as you can. I know you're with Jarret, but I hope you can leave him for a few days. Dais has had several attempts on his life. I'm worried. I need to be there. We'll be stronger together. I'm finally ready to face Casta again.

Rahuin

I fold the message in my fingers. The deep connection I feel to Rahuin sends shivers along my spine as the calling of Guardian quakes my bones. I can't ignore it. I have to go, but Jarret needs me here too. I'll just have to ask him. I know Rahuin wouldn't beg me to come unless she absolutely needed me to. I glance at my *heln* a little ways away. A glowing message from Jet lies on the surface, shimmering in translucent rainbow colors. I've already read it nine times.

He asked me to come home and help him protect Dais . . . or

knock some sense into the boy. He's got it into his head that he can help his people respect him by going after traitors. The entire nation is in turmoil, and Jet can't get him to see reason. They both need me. Really, all three of them do.

I stare up at the ceiling, studying the jade, pink, gold, and purple stones that I had requested specifically for my room. The gold always reminds me of my father. I miss him and wish he were here so I don't have to feel so divided.

I take a deep breath and head to the small table in the center of my room where my *heln* sits beside a steaming cup of tea. The smooth, herbal notes always calm my nerves and bring my mind back into a sense of peace. I take a sip of the warm liquid, thinking again what I must do.

Jarret will have to be okay without me. I'll speak with some of the council, my father's most trusted, and hope they'll be enough to watch and guide him. I've really done all I can. I haven't been a part of Treían politics for over twenty years. I hardly know what he needs to be aware of, but I don't want to leave him. He's my son, and for once in his life, I get to be there for him. I get to be his mother, but once again, I'm leaving him to be a guardian for Rahuin and now Dais. Even without the official birthright, Rahuin and Dais are like children to me as well. All I want is to protect them.

I set my tea down and spin toward the door, flicking the train on my light green gossamer dress. Surprisingly enough, most of my old wardrobe still fits. I can't believe my father kept my room exactly the way it was after I left. I assumed he would have had it repurposed for someone else, but it just goes to show that I didn't really know him at all. He loved me so dearly. Yes, he expressed it in all the wrong ways and drove me away for too long. He apologized too late, but I'm grateful I found it in my heart to forgive him. I will always cherish the last few moments we had together.

I step out of the room, heading down the hall to Jarret's room. He has a council meeting shortly, but hopefully, I can slip in my question before he's pulled away by the affairs of court. His guards nod as I enter. He's tying his black council robe at the knot of his neck.

He smiles at me. "You're here early." His teasing brown eyes glisten as he pulls his black and blue hair back into a ponytail at the nape of his neck. His hair is so long. I think becoming a Garon king has something to do with it. All the portraits of past kings have style of long and braided hair as a sign of wisdom and strength.

"I have something to ask you."

"What's wrong?" He stands in front of me.

"Your father and Rahuin have both called me back to Casta. Dais is in trouble, and Rahuin wants to go after him, while Jet wants me to keep them both in line. I don't want to leave here without your permission. There isn't much I can do for you, but I want to be here to support you because I never got the—"

"Mother, it's okay." He grabs my hands, a gentle smile on his face. "I know you want to be here, but they need you more. I'll be okay."

"I'll assign a few of my father's most trusted council to watch over you. They'll be who you can consult with hard decisions. I'll speak with them after the meeting and then go." I busy myself by fiddling with his robe and straightening the silk edges.

He hugs me. "I love you. Please don't think you're abandoning me. I know Rahuin needs you too. I'll spend most of my time learning anyway."

"I know. I love you too." My voice cracks.

He leans back, looking deep into my eyes. "I'll have Kyira send you updates. I'll be okay."

"I know." I set my finger against his stubbled cheek. I can't believe how much he's matured over the last few weeks. His entire world has been turned upside down, but he hasn't broken. It's only made him stronger, and he'll continue without me. I'm just glad I got to witness it and tell him how much I love him.

Chapter 29
How to be King

Jarret

"Now that you are the king, you should choose a mate. No king goes without a mate, an heir must be produced so the kingdom can be secure," one of the council members says, Etherl, I believe her name is. There are only thirty I need to memorize, and with everything else I've been learning, names have fallen to the back of my mind.

Rainbow lights reflect around the Treían council. I stand on a high platform with my mother, and the other advisers stand in little fissures cut in the stone around us.

If only I could tell them that I already have a mate and a baby, but I haven't heard anything from Renell in weeks, and it's killing me. She usually responds, even if it's short. Did something happen to her? Or is she ignoring me to keep me safe? The thoughts keep plaguing me. They revolve around my mind over and over. I can't even leave to find out if she's alive.

And what of our child? Was she able to hide the pregnancy? The thought makes my stomach sour because the only way she can keep the baby safe is by pretending it's her husband's, and that means . . . I swallow, trying to remind myself she's doing this because of me. If I hadn't stepped in, I wouldn't be feeling this pain.

A hand waves in front of my face. "Your Majesty?" Mother's voice quivers.

All eyes are turned on me, and they're not amused. I realize I hadn't responded to Etherl's comment, nor had I heard any responses from the council.

"Pardon me. I have too much on my mind." I sigh to prove my point. "It's a lot, as you all can imagine."

"If it's too much for you, Your Majesty. We can ask the stones to choose again. Perhaps something is muddled," Erix comments.

My mother bristles beside me. "Council Erix, I think it will benefit you greatly to keep that treason far from your tongue. You know the stones can't choose again unless the king is dead. How could you be so bold?"

Other council nod at her words.

"Because he will never be a worthy king. He knows nothing of our traditions. He can hardly morph correctly. How is he expected to lead?"

Arguments from the other council members, including my mother, erupt around the room.

Part of me wants to agree with him. I'm not sure I even want to lead. I just want to find out if my wife is safe, but is she even my wife anymore? Can I really call her that?

"Guards!" I hear the words come out of my mouth before I have the foresight to think about them. "Arrest Council Erix. He's shown true treason to this country, and I won't allow it."

Other council members around me fix their eyes on him, their heads held high with sneers and haughty looks.

He falls to his knees as sentries swarm his hollow. "Please, Your Majesty. I—I didn't mean anything by it!"

The guards take him by the arms, seizing his wrists behind his back.

"From what I've heard, Council Erix, you have sought the crown for years now. The stones could have chosen you if they thought you were worthy. Though your actions would say otherwise, and that is why you weren't chosen. Yes, I have no idea what I'm doing, but I'm trying to learn. I'm willing to learn."

It's not like I have much choice. Either I do this, or I die. The stones won't pick someone else unless I'm dead, and there is no way to forfeit the crown . . . I've already checked every archive I could find.

"I take it back! Can't you show a man mercy?" He struggles against the guards, glaring up at me.

All eyes are on me again.

"Mercy? Have I commanded your death?"

"You should . . ."

I ignore the voice. "You will be given a proper trial. You have the right, but I will not allow you to get away with speaking of such rebellion. You've threatened me too much, and if you think I will stand for it just because I'm inexperienced, you're sorely mistaken. Let a jury decide your fate." I nod at the sentries, and they take him away while he screams profanities.

I take a deep breath, before continuing, "I appreciate your concern about the bloodline, but as of now, I will not choose a mate. Allow me to be the king for a little while longer without having to worry about a family." The irony in those words. I'm constantly wondering about them. I can't even focus on the task at hand. I can't even learn to be the king I've been chosen to be. I'm trying to learn as I go and hope that I can pull it off enough so I can leave this place and get Renell... That is, if we find a way to break her curse.

"If she's even alive . . ."

I shake his sinister voice away. She has to be alive. Clòz won't kill her just because she did something wrong. He'd end up dead too. If anything, he . . . I try not to think of it. If he found out she saved me and the child isn't his, he'd probably lock her up and torture her. My breath quickens. How can I sit here? How can I focus on this when she might be in terrible suffering? Why did I have to step in? Why didn't I just let her do this on her own?

"That seems wise, Your Majesty." Council Miv's voice draws me out of my thoughts. He nods his head of orange and yellow hair as his blue eyes meet mine. "Forgive us for offering such mundane advice.

Your energy must go to Treía first. If I can encourage His Majesty, I'd say you are doing a splendid job so far. It's never easy for someone who has experienced, and you are doing marvelously."

"I enjoy the flattery, Council Miv, but you don't have to go to such extreme lengths. If you are loyal to the stones, then you will choose to follow whoever they pick."

"Does His Majesty intend to keep the Treían alliance with Casta?" Another council member asks to my left, I can't remember his name though. Other council nod their assent, and their colorful eyes reflecting the light of the Treían halls. Casta reminds me of Rahuin, and I can't help but wonder how she's fairing right now. Mother said she's in Färrin. Where she's supposed to be finding some peace, but how can anyone find peace in this world of turmoil?

"Yes, Casta will remain our allies. I'm not sure we're free of the Darkness's reach yet." I look at all their faces. "If that's all, I'll call this meeting to a close."

They nod, and I'm finally dismissed. Funny how I'm the king, yet I have to wait for their approval.

I turn, heading to my cavern.

Mother falls into step beside me. "You handled that well." She smiles, slipping an arm into mine.

I face her. "Thank you. I—I thought it would be wise not to tell them about Renell yet. I just . . ." I trail off, looking away.

"You haven't heard anything?"

I shake my head. "I want to go get her, but I have to find a way to break the curse. I just don't know if she's okay, and. . . ." I try to hide the quiver in my voice, but I can't.

"It's okay." She pulls me into a hug, and I swallow to keep the tears at bay.

After Erix's accusations, I don't need anyone else to see me in this state of vulnerability. They'll think it's about the monarchy and not about my wife. They'll think I can't do this, but I can. I just need to get my wife first. I pull away.

"How can you say this is okay? None of this is okay." I pinch the bridge of my nose.

She touches my cheek. "I meant it's okay to be worried. You love her."

"I know. I just can't help her. I can't be with her and it's killing me. All this is . . ."

"Too much, I know, but you'll find a way to break the curse. You'll find a way to save her." She squeezes my hand, her jade eyes sparkling under the lights.

"There you two are! You had me traversing the entire city just to find you." Wen rounds the corner, white tattoos lit up in the cavern.

I sigh, rolling my eyes at his antics. I've become more and more grateful for him, but he's still a pain in my neck.

"It doesn't stop you from running your mouth," I mutter.

"It's nice to see you too, Jarret. You know, if you don't start acting nicer to me, it's going to come back and bite you in the ass."

"What do you want, Wen?" I try to hide the annoyance in my voice, but it doesn't work.

"Aren't you just a ray of sunshine? You'll be pleased to know that I found a way to break Renell's curse." He looks me dead in the eyes, his mouth forming a tight line.

"Really?"

He nods. "Yes, but . . ." He looks away. "There is a high probability that if we break her curse with Clòz, it will break her curse of death as well."

"Of course," I whisper, sighing. "It's her choice. If we have a way to break the curse, then we have to tell her. She'll have to decide if it's what she wants."

"Of course it's what she wants. She wants to come back to you right? Or maybe she's having too much fun with Clòz . . ."

"But how will you get her a message? She hasn't answered her *heln* in weeks," Mother reminds me.

I thought she was leaving after the meeting. Why is she still here? I sigh. I shouldn't direct any of my annoyance at my mother. "We'll have to find her. Last I heard, they were in Onar."

"That was weeks ago. They could be gone." Wen crosses his arms over his chest, leaning back against the cavern wall.

"It's not like I can't fly," I quip, annoyed at how nonchalant he's being.

"You can't leave," Mother interjects. "You just—"

I look at her. "The monarchy will wait for me. I'll be careful."

"That's not what I'm worried about. What if you don't make it back?" She glances at Wen, her black eyebrows furrowing. "What if…"

"Then I don't make it back. I can't leave her. I can't sit here when I know I could be out there bringing her home. The time for worrying is over. I have to act, and if they deem me unfit, then at least I saved her first." I run a hand through my hair.

"I'll take care of him," Wen whispers. "I know you don't trust me. You have every reason not to after what happened with Rahuin, but Renell believed in me, even though this idiot loathes me."

I scoff, crossing my arms over my chest.

"I would do anything to keep him safe because I owe him life, even if it was only at the behest of Renell." He smirks, white teeth flashing.

I hug my mother. "I'll make it back . . . We all will."

"I love you, be safe."

"I will."

Renell

It's dark in the camp. A small fire blazes a few feet away from the tent I share with Clòz. I can see the glow from the cracks in the animal skins. He snores beside me, his arm caressing my waist. I haven't been able to fall asleep since we got back. I can't sleep when I need to get a message to Jarret. He doesn't know what happened, and I'm sure my *heln* has several messages from him.

Though, I'm not sure how many I'll be able to see. I hope he still believes I'm alive. I hope he's not on his way here to kill whoever might have hurt me. No, he wouldn't. Wen told him about my curse. He said they'd be finding a way to save me, but what if they can't? What if there is no way to break this curse?

To my surprise, Clòz didn't find my *heln* like I thought he would.

I just haven't been able to check it.

Finally, Clòz releases me and tosses to his other side, snoring as loud as a bear. I slip from the covers, carefully putting the blankets back in place so he doesn't wake up. I slip outside, heading to the tent where they have all the horse tack stored. The guards outside the opening nod as I pass them. I head inside and search until I find Heefe's tack. I kept everything strapped to his saddle. I sigh when I find everything still there. I assumed it was since Clòz didn't abuse me for my treachery. I slip my fingers into the bag, feeling the pack of herbs the healer gave me for the baby. I haven't used them in a while. I slip it into my other palm. If Clòz wakes up before I'm back, I can use these as my excuse.

My *heln* glows dimly in the dark. I pull it out and run my hand over its surface. It shimmers for a second before a message appears.

"My love, I hope you and the baby are safe. I hope it went well with the Queen."

I swipe my hand over it again and a new message appears.

"My love, why haven't you responded? Did he find out? Are you in trouble? I miss you. Please let me know you are okay."

Swipe.

"You still haven't responded. It's starting to scare me. I don't know if you're okay and it's killing me. I wish I could be there with you. Is this all my fault? Did I do this to you? Did I lose you for good? Please answer me."

"I should come for you. Treia can wait for me, but we haven't found a way to break the curse. Wen went to Casta to search their libraries. Please answer me. I love you."

"I heard the Queen of Onar died? What happened? Did you get the alliance before then? Please tell me what's going on. I love you."

"Are you distancing yourself? Are you doing this so I don't come for

you? I'm sorry for what happened, but I'm never going to let you go. I lost you once and I won't lose you again. So do what you want. I'll still find you."

"I don't know if you'll get this. Wen found a way to break the curse. We're coming for you. I miss you so much. I love you."

I swipe again, but the *heln* goes blank. That's it. I shudder, a shaking breath releasing from my mouth as the smell of smoke and that horrible Y-ak malt drink permeate the air. They boil it over a fire and drink it to keep them awake and warm on night duty. It smells almost as bad as the dungeon. I try not to cry and gag at the same time, but my emotions are all over the place. Jarret's coming for me. No more nights in despair. I reach into the saddlebag again, pulling out one of Jarret's scales.

"I'm alive. I'm still in Onar. I was captured by the Onarian Prime Minister. He thought I killed the queen because she was murdered. The—"

"You whore."

I gasp at the voice and spin around only to feel a blow against my cheek. I fall against my saddle, the stirrups dig into my side as I scream.

"Get up!" He lifts me by my hair. Tears stream down my face. It feels like my head is about to be ripped from my shoulders.

"Clòz this isn't what it looks like. This was just a gift!" I hold the herbs up. "I came to get my herbs. I felt sick from the baby." My voice trembles and I hate it. I hate that he terrifies me.

"I'm not a fool, Renell. I know what the stone is for." His eyes are black holes of misery.

My lips quiver. "Then what is it for?" I grit my teeth, meeting his eyes.

He leans down just so he can see me squirm, but I refuse to give him the satisfaction.

"Communication. Communication between lovers." He grabs the stone I threw when I heard him. He taps it, and I hope he can't see the message I've just sent.

"You're a fool, Renell."

I realize he's calling me Renell, he never calls me my first name. My stomach drops. He knows. He knows the child isn't his. He knows my treachery.

He grabs my neck, and I claw against him. I wish I could tap into my curse and kill him. I wish I could destroy him. "You helped him escape. He's alive." He lifts me up again, and I gag, his eyes trailing down to my stomach.

No. No. Please no. I have to convince him the child is his.

"Clòz. P—please. The baby is yours."

"Shut up." He squeezes harder.

"Please," I gasp. "He's yours. You wouldn't kill your own child?"

"I can't be certain this child is mine," he growls, shaking me with every word.

My vision blurs, and pain flares down my throat. "Then let him live. You will know when he's born if the baby is yours or not."

He screams, punching a post behind me with his other fist as he sets me down. The wood groans under the force, and the *heln* in his hand shatters to pieces.

No. But Jarret will be here soon.

"My promise still stands," he hisses. "*I will break you . . .*" He exits the tent, calling for a healer. "Lock her up. He's coming for her, and we'll be ready when he gets here."

I wheeze, rubbing my raw throat as I lean against the post. My entire body feels heavy. Jarret will be killed when he gets here. I shouldn't have sent the message. I shouldn't have let him know where I am. I'll lose him for good, and if I lose him, then I will lose our baby too. Once Clòz sees that the child isn't his . . .

Tears stream down my face. I don't have the strength to think about it now. I just have to keep my child alive long enough. Hopefully Jarret will be smart about it and find a way in without getting himself killed. If he'd just trusted me last time . . . I don't want to blame him. He was scared, and so was I.

Esther

". . . and don't forget to write." David's words ring through my head as I stare at the blank parchment in front of me. I still see his teasing grin and sad eyes. I wish I hadn't had to leave him, but we survived without each other for two years once. We can survive this too. I miss him so much, but I can't begin to write everything in the letter. I shouldn't have promised to write. My thoughts are too scattered to form a coherent sentence . . . even on paper. I've been staring at this page for what feels like hours. It's probably been closer to twenty minutes, but I need the exaggeration. It makes me feel like I've done more than I actually have.

I set my pen down, tucking my knees to my chest and leaning my cheek against them. Perhaps a different angle will help. It doesn't. It only makes me incredibly hot. A breeze flutters from the balcony, making the thin yellow curtains dance, but the movement of air is deceiving, not refreshing. I stare at the cool tea Lami brought me earlier. Iced tea, she called it. Perspiration drips from the glass. I pick it up, running the cold cup over my forehead before taking a sip. Smooth notes of fresh pine mixed with a hint of honey burst in my mouth.

Lami has been distant with me since the other day. I was able to convince A'zre to allow her to stay, but I lost her friendship. She doesn't speak directly to me anymore, aside from the occasional wardrobe question. She always meets my gaze with a sorry expression, and I wish I could tell her I forgive her, that it's not her fault. She was just looking out for A'zre and it almost cost her the job she's had for years, cost her the son she gained.

A'zre must have told her not to fill my head with any more ideas. Neither of them voiced that, but I know all the same. So to make it easier for her, I keep my mouth shut, even though it kills me. I miss her kindness and friendship. It cuts my soul, leaving me broken and alone in this wretched place. I'm the outcast, and I've only become more of one. Clis has even stopped talking to me.

I want to blame Lami for everything that happened, but that's unfair. She loves A'zre, and she just wanted what was best for him. She wanted him to feel and be kind again, but I'm the one who's paid the price. She almost did, but I knew I couldn't allow that. So, I chose to become the outcast once more. I've been put in my place just like A'zre promised.

He hasn't talked to me since then either. He hasn't come to see me, nor has he called me to him. I hate that his personal war has destroyed all the work I've put into gaining his trust. I've taken one step forward and two steps back. I'm afraid I'll never reach him now. I'll never be able to stop him from hurting Casta. I'll find a way, surely, but I wanted to give him a chance. I wanted to save him from his own darkness, but maybe he doesn't want to be saved. Maybe he doesn't want to leave the pain behind.

But I can't put all these fears into a letter. I can't write those words to someone I love dearly. I'm sure A'zre is having my communication intercepted. I wish we could put things behind us, but wishing is for little girls. I'm not a little girl . . . I never was. I never came here to save him. I came to save my country. I came to keep a close eye on him, but I'm the worst spy.

I can't even get close to the man I'm married to, let alone stand in his court decisions, and that's why he's confined me to my quarters. He knows I'm not here for anything else other than to keep Casta safe. He knows I want nothing to do with him aside from changing his mind about a war he doesn't need to wage.

He claimed it was about resources, but I've come to realize that's a lie. Sun'Ar has all it could need and more. From what I was able to glean from Lami and some library ledgers, Sun'Ar's trading has never been stronger. Sure, it's fluctuated, especially with the war, but their commerce has only grown. A'zre's pointless war is only for his own greed . . . or his father's greed. It's a destructive dark cloud that controls him.

Sometimes I see his caged red eyes begging to be set free, but no one can release him except himself. It makes my hatred for him run deeper. He's sent countless men to their deaths just to extend his horizons. I've seen the good man inside him, but unfortunately, the monster controls the man, and that will never change. It would be easier if he never changes. I can defeat a monster, but I can't defeat a man.

Wen

"They've got everything blocked off," I say, looking through a spyglass. Jarret crouches beside me, and I know his eyes are fixed on the woman the barbarians have tied to a post. Guards circle her prison, six in total. They're expecting us. Her arms are draped stretched above her and her black hair is ratted and matted to her head. A bruised cheek swells the left side of her face, and an abrasion splits her lower lip in half, leaving coagulated blood on her chin. She rests her head against the back of the post, her eyes closed against the sun.

It's humid in Onar, and the warm day makes it feel like we've stepped into a lit oven. I glance away, looking at Jarret. His dark eyes are full of hatred, his mouth set in a thin line, nostrils flaring. I know what he wants to do, and I can't blame him. If I were in his position, I'd do the same, but we can't kill everyone. Clòz has a third of the Cay-Llek army down there. We'd never make it out alive, and we can't challenge him without killing Renell.

"I have a plan," I tell him, just to see if he's listening. Though, I'm certain he's too buried in his own thoughts to even hear me. When he doesn't answer, I know I'm right. Pine and spruce trees dangle above us in a swaying curtain of green, and their floral scent permeates the air. The Cay-Llekians have made camp in a little valley several yards away with Renell as their prize on a pike. It makes me sick just looking at it. They truly are barbarians.

I look at Jarret again, and I can almost see steam coming out of his ears. For a moment, I think about poking his cheek just to get a rise out of him, but now is not the time or place. Ah, won't Renell be pleased to find that I'm learning? I just have to get her out of there. I grab his shoulder, forcing him to meet my eyes.

"I have a plan," I state again.

"What will you do?" he asks, trying to hide the edge in his voice, but it's there like a sharp blade.

"I'm going to study the area with the spyglass, and when it gets dark, I'll teleport over there and unbind Renell and bring her back. They won't know what happened to her, and then we can break her curse." The plan sounds so simple when I speak it aloud, but it's not. I have to be careful. I'm Renell's only hope.

"What happens if you get caught?"

I drop my jaw in mock shock. "I won't get caught."

"You're so sure of yourself. We can't afford to lose, Wen." His voice cracks, his dark eyes flashing wild and hungry for revenge.

"You think I don't know that? Renell is important to me too, Jarret. She saved my life, and I will save hers. I don't doubt I can do it. When I doubt, it means I'm not confident in my abilities, and if I'm not confident, I will fail. I will get her out, and then we'll break the curse."

"What about the chief?" He spits the word like it's poison, his lip curling.

"Once we have the curse broken, you can do whatever you want with him. They might come after us or start searching the whole area for her. I'm sure she's convinced Clòz the baby is hi—"

"If she's still pregnant," he whispers, looking out at the valley again even though I know he can't see her from this distance without the spyglass.

"Either way, they'll come after us, which gives us a very small amount of time to break her curse before you can contest the chief."

"What if I can't defeat him?" He looks back at me, fear shrouding his eyes.

"What did I just say about doubt? We've been training day in and day out. You will defeat him because you know what's at stake. You know he will kill your child and make her suffer for the rest of her days. If that doesn't give you enough confidence to overcome your doubt, then I don't know what will." I glance away. I can't believe him. How can he think about anything other than success? He has to succeed, there is no other alternative.

"You're right. I will defeat him. I won't lose them again." A raging inferno of revenge blazes in his eyes. I know I wouldn't want to be the man at the end of his blade. He understands what he has to do now, maybe even more than just with this upcoming battle. Maybe with his kingdom too. He'll succeed because he has so many other challenges to overcome. He has a family to protect, and a kingdom to lead. The stones were right when they chose him.

"That's the face I want to see."

He shifts his gaze sideways, glaring at me. There, now he's back to normal.

Chapter 30
Finally Home

Renell

I try to force my eyes open, but they feel like they've been glued shut. I can't even wipe the grime away from them. Crusty bits fall from my lashes and it feels like they're being torn apart when I finally catch a glimmer of light. It's hard to see out of my left eye, since it's puffy where Clòz struck.

Night has fallen, but small torches and fires illuminate the camp around me. Guards surround the post I'm tied to. My arms ache, and my shoulders burn like a sword has been plunged between them. I can't feel my legs. I twist my neck to see, but sharp pain shoots down the length of my back and up through my head. I wince, and the guard closest to me shifts, glancing at me with a wary eye.

Clòz had them tie me up to a post on a little platform in the center of camp. A tease for Jarret and Wen. If they're here, I know they can see me. I just hope they'll be smart about it and try not to rescue me while the entire camp is watching. I hope they wait just a little longer so Clòz doesn't believe Jarret's a threat.

The healer moves into my peripheral vision and steps onto the lit-

433

tle platform. He gently leans my head toward him, holding a cup of water to my lips.

"Drink slowly," he says, blue eyes reflecting the torch light.

The cool liquid slips down my throat, some of it dribbling past my cracked lip, but I don't care. I slurp again, coughing some of it up.

"Slowly," he warns, tilting the cup away from me.

"Thank you," I rasp.

He nods. "I'm sorry I can't help you further. I tried to suggest letting you rest, but . . ." he trails off.

I nod because I know what he would have gone through if he'd questioned Clòz. He could have been the next one tied to a post, or worse.

He gives me a little more water before slinking away into the dim camp. I lean my head against the pole, closing my eyes, but I'm in too much pain to be swept away with sleep. I open my eyes again to find Wen in front of me. I jump and try not to gasp. He holds a finger to his lips. His gray eyes shift as he reaches up and cuts the binds tying me up. Once the ties are cut, I stumble against him, my legs giving out from holding me up all day.

The guards notice the commotion now, turning with shouts, but they're too late. Wen has me in his arms, and we vanish from the camp. It feels like I'm being dragged underwater as Wen takes me to where he and Jarret are hiding out. When trees and rocky outcrops begin to appear in the corners of my vision, it feels like my chest has expanded. We fall to the ground, him trying to protect me from hitting the cold stone by holding me to his chest. Pain spikes up my spine and my exhausted body just wants rest, but Wen shifts underneath me.

"Get off me, woman. You can't rest here," he teases as a familiar pair of hands wrap around my waist, helping me up.

I fall into Jarret's embrace, my legs still too weak to support me. I sob into his shoulder once the warmth of his arms surround me. I don't care that almost every part of me hurts. I'm just so happy to hold him again.

He kisses my temple, my forehead. His tears mix with my own. "You're here. You're all right. I've got you. I love you. I missed you so much," he whispers in between his kisses, and I can't believe how much I missed his voice. It feels as crisp as sharp winter air. It reminds me of our wedding night. I feel the cold air I breathed in after we were submerged in the hot spring. I feel his lips against mine when he became my husband.

I lift my chin, catching a kiss, and I melt into his embrace. I missed him so much.

His fingers pull me closer, desperate to keep me from disappearing again.

"I missed you so much," I whisper against his lips, finding my voice to be stronger even as I sob. "I love you, Jarret." Even saying his name out loud makes my heart soar. I no longer have to be afraid of every little sound and disturbance. I no longer have to look over my shoulder for the monsters that haunt me. I'm safe. I'm secure. I never have to leave.

"I love you too," he says against my neck. "I'm so sorry. I was so worried I'd never see you again."

"I thought—" I stop, because I can't force the words through my tears. "I thought I would lose you for good when I sent that message. Clòz found me. H—he—"

"I'm so sorry. We got here as soon as we could." He leans back, looking at me closer, his fingers gingerly grace my cheek. I wince at the contact. "I will kill him for what he did to you."

"Jarret—"

"No, I won't fail this time, and we still need Cay-Llek's help."

"But it's my fight . . ."

"Renell." His hands steady my shoulders, his dark eyes boring deep into mine, and I realize there is a small fire behind me. I'm so glad I can see his face. I've missed every little detail for too long—the little scar on his right brow, his deep brown eyes, his chiseled jaw, his slightly crooked nose. "If we break the curse between you and Clòz, it could break your gift of death."

I'm silent for a second because I'm not sure I heard him correctly. Both of my curses could be broken? "What?"

"We're not sure, but if we break the curse Clòz put on you—"

"I understand, but my curse has always been a part of me. I used to be so scared of it, but I just learned to control it, and . . ." There is no way I want to be bound to Clòz any longer. I want him to perish. I want him to suffer. Then I remember my curse of death was my mother's. She passed it on when she died giving birth to me. It transfers through women. If Jarret and I have a girl, then I will die, and she will be forced to live with my curse, but if we break it . . .

"Do it," I tell him. "Break the curse. I refuse to be tied to Clòz in any way any longer. I trust you."

The night embanks us with its dark touch, but I'm no longer scared of the monsters that used to lurk in the shadows. In Jarret's arms, I'm safe. The night has become a beacon of freedom instead of confinement. Soon, I'll no longer be bound to the curse that first appeared with the full moon. Soon, the night will be a reminder of the sweetest memories—my wedding, this escape, and the moment of freedom when I'm no longer shackled to the creature of death and Clòz.

His soft eyes fill with tears again. "How can you still trust me after I forced you to marry him? I don't trust myself. I—"

I touch his cheek, and he leans into the touch. "Jarret, I forgive you. You did what you thought was right. Yes, I was angry at first. Clòz is a terrible man, and he treated me worse than the ground he walked on, but I survived. You came back for me. I get to hold you again. Our child gets to live." I take his hand that is around my waist and place it on my belly. I've only just started to show. "And that is something I will never forget. We can't focus on what could have been. It's over and done. We made it through."

He nods, rubbing his hand where our child lies. He kneels, kissing my belly. "Forgive me," he whispers before he stands, taking my hands. "Let's get this curse broken. I'm challenging Clòz in the morning before he finds us. We should be safe here until then." He leads me toward the fire, and I get a chance to look at the evergreen trees towering around us. I breathe in a sigh of awe but can't strain my neck upward very far because of the pain. Jarret and Wen have set up a little camp complete with two tents and fire with a bubbling pot of stew sitting on the coals.

Wen sits over it, stirring in spices and tasting the broth with a wooden spoon. He looks at me as I sit down beside him,

"You two finally done being all lovey dovey? I had to try so hard not to hurl into the stew." He shudders.

I missed this *dir flak*, but I'll never say that to his face. I pull him into a hug, my tired muscles protesting. He stiffens before returning it. "Thank you for getting Jarret to safety. Thank you for helping me. Thank you for everything," I say, my throat closing. I knew there was good in him. I'm so grateful I saw his light before it was too late. He's become an invaluable help to Jarret and me.

"Well, I definitely didn't do it for him." I hear the smile in his voice. "It was purely selfish reasons. I knew you would kill me if I didn't help him, and . . . you both saved my life. I had to do the same for you. We're even now, so you can't expect anything else from me." He pulls away.

"I never expected anything from you, but I couldn't have done this without you. I wouldn't have survived."

He looks at the stew, stirring it and pulling out a spoonful. "Don't get sappy on me now. Taste this." He holds the spoon out to me.

I taste it, and after two days without food, it is the most delicious sip I've ever put in my mouth. "It's perfect."

"Now I know you're just stroking my ego. It's not that good." He grabs wooden bowls he has lying behind him as I go sit with Jarret.

He pulls me close, his fingers entwining with mine as I lean my head against his shoulder. For once in several weeks, my mind is at peace. Panic no longer overturns my every thought. I know there are battles to come. I know there are things to worry about, but for once, I don't care. I'm finally home.

Dais

"Please, Your Majesty! We didn't do this! We never hurt them! We were at the pass and then . . . ." the man trails off, his eyes becoming glassy, his mind far away.

I growl and point my sword at the next soldier kneeling before me. He shivers and gasps when he sees the blade aimed at him now. Wide brown eyes reflect off the polished metal.

"I'm going to ask this once before I get drastic. Did you murder, rape, and destroy the people in the village of Grayscale a week ago and Sil Haven three days ago?" We found the traitors heading into our camp this morning. We'd just gotten word they pillaged the town of Sil Haven as well. I'd sent the refugees on to Morough.

Now, not one of these men can tell me what happened. It's like they were controlled without their consent, but how? And why? Is it just another ploy of the Darkness? Maybe I'm giving him too much credit. Maybe I'm just insane, or maybe they are. Reality seems like an unattainable aspect anyway.

A breeze blows across the plains where we'd set up camp, rustling the grass that is already tall for the early summer.

"Your Majesty, we did no such thing. We went to sleep that night, and when we woke, we weren't in our camp. We were in the plains of Ei-Kar, but none of us could remember how we got there." He lifts his head. "I swear, Your Majesty! We didn't do anything they said. We don't remember. When we woke up, we decided to head to Morough, but once we slept again, we—we woke up somewhere else. There was a village burning, and I don't remember any of it." Desperate tears appear in his eyes.

I look down the line of men, they avert their gazes, their faces filled with uncertainty and shock. Some are covered in bruises, burn scars, blood, and soot.

I step back, telling the other soldiers. "Chain them up. We march back to Morough today. We'll get to the bottom of this." I sheath my sword, limping to my horse. Despite Jet's protests, I left my cane with my supplies, only to be used when absolutely necessary. I won't let them see me as weak any longer. I'd rather walk with a limp. I swing into the saddle, ignoring the sharp pain that spikes from my knee, up my thigh, and finally resides in my hip. I scowl. I should be able to walk on my own, support myself. If I can't do that, how can I do any of this?

Jet swings onto his own mount, trotting beside me. "It doesn't make sense. What do you think happened to those men?"

I glance back as the platoon of soldiers with us shackle the traitors . . . or the men I thought betrayed this country. I'm not sure anymore, and I'm tired of the uncertainty. "The Darkness must be behind it. Perhaps it is something like the Corrupted. The traitors don't seem to know what really happened to them. They're as lost as we are. How can I convict men who don't remember the crimes they committed?" I mutter, more to myself than to Jet. He's right, it doesn't make sense . . . Nothing makes sense anymore.

"Crimes were still committed, and witnesses placed them at the scene . . . or I'm sure they will once the survivors from Grayscale and Sil Haven see them. You might not have a choice. Someone must be held responsible," he answers as more guards take position around us. Jet refused to let me ride without an entire entourage. It makes me feel like a pompous *maerk*. I miss the days when it was just Jet and me riding side by side with a platoon behind us. Those days were simpler.

I didn't have befuddled men who couldn't remember their crimes. I didn't have to deal with citizens thirsting for blood. I didn't have death threats and assassination attempts. I didn't have to be constantly checking over my shoulder. Father said I would make a better king than him, but he was wrong. I have no idea what I'm doing, and according to my people, I'm failing. Everything was better when he was here. Why did he have to leave when he did? Why can't he be here to guide me through? My biggest regret is not sitting in more meetings with him, not learning all I could while he was still here. I was ignorant and foolish, and now I'm paying the price.

"But what if they're innocent? If they had no volition to destroy those villages, then was it really their actions?"

"I guess that's something you'll have to discern. If we can find a plausible reason for their forgetfulness and terrible actions, then maybe there's a way to save them. I don't want a whole platoon of soldiers to die for this, but you know everyone will call for their blood," Jet mutters, black and gray hair blowing in the breeze.

"Spill their blood to appease the masses?" I spit the words from my mouth, accompanying the sick feeling in my stomach. If only my people knew the choices I had to make. There never seems to be a correct choice. There is always a compromise. It's a thin balance that I have a hard time trying to keep, and in my short reign, the balance has toppled too many times. I never seem to make the right choice to calm my people. I hate their version of peace. It always seems to require extremes . . . like death. Why does it always have to be something so permanent?

"That's not what I'm saying, Dais. I'm saying I want you to be safe. Unfortunately, you'll have to do what makes them happy. A king is only as powerful as his people, and if your people don't see you as someone who is for them, they'll never trust you."

I glare at the back of my horse's head. That's why I came out here in the first place . . . to show my strength, to show that I can be trusted, but now I'm more confused than ever. I can't kill all these men. Sure, something terrible happened, but do I really have to kill them to avenge their actions? Are their actions something I can really avenge when they don't remember committing the crime? Will I still have to put them to death? Will I have to put their blood on my hands as well as the blood they spilled?

Please the people. Save the kingdom, but at what cost?

Rahuin

"Your Highness, Princess Thesa has arrived," a servant says as she steps into the Färrin library. It's one of the most beautiful places I've ever had the honor of seeing. Thin steepled windows with stained glass shimmer golden sunlight into the huge room. The trunk of the huge Silfras tree creates a circled dome for hundreds of volumes. Curved shelves line every available space, and around the room, little nooks in the branches have been set up for readers. That's where the servant finds me, buried among royal purple pillows on a giant swing hanging from the ceiling.

I look up from the book I'd been reading, though I'd hardly comprehended any of the words. I haven't been able to focus on anything since my dream about Dais. I sent Thesa the message a week ago. I thought I'd receive a response before she came, but her presence is the most wonderful answer. I set the book aside, smiling as I gently slide off the swing and follow the servant to the main foyer of Silfras. Hundreds of elves leisure around the halls, taking in the architecture or admiring the foliage surrounding the city. Even the city itself is covered in thousands of plants in every variety. Bugs and birds nestle in the indoor gardens and fly around the halls like they belong here just as much as we do.

I see Thesa before she does. She's conversing with another elven couple who just entered the great tree.

"Thesa!" I call, rushing toward her.

She spins around, her eyes filling with tears when she sees me. A hand flutters to her lips before she opens her arms wide, meeting me in a long-awaited embrace.

"I missed you so much," I say against her shoulder.

"I missed you too." She pulls away, smiling at my belly. "May I?"

I nod, and she places a gentle hand on my stomach. Sira kicks her hand, and I giggle when Thesa's eyes widen with excitement.

"Oh, it's the most wonderful feeling." She chuckles, her face glowing. "And you're so far along. I thought you still had a few months left."

"I do, or I think so. I often wonder if I'm further along than I thought. I kept her hidden for so long when I was with the Darkness. Maybe coming here and finding time to breathe has allowed the concealing to disappear completely. I haven't had a midwife check yet, but I will when I get to Morough."

Her brow furrows. "Are you sure you want to fly in your condition?"

"I think I'll be all right. If it's too much, I'll ask you to stop. I just want to get to Dais as soon as possible. I fear he's in great danger."

"You're right. Jet sent me a message the same morning I received yours. He wants me to come help him keep an eye on Dais. He didn't say anything about you, but I'm sure he won't be pleased you're coming with me. You'll be safer here."

"I agree, but she won't listen to me either. Stubborn like her father." My mother walks over to us. Elves bow their heads to her as she passes them, but she nods to them.

"Queen Aleetha." Thesa bows her head as well.

"Mother."

"I thought I felt my ears burning." Father enters from another hall, no doubt summoned by Mother calling him stubborn. My parents have an uncanny gift of inadvertently insulting each other and then appearing once the insult is made. It's like they appear just to defend themselves. "And I seem to recall you're way more stubborn than me."

"Oh really, name one time I was stubborn." She holds up a slender finger.

I roll my eyes. Here we go.

He stands in front of her, crossing his arms over his burly chest. "The tree."

"There were chickadees nesting in it."

"Yes, but they could have been moved to a nicer, not dead tree."

Mother sticks her nose in the air. "The tree still had life. I could feel it."

"Yes, in the form of chickadees and that's why it's gone now, but you had to stand in front of it for days. Skipping meals and crying over a tree whose wood was eventually used as fertilizer for four new trees!" He holds up four fingers.

I sigh. "We should go. They'll be here for a while, and then they wonder where I get my stubbornness from."

Thesa tries to hide a smile with the back of her hand.

My comment gains my mother's attention. "You can't go yet. I have to say goodbye." She envelops me in a hug and then I feel Father wrap his arms around both of us.

"We'll miss you, *Aihha,*" she says.

"Tell us the second Sira is born. We'll be there as soon as we can," Father says, pulling back. I look into his green eyes that are so much like mine. "I love you."

I hug him. "I love you, Father." I pull Mother in. "I love you."

She steps back, blinking tears away. "We'll see you soon."

"I know."

Renell

Wen stands in front of me, holding the scroll he'd taken from Casta. The fire glows behind us, and Jarret adds more wood to give Wen plenty of light.

"The way this works is you have to have the intention of breaking the curses on you. It helps if you can remember part of the binding Clòz whispered when he cursed you. We're trying to reverse what he did—well, reverse everything. You have to be completely ready to let your curse go. Let the power go. Let it all go."

My thirst for controlling this power is what got me into this mess in the first place. If I had been honest and let others know, if I hadn't been so selfish and gambled with my country, none of this would have happened. I resent it. I deserve to lose it. It won't make me any less of a leader. I will still fight until my dying breath, but I won't let it control me any longer. I won't let Clòz have his power over me anymore.

"I'm ready." I meet his gaze, hoping he sees my sincerity. "I'll try to remember what he said." Everything happened so suddenly that night and I recall Nella telling me to pay attention to the bindings when Clòz said them, but I only remember a handful.

"A few words will be fine." He nods, gray eyes searching the scroll. He reaches to his side and pulls out a dagger, handing it to me. "As I recite this verse over you, I want you to mutter the words you remember and cut your palm the same direction he did. I know it'll be a bit backward, but that's the point of this."

"Okay." I hold the dagger steady, turning my palm over to see the scar Clòz left a few months ago. The jagged flesh looks like a bolt of lightning streaking across my hand.

"Now what I recite will sound strange because it's an ancient language, but you might recognize a few words since Onarian and Castian are based off it."

Forever. Bindings. Nothing will be able to break it. Love . . . Some words from the ceremony appear in my head.

"I'm ready."

Wen nods and begins to read the ancient text. As he does, the words I can remember from that night flow from my mouth, "Forever. Bind. Bindings. Break it. Love. Death." I slide the dagger across my palm, imagining the bindings breaking completely and vanishing.

Wen stops, sliding the scroll closed. He looks at me expectantly.

"That's it?" I ask, looking down at myself. Besides the pain in my palm, I don't feel any different.

"That's it. Aren't you going to see if it worked? Because if it didn't, we just turned the entire Cay-Llekian army on us until Clòz gets you back." He points behind him.

I take a deep breath, terrified to find out if it didn't work or not. I do what I normally do, envision my curse slipping over my skin like a blanket and then open my eyes. My heart thrills when I don't see Wen's veins. I look past him to Jarret, who sits watching us by the fire. Nothing. Tears appear in my eyes, and I smile. "It worked." I start to laugh. I'm free! Our child is free.

Jarret stands, crossing over to me in an instant. He pulls me into his arms, kissing me with reckless passion. His hungry lips devour mine, and my fingers dig into his shirt as he pulls me closer, lifting me up slightly. His tender touch is an elixir to my soul, like it's erasing every horrible glance, touch, and kiss from the last two months. The constant panic I'd used as a shield starts to dissipate, replaced with sweet relief of knowing I'm right where I need to be. Gone is the guilt. Gone is the fear—all in the embrace of the man who loves me in spite of it all.

Wen gags. "I think it's time I bow out for the night. If you two are going to get all nasty, I'll take my chances with the ominous forest." I hear him start to walk away.

Jarret pulls back a little, his hands under my hips.

"I missed him more than I care to admit."

"Please don't tell him. His head can't get any bigger." Jarret rolls his eyes, setting me down.

I kiss his chin. "I'm free. We're finally free."

"You'll only be truly free when he's dead. Then we can start getting Lanckest back." He leans his forehead against mine, his hands rubbing circles on my belly now.

"I'm so proud of you . . ." My voice cracks. "My husband, a king."

I swallow, kissing his cheeks.

He pulls back a little, his dark brown eyes searching mine in pure adoration. The corner of his lips lift. "And my wife, a queen."

I smile, my knees growing a little weak in his gaze. He could stare at me forever and I'd never feel exposed. "Aren't we quite the pair?"

"A perfect match." He kisses me once more, and I melt into his arms.

Jarret

Clòz is every bit as menacing as I remember, but somehow he seems smaller. Before he was a giant and now he's just a man—a man who can be defeated. A man I will destroy like I failed to do the first time. He circles me in the Onarian plain they'd set up camp in. His men stand behind him, watching me with confusion. Renell slept in my arms for the first time in two months last night, and I will never let her be taken from me ever again.

"So you're the one who stole the whore. I should have killed you when I had the chance," Clòz says to me. His eyes blaze like a fire as his gaze settles on Renell standing a little ways away with Wen. "There's the *caldig*."

"You'll regret ever calling her those words." My voice goes low as I glare at him.

"You'll regret challenging me again. I won't hesitate to rip you limb from limb this time! She's mine, and I will never let you forget it." His face turns as red as the tattoos marring his cheek as he grips the hilt of his sword, pulling it out with unbridled fury.

Some of his men look around uneasily, as if they're unsure why he didn't finish me off the first time. Well, that was his mistake. His pride will be his downfall.

"You shouldn't be so sure of yourself . . . he could defeat you again."

"He will," I say to the voice in my mind. Nothing will hold me back from killing him this time. I will never let him hurt or be tethered

to Renell ever again. I will win. I will control Cay-Llek. I will help her get Lanckest back. I will keep her safe, even if it kills me too. Everyone turns their back on a dead man, and Wen taught me to use my strengths. If all I'm good for is to die, then that's what I'll do.

He steps toward me, his entire being shaking as he raises his sword.

"What will the rules be, High Chief?" one of his men has the gall to ask.

A flash and a spurt of blood later, the man falls to his knees, gripping his sliced open throat.

Clòz wipes the blood from his weapon against his arm, leaving a trail of red as he faces me again. "No rules! A merciless fight to the death."

I stifle the smirk wanting to play on my lips. He's played right into my hands. "I accept." I brandish my sword, bending my knees slightly so I can spring into action.

His eyes are deep pits of soulless darkness as I hear the whoosh of wind in the wake of Clòz's swinging sword. "I'll tear you apart! You're nothing but a mouse under my boot!"

I spin, blocking his blow with a clang of steel.

He steps forward, our swords grating together as my heels dig into the grasslands. Dark clouds swirl overhead, bringing an ominous promise of rain.

"You aren't strong enough to defeat me! You should have learned that the first time," he grunts, grinding his sword against mine as he shoves me back with a foot to my chest.

I stumble but don't fall completely. Weaker me would have fallen. He would have died right then and there, but I'm not weak anymore . . .

I step toward him. "There shouldn't have been a second time." I smirk, parrying his next blow and sidestepping as he swings to my right. His movements are choppy and stiff, blinded by the rage seeping off him in waves. I step toward him, ducking under his next attack, spinning with a blow of my own he deflects.

He howls, a blood curdling scream that would make anyone's hair stand on end. Our swords cross against each other as he steps forward.

I grunt, slashing his weapon away from mine and jumping back before his next attack. We exchange blows until sweat coats our skin and clothes. Neither of us manage to draw blood. We're more evenly matched than I thought. Rain starts to drip around us, and I hope Wen at least takes Renell to some shelter. I honestly don't want her to see my next move either. Because it will either be really stupid or completely genius.

Mud forms under our feet as the heavens open, drenching us with torrents. I don't have time to look back to make sure Renell is secure before my feet slip in the sludge, sending me to my back and knocking the air from my lungs.

I hear Clòz yell before he appears in my vision, water dripping from his braids and face as he plunges his sword downward. I roll in the mud, dodging the blow. I think I hear Renell yelp, but I can't tell through the rain pounding the ground near my head.

"You're dead. You can't defeat him."

That's precisely what I want. I want him to underestimate me. I'm not a threat . . . not really. I stare at the mud my hands and sword are sinking into.

"Stop rolling away like a coward and face me!" Clòz rips me up by my hair. Fire rips along my scalp, and I hold my scream in as his blade aims straight for my neck. Bloodthirst shines in his eyes, and I meet his gaze as my cold fingers grip my weapon. Rain scatters across the steel blade heading for me, but it won't reach me, not yet.

I morph, and Clòz is forced to let me go as my massive form of blue scales reflect in his brown eyes. I catch a glimpse of Renell and Wen a little ways away. Confidence builds her gaze, strengthening my resolve. I screech, my roar billowing to the sky. Finally, fear fills his expression. It's the first time I've seen an emotion other than anger on his face. I'll enjoy this. Fire erupts from my veins, consuming the rain and his soft flesh as it passes from my maw. His scream is lost in the roar of the flames.

"You shouldn't have killed him so easily. You should have made him suffer like he made Renell suffer. You should have done all that he did to her back to him . . ."

I ignore the voice because I'm not sardonic like he claims me to be.

"We're one and the same. I don't know why you keep questioning that."

"I'm nothing like you," I think as my stomach turns after I see the charred lump that used to be Clòz. The smell of his burnt flesh tingles my nostrils, and I hate that my senses are heightened in my dragon form. I morph again, finding the rest of Clòz's men watching me with careful apprehension. I wait for them to say or do something against me. Clòz said no rules beyond fighting to the death and that's what I did. They stare uneasily at one another before dropping their weapons and falling to their knees with arms crossed above their heads . . . a sign of submission. I'm their new chief now.

"Jarret." I spin to catch Renell in my arms. We slip in the sludgy ground, and it takes all my strength to not drop her in the mud.

She's kissing me and shaking me at the same time. "I was so worried for a second. I thought he was going to win again. I thought I was going to lose you for good."

"You could have. Wouldn't it have been beautiful to see her crying for you? But, oh wait, you wouldn't have been around to see it. Now she'll always be around to see what a monster you really are . . ."

I ignore the voice. I'm not a monster, and he'll never make me. "But you didn't. I'm still here. We can finally get Lanckest back."

"Home," she whispers, her green eyes shining in the cool rain.

I smile. "Home. But first, we need to get you somewhere warm and dry.

Chapter 31

Defiance is a Valuable Weapon

Rahuin

Everything looks different in Morough at night. During the day, the city looks enchanting and beautiful, but at night, darkness overtakes the land, leaving an unsettling feeling in my bones. Last time I was here, the citizens wanted my head. I'm sure they still do, and maybe that's where my uneasiness comes from.

He's fine, Thesa says in my head. Her wings flap, sending gusts of wind around me. I shiver despite the fact that it's a fairly warm night. Moonlight shimmers over her scales and the sea in the distance, reflecting off the castle turrets that reach into the night. Light behind the windows illuminate the ivory towers and cast an eerie glow on the courtyard below.

Thesa lands there, and several guards rush to see who has graced the palace with their presence. They all bow their heads when they see me. I slip off Thesa's back, nodding at them while I head up the steps. Thesa and a few guards soon follow.

"Your Majesty, we weren't expecting you. I—It's very late," a general with the sweeping cerulean colors decorating his cape says.

449

An emblem of the ocean in gold adorns the left shoulder of his armor, showing his rank.

"I know. My journey was unprompted. I didn't have time to send a message." I wander down gold and amber gilded halls, passing statues of previous royal family members that look down like hidden guardians. I notice more guards than usual lining the exits of each corridor. I move toward the royal family's wing which is just before Dais's office. I slip inside. He's not there and neither is Jet. I doubt he's resting. Maybe he's not even back yet. Did he make it back? Will he? The thoughts weigh me down.

"He's here, Rahuin. Something has happened again. He's with Jet," I hear Fire speak from the lamp as I step back into the hall.

The general and Thesa are still there.

I nod him. "Thank you for accompanying me, General, but I think I can go from here."

"As you wish, Your Majesty." He bows and leaves.

Jet walks by at the end of the hall, halts, and turns toward us.

"Rahuin? What are you doing here? What—" He stops short when he sees Thesa, his eyes searching hers as if asking why she brought me.

"Don't blame her. I told her to come get me. I need to see him. Where is he?"

"Rahuin."

"Is that all you can say? What happened to him, Jet? Is he okay?" My voice cracks. Why is he being so cryptic? Why is he trying to hide my husband from me? Does he not want to see me? No, that's stupid. He didn't even know I was coming.

"He's fine. Well . . . perhaps you should see him first," he says, glancing at Thesa before spinning on his heels and heading toward the room I share with Dais.

It's dark when we enter and one dim candle glows on a bedside table. I expect Dais to be in bed, but when my eyes adjust, he's not there. My heart sinks.

Jet walks past me, heading toward a spot in the middle of the room.

I step toward him to find Dais sitting on the floor with his knees tucked to his chest and his arms holding his head. He rocks back and forth, his blue eyes worn. His curls are matted to his head and his beard is an unruly jungle on his face. Dark circles underline his eyes, and he's thin, so thin. His shoulders are hunched and he looks so much smaller than I remember.

My lips quiver. "Dais?" I whisper, but he doesn't seem to hear me.

Jet nudges his shoulder, but Dais doesn't move. "He's been like this since this morning." He straightens himself, looking at Thesa. "We got back the other night with the traitors. They came to us willingly and had no recollection of what they did. Dais was at a loss. Since then, healers have determined they were drugged. We kept them overnight, and sure enough, when the darkness fell, they're quiet demeanor turned into howls of derangement. They started clawing and biting themselves when they learned they couldn't escape.

"The healers say there is a cure, but they're working on getting the concoction to ferment. That all happened yesterday, but I found Dais like this this morning. The healers couldn't help him. They said he needed rest, but he refused to close his eyes. He refused to do anything, and then he stopped responding to me. It's probably good you came, but he didn't want you to be here."

"Why? Because of assassination attempts you didn't tell me about? Because I'm his wife? Because I could have been here before this happened? When was the last time he slept, Jet?" I glare at him even though I know it isn't his fault. Dais is more stubborn than a mountain. My hands shake so I burry them into the fabric of my blue dress. Now is not the time to breakdown. Dais needs me. I have to be strong for him.

Jet looks away, guilt stampeding across his face. "I—I'm not sure."

I take in a deep breath, glancing at my husband. Tears form in my eyes, and I can't make the pit in my stomach go away. I try to swallow the lump in my throat. I have to find a way to reach him. I have to save him like he saved me so many times in the presence of the Darkness. Though I don't feel the Darkness now, he could still have a hand in it. "I knew I never should have left. I knew he was lying to me." I kneel beside him, but he doesn't lift his head. He's muttering something, but I can't hear what it is.

I look up at Thesa and Jet. "Leave me with him. I'll let you know if anything changes."

"Rahuin." Jet reaches for my shoulder.

"Please," I beg. He nods, taking Thesa's hand instead and leaving the room. "Dais?" I grab his hands that still hold his head.

His blue eyes don't even meet mine. They continue to look off in the distance, as if he's seeing something no one else can.

"What should I do? How can I help you?" I ask, but he doesn't answer. Is my husband even still in there? His body looks like a shell of his former self. No. I can't lose him. Not like this. Tears stream down my cheeks unbidden.

"I have an idea. Give him a bath and put him to sleep. Don't leave his sight. Let him know you're here, even if he doesn't comprehend it," Water says, and I hear its voice coming from a wash basin on the other side of the room.

Wiping my eyes, I stand and ring for a servant, telling them to draw a hot bath for the king. I run a hand down the length of his chin, feeling his unruly beard between my fingers. "Please stand, my love. I'm going to take care of you. You don't have to do it alone anymore. I'm right here. I'm sorry I left you alone. Please don't go like this." I kiss his forehead, and then lift him up underneath the shoulders.

To my surprise, he stands, letting his arms fall to his sides. He still doesn't seem to acknowledge I'm here, but at least I got him to his feet.

The servants arrive a few minutes later with steaming hot water, pouring it into the tub we had in a little room offset from the bedroom. I help him out of his clothes, and then settle him inside the warm water. I add oils and herbs to the bath before I grab a scissors for his beard.

"I'm going to trim your beard," I say, patting his cheek. His eyes drift over to me, but they don't recognize me yet. He looks so much older than I remember. It makes me think I haven't seen him in years instead of a few months. Slowly, he nods, but there is still no light in his eyes.

I clip away the long whiskers then take some shaving oils and shave his chin down to bare skin. Next, I start on his hair, cleansing and trimming it before adding oils to reform his natural curls.

"Rahuin!" He jumps, splashing water over the floor as he twists to look at me.

I drop the strands of hair I'd been working with. "You're lucky I didn't have the scissors in my hand or you would have had a hole in the back of your head." I smirk even as tears fill my eyes. He's back. He's okay.

He looks at me with recognition. "You're here." He takes my cheek in his shaking hand.

I lean into his touch, blinking away my tears. "I'm here." I kiss his forehead before I wave an oily hand. "Now, sit still, I'm almost done."

He turns back so I can continue working, sloshing water. "What happened? When did you get here? When did I get into the tub?" He turns his head in contemplation, pulling strands of hair from my fingers.

"You don't remember?" I ask, scrunching his curls like I have to do with my own.

"No. I was . . . Rahuin, I—"

"I know, Dais. I came because I was worried. I got here just in time too. Jet said he found you curled up in a ball on the floor since this morning. When I arrived an hour or so ago, you were still there. You don't remember anything before that?" I move to the side of the tub so I can lean against it and stare deep into his eyes. I never want to forget his gaze. I never want to feel the fear of losing it again.

"We got back, and the healers . . ." His eyebrows lift as he nods. "I remember. The healers made a concoction of what they think influenced the men."

My mouth falls open. "And you took it?"

"I had to understand what happened to them so I could vouch on their behalf."

"Without telling anyone? Do you understand how stupid that sounds? Jet didn't know what happened to you. I was worried sick. What if you had turned out like them?" Like the crazy, deranged men who ruined villages and murdered and raped people. The thought causes bile to rise in my throat. What would have been left of him if he did something so heinous? Even if he was drugged.

"I didn't take much. They gave me a little and then gave me the cure they made. They were monitoring how it worked . . . if it worked."

"And if it hadn't worked? What would have happened, Dais? You would have been stuck like them!" I scream, pointing toward the door. "Why didn't you tell Jet?"

"I didn't want him to stop me. I had to understand what those men went through for me to say they were manipulated. No one would believe me unless I experienced it for myself. If things got out of hand, the healers would have locked me up. They wouldn't have let me go rampant." His voice cracks as he breathes heavily. "I had to try, Rahuin. I won't let them call for the death of those men too. I had to do something."

I look away because I can see the conflict in his eyes. He was so upset at the people for choosing death as the only solution for their anger and grief. He's trying to keep that from happening again, but what if he can't? What if they still choose death? Will it drive him off the edge?

"I don't want you to put yourself in danger just because of them." My fingers caress his clean cheek.

"I didn't want you to either, but it's not like you gave me a choice," he hisses, getting out of the tub and reaching for a robe. He wraps it around his thin frame.

I stand. "Dais—"

"I met Wen." His shoulders slump as he turns his back to me. "I know I shouldn't have, but I did. I understand why you loved him. I know why it was so easy for you." His words sting like venom from an angry hornet.

"Easy for me? Dais, it was the hardest thing I ever did. I did it to protect you, to protect Sira, to make it back home." I step toward him.

He whirls around. "Exactly! And you didn't have to do any of those things if you'd never left." He stands over me, anger cutting the angles of his face and making his beautiful blue eyes seem harsh.

I clench my teeth. "I had to learn."

"Did you really? What did it cost you? Was it worth it? The war isn't over, Rahuin. I lost my father because of it. I'm losing my people because of it too, because this heart"—he grips his chest—"loves you. Why"—his voice breaks—"Why didn't we try together? Why did you have to leave me?" Tears appear in his eyes.

I want to be angry. I want to scream and tell him that clearly it was for Wen, but I know that's not what he's implying. He wants to know why I left at all, and maybe he's trying to be certain it wasn't all for Wen.

"Because I thought I was protecting you. I thought I could make everything better for us and for Casta, but I was wrong. Yes, I should have consulted with you. You are my husband, yet I left you out of it." Tears choke my throat, but I swallow them down. I don't deserve to cry right now. He does. "I should have told you my plan. Yes, you would have tried to stop us, but we still would have gone through with it. Then we'd still be here, fighting over things that have already passed. Things I'm trying to forgive because I can't take it back now. I can't go back and fix what I did. I will live with it. I will survive because I made my choice."

He sits down on the edge of the bed, wiping his face, his wet curls dripping onto his robe. "Tell me honestly. Did you know he was going to be there?"

"I assumed he would be, yes." I sit beside him. "Is this about me or Wen?"

"This is about you. I don't give a *velk* about Wen. I just don't want there to be any more secrets between us. I don't want anything that will tear us apart."

"I don't think it's the secrets tearing us apart, Dais," I whisper, wanting to get up and walk out of this conversation, but I know that will just upset him more. He wants answers and he'll keep asking until he gets them.

"Did you want to see him again?"

"Yes, I wanted to know why he lied to me. I wanted to understand."

He scoots closer, taking one of my hands into his own. "Did you know you were pregnant before you left?"

I pause for a moment, thinking back to just before the battle in

Lanckest. "I'd had a dream about Sira, but I'd always had dreams about her. She was a part the future I knew was going to happen. Dreams about her weren't new so I thought nothing of it. I didn't know before I got there. Wen had been training me for a few days, and then I bled a little. I thought I killed her, but she survived.

"I knew I had to be careful, but I also had to thwart the Darkness. He couldn't know she was yours. If he did, he would have killed her. Renell confirmed it when she came to kill me. The only reason she saved my life was because of Sira. Well, Sira and Elrian, but I didn't know that at the time either." I entwine my fingers with his.

He leans his head on my shoulder. "I'm sorry for shouting. I just can't tell what is real anymore. I'm tired. The Darkness has visited me—"

"He has?" I turn to meet his eyes once more, they are so full of pain.

"Yes, and you had to do it all alone. I never knew, but now I do. I understand it was hard, doing what you did, but I couldn't help but feel like I . . ." he trails off.

"Needed the assurance?"

He pulls me into his lap, rubbing a hand over my belly. "Yes, us men, you know. We need that stability."

"Speaking of stability and honesty, Wen asked to come back and stay with us in Morough. He wants to help us. He wants to protect us both and do what he can to stop the Darkness with the knowledge he has. I told him I had to ask you. He agreed and said he would come back to learn your answer after he finished helping Jarret."

Dais nods. "I'll think about it." He pulls me close, kissing my neck. "How long will you stay?"

I smile, kissing his forehead. "I'm staying here, Dais. I'm not going back to Färrin. We'll do this together, like we promised. I won't let the Darkness isolate us anymore. I'm sorry I had to go again, but I found peace. I know why I'm fighting. The Darkness will not win."

He takes a deep breath, letting it out against my skin. "No, he will not."

Dais

Hundreds of people stand in the courtyard below. A sea of colorful clothing and clean faces stare up at me. Eyes watch me in careful contemplation. I see no hate. I see no fear. I see admiration. Admiration I might destroy with the announcement I have for them. The Darkness was wrong. They do trust me, or they want to, at least. They loved my father, and I can tell they want nothing more than to offer me the same sentiment. But doubt creeps in, saying they never will, saying they'll constantly change their minds and their love will never be genuine. Their hatred turned to admiration so quickly just because I brought home a few traitors, but now, I'll have to destroy it.

The sun crests over the people, washing them in its bright warmth. I speak, "I stand before you today to announce my verdict regarding the traitors who pillaged the villages of Grayscale and Sil Haven. After careful consideration, the royal healers have found that the traitors were influenced by a concoction of herbs once known as *Eríd*.

"It's an ancient remedy used to turn men into monsters with the night. They become unaware of their actions once the night falls and are allured by bloodlust and the evilest influence. In this state, men are easily manipulated. In light of this discovery, I have decided not to severely punish them with a death sentence. They will instead be imprisoned for a time until all the poison has left their system, and the healers have carefully monitored the cure. They will then be reinstated."

Boos and exclamations arise from the crowd. I lift my hands, one of them holding onto my cane so I don't drop it past the balcony railing. I'd done it once previously and don't want to repeat the embarrassing mistake. It's enough that I have to use the tool at all. The shouts cease.

"I know you're angry over what's happened, and I know you're wondering if it's all true. I have taken the herbal concoction under scrutiny of the healers, so I can say it's real. It's a horrible concoction I never want to be found again in Casta. I've ordered all known recipes burned for the safety of us all. Those men did nothing wrong, and they don't deserve to be punished for it. We have no idea how they were drugged, but we are carefully questioning all involved until we have an answer.

"I have reason to believe this is another work of the Darkness, who is doing all he can to cause distress in Casta by turning loyal soldiers against us. A recipe of the cure will be distributed to all healers within regiments and villages to keep this dreadful occurrence from happening again. In compensation for what happened to Grayscale and Sil Haven, I have sent a caravan of blacksmiths, carpenters, iron and stone masons, and weavers with loads of supplies to the affected cities to be rebuilt. That will be all the announcements." I take a deep breath. Somehow I got through all that, and my words hadn't faltered once, though I'd felt the quivering in my heart. The fear that begged to be released in the form of stuttering speech and sweaty palms, but I held my ground. I got through it.

The people converse amongst themselves down below, some turn to leave, others look up at me with worried expressions. They want to trust me. They want to know they're safe, but I can't promise them that . . . not until this war is over. There is only one of me, and thousands of them. I can't promise to protect them. Poisoned men is enough proof. There will always be more ways they can be harmed. The enemy is cunning, and he will destroy all who cross his path. Right now, Casta is in his path. There will be no guarantee of safety when the enemy has set his eyes on our annihilation.

"How can you protect us? How can you keep us safe?" a voice cries below.

My steady breath of relief seems to suck back into my lungs. I'd hoped none of them would question me before I decided to head back into the castle, but I knew it was wishful thinking. I look toward where I'd heard the voice.

"I can't," I speak the truth, and it draws a few gasps from the crowd. "I'm just a man. I'm doing all I can to ensure your safety, but if I promised you safety, I would be lying. I will not lie or fill your heads with empty promises. We face a powerful enemy who hasn't been vanquished yet, and no safety can be assured until he is gone. I urge you all to take part in the local trainings happening in every village. We have to be prepared. It's the only way I can start teaching you all to protect yourselves.

"This war is not over, and the biggest fight of our lives will be here before we know it. All we love is at stake, and you must be prepared. I cannot protect you all, even though it is something I dearly wish I could accomplish." I study their faces, and the fear I'd felt slips away.

Once again, admiration lights a few of their gazes along with something like determination. I know because I'd seen the look on young soldiers I used to train. Some still hold scared glances, and I can't blame them. They know they aren't safe, but will it push them to fight or cower? I'm hoping it's the former.

Someone touches my elbow, gently nudging me toward the door. "Your Majesty." Jet's voice. "Rahuin has called for you. An assassin was apprehended in the garden while they were walking. The guards found him before something could happen."

I feel the blood drain from my face, leaving me cold and hollow as I follow him back into the castle. The elation over my victory has now turned into a heavy stone sinking into my gut.

Jet takes me to my quarters.

Rahuin sits comfortably in her favorite chair, her arms resting on her belly. Her eyes stare into the flames of the lit fireplace. I pull at the collar of my shirt. It must be a thousand degrees in here, but Rahuin seems to always be cold. Maybe it's the fear we both feel.

Thesa stands a little ways away, her jade eyes glaring at the doors leading to the terrace as if someone might smash through them and claim one of our lives. I wouldn't put it past anyone at this point. I notice she's already placed a steaming cup of tea at Rahuin's side. The little detail gives me more peace than Thesa will ever know. Her constant care when Rahuin was with the Darkness always consisted of a hot cup of tea.

Rahuin turns to look at me as I approach and holds a hand out.

I take it, feeling warm flesh and blood. "You weren't hurt?"

"No, I'm all right." Her words are nonchalant, but her fingers tremble in my hand. I was terrified after the first assassination attempt. I can't imagine how she feels, but she was aware of the danger when she came home. I should have sent her back immediately, but I need her here. I refuse to let them keep us apart any longer. Sira will be here before we know it, and I want to be present. I won't let them take that from me.

I kneel beside her. "Rahuin." I want to reprimand, but I know it won't do any good.

"Dais, I'm fine. We're fine." She rubs her belly, and I do the same, feeling Sira kick my hand.

I chuckle, some of the dread fading. I kiss the place where she'd kicked before I lift my lips to Rahuin's. "I've decided to let Wen come here to help us."

She leans back a little, searching my gaze. "Are you sure?"

"I am. He wants to help. I'm not going to turn the offer away because of the things he did when he was with the Darkness. I've experienced how the Darkness manipulates us. For him, it was no different. I can't blame him for that. I, also, can't blame you for it."

She kisses me again and tears shine in her eyes when she pulls away. "I love you."

"I love you." I smile, and for a moment, I forget about the looming threat of Darkness. For a moment, it's just us.

Carrie

CITY OF PËR, KÄS

My heart palpitates so loudly I swear Aiden can hear it from where he stands beside me. I dig my nails into my palm, certain this isn't happening. It shouldn't be happening, right? We only just met a month ago. Okay, there are some extenuating circumstances like he saved my life and we're tethered so I survive. Plus, we've spent every waking second together since the day I was 'accepted' as his assistant at the clinic, but isn't this too soon?

The courthouse blurs around me, I can't focus on the dark wood desk in front of me that has nicks and cracks studding the wood. I don't see the white and black checkered tiles with gold flecks I'd been admiring earlier. I don't hear the chatter of others as they bring their problems to the clerks in hopes of resolution.

Aiden grabs my clenched fist, rubbing a gentle circle on the top of my hand. I entwine our fingers together as he leans over, whispering, "If you want to leave, we can. We don't have to do this if you're not ready." His blue eyes reflect the chandelier light above us. "We can still talk to Rave if it's fake."

I smile, my stomach doing little flips as he looks at me. Since our hasty meeting a month ago, a deep understanding and connection has formed between us. It was fun and a bit exciting at first with the attraction we shared, but it's quickly become so much more than that. It might seem fast, but I know I love him with every fiber of my being. Maybe it's because of those extenuating circumstances or maybe it's not. If I ever tried to find out by asking him to let go so I could leave, I'd die. So what does it matter?

Originally, we were going to provide some fake marriage documents to appeal to King Rave about adopting some of the Walk children he stockpiles, but after our month together, we realized we loved each other, so why not get married for real?

"I'm ready," I whisper back. "Plus, they already started the paperwork." I reach up, straightening the collar of his tan coat even though it's not crooked.

He grabs my hands. "That doesn't matter, they can burn paperwork if we walk out of here."

"Are you saying you don't want to marry me for real then?" I quirk a brow.

He huffs. "You were trying to trap me the entire time weren't you?"

"Maybe." I smile, leaning against him as I stand on my tiptoes to be eye-level.

He wraps his arms around me. "Then I'm going to trap you. I want to marry you for real, but only if you're absolutely ready. I don't want to force you just so we can try adopting some of those kids."

I cup the sides of his face, rubbing my thumb along the stubble of his jaw. "I want to marry you for real too. I love you."

"I love you." He starts to lean down as a throat clears behind him.

We break apart and Aiden faces the court man as he comes back to the desk window we'd been standing by. My face flushes as I stare down at the black and white tiles under my feet. Other people bustle past the window holding stacks of paperwork, someone mutters to another clerk to my right about property rights. I'd been so nervous before that I forgot we aren't alone.

The court man in front of us taps the papers in his hands against the desk with a clack, clack. "I'll have you both sign these. One copy for you." Clack. "One copy for the courts." Clack. "And one for the officiator." He slaps them down before handing a fountain pen to Aiden, who scribbles his signature on all three documents. He hands me the pen as I step up to the desk. I see the officiator has already signed. I assume the man in front of us is our officiator, guess I didn't think about that before. I hastily put my signature on the line under Aiden's name on all three, signing with my middle name first—Alianna.

Since that fateful day a month ago, I've henceforth changed my name to Alianna. We appealed to Mr. Kampf for a face-altering mask and wig. Now I have blond hair with rounder features and wear it any time I'm in public or at the clinic. King Rave doesn't know that I know, and if we came to him without my disguise, he'd know that I know. It all seems so confusing, but I have to play this part for now. King Rave won't control us forever, and one day, I'll go back to being Carrie, just Carrie.

"Congratulations, Mr. and Mrs. Brachus." Clack. He hands us our copy and turns away from the window.

I stare at the thick piece of paper. We're married. Aiden waves it in my face. "Ready to go now, Mrs. Brachus?" He wiggles blond eyebrows as he offers his arm for me.

I take it. "Absolutely, Mr. Brachus."

Aiden

ÄLBRECT CASTLE, KÄS

"You want to what?" King Rave raises pencil thin black brows, his arms clasped behind his back as he takes a turn around Carrie—Alianna and me, circling us like the vulture he is.

I keep my gaze trained on his dark eyes. "We want to adopt Walk children you have in the university."

"And why would I allow that?" His purses his pale, thin lips.

The dazzling obsidian pillars and gold accents of his office seem to blur together as I try to keep my face from betraying my frustration. "I was raised in that university. All I wished for was a family. I believe your Walk children will perform better for you if you allow them the chance at a normal family . . . or at least the illusion of one. We can encourage them to apply for work in the castle and establish a love of king and country while also growing their abilities naturally." The words taste like poison in my mouth as I say them, but if I don't try to convince him of my sincerity, he'll never let me do this. King Rave has one downfall—pride. If I can appeal to it, maybe he'll let this happen. He's not aware that the King I'll teach the kids about has nothing to do with him, but he doesn't have to know the details.

He narrows his eyes, stopping in front of me. He glances briefly at Carrie as a sick smile spreads across his face. "I don't believe I've had the pleasure of meeting your wife." He turns toward her.

She dips her head, blonde hair framing her face as she batts brown eyes. "A pleasure, Your Majesty." She holds a hand out, and I can feel the way her heart palpitates. I bet it's taking everything within her to keep her hand from trembling. "Alianna Brachus."

He takes her hand, kissing it. "Charmed." He grips her tighter with a quirk of his lip. "Hello, Carrie."

Her face pales as her eyes go wide. She barely has to act as I know nervousness overtakes her. "H—how did you know? I—I was free." She rips her hand away.

"Oh, I only gave you the illusion of freedom." He slaps me on the shoulder. "Aiden, played his part well, wouldn't you say?"

She glances at me with a teary-eyed gaze. "What?" She croaks.

"I had to lie. He would have killed you. I couldn't live with that."

Carrie clenches her fist, looking away, and I know she's feeding this performance from all the emotions she felt the day she realized she'd never be free. She finally looks back at Rave. "What do you want, King Rave? Have me kill more Walks? Join the number soldiers again? Take away my happiness? What?" Tears spill down her cheeks, and I step up, wanting to comfort her even though I know it's all a show.

King Rave stops me as he contemplates her. "Actually, I want you to be happy. I want you to remember this fear you're feeling every time you think about defying me. I want you to be petrified that I can take it all away in an instant if I choose." He caresses her chin, and I step toward him, grabbing his shoulder.

"Take your hands off my wife."

He steps back, releasing her as he glares at me. "A foolish thing to say, don't you think?"

"Please," Carrie speaks up, even though she's visibly shaking. "We knew what might happen if we came here, but still we risked it. If you're not willing to hear us out, then we'll leave. We'll live our happy lives with constant fear of when you might take it away."

He smiles. "What a thrill this is!" He throws his arms out wide, purple and black raven feather cape rustling against the quartz floor. I wonder if he flaps enough would he take to the skies as the infamous bird? I wish he would. Then he'd be gone from our lives forever and we can finally live in peace.

"Fine. I'll play your little charade. A trial first. You'll be given three children, and if their performances with their Walk abilities prove to be stronger at the end of one month, I will allow you to take more, but only for a year. Three children a year if you can prove your claims." He holds up three fingers, a mischievous glint in his black eyes. "If you cannot, then you will go back to your regular existence waiting in terror for the day I will take everything from you." He stares at me, knowing I have the most to lose. Carrie will feel no more pain if she's forced to leave this world, but he knows the loss will rip me in two.

"Deal."

Chapter 32
Losing It All

"I'm telling you, I can take you both to his castle if you want to know where it's at. I'm not sure it will help you, but maybe we can have spies keep an eye on it since you no longer have my genius presence there being informed of all his sinister plans. Not that I would have guessed he would poison your troops, but whatever he can do to get your people to turn against you . . ." I trail off, pondering again if the Darkness really came up with that plan or if someone else did.

I can't ignore the nagging thought wondering if David and the nymphs had something to do with it. *Eríd* is an ancient concoction the nymphs would have known about. Dais asked me to think of any others the Darkness might use against Casta and to destroy any recipes of *Eríd* I find. But if the nymphs are influencing David and using him to create these things, there is no telling what horrible concoctions they could use. They used to create and study them on gifted subjects for hundreds of years.

I'd been trying to keep a close eye on him since I got here a week ago, but in between meetings with Dais and Rahuin and getting settled into Casta, I'd hardly seen him. And I don't want to voice my opinions until I know for sure. I know I felt the nymphs when I touched David, but I'm still not sure if they can possess him.

Dais sighs, glancing at Rahuin who sits beside him, a hand resting on her giant stomach. Their baby will be here soon. Maybe I'll just take Dais with me. She should stay here and rest. Right? I don't know anything about pregnant women, but I have a feeling that if I suggest she stay here, she'll be upset, and I do not want to see angry Rahuin. Pregnant Rahuin is bad enough.

I'm not sure I can take her and Dais together too. I'm almost certain they'll hate that idea though. I don't think Dais trusts me doing anything alone with Rahuin yet, and Rahuin doesn't want anything that could possibly implicate us any further. I don't blame her. I'm walking a thin line as it is. I'll have to take them all together then.

"I think it would be good. I hate not knowing everything about him when he knows all about us," Dais says, running a hand through his curls. He still looks a little gaunt from his tryst with *Eríd*, but he seems to be recovering. If you call hollow cheeks and dark circles under his eyes recovering, but we can't all have my great complexion. I can't believe he tried it after what he knew it did to his men. Noble, but stupid. Seriously, I was only gone for a few weeks and he nearly condemned himself to a life of drugged influence. Not that I could have stopped him, but I could have convinced him to let me try it instead. Make up for the past and all that.

"Fine. Then let's go," Rahuin says, heaving herself out of her chair.

Dais stands quickly, trying to help her up, but she waves him away with a cross stare knit in her red eyebrows.

"I've got it."

"Maybe you should—" Dais starts, but another glass-shattering glare from Rahuin snaps his mouth shut.

I try not to laugh at their antics, but I fail miserably, turning Rahuin's scowl on me. Her green eyes cut me like a knife when I don't look away fast enough.

"Laugh at me one more time . . ."

I put my hands up in surrender. "I was laughing at him." I look at

Dais, who frowns. "Not you."

"Ouch." Dais rolls his eyes.

Rahuin watches me skeptically before waddling around Dais's desk. "Fine. I believe you. Let's get this over with."

Dais joins her.

"Um, I—I've never teleported two people before . . . And Rahuin, you're technically three." I find the dark green rug in Dais's office extremely important at that particular moment. I never realized the gold and auburn strands in it, it's beautifully woven. Almost—

"If anyone can do it, you can," Rahuin says, and I glance up to see Dais shoot her a jealous glance. Oh boy. I shouldn't have suggested anything with Rahuin around. I should have just talked to Dais, but they're never apart. Maybe I shouldn't have come back to Morough. This tip-toeing is going to drive me insane.

She catches Dais's eye. "I didn't mean anything by it. I trust that his magic is strong enough to get us all there in one piece. Plus he's jumped me before when I was pregnant. So he has jumped two people. Granted, he didn't know, but . . ."

That's right. How come I'd forgotten about that? Probably because a few hours later she ripped my heart out and left me for dead. That makes one forget the minor detail of her being pregnant when I jumped her off the battlefield all those months ago.

Dais tosses a resentful glance at me.

Great. Now he's angry at me too? What did I do?

I toss my hands up again. "I forgot about that. A lot's happened since then." That's an understatement. My entire life turned upside down.

Rahuin sighs. "Can we please stop arguing like children and go? You two are getting on my nerves!" Rahuin pinches the bridge of her nose with her fingers.

Dais's shoulders fall, and he takes his wife's hand, looking at me.

I step toward them. "May I?" I hold my hands toward their empty ones. Dais takes mine and Rahuin follows suit.

"This isn't awkward at all." I laugh.

"Wen!" They start together.

"All right. All right. Both of you close your eyes. I think it'll be easier for me to teleport us all if you aren't looking."

They give me identical skeptical glances before closing their eyes.

The world warps around us in an array of vibrant colors, and I feel the in-between tugging me as I try to hold onto them like my life depends on it, and in some ways, it does. I imagine everything about the Darkness's castle, but a dark cold wall blankets my mind. My heart plummets and my breath vanishes like someone pummeled my chest with a hammer. The warping fades, and when we reappear, I find that the Darkness's castle is nowhere to be found. Just a plain with green flowing grass and wildflowers of all shapes and colors.

The place where the castle should be, right up against a mountainside, is gone, replaced with nothing but a sheer rock face. Hmm, this explains why the teleportation felt different. I remember the castle being here, but I wanted to go directly to my old room in the castle. He must have cloaked it enough to keep me from doing that.

"Where is it?" Dais asks, looking around. A breeze flits by, tugging on our clothes and begging us to come play.

"It's gone. He moved it." Rahuin's fingers dance along the breeze.

That's right. She told me she can hear the elements. I wonder if they can tell her where he moved it. It doesn't matter. Even if we found it, he'd probably just move it again. He'll never let us have the upper hand, but we already do. We're fighting for the winning side, and that's something he'll never understand. He'll fail. That's why he has to hide.

"He probably knew I would take you here. That means he sees me as a threat." I smirk, feeling a little accomplished with that fact. It proves my sincerity.

"Well, spying on him is no longer an option," Rahuin says, her brow furrowing, green eyes locking on something in the grass.

I follow her gaze and see a rainbow stone no bigger than my wrist shining in the foliage. It reminds me of Treía, but where the Garon stronghold had stone in all colors and sizes, this stone swirls with every color imaginable at once. The gradient is familiar, but I can't put my finger on why.

She steps toward it, her hand trembling as she picks it up.

Suddenly, it hits me. It looks like the in-between, but what is it doing here and why?

"What is it?" Dais asks.

"A Fate stone. I'd seen them when they used to visit me. Wind says the Fates help hold the balance of time in all the Otherworlds for the King." The stone in Rahuin's hand vanishes.

I meet her gaze as she looks around us. "You've met the Fates."

She nods. "They left me messages, telling me how I would have to fight the Darkness, but I haven't heard from them in a long time."

Dais takes her hand. "Perhaps that's a good thing. Maybe we're finally gaining something."

"Or losing it all," Rahuin mutters, looking back at me. "Take us home, Wen."

David

"You're doing well with him. I'm mightily impressed." The Darkness's deep voice haunts the room around me. I'd grown accustomed to his visits over the last few weeks. He always speaks to the others though, as if forgetting I'm here too. We always wait in a dark room completely void of any light. The others say it's the best place where no one will find us or know what we're doing.

"We promised we would, oh gracious master! Did you enjoy our little stunt with the human's army? What fun we had." The hissing voices chorus around me.

Not so long ago, their presence brought fear, defeat, but now, their influence has only made me stronger. I no longer lose control of my gift. I no longer hurt the people I love. I no longer fear that my gift will destroy them. I no longer feel the cold. Instead, the voices have been teaching me how to control it, enhancing it, like they said.

Recently, they've been letting me be a part of their missions. Before, I'd blackout and forget, but now they're starting to trust me… just like I trust them. I'm keeping what I love safe, and they're the reason why. They've made me stronger, just like I've made them stronger. It's a gruesome business, what they do, but I no longer worry whether it's right or wrong. All is fair in love and war. Now, I see the value. That's the beauty of it. They've seen my full potential and whispered their grand ideas. I'll be king one day, all in the glory of our master. I just have yet for him to recognize my role in all this.

"I agree. It was a wonderful idea. Sewing more doubt into Casta's king." I feel a cold hand touch my face, gripping my chin. "Ah," the Darkness starts. "Interesting, he's awake."

"Yes, Master. He's a valuable asset. Mixed the concoction on his own. He's done well keeping his family from being suspicious of what we're doing. After all, he knows them best."

His nails dig into my skin—the only substance in the comforting dark. "Hmm, tell me. Can I trust you to kill for me?"

For a moment, a breath of an almost-forgotten voice whispers, *"No, David."* It's my voice, or it was . . . but I hardly recognize it. A stranger's voice can't be mine.

"Your wish is mine. Anything you ask, I will gladly do," I say in a tone I've become much more familiar with these last few weeks. It's confident, clear. No longer afraid. No longer a coward scared of his own power.

"Ambitious. I'm glad you finally came to your senses." He pats my cheek. "I have a mission for you. All of you. I'm bringing you to Sun'Ar with me. I have a few loose ends to tie up, and only you, David, can accomplish it for me."

A'zre

"Your little fallback plan has officially become a thorn in my side. You shouldn't have defied me." His dark voice lacks the authority I usually found confidence in. The red curtains in my office shift around his dark form as he slips into the room. Lights from the multicolored lanterns outside shimmer over the red and gold mosaics of lions and suns.

I look up from my desk. "What are you talking about now? I've done all you asked." I'm tired of his games. I'm tired of his lies. He promised me Partin, but all I have is one extra nation buried under warring Cay-Llek tribes, and a wife who hates my very existence. I would hate my existence if I were in her position too.

"The Princess Renell. You should have never gotten her involved, and you will pay the price." He steps toward me, black eyes boring into my soul.

Pay the price. Always pay the price. Maybe my father was wrong. Maybe we can't have it all. What's the point when you have to make deals and pay a price you're not even sure you can fulfill?

I glare at him. "What do you mean? I got Esther, didn't I? I'm following what you said. Yes, I tried to ensure that the plans didn't fail by using Renell, but it didn't matter, did it?"

"It does. She's coming after Lanckest with a Cay-Llekian army. I've heard from my spies in Onar that she made a secondary alliance with them. The insurance has now become a liability, and you've hardly followed my plans. I know you have no intention of finishing this war for me. I gave it all to you, but you want to take it from me."

"Why would I defy you? You have the power to destroy me in an instant. I'm hardly a threat." He knows this, but I still see the danger in his dark, soulless eyes. He doesn't care. He didn't give it all to me. He won't do what he claims. He wants Partin just as much as I do, but he'll be the one who keeps it. I'm just a mere man whose people will eventually turn on him for the wars he's waged. He just wanted to use me to get Partin, and now I realize it. He wants me to pay, but what does that even mean? Remove me from the throne? Well, he can. I'll finally be free of my burden. I'll finally be able to leave my father's monster of greed behind me. I'd be free to love. I'd be free to be myself.

"And you said Renell was hardly a threat too, didn't you?" he responds.

A scream pierces the night air, making my blood run cold. A chilling breeze sweeps in from the drapes, the desert nights have come to claim their dues after the reign of the sun. I stand and step toward my balcony, trying to determine where I'd heard the shout. A commotion in the hall outside my study's door draws my attention, and when I look back, the Darkness has disappeared, leaving a sick feeling in my stomach. He's not going to replace me. He needs me. So how else will he make me pay? I have nothing he can use to hurt me.

The door swings open with a crash against the wall, shattering some of the tiles.

I jump, glaring at the guard who just entered.

"Your Majesty, p—please forgive the intrusion, but your children. They—they're all dead."

My heart sinks to my stomach, and I can feel the blood draining from my face. I take two careful steps forward. "You're certain?"

"Yes, Y—Your Majesty. Healers have been called in, but I'm not sure they can do anything." He gasps, fear causing him to tremble.

I stand in front of him. "Were you the guard on duty?"

Tears appear in his eyes, and he swallows, falling to his knees. "Yes, Your Majesty. I heard nothing. I—I saw nothing. Then one of the servants came in to gather the children for the goodnight procession and she found them all still and . . ." He pulls his sword from its sheath. "Please end me now, Your Majesty. I don't deserve to live. I couldn't protect them."

"Put it away," I spit. "You had nothing to do with this." I step past him, heading into the hall where flickering sconces blaze over glass tiles, making the depictions of the gods on the walls look like nightmares. There are no blessings—only pain. Children are a blessing, but they have become my pain. The one thing the Darkness could take from me. The one thing he could destroy me with . . . my legacy.

I find myself in the children's wing. The two giant doors leading into their quarters are wide open. My wives crouch over their children's limp bodies, wailing and shaking them as if it could bring them back. I fall to my knees once I pass the threshold. The stench of death permeates the room. I don't have to know how they died to know that the Darkness had a hand in this. I defied him. So he destroyed them. He took them from me.

I look up to the mosaiced ceiling, chandeliers hang with the dark reality of what happened in this room. A cry of anguish that's been locked in my soul since I myself was a child escapes my lips. My innocence was torn from me and their lives were stolen. All I wanted was to provide a better future for them. I didn't want anyone to challenge them ever again. I wanted them to be the most powerful nation in Partin . . . They would have wanted for nothing. They would have had it all. Now fourteen lives have been lost because of me. Fourteen innocent lives. They never asked for this. They never asked to be my children. They never asked to become the most powerful. They were children. They didn't know any better. They didn't know I would kill them because of my greed.

"Find who did this. Make them pay!" Mira yells at me, holding my oldest son in her arms. He is—was twelve. My first child . . . our first child. "Make them pay," she wails, falling into me.

I take our son from her, holding his lifeless form. For the first time in twenty years, tears fall down my face, landing on his cheeks. "I'm sorry. I'm so sorry," I whisper as my other wives chorus Mira's cry for justice, but their cry can't be met. I'm the one who killed them. I can't bring myself to justice. I will have to live with the pain, and that will be penance enough. They'll want someone to pay, and I'm sure I'll find a criminal worthy of it, but maybe enough innocent blood has already been shed.

Wen

I lean back in my chair, enjoying the crackling of a warm fire. It's not even that cold, I just like the ambiance of the flames flickering over my room. After being stuck in Treía for several weeks and then camping in the cold winter before that, I'm finally ready to enjoy the warmth of a roof over my head surrounded by opulence. I take a sip of warm tea a servant left a few minutes ago. It settles down my throat, warming my stomach.

I breathe a sigh of relief and lift my gaze to the painting on the roof. It's a depiction of the King of Light sitting on his throne over-looking all of Partin. There are detailed portions of vibrant cities and citizens toiling over their wares in forms of seafaring, farming, study-ing, and selling.

I still can't believe Dais said yes to my request. I sigh, my mind wondering about my fruitless library search today. Dais wants me to find more ways the Darkness might be able to harm his men, but I've been looking for evidence to support my claim about David and the nymphs. I haven't seen him around much since we looked for the Darkness's castle two days ago. I can't shake the uneasy feeling in my gut, but I still have yet to find truth for my suspicions.

Maybe there are none to be found and I'll just have to catch him red handed, but I don't have much freedom to go off on my own. I have to prove my worth to Dais and Rahuin. If I make accusations about a member of the royal family without proof, I could lose what little confidence they have in me.

After a full day of finding nothing, I decided to come back here and rest a while after dinner. Night has fallen and the stars wink outside my window, watching over the castle like glittering guards. I missed the stars so much when I was with the Darkness. I never had the time to look up and admire them. Where I grew up on Is'Er, stars were a huge part of the fishermen's lives. We did everything by the stars and were expected to know them well. Treía didn't have stars cause we were buried in a mountain, and Cay-Llek was constantly covered in clouds. Finally, I get to admire all that I've enjoyed for years.

"You know the contentment won't last." The familiar voice leaves a plunk of dread in my stomach.

"That's what you like me to believe," I say, taking another sip of my tea.

"They'll never really trust you, you know. You came here because you wanted to be close to her, and he hasn't even let you come near," the Darkness hisses in my ear.

I turn my head, looking him dead in his soulless eyes. "Nice try, but I didn't come here for her. You think that just because I loved her once that she's the only reason I do anything. Your misconception has made you lose touch."

"You'll always be alone, Wen. Once you realize that, you'll come running back to me. I'm all you'll ever need." His voice starts to fade.

"No, not all I'll ever need, because you can't offer love in any capacity."

A frustrated sigh echoes throughout the room, and I almost burst out laughing. He sounds like a pouty two-year-old who didn't get his way. Well, he can sulk all he wants because I'm not giving into his taunts. I have no reason to. He may think Rahuin and Dais will never trust me, but they've already started to.

Dais even considers me his friend, which I never thought would be possible. I thought he would never let me talk to Rahuin, which I would have done in his position, but his trust has only grown since I've come. I expected him to be jealous, but he's proven me wrong time and time again. He's a fair man, and I can't blame Rahuin for her choice. He makes me want to be better. If anything, I'm happy for her. She deserves someone like him.

"You're right. I can't offer love, but I can offer power. Something you'll need in the future. I've got big plans for you, Wen."

I should have known he wasn't gone yet. "I don't care what you have planned for me, because I'm not falling into your trap. I don't serve you anymore, and I never will again. I've found a place where I belong. They care for me, and that's all I've ever wanted." I stand, annoyed that he's ruining the atmosphere and my tea's getting cold. He stands on the other side of the room by the door leading out to a balcony.

"They won't care after I'm done with you. Be ready, Wen. I'm coming for you." He points a shadowy finger at me.

"I'll count on it," I say as he disappears. He's not all I have anymore. I won't go back to him, even if it means power and stability. I'll gladly take his taunts and hate-filled promises if it means I can live and find people who love and care for me. All I've ever wanted is to belong, and he only needed me to fulfil his desires. I know his future plans don't include me. He'll try to manipulate me to his will, but he'll fail. This is what Renell meant when she said I'd have to fight against the Darkness, my old master. She was right. I can fight, and I will continue to do so until the end of my days.

Chapter 33
Not Yet Time

Rahuin

"Hello, Rahuin."

"I'm not scared of you. I won't listen to you," I say out loud, drawing Dais's attention from where he sits at his desk. He lifts his head, moving to stand beside me. The warmth of the cushioned chair swallows me whole, and Darkness stands beside the crackling fireplace. He smirks, pulling at the gray skin on his face. The night fills the room with dim shadows, but perhaps it's coming from the Darkness himself. I don't want to give him that much credit.

"You should be scared of me. I will destroy you."

Dais helps me stand, and I lean heavily against him, placing a hand behind my back as I lift my heavy load. Sira should be here soon. Thesa and the midwife both agree it's any day now.

"Your threats are empty. You cannot harm us." I stand defiantly before him. Dais holds my hand, grounding me to the present. The Darkness can't take me to the space between, not both of us any way.

He laughs. "How cute. You think I can't hurt you because you have each other? You think I can't make it all come crumbling down?"

476

"You haven't succeeded, and you never will," Dais speaks this time.

"Very well. You shouldn't have underestimated me." His form blurs before my eyes, and before I can blink, his arm is around my throat, and I'm torn from Dais's grasp.

"Rahuin!" he screams, joining the chorus of other voices.

"He can't do that!" Air cries.

"He's getting stronger," Earth continues.

"He shouldn't harm her like that. There will be hell to pay." Fire blazes brighter in the hearth, and I see the flash before the Darkness swings me around, launching me toward the stone fireplace. I don't have time to react. I can't breathe. Panic overwhelms my heart as I try to focus my intention magic on softening the blow, but it comes too soon.

Whack!

The sound reverberates in my ears, rattling my bones. What just happened?

"Rahuin!" Different voices bombard my head, but I hardly hear them. My vision blurs, and I try to turn my head, but I can't move. No. I'm frozen. My body won't respond. My heart starts to pound. I feel the darkness pressing in. Dark swirls appear in my vision, radiating around me. They seem beautiful in a way, comforting. Is this what it feels like to die?

"No, Rahuin! Don't give into the fear! Stay with us! We're with you. We're—" A bright flash of light cuts Fire's next words off, and even though I can't move my head, I know what the light means. He's here. The King of Light. We succeeded. We won.

Dais

I rush toward the Darkness and Rahuin. I see what he's going to do, but it's not possible. He can't do this. My insides twist, horror spreading through my bones. I'm not going to make it.

Whack!

The Darkness throws Rahuin against the stone hearth. Her head reverberates against the surface and she crumples into a heap on the floor.

"Rahuin!" I scream, rushing toward her, but the Darkness sets his eyes on me. I hardly notice when he takes my throat too because I can't take my eyes off Rahuin. Her eyes are open. They're looking around. She's not dead. She's alive!

A light brighter than the sun appears in the room, and the Darkness shrieks, dropping me before I can even blink the spots away in my vision. What I see causes me to stop short.

It's Him. The King of Light. His hair is white, flowing down His shoulders and standing out against His bronze skin as light seems to radiate from His entire being. Now He's got the Darkness penned in His own fist. His eyes blaze like fire, consuming the Darkness whole. The Darkness actually looks terrified.

I rush to Rahuin, gently taking her hand into mine. Blood pools out underneath her now. No. No, this can't be happening. This isn't real. It's just a dream. It must be. I'll wake up soon. The Darkness can't physically harm us. That's why he always manipulates us or someone else around us. How did he do this? It has to be a dream.

"You tried to harm My child?" the King speaks, His voice commanding the whole room and resonating in my soul. I look away from Rahuin, watching their exchange.

The Darkness gasps, trying to pry the hand away from his throat. "All of Partin will soon be mine. They will all be mine. I can do whatever I want now. I will rule it all."

"Your misconception of boldness has made you weak. You certainly don't own it all yet, and you never will. I'm coming for you. You will pay for what you've done to My people."

"What have I done? You're the one who left them. They didn't want You. They wanted me, and soon, I will have them." The Darkness sneers.

"You'll have to be ready. Nothing will save you from My vengeance," The King of Light says, releasing the Darkness, who disappears in a cloud of black smoke.

Everything suddenly seems too bright. I look back down at Rahuin, but she's fading. The light in her eyes starts to dim. No. No this can't be happening. This is all just a nightmare. I'll wake up soon. I'll wake up . . .

"Rahuin, no, please don't go. Please stay. Stay for me. I can't do this without you. You promised you wouldn't go again. You promised—" I break down into sobs, holding her close to my chest, her warm blood soaking my shirt. Dreams have blood in them too, right? But they never feel this real. My heart never seizes with the dread of deep understanding in the nightmares. She's leaving me. She's dying.

Her green eyes look at me. "I can't move. I can—am I dying?"

"No, no. You're going to be okay. I promise." I swallow the lump in my throat.

"You just said. You just told me not to—to go."

I blink away tears that blur her beautiful face. "I did. It's just because I love you so much. I was just so—so worried at first." I run my fingers through her hair, but it's covered in blood too. Too much blood.

"I'm not going anywhere," she whispers, her eyelids drooping. No. No. No. "I love you."

I kiss her lips, believing this is all too real to be a dream. She goes limp in my arms.

She's gone.

Gone.

A hand grabs my shoulder, and I gasp, thinking that the Darkness is here to take her from me. No. He won't have her. He'll have to kill me too. Too? No. She can't be dead. This isn't real.

When I turn my head, the King of Light crouches beside me. His other hand holds Rahuin's. He no longer radiates light. His white hair has changed to dark brown and His eyes are no longer on fire, but swirl in a mix of brown, green, and blue.

"This should have never happened," He says, and His commanding voice sends chills of awe along my skin. Light erupts around His hand, momentarily blinding me.

Rahuin stirs in my arms, taking a deep breath as the light fades. Her chest heaves with gasps, as if she can't get enough air.

"Rahuin!" I breathe, pulling her closer to me and kissing her lips.

She reciprocates, her arms wrapping around me. "Dais! I was so scared. I thought—"

She pulls back, tears streaming down her cheeks as she looks up at the King of Light, Who has now stood. Her mouth falls open. "Your—Your Majesty."

I look at Him too, and we both bow our heads together.

He smiles, eyes shimmering. "I have to go now."

"But you're here. We've won. Please don't go. We can't win this war without you," Rahuin mummers, her voice struck with awe.

"It's not My time yet. I had to keep you safe from him. He should have never laid a finger on you, and that act summoned me, like when I visit in your dreams." His voice feels like warm tea on a chilly evening, bringing life into my own veins and calming the nerves over the night's events.

"Is this a dream, then?" I ask, because I'm still not certain. Rahuin just died in front of me. Her blood is caked on my clothes, but I refuse to believe any of this was truly real.

He focuses on me, crouching down once more. "It's not."

"Then why can't you stay? Why do you have to go?" Rahuin asks, grabbing His hand.

He glances down at their fingers before meeting our gazes. "The way hasn't been prepared yet. I don't expect you to understand, but soon the gateway will be open, and I will come. I will claim this land back as My own."

"So we must keep fighting?" Desperation cracks Rahuin's voice, and the fire pops loudly behind her. I jump.

"Yes, for a little while longer." He caresses Rahuin's cheek, His other hand lying on my shoulder. He leans His head down, touching our foreheads. "I will see you both again soon." Then He's gone. I blink, thinking it will make Him reappear, but He doesn't.

I peer at Rahuin, seeing my own wonder wrapped up in her eyes. The fire warms the room around us, becoming the only light once again. I pull her into my arms, refusing to let her go. I didn't even get to thank the King for saving her.

"Dais, did I die?" The words are spoken with so much fear it sends my own heart to my stomach once again.

"Yes," I whisper into her neck. "He saved you. I was so scared I'd have to live without you. I couldn't have survived."

"That's not true." Her warm breath grazes my skin.

"It's true. I can't do this without you. Together. That's what we promised. Before, there was always hope you would come home, but you dying in my arms . . . it was too real. There is no hope in that." My throat chokes like someone wrapped a vice around it.

"Dais," she pulls away. "You can't just continue to only live and fight for me. I'm not—I'm not your duty. Casta is. The King's return is. You aren't just fighting for me, and I don't want you to. Tonight proves that. You would have given up, given it all up and let Darkness win if you let my death destroy you." Her fingers caress my face.

I look away, watching the flames lick the coals and dance in their odd sway. She's right. She's not my only reason, but it would have been harder to carry on without her. "I meant it would have been hard to do it without you. You're right. I don't want him to succeed, and I never would have wanted your d—death to be in vain."

Even speaking the word causes my heart to quiver. It's a part of life. I could have lost her, and I would have had to learn to live and fight without her by my side. What would I have done? Would I really have given up? Or would I have listened to the council and learned that the Darkness wins without someone to fight him? Or would I have been too grieved to care?

Rahuin is right. I can never let this happen again. I can never let my love for her destroy me. Otherwise, everything we fought for, everything men, my father, Rahuin died for would have been in vain. I will never let that happen. No, not while I draw breath.

"Good." She kisses my cheek "Now help me up. I . . . want to get out of these clothes."

I help her up, thinking about Jet. How come he hadn't come in during the fight? Oh no. Is he gone too? Did he get harmed? Usually he comes in at the first sound of danger.

I help Rahuin lean against the hearth, while I head to the door. I open it, expecting to see Jet crumpled on the floor, but he stands tall and proud.

He glances behind him. "Is something—" he stops, his brown eyes taking in my bloody hands and shirt. His mouth falls open. "What happened? Is . . ."

I pull him inside, letting the door swing closed. "Everything is fine. The Darkness came. He hurt Rahuin. He—"

"Dais." Rahuin's desperate utterance draws my attention. She stares down at her feet where water now pools over the coagulated blood on the floor. She lifts her gaze, her mouth open in astonishment. She starts to take deep breaths.

Sira. It's happening.

Thesa

Five hours and forty minutes later, well into the early morning, Rahuin gives birth to a beautiful baby girl. I'd hardly believed it when Jet ran to get me, saying Rahuin's water broke. Dais briefly informed me of the night's events when I arrived to find them both drenched in blood. Rahuin's blood. I'd nearly fainted but kept myself together to help Rahuin change into a cotton birthing gown that wasn't stiff with dried blood. A midwife came in a few minutes later to check on her. Her contractions were few and far between, so she said to come get her once the contractions were one on top of the other.

Rahuin then told me of the King of Light. How He saved her life. How He promised He'd be coming soon. For her sake, I hope that's true. I don't want her and Dais to suffer any more. I just want them to be happy and able to take care of their little girl in peace, but I know those wishes aren't for the wise. This war is nowhere near over, and they'll never be safe until He comes back for Partin. So much can happen in that span of time. Last night was proof.

I almost lost Rahuin. I wasn't even here to protect her. Again. But even Jet said he hadn't heard a thing. He didn't know the Darkness was in there, even though Dais said he shouted Rahuin's name several times. The Darkness somehow blocked them in. There would have been nothing I could have done to save her, but I never would have forgiven myself if she died.

Now, I hold a bawling baby girl in my arms. My heart sings. The last time I'd held a child, it was Jarret, and I had to give him away. It makes me wonder what would happen if I had another.

Rahuin gasps with relief, tears streaming down her cheeks while I help the midwife clean Sira off before I pass the little red child off to her mother. Sira's screams immediately quite once Rahuin holds her.

"Hi, my baby girl. I've waited so long to meet you." She kisses Sira's forehead before handing the swaddled bundle to Dais, who sits beside her.

Tears form in his blue eyes, and I can't help but smile at the display.

I kiss Rahuin's forehead. "Well done, *Elleha*."

"Thank you for everything." Her green eyes meet mine with unshed tears before they go back to her baby. After all that happened, I wouldn't want to take my eyes off my daughter either.

"I'll leave you two to it," I say, squeezing her hand before I go. The new family needs this time. It's one of the most precious moments and they'll only have so many.

Jet paces outside the door. The end of the hall starts to illuminate with the rising sun. He pulls me into his arms once I cross the threshold, letting the door close behind me.

"Wha—" I start, startled by his display of affection.

"I'm sorry I wasn't there for you during Jarret's birth. That sounded awful, and I can't believe you were alone."

I smile. Oh, that's what this is about. I wrap my arms tight around his waist. "I wasn't alone. I was with Jarret, and Klash was there at the time. He helped."

"That's not what I meant." He pulls back. "I meant—"

"Jet," I grip his forearms, looking up into his eyes. "I know what you mean. I wish you could have been there. In fact, I dreamed you were and that made it easier. At the time, I thought you were dead. You didn't know anything about the pregnancy. You couldn't have known. So don't say you're sorry, you did nothing wrong."

"I just—"

The sun dances across his face, catching his long hair and casting wispy shadows over his face.

I cup his chin. "I love you. Let's agree that we're not going to talk about the past anymore. What's done is done and we can't change what happened. All we have is now." I smile.

His fingers around my waist pull me closer as he leans his forehead against mine. He kisses me. "Would you ever consider h—having another?" he asks, his brown eyes wide with hope.

"Aren't we a little old for that?" I tease, entwining my fingers in his hair.

"Not yet." He raises his eyebrows. "We're Garons. Time works differently, remember?" His voice sounds deeper than it had a moment ago.

"Maybe you should have been in that room with me. Then you'd never want another baby." I kiss his chin.

He throws his head back. "You can say no." He meets my gaze. "It was just a suggestion."

I study his eyes. A million thoughts whir through my head. Rationally, I should say no. We're in the middle of a war. Now is not the time to be thinking about babies, but I throw rationality out the window. Because rationality says I probably won't get pregnant again. I hate being rational, and holding Sira made me want nothing more than to have another. Once again, Jet read my mind.

"No, I want another." I want to experience all I didn't have with Jarret because I had to let someone else raise him.

He laughs, and the sound gets caught in my throat with another kiss.

Epilogue

Wen

Sira coos from her crib, turning into a screech as she wakes fully. I stand, reaching for her and swaddling her in my arms. She quiets a bit, soothed by the sound of my voice as I hum, my tattoos glowing slightly. She watches with wide green eyes she got from her mother. She loves this little trick. It always calms her. A breath of a smile appears on her face.

Dais and Rahuin are off planning their christening for Sira in the temple in Morough. Thesa and Jet went with them, and I got the privilege of watching over Sira while she took a much needed nap. When I met this little one, my heart instantly melted. For some reason, she took a liking to me. Since then, Rahuin has allowed me to watch over her in little bits at a time. It's an honor I cherish. I know Dais and Rahuin appreciate it because it gives them some time to recover and continue running Casta. Thesa and Aleetha often care for Sira, but every once in a while, I get to enjoy a little one-on-one time with her.

I bounce her a little. "Did you have a nice nap? Are you ready to go see, *Elleha*?" I whisper, though I'm not sure Rahuin and Dais are back yet. Normally, she comes to get Sira straightaway.

"How cute. He's a baby whisperer now." A cold Darkness fills the room, and I look up at him. Sira's cries begin again.

"What do you want?" I hold Sira closer to my chest as if that will keep him away. We're all on edge after what happened to Rahuin. He shouldn't have been able to cause her any harm, but he did. Dais was furious after the whole ordeal and asked me several times if it was possible. I assured him it shouldn't have been. I then scoured the library for answers.

Sure enough, ancient texts said the dark one could appear in physical form and even procure physical harm if he had enough evil reverence behind his name. He's not allowed to harm others, especially under the protection of the King of Light, but he tried anyway. That was three weeks ago, no one had seen him since.

"I've just come to look upon the new child. She's precious, isn't she?" He steps toward us.

Sira's screeches grow louder.

My heart palpitates. "Again, what do you want?"

"Finally, he's afraid of me. You saw what I can do now. You know you're not untouchable." He's suddenly beside me. I teleport right then and there, appearing in Dais's office. Dais and Rahuin aren't here yet. No. I need them. I just need to stall him until they get here. It can't be much longer.

"They're not coming, Wen. I already took care of that."

"What did you do to them?"

A sick smile spreads across his face. "You should be more worried about what I'll do to you and her." His eyes fall on Sira.

"You won't touch her." I teleport again. The in-between rushes around me in a world of warped blues and purples, but darkness tinges the edges. What? My stomach sinks. I feel something grab my ankle and the clear destination I had in my mind vanishes. No. This can't happen. We could be stuck here forever.

"Let go of me!" I shout, trying to kick him off.

"It's too late, Wen. I told you I had big plans for you, but you underestimated me." Another portal opens to my left, and the Darkness flings us into it. I see nothing as we fall and fall. Sira vanishes from my grasp, and desperation clings to my heart as I try to find her, but she's gone.

No.

No.
No.
This can't be happening. I try to teleport again, but it's too late. I'm lost in the vast expanse of the Otherworlds.

Acknowledgments

This book was one of the hardest I've ever written. Much of my experience has become trapped in these pages and I hope they've resonated with you. I hope it brings you courage in the face of fear and strength to persevere through trials and grief. First and foremost I have to thank my Lord and Savior, Jesus Christ. For without Him, I never would have written or even published this book. It would have stayed a rough draft with plenty of tears shed over it.

To Quaid, for being my constant idea bouncer and helping me rethink this plot more than once. Thank you for creating my chapter header!

To Gaelle, I'm so grateful to call you my sister. Thank you for encouraging me always and for taking my author photo.

To Raphiel, there are so many things I could say about you girlie! You are such a sweet sister in Christ and constant companion. Thank you for listening to my idea dumps, spoilers, and my nine million renditions of the case hardcover. Thank you for sticking it out with me and creating something so beautiful. Thank you, as well, for my wonderful character art, and for reading this book as an alpha and beta reader, I always look forward to your reactions!

To Mom and Dad, thank you for your constant support, driving me to events, helping my buy books for the events, and always believing in me. I'm so grateful to have you in my corner.

To Braeden, for my map! Thank you for supporting me and cheering me on from the sidelines even if you can't figure out why everyone in my books is royalty.

To Kyah, for my character art of Dais. I love him so much! Thank you for always being a constant joy to work with.

To Kenzi, for the character print. It's so beautiful and I'm so glad I got to work with you again. Thank you for doing it on such short notice, it really means so much!

To my alpha readers, Jeffery, Hannah, Raphiel, Adam, and Dori. Thank you for helping me make the plot so much easier to understand and reminding me to add throwbacks to the first book so no one would be confused.

To my beta readers, Sara, Caitlyn, Genesis, Hannah, Kayla, Glory, and Raphiel. Thank you for helping me polish the story and make it even better than before. Thank you, always, for your constant encouragement.

To Caitlyn, thank you for reading this book not once, not twice, not even three times, but four times to help me fix typos, plot, and character arcs, thank you for being willing to help me on such short notice. It means more than I can ever express, and your constant love of this book and Partin: the Chosen has kept me going!

To Dorothy, this book is ten times better because of you. Thank you for pointing out that this story needed some work even though I was ready to publish it. It was truly needed and so appreciated.

To Sera, for being my fantastic editor. It's always a joy to work with you. Thank you for your attention to detail, world building, and plot. This book just wouldn't be the same without you.

To my readers, some I have met, some I have chatted with, some I will never meet. Thank you for picking up this book and giving it a chance. You make this all worth it.

And finally, to the girl I was before I wrote this book. Thank you for getting up everyday and putting your God-given stories on paper. Never forget that the world still needs your stories.

Love This Book?

Please consider leaving a review on Goodreads and Amazon! If you can't, please connect with me over Facebook or Instagram @author-rileyperrie! I love hearing from my readers!

About the Author

Riley J. Perrie lives among the fields of Nebraska with her family and cat. She's an avid reader and writer and you'll often find her soaking up sunshine with a good book or a pen and a page. She's been writing since she was seven and shows no signs of stopping anytime soon. You can connect with her over Instagram @authorrileyperrie or at authorrileyperrie.com.

Other works by Riley J. Perrie
Partin: the Chosen
Inspector Pim and the Blood of Inferium

www.ingramcontent.com/pod-product-compliance
Lightning Source LLC
Chambersburg PA
CBHW030013010826
48973CB00009B/2793